Happy Birthday

FLIGHTPLAN

Safe

I

FLIGHTPLAN

Mike Jordan

FLIGHTPLAN

First published in the UK in 2001 by IMAJI-NATION PUBLICATIONS.
Edition 1
Copyright © Mike Jordan 2001
'Faction'©
All rights reserved

ISBN 0-9540185-0-8

Printed and bound in the UK by
NOTAPRINT
Studio House
40 Oakwood Hill Industrial Estate
Loughton, Essex IG10 3TZ

IMAJI-NATION PUBLICATIONS
The Treehouse
155 the Maples, Harlow, Essex CM19 4RD

At time of going to press, all information and technical details are believed to be correct. Any amendments will be posted on the website if, and as, they become apparent.

www.imaji-nationpublications.co.uk

THIS BOOK IS DEDICATED TO THE
MEMORY OF MY TWO FRIENDS,
LAURENCE HUGHES, AGED 10 AND
CAPTAIN ANDY DUFFILL AGED 39

'GRANT ME LORD, BEFORE I DIE, A SMALL PIECE OF HEAVEN, IN WHICH TO FLY.'

Mike Jordan.
©2001

This inscription can be found carved into a bench outside 'The Squadron' at North Weald Airfield Essex, in memory of Laurence Hughes and Captain Andy Duffill.

INTRODUCTION

'Flightplan' is the first of a new type of book to be generically known as *'Faction.'* A blend of 'Fact' and 'Fiction' that encompasses actual events within the framework of the story to add realism and credibility.

Essentially an aviation-based thriller with all of the classic ingredients included, 'Flightplan' is also a reference tool including within its text, information, which offers a practical insight into the art and joys of flying. This is further supplemented by a comprehensive glossary and reference section, which begins on page 211. Wherever a topic is suffixed by the symbol (*), further explanation is given in this section and your attention is directed to it.

'Flightplan' can be approached on two levels: firstly, to be simply read and enjoyed as a traditional action adventure novel, or secondly, to be studied as a 'jargon busting' exercise for those wishing to become private pilots who are confused and intimidated by the esoteric terminology usually found in conventional training manuals.

Although not designed to replace any such formal training required for the safe and legal issue of a pilot's licence, Flightplan is an ideal accompaniment to any such study, adding enlightenment, simplistic explanation, entertainment value and the all-important inspiration for students to pursue their dream of becoming pilots. However, whichever way it is viewed, the emphasis is on enjoyment.

Care should be taken to note the smallest of the many details, which essentially appear within the diverse and seemingly fragmented opening chapters, details which may well have great significance to the complex story and your enjoyment of it when it begins in earnest, as the various elements are brought together for the exciting conclusion.

Emphasis is placed on the use of acronyms and mnemonics, which are fundamental and of paramount importance to a pilot. 'PILOT,' of course, stands for *'Person In Lots Of Trouble'*…should he forget his acronyms!

You are invited to visit the website for further information, upgrades, pictures, amendments etc. as they become available and determined.

www.imaji-nationpublications.co.uk

Welcome to the fascinating world of Aviation.

CHAPTER 1

Vittorio Bartelli parked his red Alfa Romeo saloon on the drive of his family villa among the vineyards of Frascati, in the southwestern foothills of Rome, Italy.

He loved his wife and family very much. He had flowers for her and sweets for his children. Vittorio had left the laboratory of the Servizio Sanitario Statale, where he worked as chief chemist in the Italian Government's pharmaceutical department, early this Friday afternoon, rushing home to be with them.

Vittorio's daily return from work was always announced by the 'crunch of tyre on gravel' as he pulled into the drive, normally followed by the screams of several over-excited children, who would leap into his arms delivering welcome-home hugs and sticky kisses. On this particular night, none such welcome was received.

The house appeared empty and unusually quiet.

Vittorio slowly and methodically untied the blue ribbon and opened the box that he had found on the dining table. He was used to little surprises left for him by his adoring family so, suspecting that the children were watching from nearby, he uttered 'I wander what this can be' to tease them and prolong the excitement.

"Sweet Sofia no, no!" He slumped to the floor weeping uncontrollably.

The phone had rung continuously for several minutes before Vittorio found the courage to lift the receiver. He did so almost in slow motion, as if to delay the inevitability of his fears. "Yes, I understand. This time I will do as you say."

He replaced the handset and sat motionless in his chair. He stared at his wife's wedding ring as he lovingly cradled the box in his lap. Her recently amputated finger was still in it.

"Mayday, Mayday, Mayday (*) - Manston Airport, - Golf Mike India Delta Romeo, - Beagle Pup, -engine failure, - attempting restart, - eight miles south west of…" The Mayday message ended abruptly.

The Manston air traffic controller was only ten months in the job, his training still reasonably fresh. The Mayday procedures were drummed into him during his studies at NATS (National Air Traffic Services) in Bournemouth, yet, faced with the actual words 'Mayday, Mayday, Mayday' his thoughts raced along with his pulse. He mentally turned back and forth the pages of notes that had been his companions during those twilight study hours on the south coast of England. He questioned his recollection of the Mayday sequence when 'Golf Mike India Delta Romeo' failed to complete its position report. What seemed an eternity of silence was broken only by the sound of his own voice as he shouted and repeated "Attempting restart eight miles south west of…" in a vain attempt to finish the call for the stricken pilot. The eerie

1

silence of the usually crammed radiotelephony frequency (*) ('RT' for short) was, in its own way, deafening.

Manston was a half military; half civilian, international airport on the south east coast of Britain near Margate and the radio frequency was usually very active. Military and private training flights barked their position reports in between scheduled service flights that, in turn, competed with commercial freight traffic requesting circuit-joining instructions for landing. Only one transmission can be made on any single radio frequency at any one time and anxious pilots, eager to make their call, often clashed with one another, jamming the frequency with garbled, senseless, white noise and tangled carrier waves. This resulted in much confusion and further, unnecessary transmissions to clarify who said what and why, yet, suddenly, this time, there was nothing to be heard at all. Even white noise would have been a comfort to the controller to compete with the loud, quickening, rhythmic pulse of his adrenaline filled system. This time, he had a pilot down for real.

Pilots and air traffic controllers were selected, amongst other abilities, for their retentive memories and a basic affinity with numbers. His mind played a cruel trick by presenting him with just one particular set of figures on this occasion, a percentage statistic: 85 %. He recalled his NATS lecturer summing up the Mayday procedures sessions:

"Of course, these routines are vital and are to be wholly committed to memory but, in actual fact, 85% of 'ATC' officers will live and die without any practical involvement in a real Mayday." He was unsure whether to feel proud or 'hacked off' that he was numbered amongst the remaining 15%.

An immediate comfort was afforded by his next recollection that the Air Navigation Order (ANO- the rules of the air by which all of its travelers must abide) states quite clearly that once a 'Mayday' is called, no other station is to transmit on that frequency until the situation is resolved and the 'Mayday' has been duly cancelled by the pilot who initiated it. Hence the unusual degree of silence in his headset, as nobody else dared to intrude in the crisis, leaving the channel open for those that needed it most. In fact, the controller would also have taken great comfort had he known that twenty or so other pilots, also on frequency, had heard the call too and were similarly anxious.

Snapping himself back to a level headed consciousness, stifling the incipient stages of panic, he said out aloud, as if to emphasize the point 'just keep your head and follow the procedures.' He composed himself and made the call; "Golf Delta Romeo, (the aircraft's, call sign (*) now abbreviated for expedience) say again your position." A calm, textbook reaction from the controller but, sadly, it elicited no radio response.

He considered what must have actually been happening on board 'Golf Delta Romeo.'

If he himself were at the controls of a light aircraft when the engine stopped, the last thing he would want to do would be to make polite position reports. Part of his training as an ATC officer included basic flight training and he was always wary of the practice engine failure procedures. The prime consideration however, was to fly the aircraft with a dead stick (no engine) and this alone was all consuming. He recounted the old adage 'Aviate, Navigate and only then Communicate.' 'How the hell' he thought, 'am I to make radio calls and do all these other things as well?' Those all-important numbers on the various instruments have to add up to the best glide ratio and the first thing to do is to trim the aircraft for the correct speed. 'Which direction is the wind coming from? - (Aircraft should always take-off and land into wind) - is there a suitable field within range to make a forced landing that is unimpeded by power lines / trees or crops?

'Trouble checks (*)! – Carburetor ice? This was the first thing to check. Carb' ice was a favorite engine stopper if neglected and all aircraft are prone to it under the most unexpected of conditions, including the hottest of summer days. Many anxious pilots, at the first sign of any trouble, yank the Carb' heat control so hard that it comes out in their hand. – Next - Fuel check - tank selector cock on the 'both tanks' position - fuel pump 'on' - sufficient fuel present -mixture set to 'rich' - Then check magnetos are on 'both'… Electrics? Is there any sign of an electrical fire? Shall I switch off the master switch if so I'll lose the radio…'The list of 'what to dos' and 'keep a cool head while your doing them, as your aircraft plummets out of the sky' went on.

The controller reasoned that, with the cockpit workload at hand, he couldn't reasonably expect a radio response from 'Golf Delta Romeo' in such a short time frame so he held his breath and waited.

Seconds seemed like minutes when suddenly, the call came through from the airborne soul in distress. No standard procedures or calls this time just sheer panic!

"We're going down! Manston we're gonna get wet…" From that point on, the last transmission was only noise. Not the familiar, annoying white variety but a more nauseating high-pitched wine. It suddenly dawned on him that the only thing about 'Delta Romeo' that was in 'full flight' was its stall-warner. This was a simple reed like device, similar to that found in a saxophone, fitted to the leading edge of the port wing, whose job it was to 'bleat' a warning in the cockpit that all was not aerodynamically well if in fact it wasn't.

It, along with the rest of 'Delta Romeo' was indeed about to get wet.

CHAPTER 2

Guiseppe Marcantonio was ready for his lunch. Whitebait and olives, red wine from a local vineyard and, today, he had an orange for a treat. The local orange grove stocks had failed this last year and there were few left to share. He was a man of routine and he would rest a while after his meal before going to the chapel to pray for his dead parents, his sick wife and for a miracle to help him pay for the repairs to his ageing fishing boat. He also went to the chapel to seek refuge from those he owed money and from the relentless stare of the midday sun.

For over fifty years the sea had been his mistress and he had used her each day, taking what he wanted when he wanted. He extracted his living and her fish. She, in turn exacted her revenge on, not only his body, but on that of his boat. Urgent repairs were needed on both. His hands were skinned almost to the knuckles, his legs were bent in directions that they were not intended to go and his eyes wore a permanent glaze awarded him by his mistress and her ally the sun. His home on the isle of Capri in the bay of Naples had little to offer him by way of alternate employ sensitive to his frailties. He was a fisherman and could not give it up but at 65 years of age, he knew in his heart that the ocean would soon give him up. What would he do without help?

The olives were bitter and the orange sweet. As he sat on the harbour wall tending his frayed, rotting nets once again, he mused that his life was one big lunch of olives and oranges with the latter in short supply.

Mario would return soon. Sweet Mario, his only son, his 'orange.' He would come home to help nurse his Momma and Mario would know why the engine makes so much black smoke and goes so slowly that the other fishermen in the village always reach the shoals of sea bass first.

Mario was an engineer for a ferry operator running a service between Capri and the many other ports that the islands and bordering countries of the Mediterranean and Tyrinean seas had to offer. He would be gone for a week and then return for a few days at a time. He would go to the chapel with Papa to help him pray. This time though, Mario had been gone two weeks without a word. Guiseppe was worried, probably more for himself than he was for Mario. Mario could look after himself but Guiseppe could not. He would say extra prayers in the chapel this afternoon.

The local catholic chapel was itself in need of some attention other than spiritual. The roof repair fund had an IOU in its box, drawn on the Santa Maria statue repair fund box cited in the annex. The roof had always leaked and probably always would but the statue had to be urgently repaired in readiness to be carried through the streets for the upcoming festival of 'togetherness,' where each and every person in the village paraded alongside their neighbour in a splendid display of community and pageant. These festivals were paramount to the villagers who rigidly stood by and supported each other as if all were one great family. However, the truth was, that the once proud, active, and prosperous little fishing village of Niapello was falling apart, gradually disappearing along with the fish stocks and the orange groves.

Guiseppe would light a candle and pray that Mario would return soon. He ate his orange.

CHAPTER 3

Rebecca H. Washington was blond, beautiful and very sexy. She was the kind of woman that men dreamt about every night and twice on Sunday. Rebecca also possessed 'that' which blondes were generally rumoured to be short of; brains. She was the perfect example of femininity and men simply adored her.

Rebecca was well aware of the effect that she had on men and had learnt at a very tender age the amount of control she could command over the opposite sex, yet, she wasn't blatant in her use of it, unlike the 'if you've got it, flaunt it' approach of her counterparts. She didn't take advantage of her good looks nor the men who were captivated by them. Instead, she had a sensitivity and respect for the men-folk she encountered. It was simple. She knew their hearts would break at the first encounter. Ipso facto. Her sincerity was apparent and this, added to her appearance and independence, made it conclusive. Instead of running shy of her, men felt totally at ease in her presence. They bathed in her charisma. The basic warmth of her personality eventually melted the very heart of them.

This was some woman. Blessed also with an above average IQ and a solid helping of good old common sense, Rebecca was a formidable presence in any situation. As such, she was also a considerable asset to anybody lucky enough to employ her and retain her services. Sir Freddie Laker was the first major entrepreneur to recognize and harness her talents. The first Skytrain flight was attended by Rebecca and her carefully selected and trained cabin crew. Her role was actually quite formative in those initial, successful Laker days.

As the fleet grew, Rebecca's charm and influence moulded and trained all of the company's flight attendants, elevating her to a position of enormous respect within the company. Respect not just from her superiors, who were quick to recognize that empires were built on such people management skills, but also from the crews she trained and worked with.

Far from operating solely in a managerial role, Miss Washington was an active stewardess and worked the rota with the others, despite the pressure from her superiors to 'fly a desk' with a more social working timetable. She reasoned that she couldn't possibly advise others on attendant skills that she herself would be out of touch with if she didn't actually get her 'hands dirty on the job' as she phrased it, on a regular basis. Besides, Rebecca was simply a great stewardess. It was her safest and most familiar environment and how could she work her magic on people from behind a desk?

Becky was a flyer. It was in her blood to 'be in the sky' and to travel. She was brought up on a strict regime of both. As a RAF pilot, her father was forever being posted abroad, serving 6 months here and 10 months somewhere else. Never long enough to form any kind of friendship or bond in depth; she developed a self-contentedness and independence, which, in later life, simply added to her general appeal.

Rebecca formed a love of aircraft too. Her technical and practical know how of the machines was almost equal to that of most commercial pilots although she herself had never actually learnt to fly. She had promised herself that she would one day, as her fiancé, Danny Michaelson was a flying instructor at a small airfield in Essex, but she simply couldn't find the time for the intensive training needed to gain her PPL although she was pretty familiar with the principles involved.

Rebecca's mother had died whilst giving birth to her younger brother Peter and her father had no choice but to cope on his own. It was a common site on the flight line to see Captain Douglas Washington attending and pre-flighting a Jaguar, followed swiftly by a walk round and undercarriage check of a Silver Cross pram with little Rebecca safely harnessed aboard. There was never a shortage of eager WAAFs acting as surrogate mothers and 'would be' lovers.

Douglas Washington was every inch the hero. Not the stiff upper lip, textbook type but a practical, sensitive and popular man. Morale was sometimes the only commodity that was not in short supply on the occasions that Doug Washington was commanding officer. When a young, low-houred pilot was suddenly catapulted from blackboard theory level to an active, war zone situation, there was no better place for him to be than, literally, under the wing of CO Douglas Washington. Doug knew how to calm these burdened souls and how to help them come to terms with the importance of the job, even though many aspects of it were in conflict with the very essence of their being. Doug would always manage to put things into perspective for them and offer them great peace of mind. He would tell them that pilots were a special breed. They are not 'made' but 'born.' They were sensitive, caring people, sometimes at odds with their wartime duties but selected for, not only their flying skills, but also their undefined humane qualities that brought perspective and judgment, understanding and authority to a world so often on the brink of anarchy. Wars were won in the air he would tell them. The balance of world power and its well-being were decided from the air. Their roles were paramount to the very structure of society and they were special people. He left them with no doubt. They were indeed.

Doug Washington was a great man and an awesome pilot. Not only could he make the others in his command give more of themselves than they believed they had to give, but his uncanny relationship with the aircraft he flew was nothing less than magical. Whilst most explored the extremities of the flight envelope, Doug would expand it. Published performance figures were meaningless to Doug. He would determine his own. It was a total bonding of man and machine. If the maximum permitted published speed (known as VNE (*)-never exceed) was 400 knots, Doug, somehow, would elicit 450. He exercised a ruthless control over a sometimes overstressed airframe but was quick to reward with a sensitive, delicate manoeuvre when required and no one questioned his superior understanding of aero- dynamic forces.

7

As a young pilot, he first saw active service during the Falklands conflict. His own C.O. at the time, on the carrier H.M.S. Hermes, was 'old school' and unforgiving of this new breed of hot shot 'Top Guns.' In his day, he flew by 'the seat of his pants' and didn't rely on ground based back up forces to wipe his nose.

Many ungracious stories were swapped each night in the ships Galleys and mess decks about the handlebar moustachioed 'old vet' William J. Tomlinson. Rumours were circulated that he invented the infamous 'QFO' code. Lots of 'Q' codes (*) were invented and utilized, many remaining to this day, to facilitate swift communication of necessary information to pilots on sortie. For example, a pilot requesting a 'QDM' would be given a magnetic heading to steer in zero wind conditions that would point him back to the transmitting base.

It was widely believed that Tomlinson himself invented 'QFO' on a mission in Korea when inadvertently straying into restricted, highly dangerous, enemy airspace and finding his squadron of Hawker Sea Fury's suddenly engaged in heavy ground to air missile attacks. He is believed to have conceived the concept of 'QFO' at this point shouting it repeatedly over his wireless. QFO - QFO! Literally translated it meant 'Quick Fuck Off!'

As a young flight lieutenant seeing active, aggressive duty for the first time in the Falklands, having trained and flown in peacetime only, Douglas Washington was about to rapidly mature in the job. Having been hurriedly assigned a detached service to the Royal Navy, Doug's legendary handling of a Harrier Jump jet made him first choice for the task at hand. He had previously been junior flight crew on the massive C130 Hercules transport planes and had flown aid missions to Africa dropping basic famine reliefs and clothing to the needy. The amazing sense of fulfilment of these missions was about to be countered and balanced by the word 'SCRAMBLE.'

The flight line of eager Sea Harriers (*) was pre flight checked and the aircraft were anxiously awaiting their commanders. No time for flight plans, Met checks or cold feet. There was a job to be done. The only brief was to get airborne and go South West awaiting further instructions. Those instructions were academic. As they were given, the four Harriers rounded the promontory of Bluff Cove to see a flaming Sir Galahad being bombed at anchor by an Argentinean Skyhawk fighter. This was no simulation. People were dying. He recalled that people were dying in Africa and he knew what to do then instinctively. It should be no different now. The Sir Galahad could not 'QFO.'

In a spontaneous, reactive moment Doug plunged the Harrier into a VNE maximum speed dive, simultaneously shouting his instructions to his wingmen, reds, two, three and four to ascend. Seconds later the fresh-faced Argentinean pilot saw three British bogeys in his two o'clock high position, the outside pair separating to the left and right. The Argentinean's own wingmen had finished their attack runs and could offer no immediate support. He broke off his attack of the Sir Galahad, which was already crippled and well ablaze, to engage Red three. Red four, acting on his own initiative, 'broke off' from his middle position to pursue an Argentinean, French made

'Super Etendard' fighter. The Argentinean air force was believed to have only five of these devastating aircraft, which were the harbingers of the deadly Exocet missile. A truly fearsome combination, the Entard itself, capable of speeds up to 650 miles an hour, could launch its radar guided Exocets up to 30 miles away from their intended target. The missiles would skim the top of the waves at 700 miles an hour and once launched, they were almost unstoppable. Only three courses of action were available once an Exocet had 'locked on.' The first would be to shoot it down, almost impossible given its cruise speed. The second would be to release a cloud of 'chaff,' a 'metal mist' to confuse its radar guidance system. The last option was to pray.

On the morning of May 4, 1982, the royal naval destroyer H.M.S. Sheffield had time only for the third option. It was duly sunk.

Red four seized the opportunity to reduce by one, Argentina's quotient of such aircraft and he duly exacted his sweet revenge.

The Skyhawk, which had bombed the Sir Galahad, was now only in direct confrontation with Reds Two and Three. Both the British pilots instinctively turned to face their Argentinean aggressor and 'head on' (*) intercept courses were adopted. With closing speeds of 800 knots (920 miles phr) the young airman from Buenos Aires had little time to rationalize. He was naturally right handed and chose to launch his heat seeking, French made 'Magic' missiles on Red three, still in his two o'clock high. They 'locked on' immediately to Red three's heat signature and the HUD (head up display) on board the Harrier illuminated, barking the appropriate warnings

'MISSILE LOCK – MISSILE LOCK!'

It was in fact, far too late for any avoiding action. This was 'point blank' and nothing short of a miracle could prevent the inevitable. That miracle came in the form of Red One, courtesy Douglas Washington. His orders to Red Three were clear

"Red Three! Roll and break left now!"

Red three duly complied. The Skyhawk was unaware of the Harrier that had dived beneath him and obligingly exposed his fleshy, crocodile- like undersides for Red one to attack. Douglas Washington instantly dispatched his own sidewinder missiles, which obliterated their target seconds later. Red three saw none of this as his attention was on the two, heat seeking 'Magic' missiles, currently seeking him.

"Red Three Mayday" he cried constantly in vain, over and over-"Red three Mayday- I have incoming lock!" He had little time to realize that he was in fact jamming the frequency and that Red one was trying to call him to 'work his miracle.'

The two Magic' missiles were only moments away from impact when he let go of the transmit button, clearing the way for the call to come through. It was not the call Red Three had wanted and he delayed his reaction until Doug Washington repeated it as an order,

"Close your throttle now, that's an order!" At a time when he was trying to out run two heat seeking missiles, the last thing he wanted to do was to slow down.

This time Red One jammed the frequency. Again he ordered "close your throttles now!" Red Three had no other action available to him and duly responded to his commanding officers requests applying full back throttle. The great beast of a machine responded instantly as the massive power plant became docile but the Harrier remained straight and level due to the effects of considerable velocity. The commander of Red Three then experienced a moment of great religion disturbed only by the sight of the two 'Magic' heat seeking missiles (so close that he could practically see their serial numbers), veering off his starboard wing and locking on to the ball of fire that was once the Argentinean Skyhawk that had launched them. They sought, they locked on and they finished the job started by Red One. A poetic justice and somewhat of an own goal.

Douglas Washington was a snooker fanatic. He loved the skill of the game and he loved the strategy. He was a natural at playing three shots in front. The moment he saw the lone Skyhawk with the Sir Galahad at its mercy, he had it snookered. The game plan simply presented itself to him in an instant. He knew that by sending his wingmen aloft as he dived, he could effectively sandwich the foe between them and there was no escape. Red Three felt initially that he was a sacrificial lamb, as the Argentinean pilot would statistically fire to his right. On returning to the carrier, he vented his anger and adrenaline on Doug and had to be restrained while Doug explained that it was just a game of snooker. He had every shot worked out in advance. He knew that by cutting the power to the Harriers engine meant that the greater heat source was the burning Argentinean jet. The magic missiles simply couldn't 'see' Red Three any more and went after their host instead. Doug called it 'potting the black.' Red three called it something else. Douglas Washington was awarded the Distinguished Flying Cross for this particular occasion and was subsequently commended for many others. The casualties of the Sir Galahad were atrocious. If it hadn't been for Doug they would have been conclusive. He was a hero.

At the time of their surrender on June the 14th, 1982, Argentina had lost 109 of their aircraft while Douglas Washington and his British colleagues had lost just ten. In 1995, CO Doug Washington's home squadron at RAF Wittering, Cambridgeshire, were shocked at the news that he had been shot down over Bosnia Herzegovina and was missing, presumed dead.

Chapter 4

Of all the Medway towns, Rochester seemed to many, to be the most interesting. It was a testament to the many and varied architectures and influences that peppered lands south of the Thames and it had a definite, diverse appeal. Not so much a blend, more of a punch bowl of old and new styles and designs.

Rochester had a cathedral and, as such, was determined to be a city. Not a bustling, heaving urbanization as the title would suggest, but a town with a strong sense of community, although struggling to find its identity. In a single street there could be found a casino book-ended by an antique shop and another, acting as a specialist outlet for those interested in the occult. There were also myriad afternoon tea 'shoppes' accompanied by art galleries and craft shops, all of which fell under the shadow of the city's own castle. There was a privately owned airfield close to a speedway track and, of course, the Medway supported a large marina and dockyard. There seemed to be plenty of everything in this Medway town. Most visitors would call it a 'midway' town as it appeared to be neither this nor that, but all would say, 'interesting.' As such, it reflected the personality of its indigenous population. They too, were interesting and seemed to have an accent all of their own. It didn't seem to owe its influence to any particular county or region. It was unique. In fact, it was almost a non-dialect. It belonged to Rochester.

It didn't take long that afternoon for Doris Turner and her colleague behind the scone counter of the local bakery, to decide that the olive-skinned gentleman who had sat in the window seat every afternoon this week, drinking strong black coffee, was not from Rochester. These retired old ladies manned the shop six days a week. The wages were negligible but the gossip was champion. The two old dears could 'natter' for England if there was indeed a team. Sadly though, this week, the girls felt somewhat short changed. The interesting stranger in town would just sit in the bay window, drinking coffee and duck whenever an engaging 'not from round here then?' came his way. He was always preoccupied with his watch and would suddenly just get up and go without a 'bye your leave.' He always left far too much money on the table to pay for two cups of black coffee. In the end, the girls gave up on him. If they couldn't chatter with him, it was no bother, they would simply gossip about him! They would sometimes start before he had actually left the shop. He would usually head up the street in the direction of the cathedral.

It was in the shadow of that very cathedral, as the choir sang, that the check - shirted driver climbed into the cabin and primed the diesel charged Iveco 32 toner. He turned the ignition, settled his left boot on the massive clutch pedal and placed both hands on his knee to assist with its depression. As the engine fired and caught, he was sympathetic to the strains of the choir this Sunday afternoon and warmed the massive power plant by revving it to the metre of the hymn during the refrain. That way, he would be less of a nuisance when everyone joined in singing. He went through his final checks. Route, passport, carnet for passage through France, export license for English customs at Dover, import license for the Spanish authorities, cash, some francs and more pesetas than he had taken last time as he'd run short then, and, of course, the ubiquitous Mars bar.

Having made many trans -continental trips before, the driver was quite aware of the customs difficulties usually encountered. It was in the nature of the job. He had hoped for a slackening of 'UCD,' as he called it, 'Unnecessary Custom Delays,' in light of the recent EEC directives concerning freedom of movement for member state passport holders. Not so, it would appear, at least for the British truckers, who were constantly subject to petty checks and delays, particularly in France.

He had made it a practice to add at least one day to his projected job time. He'd made the run to Madrid on several occasions and his firm, 'Forward fast freight' at any one time, would have six or seven container lorries somewhere in Europe, all of whom would have had experienced similar delays at some time or another. He knew the score and was prepared for the usual delays as he left Rochester a day early and headed along the M2 to Dover for an evening rendezvous with a roll on, roll off ferry. He didn't notice the silver BMW that pulled out from behind the rugby club with its single, Mediterranean occupant, also en-route to Dover.

Chapter 5

The Balearic Islands, namely Majorca, Ibiza, Minorca and Formentera were the prettiest islands in the Mediterranean. Enjoying a more North Westerly orientation than Sicily and Malta, they were greener and slightly more temperate, making them attractive to a wider range of vacationer and not just the hardened sun worshippers. Popular also because of their proximity to mainland Spain, where the vast network of established holiday charter flights was easily extended, offering consequent cheap air fares to the islands. Palma alone would attract a staggering 3 million passengers in just 6 months of summer season.

Against this culturally and geographically spectacular setting there was also, sadly, a seedier, sinister side to the islands. Hundreds of late night bars, clubs, and discos played host to thousands of the islands' less desirable visitors and the inevitable parasite trades grew. Ranging from slum apartment holiday 'rip–offs' to black market blood donation, through prostitution and of course, alcohol and drug abuse. The Spanish authorities were not noted for their subtle, 'politically correct' handling of offenders who they would treat harshly in the best traditions of 'zero tolerance' but still these young revellers came in their thousands. From Britain, Germany, Holland and a few from France. Armies of young ' no hopers' who demanded their Balearic fortnight of the four S's - Sun, sand, sex and usually sickness through over indulgence in the other three.

Jose Viladro had run the golden gate nightclub in San Antonio, Ibiza for eight years. It was the town's biggest nightclub and ran to capacity every night starting at 11 PM and running through the night to 6 AM, when the first two of the four S's would steel his trade. Many young revellers could just make the cost of the flight and would actually live on the beach for the duration of their stay. They would simply bop all night and adjourn to the beach as the sun came up and the clubs went down, repeating the cycle for the full two weeks. Many were refused carriage on their return flights until sober causing chaos at the terminal. This was such a common occurrence that a special, high security departure lounge was constructed to hold them. The rules of the air state quite clearly that 'a person must not board any aircraft when drunk or be drunk in it'. The airlines trod a thin line between adhering to this directive and selling the passengers as much alcohol as they could to increase their turnover. Jose took easy pickings from these 'two-weekers' as he called them, as he played on the definition of 'too weak.'

In those 8 years, Jose had seen it all and nothing could shock or offend him. He was used to the sight and sounds of drink and drug crazed, foul-mouthed revellers. Although any violence was dealt with swiftly, he turned a blind eye to the prostitution and soft drug trade taking place in the club. He realized that these were peripheral 'nasties,' necessary for his own existence and looked, if not away, at least sideways. His security staff were quick to eject trouble-makers at the first sign of any violence yet

13

it was not uncommon for sexual acts to take place, not only in the darker corners of the club, but quite openly in the foam party session which was the highlight of the nights entertainment. The local authorities seemed to prefer, and indeed, encourage this behaviour in the clubs, in an effort to keep it off the streets. The security staff, simple muscle to most, were actually quite drug wise and could usually tell the type of substance being traded simply by the manner in which the deal was conducted. The new breed of chemical designer drugs such as Poppers, Ecstasy etc. were allowed but heavier organic drugs, Heroin, Marijuana etc. were 'dirty' and unwelcome. Any caught trading these 'dirties' were not only ejected, seen to be ejected but were seen to have *been* ejected for several days until the swelling subsided.

The definition 'dirty drug', as Jose had instructed them, was not a reflection of his personal disapproval, frankly, he didn't give a damn what the 'too weakers' took or did to themselves, but he knew that the licensing authorities drew the line at the organics.

Recently, there was talk in the club and the town of a new hybrid, half organic yet chemically enhanced, designer drug that not only gave the user the normal euphoric sensations but also reputedly worked directly on the sensory area of the brain responsible for sexual stimulus. Many wild stories were circulating about what effects this new pill did or didn't induce, but there was no doubt that most stories told of endless orgasms experienced by those who took it. It was rumoured that, such was the potency of the drug, reputedly named *'Destiny,'* that uncontrollable, spontaneous ejaculations were experienced within minutes of it being taken and some girls, it had been said, had actually menstruated. Just the smallest amount was necessary and the pills were reported to be one tenth of the size of an Ecstasy tablet. Although there were no reported dealings of the drug, as yet, on the islands, the recent reports from the clubs in Malta suggested that it wouldn't be long before it arrived. Jose Viladro mused as to how his superiors would receive it and whether they would classify this one as 'clean' or 'dirty.'

At 4 am, the house DJ at the 'Gate,' actually a Brit' contracted for the season, pressed the final program button of his disco console and the grand finale began. The familiar garage music overture accompanied by a spectacular laser show heralded the usual five-minute warning before the dance floor was lowered and subsequently filled with foam. This really was the highlight of the evening and the foam acted as a screen, hiding all manner of 'goings on.' Every one got carried away at this point. Even the otherwise most respectable of girls who were secretaries and receptionists in other lives, succumbed to the moment and, at the very least became wet T-shirt contestants. The drug dealers were quick to take advantage of this cover and sexual intercourse 'en -foam' was commonplace.

Jose was in his office when he heard the screams. Not the usual type associated with the high spirits generated by the foam party. These were of a more sinister, threatening strain prompting him to run immediately into the DJ booth which offered, not only a total visual panorama of the club, but a degree of protection from any

14

potential dangers. He arrived just in time to see the first dead body being pulled from the foam. Two more were to follow. Although Jose did not realize it at the time, *'Destiny'* had just arrived on the island.

Chapter 6

Room 155 was sited in one of those endless corridors of Whitehall offices, each charged with a particular task or duty and operated under strict security.

Lawrence Carlton sat at his desk, distracted momentarily from his duties by a picture of his wife Barbara who was tragically killed in an RTA (road traffic accident) 3 years earlier. The therapists had told him that two to three years was an average period for grieving, after which, he should find himself able to re-engage in his life. In the interim, the Paroxetine antidepressants would help relieve the symptoms of clinical depression and offer a 'light at the end of the tunnel.'

The 'mind doctors' also promoted active involvement in sessions with others who had suffered such a loss but this was not for Lawrence. His grief was private and he wouldn't presume to off-load or inflict any such trauma onto another individual. He knew that most people could not remain detached from the pains of others and he had enough on his own plate to deal with. Lawrence decided to deal with his grief alone. He cried a river in his own time but his public face was a stoic portrayal of strength, although some had said that he was 'cold.'

Lawrence's salvation would be his work. He was a pro-activist and achiever and his government superiors recognized this. Maybe they took advantage of his desire to immerse himself in all consuming pursuits in the wake of his loss. This, combined with his background, made him the ideal candidate, in fact, the only choice, to initiate and develop room 155.

Lawrence had studied law at Cambridge graduating with honours from Magdalene. During those study years, he developed a zest for politics and management and combined them by initially setting up various student bodies and clubs. His reputation as a formidable opponent in campus debates earmarked him for future positions of privilege and it was a natural progression for Lawrence to move into politics. He was, in fact, instrumental in establishing the Cambridge branch of the young conservatives and, via this involvement and much lobbying, was able to achieve the formation of the thing for which he would be most remembered in Cambridge, the 'College Air Squadron.' (*)

Lawrence had nurtured a passion for flying ever since his youth. His humble background (his father was a fisherman sailing daily out of Lowestoft,) afforded him no means to pursue the interest, other than his weekends spent at the perimeter fences of RAF Coltishall watching the fast jets manoeuvre and the civilian flights on final approach into nearby Norwich airport. He had financed his own way through university by playing in the many bars and venues that Cambridge had to offer. Lawrence was a talented keyboard player and had spent his formative years playing in bands during the summer seasons at the many holiday camps that the Yarmouth area had to offer. It was on a local wine bar 'gig' in Cambridge that he had in fact met Barbara. It was an instant attraction and a love affair that lasted until her death. She shared Lawrence's enthusiasm for most things but particularly his passion for flying. Together they developed the concept of the College Air Squadron on the notion that, the RAF could tap and nurture an instant supply of potential pilots from graduate stock. They reasoned that much money would be spent and wasted, training, filtering and subsequently rejecting applicants from those solicited by the naff 'come fly with me' Royal Air Force adds in the general tabloid press. They argued that a substantial saving could be made and, of course, Lawrence and 'Babs' could go flying more often. Viewed almost as a logical extension to the Youth Air Training Corps, Lawrence found green lights most of the way and it wasn't long before the first Chipmunk found its way to Cambridge. The Chipmunk was a stalwart military trainer and this one had seen much use and, sadly, abuse. Recognizing the potential for another crusade to get his teeth into, it didn't take long for Lawrence to persuade the Dean and the Bursar of Magdalene that they could now offer aviation based engineering diplomas and the next two Chipmunks followed 6 months later to compliment the engineering workshops. Lawrence accrued a few more brownie points too. There was no stopping him. The CAS grew rapidly and subsequent squadrons were located at Oxford, and York and many top class pilots were spotted, going on to full RAF careers.

Lawrence and Barbara had no such aspirations. She was an economist and her skill with figures helped to get the squadron off the ground, literally. Lawrence had designs on an international law career but achieved his PPL whilst at Cambridge, assuring him of hero status with 'Babs' and making his humble parents even prouder. Larry and 'Babs', as they were known on campus, were married in the chapel of Magdalene in a ceremony immediately following the one where they were handed their degrees. The whole campus attended the service and the ball where Larry joined the band and sang 'come fly with me, come fly lets fly away.'

His career moved rapidly along with law firms head -hunting and offering all manner of incentives to procure his services, one even purporting to offer Lawrence a much sought after Bulldog trainer that it could acquire. Lawrence dismissed this as Bull (dog) shit as he knew the difficulties the CAS had in obtaining their own two Bulldogs at Cambridge and to date, he was unaware of any others that were civilian registered and operated. Ultimately, Lawrence's blend and understanding of international law, politics and general strength of character made him an obvious selection for work in government and latterly, as a Euro minister based in Brussels where, sadly, Barbara was killed.

Room 155 had been established as a special investigations bureau bridging the gap between military and civil aviation matters. Lawrence was currently engaged in protracted negotiations with Brussels over the forthcoming JAR (joint aviation requirements) documents for a scheduled implementation date of January 97. Historically, most countries operated their own set of aviation rules and practices and the growth in air travel now required some standardization of these matters. As in all matters 'EEC,' there was much debate and jockeying for privilege and Lawrence and his staff were at the forefront of these negotiations. However, there were other matters that fell under his mandate for investigation and one such was causing some concern.

Lawrence returned his attentions from Barbara 's photograph to the report passed to him by the Dept. of Transport AAIB (air accident investigation board) inspectors who had exhausted all their own avenues of inquiry. It concerned the two incidents of missing Beagle Pups that bore remarkable similarities. Within 6 weeks of each other, two of these much sought after, rare, delightful little aircraft, had made incomplete 'Mayday' calls and subsequent, extensive 'SAR' (search and rescue) operations had produced no trace of either craft or occupants. Only one hundred and seventy of these highly manoeuvrable, semi aerobatic 'all things to all pilots,' pretty little aircraft had been produced in the number one hanger at Shoreham airfield, Sussex in the mid 60s.

'Beagle' was an acronym of 'British Executive And General Light Aviation' and was a typical example of British design and ingenuity craving government support and finance and receiving neither. With the companies' sad demise in 1969, a little over one hundred of them were completed, with many going abroad. The Swiss air force, for instance, used them as trainers extensively and some were only now beginning to find their way back to their homeland. It was unclear how many of them were left, with several lost through training accidents or simple attrition but those that were left were often pampered, treasured members of the family of those fortunate enough to have one. To lose two in such a short time under such circumstances was not only sad but Lawrence concluded, highly suspicious.

CHAPTER 7

The eastbound traffic of the M2 was moving quite freely, despite the previous hold up, while an overturned caravan, or what was left of it, was taken off the carriageway. He was four hours early for the 8pm ferry so the driver decided on a little detour into Canterbury city centre to pick up some tobacco for his pipe. It was to be a very brief stop; the little tobacconists literally two minutes walk from the car park. It was long enough, however to cause concern for Mario Marcantonio as he unexpectedly followed the lorry off the M2 for it's unscheduled stop. He had spent many hours recently, studying the movements of the vehicles operated by 'Forward Fast' freighting. Mario had shadowed this particular driver on several runs to the continent and he had never before made any deviation to his route or schedule. He found this disturbing. Mario pulled into the car park, staying an appropriate distance away, and waited. In the event, it was simply a harmless shopping stop, but Mario was not to know this and he pondered the ramifications of any delays to his own, carefully laid out plans. It was simply a matter of minutes before the driver returned, pipe duly primed, and the journey resumed, which remained uneventful until he was safely aboard the ferry.

Mario had waited anxiously and was needlessly suspicious, however, he followed the Iveco long enough to assure himself that it was indeed Dover bound and he then made a detour of his own.

Having previously bought a car park season ticket, the BMW now securely parked in the corner of the compound, Mario made his way to platform no 1, Southbound, of Deal station to fulfil his rendezvous with a colleague. She was there before him and was easy to spot amongst the other Dover bound commuters by, not only her stunning, long blond hair, but by the absence of a rucksack. At this time of year, backpackers were commonplace on this line, many en route to Europe via the Dover facilities. Most chose the ferry as it was the cheapest option but there was still a novelty factor to the 'Chunnel' and the persistent ones could be lucky enough to hitch a ride with a family saloon going to Paris.

Mario and his partner were booked on the eight o'clock ferry and were relieved when the train arrived at Deal only two minutes behind schedule.

The cabin of the Iveco unit was a virtual 'home from home' offering every possible comfort except a hot tub. The driver normally lived in the cab throughout the entirety of his journeys, taking advantage of the many service facilities en route when required. These new highway megaliths were expensive but saved a small fortune in overnight lodgings and far from being cramped, the bed offered a high level of comfort. The cab offered the same by way of security. In recent times, it was a sad fact that most truckers would be reluctant to leave their loads overnight unless they really had to. All manner of raids and hijacks had been reported this last twelve months and stowaways in the form of illegal immigrants were always a problem.

Safely installed on the freight deck of the Calais bound ferry, the driver gambled that no harm would come to his rolling 'home -come- work place' for the next twenty minutes so he ventured upstairs for a hot coffee. He also wanted to get some more pesetas from the bureau de change just in case. He was shocked how much prices appeared to have risen on his last trip to Madrid and he wanted to be safe rather than sorry this time. As he sat checking his currency with one hand, he managed to spill his coffee with a 'kak-handed' manoeuvre from the other. He was doubly embarrassed on looking up, to see a gorgeous blonde girl giggling at his carelessness. To date, he was an established bachelor, not through choice, but a general shyness had made him so. He wasn't unduly unattractive but he wasn't particularly handsome either. He just felt so uncomfortable with girls. He did have a romance or two in his youth but both girls eventually ran off with a rugby player and a local restaurateur respectively. Far more interesting types than he, he felt. He grew up 'girl wary' and saw them as objects of intense pleasure usually followed by an even greater measure of pain.

He felt his face flush with crimson when he looked up again as his blond tormentor continued to giggle. At this point, his biology was in a nose-dive, totally out of control. He was genuinely thirsty and tried the coffee again. 'Is she really looking at me?' he thought as he looked over to her once again. This time, her giggle had matured to a very transfixed, inviting smile at which point, the coffee cup became malevolent, refusing to even approach his mouth. What manner of trick was Mother Nature (another women) playing on him? He had no control of his arm at all and the cup began to oscillate in his hand. He could feel the girls gaze penetrating his very soul and his nerves were in turmoil. He decided on a 'forced landing' and tried to return the cup to its saucer by the quickest route. He took aim and threw his arm in its general direction and the resulting 'clack' of its arrival made several of the backpackers look up. He gave up on the coffee and stood up to return to the truck in time to see this blonde 'she devil' laughing out aloud. All of his life, girls had tormented him so.

Comfortably back in his cab, a little less flushed now, he indulged himself in a self-humiliating chuckle and acknowledged what a Pratt he must have looked back in the coffee lounge. He was still thinking of the girl as lots of other passengers rejoined their vehicles whilst the Tannoy announced their imminent arrival at Boulogne.

Docking procedures completed, the commercial vehicles were offloaded first and he was third in line for the customs terminal. He readied his paperwork and duly presented it at the window when his turn came. In an effort to limit 'UCD,' he had learned that it was best to make a small but significant attempt to converse in the native tongue by way of an opening gesture

"Bonsoir monsieur. Je parle francais en peu." The French official made no effort to accommodate him and responded with a volley of French dialogue, no doubt designed to intimidate him. It was an unsuccessful attempt, as the driver was familiar with the strategy, and he failed to take the bait. He knew the best approach from here on in was to just say 'pardon' in the right places, shrug his shoulders in the gaps and persistently present his paperwork for inspection. Eventually, this process took its course and he was on his way with rubber-stamped approval in the relevant boxes.

The immediate route out of the port area, having cleared customs, was usually most frustrating for anyone embarking on a long journey. The conflict of commercial and tourist traffic, jostling for position amongst the cyclists and pedestrians, each wrestling with their maps to check that all important first leg of the trip, led to more frustrating delays. In the space of seconds, the tap on the cab window was swiftly followed by the door being swung open. A single athletic leap landed the vivacious, blond she-devil on the passenger seat beside him.

"Any chance of a lift?"

CHAPTER 8

"Hi Rebecca, I've got you at last!"

"Oh hi Danny ' - great timing, I just got back."

" How was the trip?" Enquired Danny.

"Oh, you know, usual thing. Pretty uneventful, although I nearly missed the flight in the first place. I got held up at Whitehall, but listen..."

"What?"

"Mr. Carlton had some news on Dad."

"Oh that's great! What did he say?"

"Well, its not directly about Dad, but his sources in Sarajevo have had several reports that two pilots are being held captive in the hills near Mostar and he's trying to get confirmation."

" Well that's encouraging, but it could be the two French guys that were shot down"

"Yeah, I know Dan but I've got a feeling about this."

"Becky, come on now, we've been through this before. You're clutching at straws."

"Look Dan, if it's all I've got, then I'm gonna' clutch OK. You've got to understand. He's my dad.

"Yeah I know, but I just don't want to see you go through any more heartaches - it tears me apart to see you end up so distressed and disappointed."

" I know Dan, that's another reason why I love you, but I've got to have something to keep my hopes alive."

"OK. I understand. You go ahead and clutch. We'll talk about it later. Now, talking of clutches, we haven't 'clutched' for six days and I can't go seven I'm afraid!"

"Down tiger, down! Just be patient. I'm all jet-lagged and tourist weary. I wouldn't be up to much tonight."

"I'll be the judge of that. Anyway, all you have to do is 'be there.' Think of England if you want, just be there!"

"You're an animal Michaelson! Did you know that? Hey, I wont be thinking of Dallas that's for sure. The place is a nightmare. Im gonna' skip the next trip. Any way, it's time I went back to Europe for a bit to see what they're up to. Any chance of flying down tonight Dan?"

"Well, let's see. I've got a two-hour lesson this afternoon. Maybe you can pick me up at Biggin hill, say… five thirty?"

" Sure can, err... No Dan....better make it six. The flat's a tip. Need to sort it a bit and have a shower. Is that OK?"

"Yeah, six is fine at Biggin but skip the shower and we'll have a bath together instead. I'll give your shoulders a rub too. How does that sound?"

"Like heaven! I can't wait Dan, fly carefully and I'll see you in the lounge at Biggin as soon as I can. Bye."

Danny had met Rebecca two years ago at a dance at the Concorde club in West Drayton. He'd been attending the two-day conference held by 'Gasil.' Gasil was a periodic publication issued by the CAA concerning matters of safety. It stood for 'General Aviation Safety Information Leaflet.' Danny had been a contributor to 'Gasil' over the years and was a special guest at the conference.

Not only was Danny a full time flying instructor for a small club based at North Weald near Stansted airport but he had a background in radio controlled model aircraft and still built and flew many of his own designs as a hobby. Becky called it his 'busman's hobby' as he never stopped his involvement with aviation, even in his spare time. He was also an electronics expert having worked for British Telecom in his youth, and 'modelling' was a nice way for him to combine his two interests.

Danny was not a regular 'nine to five' kind of a guy however and did things his own way and in his own time. He had an 'off the wall' sense of humour and made light of most things. He had his own, individual approach to teaching and often relaxed a nervous student with his blend of wit and personality. He was undoubtedly the most popular guy on the field and was well respected for his flying and teaching skills. If faced with a particularly nervous pupil, he would use one of his very own, light - hearted, pre- flight briefings to calm them down. For instance, summing up the principles of flight:

"The general idea is to have as many landings as take offs' he would say and wait a carefully gauged time for a reaction. He reasoned that laughter was a great release for tension and nerves, both of which were undesirable for a pilot. "Pull this stick back and the cows get smaller, push it forward for bigger ones.' When pounding the circuit with a student practicing 'touch and goes' (*) (landings followed by immediate take offs,) he would often say, with the straightest of faces, 'try and land as close to the airfield as possible!"

It didn't take long for the students to begin to feel comfortable in, not only the cockpit environment, but also in Danny's presence.

The club he worked for operated three Cessna 152s, two 172s, a Piper Cherokee and Dan's 'other woman' as he called her, a treasured Beagle Pup. The Pup was hire charged five pounds an hour more than the rest of the fleet and Danny, doing it 'his way,' often subsidized the lesson to that amount so that he could fly 'her' instead of the Cessnas. He had eleven hundred hours 'on type' and nobody knew or flew a Pup like

Danny Michaelson. He had even made a radio controlled model of her and made guest appearances at summer shows, where he performed aerobatic displays on both the real and radio controlled versions. These were usually accompanied by one of his inimitable commentaries.

Danny was not only very entertaining but had an endless supply of useful anecdotes. He would tell students to remember the three most useless things in aviation:

'Runway behind you, Sky above you, and Fresh air in the fuel tanks.' Nobody questioned the wisdom of this advice. However, many did question why a pilot of his calibre would spend so much time playing with radio-controlled models. To some, 'Modellers' were likened to 'anoraks,' or train spotters and were considered a bit of a nuisance, not being taken too seriously. Danny would argue a strong case though, for consolidating piloting skills on a model.

'Think about it' he would say. 'You're sitting in the cockpit and you move the stick left, the ailerons roll you left and vice versa. Now, it's OK flying a model in a direction away from you because it will respond in the conventional way. Now imagine that you are stood on the runway with a small remote in your hands and the model is flying towards you. Which way are you gonna' push the joystick to roll left now?' This made most pilots stop and reconsider, not only their understanding of the control surfaces of the aircraft in its different axes, but also their respect or lack of it, for the modellers! Danny had a knack of getting the point across.

In recognition of his invaluable contributions to Gasil, Danny was a guest of honour at the evening's celebrations and was to be awarded a plaque. The impressive, important guest list also included Miss Rebecca Washington who was chosen to present it. When called to the podium to receive his award, Danny made the relevant 'thank-yous' and acceptances and then asked publicly if he could swap the trophy for Miss Washington's phone number. He actually came away with both.

While Danny had been talking to Rebecca on the phone, he had heard his mobile ring in the other room. He hadn't rushed to answer it because he always left his voice mail facility switched on, spending so much time as he did in the air. If the call were important, the caller would leave a message that Danny could pick up at his convenience. If it wasn't, he figured that they would call back anyway.

Danny surrounded himself with gadgets. He loved technology and made very practical use of it. He didn't go anywhere without his 'do it all' electronic personal organizer. This powerful pocket computer contained all the normal 'filofax' type of facilities, but it was powerful enough to run a variety of more complicated programs. Danny ran a powerful flight plan program on his which worked out distances, fuel requirements, wind drifts etc. at the touch of a button and stored them for subsequent trips. The organizer could be hooked up to a printer to make hard copies of the plans and was even capable of sending faxes via his mobile phone.

Sure enough, his mobile rang and an automated voice said "You have one new message waiting...

"Danny, it's Roger at the club. Tried you on your landline - been engaged for ages. Call me urgently, you've got a serious problem.'

CHAPTER 9

The Spanish police were quick to clear the club of any remaining revellers and the chief medical officer was immediately flown over from Palma. He issued strict instructions for the three bodies not to be moved until he had seen them for himself. The local doctor, who was first on the scene, had described the most bizarre, physiological symptoms and neither he nor Senor Mendez himself could find any record or reference of such a condition.

Senor Alberto Mendez arrived by helicopter within 30 minutes of receiving the call. The three bodies, young, white males, were lying on their backs on the dance floor in exactly the same condition, as they were when they were recovered from the foam. All three had prominent erections but their genitalia were haemorrhaging along with their noses and ears. They had apparently bled to death. Blood and semen samples were taken immediately and, when the police had finished collecting their evidence and taking the necessary photographs, the bodies were removed to the local coroner's office for autopsy.

Two pathologists were awoken at their homes and requested to join senor Mendez at once. As they worked in their laboratories throughout the night, the police were interviewing, (although interrogating was probably a more appropriate description,) several youths who were known associates of those currently on the slab. The group had apparently arrived from Malta the day before and eventually confessed to bringing a supply of drugs with them including a new one called *'Destiny.'* A pusher in Slima had introduced them to it. He had actually given them a small supply to use and some Ecstasy free of charge. They, in return, had to agree to tell their friends about this new wonder drug and exactly where they could get it. The police inspector could find no drugs on the youths at all and they confessed to flushing their remaining supplies down the toilet when the commotion started.

At 9 am, Senor Mendez was woken from a brief slumber in his chair by the sound of the laser jet printer dispatching its report containing the analysis of their night's endeavours. The desktop computer was connected via the Internet, on a secure, firewall-encrypted link, to a network of other similar terminals in government pathology labs worldwide. All were running the radically new 'Byotek' analysis program.

The Byotek program had taken years to develop and was the culmination of extensive, international co-operation between many different government agencies, pharmaceutical companies and top bio- chemists worldwide. Initially promoted by Interpol in their war against the proliferation of new designer drugs in Europe, the project heralded an unheard of level of coalition between national security forces who were normally engaged in covert operations against each other. The CIA were next in the project offering geographical data pertaining to the origination of different banned substances, even down to the location and origination of many different grades and strains of the various plants. They could pinpoint the source of the rarest blends of heroin, marijuana etc., usually being able to offer a grid reference for the seedbeds, details of known chemists / production techniques, the particular cartel and its supply infrastructure.

Israel were major contributors financially and practically to the project. This insular nation showed great prudence by their investment in the scheme. Others questioned their involvement and suspected ulterior motives. 'Why such an investment of funds and manpower when Israel effectively had no drug problems of its own?' Ever the supreme diplomat and statesman, Yitsak Shamir replied

"You are of course, correct. Unlike your own countries, we have no drug abuse problem to speak of and quite frankly, we want to keep it that way."

The biggest surprise was in fact the involvement and outstanding input from the Russians. For the first time, here was a project of immense proportions and potential that saw MI5, Interpol, the Mossad, the CIA and the KGB, the Surite and others, working together as a cohesive, productive work force.

With the demise of the Berlin wall and all that it represented, the world press buried themselves in the rhetoric of a new world order with freedom of speech and enterprise. They spoke of a new age of brotherhood and prosperity and of new markets and expanding economies. They were wrong. Areas of Middle Eastern Europe were plunged into chaos. Far from prospering, communities were torn apart and established boundaries were freshly disputed. Trading networks foundered and political regimes were hijacked, subsequently betraying each other. Without the policing presence of a central, powerful communist force and, effectively, left to their own devices, cracks began to appear in communities that previously lived together untroubled for decades. Minor ethnic community squabbles escalated into civil wars and the ugly spectre of Nazism and genocide re -appeared with the disgusting arrival of ethnic cleansing in Bosnia.

The only free enterprise market that did prosper in Russia was the black one. Where the communist party left off, the Russian Mafia took over and a sub culture of drugs and racketeering was soon established. There was a public up rising, culminating in a siege and eventual take over of the ruling government offices and buildings.

Boris Yeltsin took an initiative and ordered the military to intervene. A series of much publicized raids were broadcast world wide with brutal treatment of suspected criminals graphically reported on global television networks such as NBC. There was an obvious propaganda element to this exercise with Boris being seen to 'fight the good fight' but, to his credit, this somewhat curious, radical Russian president recognized that he had a vast drug problem gripping his country. The shrewd timing of these much-publicized raids coincided with the expansion of the Byotek project. He had, of course known of the project since its inception. He knew also that it had stalled due to a technical problem, the nature of which his scientists were aware and assured him they could overcome. Where his predecessor, Mikhail Gorbachov, had brought about change through earnest debate and lobby, Boris was an expert at playing the tactical manoeuvres game. He was adept at getting what he wanted without actually asking for it, an expert in manipulation. He wanted to be established in the world eye as a new, amenable and co-operative Russian leader who played his role in the international community. He wanted also to find a market place for Russian technical ingenuity and more immediately, he needed help with his country's own drug problems. However, Boris did not want to lose face in his previously autonomous land by going 'cap in hand' to the international community and asking for help with his domestic problems. His masterstroke was to be seen as saving the day by offering a solution to Byotek's problems when in fact; Byotek's own expertise was invaluable and more important to him. He knew he could win points at home and abroad with his timely intervention.

" You know, of course, of the manner in which we have dealt with our own drug problems. We take it very seriously and stifle it in the early stages. We too have a project similar to your Byotek operation and I believe we maybe of some help to you as I understand your project has faltered."

The Byotek administrators were situated in Brussels, the obvious place to co-ordinate international co- operations of such magnitude. The directors of Byotek sat up and begged when the call came from the Russian premier.

" My sources tell me that you are having technical difficulties interfacing the program data with the analytical hardware required. I believe we have such an interface."

In fact, at that time, the Russians didn't! However, Boris was afforded access to the Byotek system data immediately and while his experts extracted the information they needed and took the necessary action to counter their own domestic drug problems, his technicians were working around the clock on the interface. In fact, all they had to do was adapt a military sensor (*) that they had developed years earlier. This system actually 'sniffed' gaseous compounds that it may encounter in a war zone and gave an instant breakdown and read out of any known compounds, displaying appropriate procedures, treatments and courses of action. It would also issue an alarm if it came into contact with a previously unknown substance, being unable to offer any antidotes or remedial actions. The technology was so refined that it was ergonomically designed to be fitted to their MIG fighter planes as well as the hand held units that the ground forces used. These planes would make a sortie over an active battle zone and instantly relay information to a ground station of any chemical, or biological substances that were present. A suitably adapted device was soon available to offer Brussels for Byotek. Later versions and adaptations of this technology were widely used in the Gulf conflict to alert allied forces against any chemical weapons used by Saddam Hussien.

A qualified chemist could easily follow the procedures required to break down any substance in readiness for analysis. The first stage would be the sterile chamber. The substance would be entered, the chamber would be sealed and a vacuum induced. The gaseous elements would be the first to be noted. Heat treatment was next. Many compounds experienced a metamorphosis when heated to a certain temperature. Indeed, the actual point of change at a given temperature was often an indication as to what the substance actually was. Once broken down in this manner, it was subject to a period of not less than two hours in a centrifuge, to further separate its constituent parts. The atomic structures of different substances all had their own gravitational fingerprint. Each had a specific gravity particular to its type and its atoms would collect at the same point in the centrifuge. When isolated and no longer a 'compound', each would be subject to chemical reactives and again, reaction time, degree of change etc. would be noted by Byotek, plotted against the initial figures given under heat testing and then compared with league tables of known quantities resulting in a general analysis. If identified, supplementary data as to its origin etc. was also supplied. The process involved massive equations and took an average of five hours before data was available.

Yeltsin had 'pulled it off' and many orders were received, not only for the complete units, but the various components and spin offs for general use by the drug companies. He had launched a new Russian industry and collected a few international 'house points' in doing so.

As the report filed off the printer, senor Mendez was heard to mutter 'Santa Maria!' At that point, his chief pathologist, also from Palma, had joined him and they could not believe their eyes. Byotek had taken its five hours to dissect, deliberate and deliver its findings. Headed by four 'skull and crossbones', question mark icons, that warned of unknown toxic compounds, here was a schedule of the most elaborate, comprehensive and potentially lethal, narcotic substance he had ever come across. There were many surprising constituents that bore no apparent relevance to the cocktail. A domestic painkiller was present in all three victim's metabolisms along with large traces of a particular cough and cold medicine. They concluded that the three friends were all suffering hangovers from their obvious binges of drink and soft drugs and dismissed the presence of these elements in their blood streams as remedial. There were amphetamines of five different varieties along with traces of caffeine and an adrenaline compound used in the immediate treatment of cardiac arrest. This caused some concern and confusion because the three autopsies had shown myocardial infarct (heart attack,) to be one of the causes of death. There was also massive haemorrhaging of internal organs, particularly of the lungs, and suffocation was listed as another cause.

"These boys drowned in their own blood and were too high to even notice," said Senor Mendez. He considered that the initial symptoms may well have induced coughing and the boys took their cough medicine when they were lucid to sooth the condition. Another doctor entered the room and saw the consternation of the others. After a while studying the report, he suggested that the adrenaline was present to accelerate the heart beat and metabolic rate in order to ingest the drug into the system more quickly. This tied in with the police inspector's account of his recent nighttime interrogations. Those interviewed had stated that this new drug would act within minutes of being taken and this would account for the rapid deaths in the foam. They had been perfectly OK just prior to entering it. There were traces of many known narcotics in the analysis and there was a real 'nasty' too, Heroin! This ingredient was no doubt included to induce a rapid addiction.

A suggestion as to the purpose and nature of one of the unknown 'skull and crossbones' was offered by a paragraph originating from the Glasgow, Scotland terminal. They had seen recent deaths whereby cellulose capsules that had previously been melted down and injected, had re- coagulated causing arterial blockage. Many of Glasgow's surviving heroin addicts had developed gangrene and suffered amputations due to using this type of drug in this fashion.

Senor Mendez was puzzled by conflicting physical abnormalities found during autopsy and may have found the answer also from his Glasgow colleagues. On opening the chest cavities of all three cadavers, both massive haemorrhaging and regional blood clotting were found. These two conditions were contradictory by nature and biologically opposed. He retorted that there was nothing logical at all about these particular 'bio -logical' examples!

On review of the evidence before the team, a picture began to evolve of the regime of these *'Destiny'* pills. The adrenaline would ensure a swift delivery around the body of its various constituents, some of which obviously induced the sexual stimulus and resultant haemorrhaging. This unknown clotting agent was then designed to 'put the brakes on' and effectively 'dam' the blood flow at various places allowing a build up of compounds at the most reactive organs, concentrating and exaggerating the consequent effects to the user.

As discussion and abhoration continued throughout the room, the terminal bleeped once again and the printer chattered a further report onto the desk. Another possible explanation for the second 'icon' was offered from the Moroccan terminal. A similarity had been found between this unknown commodity and an organic compound used in the treatment of impotence. A derivative of a particular tree root, the Yhoba tree, used by the nomadic tribesmen of northern Africa for centuries, as an aphrodisiac and beyond, was recently seen as a periodic cure for detumescent (impotent) elder patients attending private health clinics. These were usually rich old men who had acquired 'gold digger' type, considerably younger mistresses and were desperate to copulate with them. The drugs were extremely potent, effective and consequently expensive.

The Uharu tribe of the eastern Sahara were a male dominated culture and women were considered not as partners, friends or lovers but as housekeepers and mothers. The roving nature and routine of the tribe could not be jeopardized by untimely pregnancies so a breeding season was utilized. During the spring hunting season, the strong young men of the tribe would venture south and hunt stocks of water buffalo. They would then return to the village where the women folk would prepare stocks for the winter season. The tribe would settle during December and January for birthing and the men would recuperate from the summer's kills. A ceremony to mark the start of the hunting season would begin with a weeklong fertility ritual. A preparation made from the root Yhoba bush would provide a raging erection for the young studs of the tribe that would last ten hours plus. It was a one-week orgy whilst the remaining fifty-one weeks of the year were spent celibate.

Many new additions to the tribe arrived in the New Year and were always of strong virile stock.

The Marrakesh Byotek report offered an explanation also, for the presence of the cough syrup. A popular, readily available decongestant was known to prevent erection and was offered by various clinics as an antidote to their Yhoba treatments should any embarrassing and untimely erections remain. Two teaspoonfuls were enough to return an active lover to a dormant state in a matter of minutes.

These Maltese revellers had obviously been on a cycle of sex and cough syrup for days and the drugs had an apparent cumulative effect resulting in their deaths.

The terminal bleeped again signalling the arrival of more 'E - mail'. This time it was from Washington. The CIA database offered a location for the grade of heroin that was present; Sicily.

After a long exhausting night, it was an overall conclusion by Senor Mendez and his team that this *'Destiny'* was designed for maximum, immediate impact and because of its inherently lethal and addictive nature, they could expect an extensive, rapid, marketing campaign to quickly establish it amongst the clubs and the junkies and many such deaths would result as a consequence.

Senor Mendez thanked and dismissed his colleagues. Although each of them would continue to research the drug from their own laboratories, he felt that this was a matter that had to be handled and co-ordinated directly from Brussels.

Before he left the office in San Antonio, Senor Alberto Mendez sent an 'all station address' message, with a 'priority red' designator. Via the Internet, this designator would poll every laboratory, office and Byotek station, world wide, urgently requesting information of any nature concerning *'Destiny.'* It was imperative that the drug was analysed and broken down to its base elements immediately. Not only was it essential that the unknown constituents were identified but the actual quantities and mix were also needed in order to develop an antidote. Many of these 'counter measure' remedial preparations were themselves highly toxic and a delicate, carefully measured amount was to be administered in order to cure not kill. In order to save many young lives, Byotek must prove itself, and do so now.

As papers were gathered and briefcases closed, there was one last beep. Once again the printer engaged and produced a single page for inspection. It simply read 'LOOK TO YOUR FUTURE. THE FUTURE IS AT HAND'. The document was unsigned and unheaded. It was absolutely anonymous. After brief consideration, the team decided that it bore no relevance to their task so they dismissed it as a spurious transmission taking a wrong turn on the vast information highway.

Senor Mendez made arrangements to sleep. He would then board a plane and make a full report to his superiors in Brussels.

CHAPTER 10

He had made the journey several times and the route was familiar to him. Very little reference to the map was required. Occasionally, he would take a slightly different but parallel track, and take advantage of some of the splendid French countryside on offer. However, on this occasion, panoramic France was not his priority. He sensed that his blonde travelling companion wanted more than just a lift. Just how much more, he was uncertain, but he felt a rush of sexual anticipation mixed with a slight anxiety. It had been so long since he had received any affection that he had become reasonably comfortable without it. Comfortable that is, in the absence of the distress that usually followed such a liaison on its eventual demise. After his last relationship, which ended on a sour note, he made himself one of those personal 'never again' promises which inevitably end up being broken. It was time though. This last two years of endless freighting on endless autoroutes had afforded him the space and solitude he had required but they had also awarded him certain loneliness. Yes, it was time, and this girl was so very beautiful.

His usual itinerary meant heading south on the E402 autoroute on leaving Boulogne and making Bordeaux by evening, resting in a lay-by or similar facility for the night. His schedule for the following day meant leaving the main E72 between Bordeaux and Toulouse and taking minor, but more direct country roads to cross the Spanish border at Puerto de Somport mid afternoon. This leg would take him close to Lourdes and, on the last trip, he had managed to make the necessary diversion to the famous town, visited also by the Virgin Mary. Whilst hardly a pilgrim, he had taken the time to light a candle and pray for his father.

Journey resumed, it was onto Zarragoza and eventually Madrid to dispatch his load of mountain bikes, his usual cargo for this trip. On this occasion though, he would not make Madrid.

The young, blond lady, who said her name was Ruth, seemed to be in no hurry to get anywhere in particular. When asked, she said she was 'just along for the ride' however, she inquired if the drivers route would take him anywhere near la Rochelle, a small town on the west coast of France which also boasted an eighteenth century cathedral and a small airfield. She had a friend there and, as it was so late, maybe she could arrange some overnight accommodation for them both if he so desired. He hung onto the word 'desire' and said that it would be no bother but he must make Madrid by tomorrow evening. He would have to make an early start the following morning.

Once in La Rochelle, they made a refuelling stop and Ruth made a phone call to her friends. She reported, sadly, that they were not at home but she did know a little reasonably priced motel on the north side of town.

That night, he broke his personal promise and made love several times with Ruth. He knew not why this gorgeous blond woman chose him but he wasted no time questioning it further. Every dog has his day, or night, he reasoned and this was his.

He was awakened by the sound of a vehicle being started and he turned over to make love to his companion yet again. She was gone. His immediate reaction was to check his wallet and, as he leapt out of bed to find his jacket, he felt suckered. He scolded himself for his lack of caution and reminded himself of his theory that women amounted to intense pleasure followed by a larger measure of pain. He suspected he was about to be invoiced for a night of the former. He was more than surprised to find his wallet, passport and all papers exactly where they were meant to be. His sense of relief was short lived however as he suddenly remembered the truck. He had been woken by the sound of one being started.

'How could I be so stupid!' He reprimanded himself. He ran out of the room and down the corridor wearing only his boxers and arrived in the car park to find his Iveco exactly where, and as, he left it. This didn't 'add up' and he returned to his room to double check everything. Nothing was missing.

Several cups of strong French coffee later and, after several, unsuccessful attempts to converse with the reception desk about the whereabouts of his partner, he pacified himself with the notion that maybe, this time, he would just be left with the pleasant aspect of the experience. No downside. This girl had taken what she wanted of him, when she wanted and they had both had a great time. Now she was gone. That's all there was to it.

Showered and refreshed, and a little behind schedule, he rejoined the motorway and headed for Bordeaux. As he passed the airfield, a Reims Cessna 172 was taking off and, for a moment, he swore that he could see a blond sitting in the pilot's seat.

Making up for lost time, he was relieved to arrive at Puerto de Somport by 3 pm. He had been anxious about his carnet requirements. The customs officer at Boulogne had stamped the papers with a 5pm arrival time at Somport. A carnet was a temporary import license for the goods within its schedule. If these goods were not exported from France by the given hour then a considerable fine was levied. He was well within the stated period though when he presented himself at the Spanish post. He couldn't understand why he had been asked to wait in a secure office and why he was being further delayed. Despite his protestations, no explanation was forthcoming so he prepared himself for further 'UCD'.

A further two hours passed and eventually a Senior customs officer entered the room with a police officer. The drivers' questions remained unheeded and the Spanish officer spoke in a strained English:

"You are a British citizen?" he enquired.

"Yes" he replied.

"Are you the owner of vehicle registration D226 SSA?"

"I am a co-director of the company that owns it and several others. What is the problem?" His question remained temporarily unanswered.

"Are you the driver of vehicle D226 SSA?"

"Yes, look what is this? What is the problem? I have to be..." He was interrupted by the police officer:

"You are under arrest for the transportation of Heroin."

CHAPTER 11

"Roger? Hi, it's Danny. What's up?" Roger was the flying club owner and Danny's boss.

" Dan, you better get over here straight away."

" What's the panic?"

" Look, I can't talk properly now, but, in a nutshell, I've got a Brass from the CAA (*) here going through the books. He's asking all manner of questions about you and he's not happy about something. He wants to interview you straight away. What's going on Dan?"

" I have no idea, I'm squeaky clean. You know that. What did he say?"

" Well, he's not giving anything away, but he's comparing our booking in/out log with some notes of his own. He's questioned everyone here at the field about you, your attitude and general airmanship and stuff. Naturally, we've waved several copies of 'Gasil' under his nose and your award is staring right at him in the office, but he seems to have a bee in his bonnet about something. Look Dan, I'd get over here double quick if I were you. You know these blokes don't muck about."

" Christ, I'm stunned. OK look, I'm on my way but I've simply got no idea what it's about. I'm sure we can clear it up quickly. See you in twenty."

The flat was a tip. Rebecca should have had a maid. She could afford it, but she couldn't stand the thought of someone in her home, her sanctuary, so, it was a simple equation, it turned into a tip when she was busy and back into a home when she wasn't. It was almost back to a home when the phone rang.

" This is the international operator, will you accept a reverse charge call?" The voice was accompanied by that annoying echo effect that was common on international calls, making it sound like you were having a conversation with yourself.

" Yes, of course. Who..." There was a click or two before a familiar voice came on the line

" Becky! Is that you? It's Peter."

" Peter, yes it's me. Where are you? What's the matter?"

"Becky, listen carefully, I haven't got long. I'm in Zaragoza and I'm in trouble. I've been arrested for drug smuggling."

" You've what!" ·

" Drug smuggling. Look I'm innocent, I've been framed. I've been totally stitched up from start to finish...."

At this point, Rebecca could hear a lot of shouting.

" Peter! Peter! Are you there?"

" Becky, look, they're giving me a bad time here, you've gotta' help me, there was this blond girl and...."

" What girl, where?"

" I have to go. Becky, I'm in a jail in Zaragoza. Please call the British Embassy, the British Embassy here in Spain, Madrid. Have you got that?"

Rebecca could hear more shouting and she heard Peter arguing with someone.

" Peter! Peter!......." He had gone. Rebecca still had the phone to her head when a Spanish voice started speaking. She had basic Spanish skills but her mind was in turmoil and she couldn't follow it. It was seconds before the voice changed and spoke a strained English, and said

"Three thousand five hundred pesetas will be charged to your account" and then hung up.

Becky was usually good in a crisis. She always had been. She had saved the day on many occasions, with all manner of passenger problems, but this was different. This was family. With Dad still missing, she only had Peter. They were very close. She couldn't quite accept what was going on. She tried to gather herself and think straight. She did it by the book. Her training had provided her with some useful counselling skills for distressed passengers and she turned them on herself. She was a little in shock and recognized the signs. She knew that there were three stages to dealing with a trauma and she told herself she better get on with them, for Peter's sake. One, denial. She couldn't believe what she'd just been told. It just didn't make any sense. Two, anger. She was furious that her brother was in such a predicament if indeed he was. Three, acceptance. It is only when you get to stage three that there is a potential for recovery. The whole process usually took considerably longer but Rebecca dealt with it in minutes. She reasoned that it was indeed her brother she spoke to and there was no point in his lying to her. Accept it and get on with it. Sit down and make some calls.

She had been connected to the British consulate in Madrid, without speaking to anyone important enough to help her, for ten minutes plus, when the front door bell rang. It went several times and she ignored it. Eventually, she heard Danny calling through the letterbox.

" Please hold" she ran to the door and let him in, running back to the phone, shouting at Danny as she went.

" How did you know? How did you find out?" Danny pulled a face and followed Rebecca into the lounge. He overheard a fragmented version of the story as she was, at last, connected to the British Ambassador and as she duly related it to him over the phone.

" That's right Sir, Peter Washington, son of Douglas, a decorated commander in the RAF. Yes sir, my name is Rebecca Washington, Peter's sister. Please sir, do something as soon as possible. Thank you, thank you!" She wasn't sure if she had said it twice or if it was that infernal echo.

" Dan, how did you?... What are you doing here? I thought I was supposed to...."

" Calm down Becky, it's O.k. I drove. Just take it easy and tell me what's going on."

" You mean you don't know? Then what are you doing here?"

" I don't know anything. I've had a couple of problems of my own so I just drove down. Don't worry about that just now, you must tell me everything. From the beginning, OK." He decided that, even though he was in a considerable spot himself, it would keep. Rebecca needed him alone at this point, without any additional problems of his to contend with. As he put his arm around her, the phone rang.

CHAPTER 12

Mario found his father tending his nets at the quayside, watching the others fishing out in the bay.

" The engine she is sick again papa?" Guiseppe found the mobility to run the last few yards towards his son and he cried uncontrollably in the embrace.

" Papa it's OK. I'm gonna' fix everything now. I have much money and I'm going to take care of everything, as I always do."

Mario had always been well liked in the village. As a child, he did what other children did and often got into trouble. He would be reprimanded along with the others but rarely punished. When the others raided the orchard, they would make themselves sick with oranges. Mario would take his share away for others to have. When his friend's father died, Mario took his mother a fish from his fathers catch every day for her supper until she was well enough to cope again. Every one in Niapello knew of the cheeky faced, naughty boy with a generous heart who would steal from your orchard but give you a fish. He would rather run errands for family or neighbours than play silly games with the other children. He liked to be liked and indeed he was. Nothing had changed now. He was still there to help anyone in the village with a problem and, with his new found prosperity, about which, no questions were asked, he was about to put Niapello back on its feet again. The villagers were used to turning a blind eye when it came to Mario. No one asked where the money came from when Mario gave considerable amounts to the village church for its repairs. The chapel of 'Our Lady of Suffering' was the central point of the village geographically and was its heart socially. Mario knew that the community was held together by the church and he made it a priority. The roof would have its repairs and there would be a new statue for the villagers to bear aloft and lay their offerings before.

No one questioned where the money came from to replant and rescue the orange grove, which was the village's other industry alongside the fishing trade. Mario had a long established relationship with the long, narrow orchard and felt a responsibility towards it. Having been party to those childhood raids, he progressed to working the orchard as a young man. He first made love there, to a girl from the town. He would never forget the smell of her scent mixed with that of the oranges and the sweet taste of both. Every one in the village had worked the grove at some stage or another. In recent years, it too had faltered. There had been no new plantings for several years and this season's yield from the tired over burdened trees had been poor. Mario was about to intervene once again.

When the trucks arrived with the new sapling trees from Morocco, Mario was guest of honour and the whole village turned out to receive and plant them. Under Mario's supervision, two, long, dense lines were planted in rows with a small central avenue between them to facilitate access for the motorbike cart vehicles that were common in such plantations. The foliage from the two rows of trees would provide a canopy over the central parade shielding the workers from the ravages of the sun and Mario had designed a trellis work of ropes and pulleys to hold them in place. He was, of course, a trained engineer and this system was radical in design but simple in use. He taught the townspeople how it would work and they all understood.

That night, a grand feast was held on the plantation and while the women folk cooked, then sang and danced, Mario and the village elders huddled around the fire in the clandestine fashion that was commonplace on the islands. They drank local red wine and talked of the future. This year would be a good one for Niapello.

The funeral was well attended. Felecia Marcantonio had been a lace maker and every home in the village had an example of her lavish embroidery. Her coffin was draped with a large tablecloth adorned with smaller exhibits of her work which were duly buried along with her. Mario wept for his mother and was comforted by his father, who bent down and whispered in his ear. Suddenly the tears stopped and a smile replaced the sorrow. Guiseppe had explained that there were many ways to grieve the passing of a loved one. In sorrow you can always find joy.

" My son, it is selfish to mourn the absence of a loved one without recognizing the relief death often brings to those who had suffered so much pain in life." Guiseppe recalled the way the cancer had ravaged his beautiful Felicia and the screams of pain that tore at his soul each night. Mario understood that his father would rather be without his love and companion of forty plus years than to see her suffer any more. It was the greatest of all loves. His smile then blossomed in earnest gratitude to the deliverer of his mother's release. Death was the best gift that she could have had. The best gift that he himself had ever received was his father's wisdom. He had taught him so much. Mario would repay him this time

" But papa, you don't have to fish any more. I make enough for you now!"

The old man took his son's hand

"Mario, my precious boy. Listen to me for a while. In my long, difficult life, I have worked hard for many things. Most of them have been taken away from me and I had no choice in the matter. I chose to fish as a boy and now, as an old man who can still enjoy the freedom of choice, I choose to fish. My wife has been taken from me and many other things too but, as I breathe, you cannot take my pride and I am proud to fish for my village. What you are is who you are. Do you understand my son?" Mario never questioned his father on the matter again.

As Mario boarded the ferry the following day, the engineers and craftsmen were hard at work on Guiseppe's boat. A new engine was being installed and structural damage caused by the last storm was being attended by master carpenters and chandlers. Guiseppe waved farewell to his son. He knew Mario would be back soon.

CHAPTER 13

"Hello, Rebecca speaking'' Becky was hoping that the call would be from the consulate.

A woman's voice gave a curt reply instead.

" Do you know how much trouble your brother is in Miss Washington?"

"Eh, not exactly. Who is..."

" Peter means a lot to you doesn't he?....." Suddenly, the call was terminated and Rebecca was left with a dial tone.

" Who was that?" Asked Dan.

" I don't know. Some woman just told me that Peter was in a lot of trouble and she kind of threatened me.!"

" What do you mean, threat?"

" Well, it was a bit ambiguous. She actually... Well, she just asked me, or told me even, that Peter meant a lot to me and that he was in a lot of trouble. Then she hung up. Maybe she was calling internationally from the Embassy and got cut off. It was a bit strange."

" Is that all she said?" Inquired Dan. The phone rang again. Rebecca still had her hand on the set as if to prompt a call from the Embassy. The same voice was at the other end.

" Do you realize the penalties for smuggling Heroin? Your brother could spend up to 15 years in a Spanish jail and he would not come out the same man, that is, if he comes out at all."

" Who is this? What do you want?"

" The Spanish authorities deal harshly with drug smugglers and the prisons are not the most civilized. You brother is going to lose everything. Do you know that?"

" Look, who are you? What do you..." Once again, the dial tone. Rebecca began to cry and Danny rushed to her aid.

" Becky what is it? What's going on?" The phone rang once again. This time Danny grabbed it.

" Look, who ever you are what do you want?"

" Hum, I'm sorry. Is this the right number for Rebecca Washington? This is Lawrence Carlton speaking."

Danny hesitated before replying,

" Mr. Carlton, of course, I'm sorry but she's had a bit of a family upset today coupled with some strange phone calls just a minute ago. She's a bit distressed right now and can't come to the phone. This is Danny her boyfriend. Can I give her a message for you?"

" Danny, hello, Rebecca has told me all about you. I believe we have a few things in common. Eh, if this is a bad time, I can call back tomorrow but I have some encouraging news of her father that she may like to hear."

" Dan, I'm OK, I'll talk to him." Said Rebecca. Danny passed her the phone.

" Hello Mr. Carlton."

" 'Lawrence' please Rebecca. You sound terribly upset my dear, is there anything I can do?" Rebecca unfolded the story for him. Firstly, by way of a release and secondly, in the hope that he may be in a position to offer some help.

" Well my dear, that's quite a story, I'm not surprised you're so upset. You appear to be having more than your fair share of family problems. Well, first of all, I'm afraid that I can't directly intervene. There are proper channels for this kind of thing as we don't know for sure that he's actually innocent." This remark touched a nerve with Rebecca but before she could protest too much, Lawrence continued.

" No offence intended Rebecca; I'm just playing devil's advocate. It wouldn't be the first time that a British citizen has got himself into trouble abroad and summoned the weight of the foreign office to his side when, in actual fact, he was guilty as hell. That's why there are procedures for this kind of thing. I'm sure, from what you have told me that your brother has been set up. What else did this caller say?"

" I've told you everything. She may be trying to call back now."

" OK Rebecca, I'll keep this brief. You say your brothers in a prison in Zarragoza and his full name is Peter Robert Washington." Becky supplied him with all the respective details.

" I may not be able to deal with this directly but I can make sure that the correct authorities are informed and that the correct procedures are adhered to. These things take time though, I'm afraid and you're just going to have to be patient. I'm off to Brussels tomorrow for a few days and I believe I can be quite effective there so leave it with me. I'll do what I can and keep you informed. Meanwhile, I have some news of your father that I'm sure will be welcome. We have had a confirmed report by a captured Serb soldier that he has seen two British airmen being held captive in the hills near the village of Zenica, north of Sarajevo. A UN team questioned the prisoner, currently being held by Muslims, and he simply mentioned the airmen without any prompting. They apparently sent a team to investigate but they believe the pilots had been moved just before they arrived. They said that there was evidence to support the soldier's claims though. Various bits and pieces left at the scene and the dates and timings are consistent with those relating to your father and his co pilot. We have, of course, approached the Bosnian authorities but they deny all knowledge of them."

" Did this soldier say if Dad was all right, if he was OK?"

41

" Well, as far as we can tell, he said that one pilot had a broken leg or ankle but the other seemed to be OK despite a bit of a cough. We are guessing that General Milosevic is holding them and will no doubt use them as political pawns or hostages when a situation presents itself. The Serbs wont admit to holding any member of the peacekeeping forces against their will at this stage, because they could incur the full wrath of the UN. However, general Milosevic is a shrewd cookie and we believe that he'll keep the airmen in good health. It could just work out that, if the war goes his way and he's victorious, but seen as the evil aggressor, he may want to win some international favour by being seen to rescue and return them. We're optimistic about their welfare but, of course, in a war situation, many things can happen. We want to locate and retrieve them as soon as possible."

Rebecca thanked him for his help and hung up. After five very long minutes stood watching the phone, Danny insisted that she came and sat down and he made her a cup of tea. There were no more calls that night. Rebecca questioned Danny as to why he'd driven up and didn't fly and, did he say earlier that he'd had some problems? He placated her with a tale of 'double bookings' and 'out of hours aircraft' (all light aircraft require a check every 62 days or 50 flown hours. Many pilots don't get the checks done in time and are consequently grounded until they are duly completed.) Danny didn't want Rebecca to have any more worries tonight and, besides, he just couldn't bring himself to tell her the truth.

Danny was absolutely in love with Rebecca. Having a high profile job and a personality to suit made him not unattractive to the opposite sex and he'd had many girlfriends in his time. Over the years, he'd picked up an aspect of each one of them that he'd found attractive. A smile here, a curve there. A mannerism or laugh. A hair style. A dress sense or husky voice. A particular way of walking and general body language. A vulnerability. Especially the vulnerability. If he sensed a need, his greatest fulfilment would be to come to the rescue of a damsel in distress. When he met Becky, it was instant. She was his dream woman personified. And tonight she was in distress. She was vulnerable. This night Danny would make love to Rebecca, but not in the way that he'd originally intended. The physical attraction between them was intense and their lovemaking was usually athletic in the extreme. They made love whenever and wherever the mood took them. Once, the desire was so great that they actually made love one afternoon in the car, on the top, open air storey of the local NCP car park, believing that no one would park in the 'upper regions' during the quiet of the mid week period and thinking, therefore, that they would not be observed. They were almost correct in that assumption but not quite. They had neglected the fact that the car park laid directly underneath the 'Down wind' leg of the local flying club's circuit (*).

On the next occasion that the pair went to the club together for a drink, Roger told them to make a special point of checking the new 'AICs' (Aeronautical Information Circulars) on the notice board. These notices had to be checked before any intended flight for any temporary restrictions or changes to airspace. For instance, whenever a flight of a Royal nature took place, and there were always helicopters ferrying various 'Windsor's' or other foreign dignitaries across the region, an 'AIC' would be posted notifying all airfields as to the existence of temporary, restricted,' Purple' airspace. On this occasion, a rather large notice was attached to the board advising of temporary, unrestricted, 'Blue' airspace in the vicinity of the car park and any members wishing to join a planned 'fly out' to this location on Danny and Rebecca's next day off, were to please add their names to the list!

This night however, was to be different. This night, Danny was to be 'lover' not lust. He was refuge not dominance, support not satisfaction. He held her so gently yet, at the same time, with a strength and resolve, providing an impenetrable defence. With his hands cupped around her breasts, caressing her nipples, he gently entered her from behind as they lay together under the quilt. He rocked her gently, whispering her name in her ear over and over as he did so. He paused at her every breath and pursued every pleasurable sensation she acknowledged to its climax. He spoke to her often, telling her how beautiful she was and how he would keep her from harm. This was the lovemaking of a 'true companion.' He would advance as and how and when she desired and retreat to a safe distance when she relaxed. Always there, watching, protecting, but not suffocating or stifling. A balancing act of rescue and release. As Becky drifted into a deep, salutary sleep, Danny made her a promise that he would always be there for her and that she need not worry about anything. As her eyelids fell dormant, Danny withdrew, forgoing his orgasm. It was not important enough to wake her.

CHAPTER 14

Rebecca was still asleep at 9 am when she heard a strange voice calling her name. In the twilight between wake and sleep, she thought it was her father calling her. She cried out

" Dad, is that you?" The voice kept talking to her as if engaged in a strange, one-way conversation and it didn't respond or react to her questions

" Dad, is that you? Are you home?" As sleep subsided and was duly replaced by the early stages of consciousness, a mild panic beset her. She reached out an arm but Danny was gone. In an instant she felt threatened, alone, confused. Still the voice, on and on.

" Danny, Becky, if you're there, please pick up. Its Roger and I need to talk to you!" Rebecca realised that the ansaphone in the hall was taking a message. Danny had switched the ringer off on the bedside phone as he went out that morning so as not to disturb her. He had forgotten, however, to turn down the volume on the ansaphone. She leapt from her bed and grabbed the receiver just before Roger hung up.

" Rog', hi its Becky. What time is it?"

" Its just after nine Becky, did I wake you?"

" Yes, don't worry, Its OK. I've overslept anyway. Do you know where Danny is?"

" Do I know where Danny is? Christ, that's just what I was gonna ask you. We need to talk double quick. I suppose he told you about yesterday?"

" A little. The double bookings you mean?"

" What double bookings?" Roger paused a while.

" You mean he hasn't told you? Christ Becky, you'd better sit down. Where is he anyway, I've been leaving messages all over the place for him."

" I don't know and I'm a little worried. He was here last night and I've just woken up and he's gone! What's happened Roger, what the hell is going on?"

In fact, Danny had simply popped down the store to get a paper and some basic groceries. He'd planned a good, fried breakfast today. He suspected it was going to be a long difficult one and wanted to make a good start. He didn't realise just how long and difficult it was going to be.

" Good morning sir, can I help you?"

" I think this lady was first." The woman beside him in the newsagents placed her paper on the counter and asked for twenty Marlboro.

"Thank you very much" she said" You're a true gentleman."

Danny spent a few minutes selecting a magazine or two to accompany his paper, presented them and the ingredients of his hearty breakfast to the girl on the till and stopped short in his tracks. Right there, in front of him on the counter, was this week's edition of the local 'rag', the Rochester review. The front page headline captivated him

"Christ, they didn't waste anytime here. What's going on?" He said out aloud, although it was intended only as a personal remark.

" Are you all right sir?" Said the girl behind the till.

" Yes, sorry, I'm fine. I'd better take one of these too." He put the Review' in his basket and continued to read the next copy as the girl totted his bill. The headline read' 'LOCAL MAN DISGRACED. ARRESTED IN SPAIN FOR DRUG RUNNING'. He still had his head in the lead story of the paper as he left the shop for the five-minute walk back to Becky's flat. He never made it.

Becky was now sitting on the edge of the bed and continuing her conversation with Roger from there.

" I think you'd better start from the beginning Roger, and don't you dare lie to me, spare me anything or mislead me."

" The whole picture eh?" He replied. " OK. Yesterday, some big shot from the Civil Aviation Authority turns up and starts tapping everybody about Dan. We all told him the truth, that Dan's the finest pilot and instructor we've ever had and, Christ, why don't you read your own' Gasil' reports occasionally! You know what these guys are like though Becky. He was totally unmoved. He just kept digging. I got hold of Dan and he came over to see this fella. We sat in my office for over an hour and he kept popping away at Dan, asking him if he recalled what he did on 'this occasion' and 'that occasion' when he was up flying. He asked Dan if he could remember his air law and asked him loads of dumb questions like, 'do you know what rule five of the air navigation order states?' (*) He actually cautioned him before he answered and told him that his answers could be played back in court and he then switched on a tape recorder. I thought I was watching an episode of 'The Bill', it was incredible. Dan came back in a second and said 'rule five of the ANO states that 'an aircraft may not fly closer than 500 feet to any person, vehicle, vessel or structure' Sir. This guy, Baker somebody, kept on and on but Dan simply knew his stuff. He answered everything correctly and then Baker said

'Ignorance of the law is no defence however, you seem well versed in it Mr. Michaelson. I can only assume that you have conducted yourself in flagrant abuse of it, which in my book, is worse!' Danny protested but all this guy would say is that they had been given a dossier on him with detailed accounts of flying breaches of conduct. The charges were so serious that civil criminal proceedings were likely and they would press for charges to be made. He asked for Dan's licence there and then and revoked all his ratings and privileges and his parting comments were something like 'I don't like

45

cowboys like you Michaelson. On the strength of what I have here I'm going to get the crown prosecution service to throw the book at you. At least I'll make sure you never fly again.'

Rebecca was stunned. She simply could not believe her ears. Following on from the events of yesterday she began to wonder if this was real or if it was some bad dream or joke maybe?

" What did Dan say to that?" She asked

" He just took it all in his stride, quietly protesting his innocence. You know what he's like. He didn't take it seriously at first, made a couple of cracks,' I'll come quietly officer' and 'can I share a cell at Holloway'. This just made it worse. The guy, Baker, whatever, had it in for him from the start. He drove off and Dan just clammed up. He didn't say a word except 'I've done nothing' and then he just drove off too and left me standing there bewildered. I tried calling you last night but your line was engaged for hours. I gave up when it got too late. Any way Becky, listen. This morning I turn up at the club and I've got two Inland Revenue inspectors and one VAT guy all over the place like a rash. They've grounded the planes and put a securing order on them. What the hell is going on. Where is he?"

" Oh Roger, I just don't know, I'm so worried now." She began to cry again.

" Becky, I'm sorry, I didn't mean to upset you but I must talk to him urgently."

Becky got a grip of herself and told Roger all about Peter and the woman caller.

" Oh my God, I had no idea. What on earth is going on? Look, hold tight. I'm coming down. I can't do anything here; the place is virtually at a standstill. I'll be with you within the hour."

Danny raised his head from the paper just in time to avoid a lamppost. Had he hit it, he would normally have had a good laugh but today he was a worried man. He went over his meeting with Baker yesterday and how he matched the bloke point for point in his question and answer session. At that point Danny did allow himself a small moment of black humour. He thought' I can remember my air law but I forgot about 'DABLE'.' DABLE' was one of the many mnemonics that pilots learnt to remember a sequence of actions in a particular manoeuvre. There were many of them but this one in particular related to the actions necessary when adopting a climb from one altitude onto another, considerably higher one. The 'D' stood for 'Direction'. When going from straight and level flight, where the pilot had a visual reference on the ground, say a lake or a tall building, to a nose up, climb attitude, suddenly, all the pilot would be able to see would be sky and his direction could be lost very easily. 'DABLE' in the climb, requires the pilot to ' dip his nose' every so often so that he could, in fact, see where he was going. 'D' for Direction. Dan chuckled because; it had just occurred to him that he should always remember to ' DABLE' to an extent, when walking along a street reading a newspaper! He did look up again however, just in time to narrowly avoid a lady

46

leaning against her car reading the front page of the local newspaper too. He recognised her as the blond woman in the newsagents and he bid her good morning again.

" Good morning Danny" She replied in an overly familiar fashion that made Dan stop and think.

" I'm sorry, do I know you?" he said, anxiously trying to remember her and not appear rude.

" Not yet, but we're going to get to know each other really well. Would you please get into the car."

" Now just hang on a minute..." He stopped his protestations the moment he saw the back seat passenger pointing a small hand gun at his stomach."

" Please get in Danny, there's no reason for you to get hurt."

.

.

CHAPTER 15

Lawrence Carlton's work on behalf of the government and the CAA involved many visits to Brussels. This Euro capital was the tabernacle, the very heart of the newfound, vast community. The buildings and offices of the Euro policy makers were many and various. A virtual labyrinth of corridors and walkways connected thousands of offices bearing the names of their elected inhabitants. Each office was also equipped with the latest computer hardware, daisy chained by a central 'nervous system', designed to keep the left hand and the right of this 'Euro body' in touch with each other. A daily schedule was sent to each office, each morning and was duly printed out for an army of secretaries to dissect and co ordinate and act upon. It was an epic communiqué of incredible proportion detailing meetings, seminars, new rules and regulations etc. and had to be issued in the twelve different languages of each member state. Frankly, it was a nightmare and many a thing was lost in the translation and many a directive ended up on the wrong desk.

This morning's agenda, scheduled for the great auditorium, included debate and discussion on several items including 'Radnett' and 'Byotek'. These were only two the of many projects under development that were dependent on an unprecedented high degree of international liaison and co -operation.

'Radnett' was Lawrence Carlton's brainchild. As an avid flyer, he would often pilot his own, treasured Bulldog aircraft throughout Europe, either on business or simply for recreation. Europe had so much to offer the private pilot by way of changing panorama and landscape and he quite often ventured across the channel. Lawrence often flew into Geneva and stopped overnight in his favourite resort of Lausanne. The sight of Mont Blanc on final approach into Geneva was breathtaking.

Lawrence had first hand experience of the irregularities of air traffic control procedures between these different nations and recognised the importance of a new standardisation to cope with the advent of this new community and also the major increase in traffic. With the conflict still raging in the former Yugoslavia, flights that would normally enter the Balkan air space had to be re routed. Numerous holiday charter flights from the UK France Germany etc. en route to Greece, turkey, Cyprus and various other popular holiday destinations were now being flown through Italian skies and many experts concluded that it was only a matter of time until there was a major disaster.

Radar (Radio Detection And Ranging, invented during world war 2) was, by its very nature, limited in its range and use. Radio waves travel in a straight line and cannot detour or bend around inanimate objects such as mountains. Only a body within its 'line of sight' can effectively be monitored so the actual scope of any particular system was academic, depending on local terrain and ground features. At high altitudes, its effectiveness was greater because it was unlikely that any thing could interfere with its view. Low level sensing however was particularly difficult, with trees and buildings all obscuring its path. Because of the vagaries of the system coverage, much of the en route controlling of flights was 'procedural' i.e. one station would report to another en route, usually by fax, that at a certain moment, they had traffic in their coverage and the next station could expect it at a given time. This involved lots of 'rule of thumb' guesstimating' which had always bothered Lawrence.

Many things would reflect a radio wave back to its station; even a particular weather system could show up on the controller's screen as a momentary blip. Recent developments allowed each blip to be processed by a computer and the spurious ones were usually filtered out. It occurred to Lawrence that the hardware for his 'Radnet' was already in place. All that was needed was some system of networking to link the terminals and make the necessary calculations between the different coverage areas, giving an overall picture to fill in the gaps. Surely it wouldn't be that difficult he thought. 'Christ, we can send chaps to the moon and back!' Hence, 'Radnet' was born.

Bremen, Maastricht, Amsterdam, Brussels, Dusseldorf, Rome and many other military and civilian facilities were connected to the program and there were now the beginnings of a positive, Eurocontrol infrastructure. The whole program was in its initial formative stages and Lawrence Carlton gave much of his own, personal time to it.

'It is a labour of love' he would say.

The primary, ground based, Radar system, when operating at its optimum, gave limited information to the controller. It would tell him that something was there and, by calculating the amount of time for the radio wave to be reflected and received back at the station, it could tell him how far away it was. It did not tell him how high it was or, indeed, what it was. Most aircraft were fitted with a secondary form of radar, SSR (Secondary Surveillance Radar). This took the form of a ground-based transmitter coupled to a responding unit in the aircraft, thus called a transponder. Quite simply, the pilot could select various, four digit codes from the front panel of the unit which would then modulate the incoming signal from the ground, sending an altered version of it back again. These codes could then provide more detailed information to the controller. Most controllers would talk to the pilot under his control by radio and ask him to transmit, or 'squawk' a given set of these numbers. These would duly appear on his screen and the controller knew exactly who was who, and where they were. When releasing an aircraft from his coverage, the pilot would be asked to squawk 7000 which was a general conspicuity code usually adopted in flight. There were several emergency codes too. 7600 indicated a radio failure. Ground based light signals could then be used to give the pilot important information. 7700 indicated an emergency along the lines of a hijack or similar and if these numbers appeared on the controller's screen, and subsequent efforts to contact the craft failed, military aircraft were scrambled to intercept.

'Radnet', Lawrence concluded, would be his invaluable contribution to Europe and his greatest achievement to date, far surpassing the College Air Squadron. Barbara would have been so proud of him. He stifled a tear as his secretary, Margaret, brought him a copy of the morning's agenda, supported by a cup of his favourite Belgian coffee.

" Good morning Lawrence" she said. Usually, the address was a more formal" Sir" or" Mr. Carlton" but Margaret was sensitive to his loss and aware of the days when it was difficult for him. Margaret had been his secretary in London previously and, being a spinster with no direct family, welcomed the chance for a new start in Brussels. She had even bought a flat there and was based in the office full time, holding the fort when Lawrence was in London. Lawrence saw her as a lot more than just a secretary. Publicly, he would describe her as his' girl Friday'. Privately, he thought of her as something a little more than that. Her duties exceeded the usual filing, typing appointment making, diary running, mundane, and office chores. She had been known to press his shirts, straighten his tie, and even monitor his diet. His 'all up weight' as he called it, in that pilot talk of his, was very volatile. The endless Euro lunches and ministerial cocktail parties played havoc with his own weight and balance schedule.

Last Christmas, Lawrence had bought Margaret a silk dressing gown as a gift. After a tipple too many, he presented it to her with a rather tongue tied delivery speech. Margaret was filled with anticipation. At last, was, he beginning to have feelings for her ?

" Margaret, I'm not very good with words and there's... Well I've... That is...Look I've bought you a little gift by way of my appreciation for the way you've looked after me." She was flushed with anticipation. She had been in love with him even when Barbara was alive. Now, just maybe, his loneliness and vulnerability would deliver him to her. She had been so patient.

" There's something I'd like you to know too." This was it, surely? " I want you to know that I regard you as meaning more to me than just my personal secretary, do you understand?"

" Yes Lawrence of course I do." This was definitely it, the moment she had waited so long for.

" I've come to regard you as more of a big sister and I don't know how I would have coped with all that ironing and all. Thank you so much." He leant forward and gave her a very politically correct kiss on the side of her cheek.

That night, Christmas Eve, Margaret cried herself to sleep.

Chapter 16

As Lawrence Carlton, shirt pressed, tie repositioned and generally 'readied for work' by Margaret, entered the grand auditorium for the mornings debate, nine hundred miles away, the ferry boat 'Messina Morgana' rounded the point of Bagheria and docked at Palermo on the northern coast of Sicily.

In the shadow of Mount Vesuvious, the great sentinel on the Italian mainland guarding the bay of Naples, this medium sized car ferry departed the isle of Capri, sailed due south, hugging the western seaboard of Italy until it reached the Golfo Di St. Eufemia. It then headed southwest on a course, which took it directly through a complex of seven little islands off the north coast of Sicily. These little dots in the Tyrrenhian sea were spectacularly beautiful and boasted a volcano of their very own, offering a sightseeing bonus to those on board. This part of the world hosted many volcanoes, the mother of them all being Mount Etna, overseeing her children from her home in Sicily.

Mario's duties as chief engineer for the fleet afforded him a great independence and freedom of movement, and he travelled relatively unchallenged in the islands. He had started his apprenticeship at fifteen and was a fully qualified, skilled engineer. He served many loyal years below decks and it did not take long to realise that his employers were, in fact, Mafioso.

The many different families that comprised the fraternity of the Mafia all had legitimate business interests in and around the islands. They were operated as going concerns in their own right but were initially set up with 'family' money, undoubtedly the proceeds of crime. Mario made it clear to his superiors that he did not want to spend the rest of his days in the engine room and that he was available for any extra duties where his other talents maybe of some use.

He was the ideal courier for the mob although his activities and freedom of movement were currently limited to the Tyrrhenian and Mediterranean seas. The ferry company 'DESTINIA' were hoping to expand their routes and, of course, their other services, to the Ionian and Adriatic seas within the next few years.

Mario had been elevated to his position as chief engineer, not only by merit of his skills and general knowledge of ferries, but also because he had proved his worth to his employers by carrying out some additional nocturnal activities. Amongst his more dubious talents, he was an accomplished burglar and had been an asset to the family in recent times. He had acquired various documents and information from government and industrial offices and recently had planted some very incriminating evidence in the safe of a high-ranking government official who was a prominent voice in the ever growing, anti-Mafia lobby now gripping Sicily. The official was eventually discredited and removed from office on the strength of Mario's handiwork.

Mario was indeed the golden boy and he was honoured to be included in the *'Destiny'* program.

The Messina Morgana eventually docked and began to disembark. Goods vehicles first, followed by tourists.

Whilst others endured the usual customs checks and delays, quite a harrowing experience in the company of several Carabinieri, a type of armed militia-come -police force, Mario swept through the building totally unchallenged. He was met by a chauffeur who led him to a black stretch limousine waiting to take him to his appointment. There was no attempt at subtlety. The families operated in flagrant view and defiance of the authorities and fear was the order of the day.   Sicily was on the verge of a virtual civil war. The clamp down by the government had been met by an equally strong rebellion from the Mafia. Many assassinations were carried out. Judges, politicians, priests, in fact, any body with a voice who spoke out against the Mafia, found themselves subject to the wrath of the families.

The black Lincoln looked totally incongruous with the olive groves and mountain ranges acting as the backdrop for its journey south of Palermo, winding its way deeper into the valley di Mazarra. This region boasted many of the Mafioso families, Corleone, Prizzi, Scaatchi, to name but a few. Don Marineo was the CAPO (Mafia leader) of the families in this region. Many were allies in their business pursuits, many were not. Some were believed to be allies but secretly conspired against the others. All, however, were unanimous in their battle against the Italian authorities.

Now that Italy had received full membership of the European Economic Community, it was trying to clean up its act, or at the very least, be seen to be cleaning up its act. With the numerous handouts, grants, subsidies etc., Italy wanted to purge its administration of corruption and was at great pains to do so. The families were worried. Many of their gambling and prostitution activities had been closed down on the mainland and many eyes were turning to Sicily itself, which up to now had been a virtual sanctuary for the mob.

" How dare they!" Don Marineo banged the top of his ornate oak, carved table with his fist. He had summoned the various Dons of the other families to his villa for a crisis meeting in an attempt to consolidate their resistance to the onslaught against them. There were representatives from the 'Camorra' based in Naples and also representatives from as far away as the United States. The influential, rich, American 'Cosa Nostre' families remained faithful to their blood origins and were party to the rebellion offering every assistance.

CAPO Don Marineo listened to the others in due course and was thankful for their advice and observations but he was angry when petty squabbles broke out. Once again he crashed his fist to the table.

" I have not brought you all here to listen to your childish, narrow-minded bitching. You are beginning to sound like old mommas. Do you not realise that we are at war! Never before have our families been under such a threat and you sit there and cat fight!" The Don composed himself. "I have listened to what you have said and I am impressed by much of it but no one has actually made any practical suggestions as yet except, that is, my own family, Marineo!" There was no doubt about the level of attention in the room at this point. The Don had the chair." We have been very busy this last few months and while you have fought amongst yourselves, we have developed a new product that will make us much money and strike at the heart of our enemies." The room was devoid of any sound and no one dared breathe. "Gentlemen. I have long been aware of this escalation of hostility against our families and I have been working on a contingency plan for many months. It is now time for me to reveal to you our new saviour." Everyone looked around expecting some important figure to enter the room. Instead, Don Marineo opened a draw in his desk and removed two cases. One was the size of a shoebox and bore an elaborate carving of Italian folklore figurines carved into its wooden frame. The other was a considerably smaller, metal pillbox.

" Gentleman, may I introduce you to your future, your '*Destiny* !'" With this, he removed the lid of the pillbox and a terrible, acrid smell filled the room. Most of the Dons reached for their handkerchiefs and some began to cough.

" Is this some kind of joke?" bellowed Don Prizzi." Have you invented a new pocket stink bomb that every schoolboy must have?" Despite the noxious fumes filling the air, everyone burst into laughter. Even Don Marineo managed a smile as he carefully replaced the lid.

" My friends, listen to me now. Our casinos, our brothels and even our legitimate industries are being run out of town. Are we not all agreed that we need a miracle? Well my friends, you have just smelt it! Although it is not a stink bomb Don Prizzi, I shall consider your suggestion and see if there is any return to be had from that market!" This was now a good- humoured occasion and everyone roared at the thought of a stink bomb empire.

" Tell us CAPO. What is this puerile miracle of yours?" Said Don Prizzi

" Gentlemen. This substance is simply a resin produced in my laboratory here in the valley. Six months ago, I instructed my technicians to design a new drug. They were briefed that it was to be the ultimate experience. It was to be instantly effective and highly addictive. It was to be so potent that the only smallest amount was required for a 'fix'. This would enable us to ship it in smaller quantities making it easier to transport and harder to detect. We would embark on a blanket marketing program to immediately establish it throughout this European economic community and thus, we would become part of the very thing that seeks to destroy us. It would be so popular with the users that we could name our price. I believe, my friends, that they have done it. As an added insult to our persecutors, we borrowed the government's chief chemist to complete the recipe. He was not the most willing of workers and took a little persuasion." Once again, the room applauded and laughed with approval. Don Prizzi interrupted again.

" What does one do, Don Marineo, rub it into your chest like a cough preparation? Put some on your pillow maybe?" Although the roars of laughter were genuine, the CAPO was aware of the cynicism of the remark. He and Don Prizzi were rivals of old and he was just about to even an old score.

" If Don Prizzi would allow me, I will demonstrate. This little amount of resin, when heated and processed will provide this many micro pills worth 60,000 lire (approx. £25) each!" In a simultaneous, dramatic gesture, he opened the lid of the hinged carved box and tipped the contents onto his desk. Thousands of tiny *'Destiny'* pills poured onto it, many falling to the floor. Don Prizzi was duly silenced by the tumultuous round of applause that followed. Many questions were asked and duly answered about production, supply, marketing, and of course the relevant benefits to all of the other families. Don Marineo pledged that, in return for co-operation and practical help with the project, he would finance the terror campaign against the authorities and there would be a newfound prosperity to be enjoyed by all.

He went on to explain, that the pills were being marketed throughout the Mediterranean as they spoke and that it was necessary to ship a large amount of the resign to northern Europe and the UK for processing and marketing there. This was proving to be a slight problem as the resin blocks were so noxious that even a catholic priest with the flu could detect it. However, a plan was in motion at this time and he hoped that the problem would be resolved within a few weeks. Don Marineo, having dropped his bombshell and delivered his miracle, dramatically brought the meeting to a close and said that his people would be in touch. He bade them farewell and left the room. He went into the small adjoining study and shook hands with his other guest.

" I am honoured Don Marineo"

" Mario, I am pleased to see you. Please sit down. I was sorry to hear about your mother. I trust the funeral was the finest and the most lavish?"

" It was the greatest tribute my family could have given her. I am ever in you debt."

" And your fathers boat? My people are hard at work?"

" They are, Capo. Thank you. Thank you"

" And you Mario, have you been hard at work? I trust that you overheard what was said in the meeting? You understand how important it is for you to solve our last problem, don't you. I would hate for your village to suffer further hardship without my help and I believe your father may not be able to fish again without my assistance. You have got some good news for me I trust?" Mario was fully aware of the veiled threats that had just been so expertly delivered by his Capo. He knew that tradition required a great service from him when requested by his Capo. Success would set him up for life. Failure would probably cut it short.

" Every thing is proceeding as planned Don Marineo. We have no problems."

" And the orange grove?"

" The grove is replanted and is fully functional now."

" Good boy. Do you need any more money Mario?"

" I have plenty right now, thank you."

" Plenty is not enough. You must take this." The CAPO gave Mario a leather attaché case full of money." If you look after me Mario, my family will take care of yours. I hope you are taking care of my ferries too! I believe you have one to catch!" This was not a question but an expert dismissal and Mario graciously took his leave.

CHAPTER 17

When Danny regained consciousness, the first things he saw were his keys, wallet, mobile phone, electronic organiser, handkerchief etc. In fact, the entire contents of his jacket and trouser pockets were laid out on the table in front of him. This was not an unfamiliar sight, as he would always empty his pockets onto his bedside cabinet before retiring for the night. Momentarily, he imagined he was back at the flat in Rochester but as he tried to raise a hand to rub a particularly stiff neck, he was shocked to find it, and the other one, tied to his chair.

" You have been sleeping for quite a time Danny; you're going to feel a little drowsy. Maybe you could use a coffee?" Ruth turned towards one of her cohorts "Make that two. Black. Lots of sugar in Mr. Michaelson's"

" Who the hell are you? What's going on? Where..." Ruth interrupted him.

" Calm down Danny, you're perfectly safe. No harm will come to you or Rebecca if you co operate with us." On hearing Rebecca's name, anger rose within him and he began to rock violently in his chair.

" You bastards! If you dare touch her I'll kill you!"

" Now now Danny, calm down. There's really no need," said Ruth.

Although still half drugged, Danny's mind raced. He felt that he was in a scene from one of the videos that he and Becky regularly rented from the local store. He convinced himself that he'd been abducted by the IRA and was about to be beaten, pistol-whipped or even knee capped. An enormous wave of panic and terror gripped him and he shook violently.

" It's OK Danny, its just the after effects of the sedative. Your blood sugar level drops when you are in shock. That is why you are shaking so much. Try and drink some coffee." One of her assistants untied one of Danny's hands and gave him the mug. Ruth got up and placed a blanket around his shoulders." Drink some coffee. Calm yourself and we'll talk shortly. We have a lot to discuss." With this, she left the room.

All Danny could think about was Rebecca. He could cope with most things but the thought of Becky coming to any harm was unbearable. He drank his coffee and rubbed his neck. It was, in fact, slightly swollen from a careless stab with a hypodermic. He looked around the room for a clue as to his whereabouts but there were no immediate indications. There was a desk, complete with his possessions, a computer, printer and an electric kettle on a tray. There were a few mugs and a jar of coffee. There was no phone in the room but the computer was connected to a BT socket via a modem. There was a little fan heater on the floor and a very old playboy calendar was still on the wall. There were two very simple makeshift beds separated by a large locker that had a suitcase on top and there was a mattress thrown in the corner that was so dank, the room was tainted by the odour. The place looked every inch like a night watchman's office.

Twenty minutes or so later Ruth came back into the room.

" Well Danny, are you feeling any better?" He had no time to reply." Good. We have a lot to get through." Danny was convinced that he knew Ruth's voice and just then she said

" We have spoken before. Do you remember?"

" Not exactly, look what do you want?"

" Danny Danny! Please relax. I'm not going to hurt you. I just want you to do a job or two for me that's all, just like you did before. In return my people are going to take care of all your problems for you."

" I've never worked for you before" he said.

" I'm afraid you're wrong there Danny. Don't you remember making this for me?"

Ruth unlocked the cupboard and clipped to a frame inside was one of the pair of radio controlled Pups that he'd made several months ago. He'd never actually met the client (until now) but had spoken to her a couple of times on the phone.

" That was you? What did you want them for?" He was very muddled but Dan, being Dan and feeling slightly relieved at the sight of one of his creations and also, because he hadn't been knee capped as yet, said "Look lady, if it's broken, I do do an after sales service. You didn't have to kidnap me, you know!" Everyone in the room managed a little laugh that diffused some of the tension and Dan felt a little less threatened. The tone then turned a little more serious and Ruth spoke to him quite menacingly.

"As we speak, your future brother in law is locked up in a Spanish jail on very serious charges. I understand also that you are in some trouble yourself at the moment with possible charges of your own pending." She paused for a moment to let this sink in." If you co operate with us Danny then we in turn can help you with these matters."

" Who are you people, IRA?" He inquired.

" Ha! No Danny but you should not underestimate the power of the family I represent." The word 'family' gave it away.

" Mafia!" He said, totally shocked. He was indeed fully aware of the implications." What on earth would the Mafia want of me? I'm a nobody surely?"

" On the contrary Danny, you're the only person for this particular job. Let me explain. Firstly I should tell you that my superiors are very impressed with your model design. My people have copied it faithfully and are very impressed by its performance. They are so impressed in fact, that they want you to do some additional, similar work but, shall I say, on a slightly larger scale." Danny looked totally perplexed." Come with me Danny." Flanked by her minders, she took him by the hand and led him through the small office door into, what appeared to be a small hanger. Her assistants removed two large tarpaulins that were draped over what he thought were Landrovers or small trucks. His jaw dropped in disbelief. In the half-light, he could make out the silhouette of a small aircraft. Ruth flicked a switch and the fluorescent tubes hummed and stuttered themselves awake. As they illuminated the compound she said

" I trust you recognise these!" Danny found himself staring at two Beagle Pups and he knew instantly that these must be the two that went missing earlier this year." Woh! What are they doing here, wherever ' here' is? And just where do I come into all this?"

" It's quite simple Danny; we just want you to do exactly what you're best at. For now, we want you to make some modifications to these aircraft. We know you have the expertise. We will supply you with all the relevant details and all the tools and materials that you will need. You have the use of the computer in the office and you may have whatever you require.

" What do you mean,' for now?'" asked Dan.

" Well, we require you to make a very detailed flight plan (*) as well."

" To where?" asked Dan.

" You will know all that you need to know, as and when you need to. For now, you must rest and get a good night's sleep as you will start work early tomorrow."

" But what about....." Again, Ruth interrupted

," I will answer more of your questions tomorrow."

" Just tell me that Becky is safe!" Demanded Dan.

" Miss Washington will remain unharmed as long as you co operate with us." Ruth gestured to one of her colleagues to lead Danny back to the office and she left the building.

Chapter 18

The Morgana sailed out of Palermo in calm seas and headed due east initially, before taking up a southerly course for the straits of Messina. This little stretch of water between Reggio de Calabria on the mainland and the Sicilian island town of Messina provided very little except for some all-important separation between the two. The Morgana, named after an Italian sea goddess who lived in the straits, would dock briefly at Catania before routing onwards south to Valletta, Malta.

Mario Marcantonio was primarily an engineer, having spent the formative years of his life below decks smelling of axle grease, scraping his knuckles on half shafts and bearings whilst learning his stock and trade. His family and friends, in the true village spirit of Niapello, recognising his potential and mechanical prowess, gave him the fiscal and practical support he needed to complete his apprenticeship and he would always be in their debt. They knew that in return, Mario would eventually 'make good' and repay his debt in kind to the community. However, recently, he acted in more of an 'overseeing,' managerial capacity and he rarely got his hands dirty. He double checked gauges, speeds, temperatures, calibrations etc. and would advise the crew on operating procedures. He was always readily contactable if there were any operational irregularities with the massive engines and he would instinctively know what the problem would be, simply by the tone of the turbines.

Mario made his way below decks and headed for the engine bay where he assumed the role he was principally paid for. The deep and loud, Regular cycle of the Morgana's propulsion system was a comforting 'heart beat' to Mario. Not only was it a constant rhythmic reminder that all was mechanically well, but the engine room and its accompanying noise   afforded him a comfortable, natural environment. He had spent the last fifteen years in many a similar place.

Checks done, foreman briefed and logbooks completed, Mario adjourned to his small, but comfortable, secure cabin, which lay beyond the engine room in the aft belly of the ship. To Mario, this little cabin was sanctuary. He looked upon his little room as more of a 'case' into which he put himself to remain safe while he rested. Surrounded by two-inch thick steel, he felt totally secure. He had all that he needed here and the blend of engine noise and the sea, complimented by a glass of whiskey, awarded him sleep.

At a pre-determined time, without the use of an alarm, Mario's body clock awoke him. He had learnt not to linger in half sleep, so, once his eyes were open, he immediately swung both his legs over the side of the bunk and supported himself with a hand on either side of the bed until the cologne of diesel fume and sweat, that permeated the engine bay, stung him to his senses. He gathered himself and then reached down under the bunk, pulling out a large, aluminium flight case, which he laid on the bed. He unlocked and opened the lid, took out the various components and began to assemble them. Ten minutes later, Mario placed a plastic bag containing two thousand *'Destiny'* pills inside the compartment area of the small model aircraft that Danny Michaelson had unwittingly supplied months earlier. He then opened the door of his cabin, which led onto a small, one man, steel veranda. He licked a finger of his right hand and held it aloft to check which direction the wind was coming from and simultaneously checked the watch on his left.

The Morgana had just passed the small island of Gozo and was running parallel with the Maltese coastline. Mario checked his watch once again and raised the binoculars suspended on a cord around his neck to survey the island. He released the glasses which settled comfortably in his mid chest whilst he looped his hand through the wrist strap of the remote control unit and extended its aerial. He flicked the master switch and a red 'power on' L.E.D. illuminated. He carefully picked up the little aircraft and positioned it on the railing in front of him. He maintained a steadfast grip with his left hand grasping mid fuselage whilst he pushed the start button on the remote with his right. The electric motor whirred into life instantly and remarkably quietly considering the amount of thrust being generated, even at idle speed, by the small composite propeller fitted to the sharp end of an entirely composite air frame which made the craft impervious to detection by radar. One last check of his watch and Mario pushed forward the lever on the remote unit, which acted as a throttle. The thrust was extreme and Mario gauged the moment of release carefully. In an instant, the craft became airborne and Mario reached for his binoculars with his now free left hand. He caught sight of two unsuspecting sea gulls making sudden steep, avoiding turns indicating the whereabouts of his radio controlled delivery service. The little craft was so stable that it practically flew itself. Danny's design was faultless. Mario had only to steer the craft in the general direction of the small beach on his starboard bow and this he managed quite easily, as he had done on several occasions before. Suddenly, his remote unit bleeped and the accompanying green L.E.D. illuminated. Mario watched the craft glide out of sight onto the beach, now in the control of another land based operator. Two more bleeps were heard from his hand unit signalling that the journey was complete. He placed the binoculars and the remote into the flightcase and returned it under the bed.

The Morgana made a regal entry into the vast Maltese harbour bounded on one side by the capital Valletta and the other by the town of Slima. The formidable ramparts and portals of this Maltese harbour were steeped in history. Valletta was the largest natural harbour in the Mediterranean and control of it was a distinct advantage to any who would wage war by sea. The island had seen many a great battle and had seldom been victorious. None, however, would compare with the struggle it faced, as *'Destiny'* became its latest and most fearsome invader.

The Morgana would birth in Valletta only long enough to dispatch her primary, legal cargo and pick up another for her return trip to Palermo, then onto Capri and Naples. Mario went ashore into the busy port authority area and signed the Morgana into the harbour log. The attendant routinely gave him a receipt for the docking fee he had just paid and, after a discreet look over his shoulder, a brown envelope containing forty thousand pounds. Mario didn't bother to count it. Nobody would short change

Don Marineo. Mario slipped quietly back onto the Morgana and awarded himself another whiskey below decks.

CHAPTER 19

Roger found Rebecca walking along the drive leading from her flat down to the high street. He tooted his horn twice, pulled alongside and asked her if she wanted a lift.

" Oh hi Roger. I left you a note on the door.'' Said Rebecca, a little startled. "I thought I'd see if I could find Dan. He always goes for the paper in the morning and he sometimes goes into the bakery for a coffee. If he's not there, I'm going to check at the rugby club. There might be a match on or something. You know what he's like, when he's got something on his mind, he often disappears to think it through."

" Good idea Becky, hop in and I'll drive you."

" Thanks all the same Roger, but I'd rather walk just in case I miss him coming back."

" OK. Let me park up and I'll come with you."

They made their way down the drive, bumping into a couple of immediate neighbours en route who said that they hadn't seen him either. The girl in the news agent's was new to the job and didn't really know the locals too well as yet but, when questioned, said that she believed it was Danny who bought some food and a news paper there that morning. She said that he seemed a bit disturbed by something on the front page of the local paper. Rebecca looked at the 'Review.'

" It must have been Danny" She showed the paper to Roger.

" Well, at least we know he's been here, Becky. Where else could he have gone?"

" Let's try the coffee shop. He goes there quite often but he should've been back hours ago, specially if he had bacon and eggs with him."

There was no sign of Danny at the shop but Doris was pleased to see Rebecca.

" I haven't seen him since he drove off with you this morning my dear at about 9.30" she said. Doris didn't miss much that went on in the street but her eyesight was not what it used to be.

" But I haven't driven off with anybody today, least of all Danny." Protested Rebecca.

" Well, I thought it was you my dear. She was very pretty and she had long blond hair just like yours. I must have been mistaken." Rebecca was visibly upset, and responded curtly

" Yes, you must have been" and left the shop. No doubt Doris Turner would soon be on the grapevine with the news of a missing Danny and tales of a new male companion, seemingly very close to Rebecca. Her imagination was running wild.

Roger sensed that maybe Danny was involved with someone else and had simply gone off. He was quite shocked at the notion, which was totally out of character for the Danny that he knew, but, none the less, he was sensitive enough not to say anything to Becky. He didn't have to. It was written all over his face.

" Rog', I know what you're thinking but it's nothing like that. Danny and I are still very close. I wonder if this blond is anything to do with the one my brother mentioned in France? It was a women who made those funny calls last night too."

" Could be, but it all seems a bit far-fetched doesn't it, but then again, some weird things have been happening lately? I know he was really shook-up about the 'Baker' thing at the airfield yesterday. I reckon that he's just gone off, as he tends to from time to time, to get his head 'round it. I guess that we should just sit tight for a while and wait for him to surface. What do you want to do now Becky? Have you had lunch yet, you've got to eat?"

" I couldn't eat anything right now Roger, thank you. Would you drive me to the rugby club, you can get something there if you want and then I really must go to the yard and see if the boys have heard anything more about Peter."

There was no sign of Danny at the club and when they pulled into the 'Fast Forward' yard a couple of the drivers and mechanics were already engrossed in the Rochester review article and were busy discussing it. Rebecca knew most of the people at 'forward fast' and she also knew that Peter was very popular despite his shyness, but she didn't quite know how she would be received in view of the scandalous headline and the ramifications that might befall the firm. She met with some initial, incredulous reactions but She anxiously explained that she had heard from Peter and that it was quite obvious that he'd been set-up from the start. Rebecca casually asked the lads if any of them had seen Danny today but she felt it best not to elaborate as to why. Apart from working her usual magic on the gathered men folk, who now stood at complete attention, she had also accrued a double sympathy vote, with both her Father and Brother missing. If she told them the truth about Danny as well, then the whole situation would have appeared surreal.

Peter had started 'Fast Forward Freighting' from scratch and he had struggled in the early stages until the firm became established. However, he always made sure that the staff were always paid on time, despite his hardships, and the guys remained fiercely loyal. The offers of support were unanimous and Rebecca found them overwhelming and comforting.

" Thank you all very much for your support. I really need it at the moment." Rebecca had no need to play the damsel in distress as she genuinely was and it was apparent too, despite her attempts to maintain her composure. "Could I just ask you all to please keep things up and running here until we get it all straightened out." Rebecca had nothing to worry about and was reassured that everyone would pull together in the crisis.

When Roger eventually took Rebecca back to the flat, the note that she had left him was still stuck to the door. She felt a little disappointed, as she was sure that Danny would have been back by now and would have removed it. She noticed immediately that there were 4 messages on the ansaphone and she rushed to play them.

" Come on Dan, what have you been up to," she murmured as she hit the 'play' button. The first two calls were hang-ups. They sounded as if they were made from a mobile because there was a lot of background noise. The third was Lawrence Carlton.

" Rebecca, hello, its Lawrence Carlton calling from Brussels. I'm sorry I have missed you. However, I wanted to keep you up to date. I have duly notified the British Embassy officials in Madrid and they are making arrangements to see your brother and get this mess sorted out. The Spanish authorities are notorious for obstructing our officials I'm afraid, so you will just have to be a little patient. We have lodged a complaint with the Spanish Embassy here in Brussels and demanded some immediate attention but nothing positive to report so far I'm afraid. If you need me, you can contact my office in London. I shall be home next week. Oh, nothing further about your Father as yet. Good-bye for now."

The fourth message was another' mobile hang up and Rebecca was again, sadly disappointed.

"Roger, I'm beginning to get worried now. I think I should call the Police." She was about to when the phone rang again. It was a women's voice on a mobile

" Rebecca Washington?"

" Speaking"

" If you want to see Danny and your brother Peter again, listen very carefully"

" Who are you? What do you want?" cried Becky.

" Do not go to the police. Don't tell anyone about this. If you do, you will never see them again. Do you understand?"

" Yes! But....."

" Listen carefully. Do not underestimate what we are capable of. We require your full co-operation."

" Yes, but what do you want of me? Why are you..." Again, Rebecca was not allowed to finish.

" For now, you will say and do nothing. We will be in touch shortly with some instructions." The caller hung up and left Rebecca still holding the phone to her ear in a state of shock.

Chapter 20

The offices and laboratories of the Italian Government's Health and Medical Department were situated high in the Villa Borghese region of the city of Rome, in the heart of the ancient quarter. Vittorio Bartelli would look from his window on the top floor and imagine legions of centurions marching through the ancient gates that were prevalent throughout the city, one of which was directly beneath him. He imagined he had been there before, in a previous life, at the beginning of this great place, such was his patriotism and his sense of spirituality. Much of the city was still as it was in those ancient times and his family roots were Roman as far back as the records could determine. He felt a great sense of belonging to his birthplace and it and its people always inspired him.

Rome was also the centre of the Christian world and he was himself a devout catholic. He often considered the geographical inconsistencies and ironies of this chosen place. He would look across the river Tiber, past the great castle of St. Angelo and onto St. Peter's Square. The magnificent basilica of St. Peter's was clearly visible yet, if he turned to his left, he could also see the coliseum, the great Roman amphitheatre wherein people like him were once thrown to the lions. A strange place indeed for Christians to focus upon. Surely a better site for the Vatican would have been Bethlehem, Christ's birthplace. This was some many hundred miles away, where, just as curiously, the Muslim-faithed Palestinians had settled. They were, in turn, locked in a daily battle with the occupying Israeli forces for this land, known to be the birthplace of Christ. Christmas day was certainly not recognised nor celebrated by neither Islam nor Judaism yet, here was the rightful sight of the original nativity scene, which now adorned St. Peter's square each December instead. Vittorio would take his wife and children every year to the carol service, never deterred by the weather. The sheer thrill of so many raised voices chorusing 'Oh come all ye faithful' and 'the first Noel' warmed their hearts in defiance of cold toes and fingers. 'This is the only place to be at Christmas' he would tell himself, yet the scene had always felt displaced despite its magnificence.

These inconsistencies had often bothered Vittorio and he had challenged members of the clergy on such matters on several occasions and been disappointed by their response.

Vittorio was also ashamed of his own inconsistencies. He had been in the public health service since leaving college at nineteen. He could make more money in the private sector but he was Roman. He was a citizen of the greatest city in the world. He would always be a public servant and work for his people. He had developed many medicines and preparations for his people during his twenty years at the laboratories and he had been publicly commended for his work, yet he had done a terrible thing. Using the skills of alchemy that he had pursued all his life in the role of healer, he had created the most abhorrent substance he could imagine. He was appalled by the deadly nature of the drug he had invented. Twenty years of such hard work and experimentation to find cures and remedies yet he found the irony overwhelming that it took just 6 weeks to create ' *Destiny'*.

He loved his wife, Sofia, dearly. Had he agreed to help the 'Mob' the first time they approached him, then his beloved wife would not be so ill now. The loss of her finger was bad enough but the mental damage caused by her ordeal was irreversible. His bubbly, confident, normally extrovert Sofia was so traumatised by those events that she had withdrawn from herself and was wasting away. Vittorio would visit her every day after work. The nuns in the convent would tend her by day and pray for her by night. Vittorio would hold her hand and tell her how beautiful she was and how sorry he was. He would weep, begging her forgiveness. If only he'd done what they wanted from the start. He had ended up giving them what they wanted anyway so why didn't he do so the first time he was asked. Sofia would then still be at his side. His soul mate. His only 'true companion.'

Vittorio had known only love and positive emotions in his life. He had been fortunate enough to be surrounded by them for all of his existence. 'Hate' was a word with which he was unfamiliar and uninterested in. Until now. He hated them. He pledged an allegiance to his new found hate and vowed to pursue and personify it. Don Marineo was the Devil incarnate and he would get even. He vowed to avenge his sweet Sofia no matter how long it would take. He would be thorough, yet careful. He could not risk any further damage to his family but he *would* get even.

Vittorio highlighted the 'send' icon at the top of his computer screen and clicked the desktop mouse. This time, he added two more lines to the message 'LOOK TO THE FUTURE, THE FUTURE IS AT HAND, LETTERS ONE TO SEVEN WILL HELP YOU UNDERSTAND'. He smiled and picked up the picture of Sofia that lived on his desk and graced it with her presence. One day she would come back to him and she would be very proud of her man, just as before.

Vittorio took one last look across the city before he left for the day. It was raining quite heavily so he readied his umbrella and did up the top button on his overcoat. He did not want to look like a drowned rat when he saw Sofia, not that she would notice. She would usually sit and stare at the walls, that is, when she wasn't screaming. He walked the two-mile journey to the Santo Francisco hospice every night and would take several alternate routes to change the scenery and experience as much as he could of this beautiful place. His favourite route would be to take the Spanish steps and then drop down towards the embankment. This night, however, he chose to follow the main road, as the steps would be wet and slippery. He could not afford an injury at this time. There was a job to be done.

The rain was heavy and the gutters flowed, seemingly in harmony with the resplendent fountains that graced the city at every turn. Vittorio had proposed to Sofia in front of the Trevi fountain. He had, of course, thrown in an offering beforehand as was customary, as he was about to take no chances this night. Sofia and the Fountain were the two most beautiful things he had ever seen. He believed that Michael Angelo had crafted them both. What a joy to bring them both together.

A careless driver ploughed close to the curb and gave Vittorio a good dowsing. His Italian blood rose and he shouted 'hey' and thrust a single finger into the heavens. The black stretch limo ground to a halt and a door was opened.

"Maybe I can offer you a lift and shelter from this rain Mr. Bartelli. Please get into the car."

Vittorio had been careless. Maybe he had been seen or his computer terminal traced somehow. Why hadn't he been more careful? The last time a black Lincoln continental pulled up in such a way, Sofia was bundled onto the pavement in front of him. She was catatonic. They had filled her full of Heroin and by way of a small mercy, she was too drugged to feel the skin tear from her knees and chin as she bounced along the kerbstones.

Vittorio felt a calmness descend as he accepted the inevitable. It was almost as if he was in a state of grace. Having fought and lost, he would now accept his fate. The battle was over. He gathered his self-respect and entered the car of his own volition. The Lincoln drove off into the back-doubles and emerged again twenty minutes later. The storm was at its peak and very few people had ventured onto the streets. The car came to a halt outside the hospice of Santo Francisco and Vittorio stepped out.

The Lincoln disappeared again into the night. Vittorio looked up. As the volley of rain bounced of his face, he began to laugh.

Chapter 21

Danny found himself woken by a rather crude shove from a black boot. Its wielder did offer him a coffee, which he accepted grudgingly. At least he wasn't in the chair and had been allowed a night's sleep on the mattress. He felt a lot better than he did the day before, although he 'ached for England.' The coffee soothed and lubricated his dehydrated throat and he welcomed the stimulus. The other one of his minders was sat at the desk playing with the computer. It was seven A.M. and his immediate priority was his bowel. He stressed the urgency of his request and was duly escorted to an outhouse to conduct his ablutions. The chill morning air slapped his face and chased away the remnants of sleep. There was a salty quality to the air and he sensed that he was near the coast. He wasn't particularly alert but scanned his surroundings for a clue to his whereabouts before his minder could object. With his back to the hangar he could see open green fields to his right and ocean to his left and front. Coming out of the latrine he spotted an old, obviously disused, runway in a state of disrepair and he turned to catch a glimpse of an overwhelming, towering industrial plant in the distance, just before he was ushered back inside. At that point, Danny believed that he knew where he was, but why? It just didn't make sense.

Ruth was waiting for him when he got back.

"Danny" She acknowledged. "We have much to do." She handed Danny a sheet of paper and invited him to read it. After a couple of minutes Danny said

" This is impossible, it's just ridiculous."

" You have no choice. If you want to see Rebecca again." The threat was implicit and supported by a blow to the abdomen from one of Ruth's colleagues. The mention of Rebecca's name filled Danny with fear and rage. He had no idea that Rebecca was involved in this madness. It took him a few moments only though, to appreciate the seriousness of the situation. He soon realised that any objections at this stage would immediately result in another beating and he simply couldn't risk any harm coming to Becky. He knew what these people were capable of and he had no choice at this stage, other than to do what they wanted. Dan experienced real fear for the first time in his life but remembered the essence of his training and tried to keep a cool head.

" I'll need tools, parts and help from your goons."

" Name it and you'll have it".

Danny would later regret the comment about the 'goons' as the black booted alarm clock would prove to be a little louder next time round.

" Just how far are these Pups expected to fly in one hit?" he enquired.

" Twelve hundred miles plus reserve" Ruth replied." I should point out at this stage that I'm a pilot too and you wont be able to 'blind me with science' so please don't try.

Danny began to feel a knot in the pit of his stomach. He had a feeling that they wanted a little more of him than they had asked so far.

" I take it you're going to fly one of these?" Ruth nodded a yes. "'And who is going to fly the other one?"

" You are Danny."

" Now just hang on a minute...." His protestations were worthless. Ruth reminded him that, if he wanted to see Rebecca again, he had no choice.

" I want to know exactly what you want of me and what I get in return. And I want to see Rebecca." He demanded.

"Out of the question" she replied.

"You have no choice," she reiterated, "but to do exactly what I ask."

"And just exactly what is that?"

"Simple stuff for a man of your talents Danny. Nothing you can't handle. After you've made those modifications to the Pups, you're going to fly one of them and accompany me on a little trip."

Danny had formed a pretty good idea by now what this was all about.

"Drugs" He announced. He knew he was right by the lack of any acknowledgement.

"I need your expertise both mechanically and practically to get us both to our destination and back in one piece with our consignment. Only then will you see Rebecca. Also, I can arrange the release of your brother in law Peter and you might just find that things get back to normal at North Weald."

" You were behind that as well?"

" Of course."

" Well at least that's a relief. Oh, I get it. All those questions about low flying and airspace. You were checking me out weren't you? I suppose Baker works for you too?"

" You're very perceptive Danny. Mr Baker has played many differing roles for us in the past. There is very little that we can't achieve. You must realise that.'

"Why me?" Dan enquired. "Surely there were plenty of others who would've done this for a simple pay-off? Why me?"

"We knew you had too much integrity to do the job for money so we used a little persuasion." Ruth replied, dodging the essence of the question.

"Yeah, but why me?" he asked again.

"We needed your expertise and you've already proved yourself with the radio controlled models. Time to try it on the bigger versions." Dan remained suspicious. He felt that there was another reason. Something bigger, something personal.

" Well Dan, now that we know where we stand, we had better get to work, there's a strict schedule running."

Danny spent the next forty-five minutes examining the aircraft. He didn't say a word. He made many notes whilst Ruth and her heavies watched. Eventually, he adjourned into the office and placed his pad on the table.

" Firstly, I need my organiser. I run all my programmes and calculations on that. I'll need to interface with the Macintosh too. We'll need two cruise fuel tanks. I'll have to remove the back seat to get them in and I'll need to know the approx. weight of our cargo for weight and balance purposes." Danny had recently helped fit one of these cruise tanks to a Siai Marcheti SF260, a classic Italian designed military trainer. This one belonged to a famous film star who was returning to the states after filming in London. The little craft was to be flown across the Atlantic. Navigation might prove to be a problem but fuel supply shouldn't. "We'll need two booster pumps, brackets, tubing."

" I want you to improve their 'STOL' (*) performance too" said Ruth. 'STOL' stood for 'short take-off and landing'. The Pup wasn't renowned for this although it was not the worst performer in this department.

" In that case, I'll need new adjustable propellers for a finer pitch in the take off roll, bigger wheels, tyres, new leg fairings. I'll have to enlarge the flaps (*) too. Jesus lady do you know just what's involved here?"

" I haven't finished yet Dan. I want you to adapt the radios also, to work on a frequency band outside of the normal aviation range. We will need to talk to each other en route and we don't want any stray transmissions being picked up."

" Anything else?" said Dan sarcastically

" One more thing. You must remove the call signs from the body of the aircraft and replace them with more suitable, less detectable ones. You will remember that these aircraft were reported missing and the authorities are still trying to trace them." That reminded Dan that he was actually on frequency and heard the distress call issued to Manston when the first Pup went missing. "I think I know where we are now" he said. He opened the chart that was on the table in front of him and tapped the spot. " We're here aren't we?"

He pointed to the land just south of the Bradwell bay area. That's the disused strip out there and no doubt that's the power station behind us. I didn't recognise it at first, I've only ever seen it from the air before."

" Well done Dan, I'm convinced you are indeed the right man for the job."

" Let's see now, you were out here when you made the 'Mayday' call." He pointed to the bay between Southend and Margate which formed the mouth of the Thames."

" My guess is that you were already low and well under radar and you flew around the coast into this field."

" Almost Dan. Look at the map again."

Dan studied the chart for a moment

" Well I'll be beggared! You took your chances. You actually flew through that?"

" We knew that 'Search And Rescue' wouldn't go anywhere near the place and no one else would have seen us, so we risked it."

On the northern rim of the bay at Shoeburyness, there was an extensively marked danger area (*). There was a vast military firing range cited there and no one in their right minds would fly anywhere near it, let alone through it for fear of being shot down.

Dan began to type a list of the things he needed into his organiser just as the Macintosh bleeped. Ruth and her colleagues looked at the screen as the latest Byotek circular arrived, requesting help identifying the third icon. Ruth laughed and said:

" We are causing quite a stir gentleman, quite a stir!"

Danny heard a car start and caught a glimpse of Ruth as she drove off in her silver BMW. He was hard at work and had tasked his minders, who answered to the names Johan and Franco respectively, with the less important manual jobs.

" Don't tread on that you idiot!" bellowed Dan." You only tread on this part of the wing, the bit painted black!" Johan responded by stamping his black boot firmly onto the area that Dan had indicated. Johan had been the one who stabbed Dan with the hypodermic. He appeared to be some kind of mercenary and Dan felt that this guy had some kind of military background and wasn't to be messed with. He was definitely brawn while Franco, the quieter one, seemed to be the brain. He spent a lot of time at the computer and said very little.

They worked hard throughout the day and Franco provided basic foodstuffs for them, pizza, chicken and fruit.

Danny sat in the office while he ate and tried to converse with Franco in an attempt to find out as much as he could. Franco wasn't drawn into any conversation and either answered with a basic 'yes' or 'no' or not at all. He was busy at the Macintosh and made no attempt to hide it from Danny. Danny was fully computer literate but expressed a particular ignorance of the Mac' to Franco to make him think that he wasn't.

" You'll have to show me how to use that thing" he said" I've only ever used my pocket organiser." Franco nodded and continued scrolling through the pages on the screen. Danny appeared uninterested but was actually taking in as much as he could.

71

There were several pages of diagnostic reports and chemical formulas. He noticed particularly reports that mentioned increasing mortalities in southern Europe. The name BYOTEK appeared regularly and there were several E- mail memos requesting help and information concerning a new drug called 'Destiny.' Danny was pretty sure now that he was going to be the unwilling courier of this 'Destiny' and that he was in it up to his neck.

By the end of the day, both Pups had their back seats removed and were suspended on jacks with their wheels missing. Danny had argued with Franco about the time limits involved. There was an inordinate workload for such a time frame. As the work progressed, Danny needed more equipment and parts so Franco called Ruth on his mobile phone. They had smashed Danny's and it lay in a bin in the corner of the workshop.

" Ruth will be back tomorrow with all the parts" he said and continued with the Mac. Danny decided to attend to the registration marks while the craft were immobilised.

Emblazoned across the side of each aircraft, in one foot high lettering, were the four lettered call signs prefixed by a 'G' making five letters in total. These call signs were effectively the same as a cars number plate and were unique to the bearer. They were registered in the country of origin and this was denoted by the prefix, in this case 'G' for Great Britain. The authorities would obviously be on the look out for these two, or any Pups in UK airspace with a 'G'' prefix. It was a matter of procedure to check the details with the CAA registration office in the same way that the Police readily check car number plates.

Ruth had instructed Danny to choose something suitably foreign that would not arouse suspicion and would be awkward to trace. As he sat in the office, while Franco was consumed with the latest Byotek update, Danny toyed with alternate ideas for call signs and eventually typed his choices into his organiser. He had decided on a 'K' prefix. In fact, the proper prefix for Kuwait was '9K'. Danny felt that this was suitably recognisable as a non-European call sign and would be difficult to trace anyhow. Danny was aware of at least one Saudi registered 727, which was impounded at Manston airport, for non-payment of fees The actual owners had not been traced despite ten months of enquiries. The Kuwaiti airforce were known to have ordered several Pups as trainers originally and it was quite feasible that they would have found their way onto the civilian register at this time. Many such air forces had off-loaded their ageing trainers within the last few years. The Swiss had recently disposed of four of their Pups and several Bulldogs had just been brought back to the UK from Hong Kong.

Danny chose blue lettering for the newly christened 'KILO ZULU MIKE ECHO TANGO' and 'KILO ALPHA ROMEO MIKE ALPHA'.

Sleep was a problem that night. Although Danny was exhausted from his day's endeavours, his mind played leapfrog, jumping from one problem to the next. He was quite a logical thinker so, in time, he began to prioritise his thoughts and an agenda soon presented itself. He was not the best of sleepers anyway. With the small desk light left on in the room, he found sleep impossible so he decided to make himself comfortable and afford himself some simple rest instead.

Johan and Franco had taken it in turns to sleep whilst the other kept vigil over Danny and the Pups. There was no need for physical restraint. Danny knew the consequences of any escape. His only option was to run with the whole charade until some kind of conclusion was reached. At all costs, he must not endanger Rebecca and these people were Mafia, he reminded himself. They would stop at nothing.

Dawn broke and Danny was ready for Johan's boot. As the German oaf attempted to awaken him again with a vicious kick in the ribs, Danny grabbed it with both hands and twisted it ninety degrees, forcing Johan to dive to the floor. Both were back on their feet in seconds and a standoff ensued. Franco intervened and shouted at Johan in German and he duly backed down.

" Keep him away from me or these planes are going no where!" Shouted Dan realising by now that he was important to the whole project and he didn't have to take this kind of shit anymore. Franco nodded.

" It won't happen again" he said as he returned to his desk

" It'd better not."

Danny's next job, in the absence of the larger parts he had ordered, were the radios. He had served an apprenticeship as a British Telecom engineer on leaving school and what he had in mind shouldn't prove too much of a problem.

He chose 'Kilo Alpha Romeo Mike Alpha' and removed the avionics panel. 'Kilo Mike Alpha' was equipped with a full instrument panel unlike 'Kilo- Echo Tango', which had a basic set up. Dan had an 'IMC' rating (instrument meteorological conditions) a simple but effective instrument rating which basically enabled him to fly in adverse weather conditions and he chose 'Kilo Mike Alpha,' as, both it and he were best equipped to be the lead flight.

The wiring loom soon led him to the radio. It was a simple matter of removing the casing and retuning the oscillator away from its usual VHF frequency range to the higher UHF band, as Ruth had requested.

Danny was disturbed by the sound of a van drawing up outside. He had just put the finishing touches to his job when Ruth returned. She stayed inside while Johan and Franco unloaded the vehicle. She surveyed Dan's progress in silence.

" Before I go any further with this I want some assurances" said Dan." I want to speak to Rebecca. I need to know she's OK."

" Rebecca will be OK as long as you do what we want. I've told you that."

"That's not good enough"

" What do you want?"

" I want to see her"

" Impossible"

" I need to know she's OK"

" I'll try and arrange for you to talk to her tomorrow as a small gesture of goodwill. Just finish the job." She offered as an incentive.

While Danny and Johan unpacked the items that Ruth had brought, Franco dealt with some cases of his own. It soon became apparent that he was assembling some kind of small laboratory. It appeared that Franco was a chemist by trade and he was expecting to go to work shortly.

Danny modified Ruth's radio in a similar fashion to his own and assigned a common channel to both to enable in-flight conversation between the two craft without being overheard as requested. He had asked Ruth for several electronic items, explaining to her that these were necessary for the frequency change, and he made best use of them. Danny would spend the next twenty-four hours flat out, adapting the Pups.

CHAPTER 22

From the front window of the flat, Rebecca watched life continue in Rochester as if nothing was wrong. Kids were noisily playing in the street on their way to school. Milk float passed postman and husbands kissed their wives goodbye as they left home for a day's normality. That was all that she wanted. Normality. The things that you take for granted and only crave when they're gone. Normality. Everything seemed so detached from real life, so abstract. Why couldn't things be normal again? But then, Becky's life had never been that normal. For instance, she had grown up without a mother. Her father had done a fine job but, after all, he was a man. Why was she denied the love and affection that only a mother can bring? Why was she left to develop the skills of a woman without a maternal guiding hand? Her life had begun 'not normal'. In fact, this was why Rebecca was not a normal woman. She was not her mother 'once removed'. She had forged her own persona through a difficult, unsettled childhood and she was definitely not 'normal' in the perceived sense. Although she would not think of herself as such, she was in fact extraordinary.

She often thought of her mother and what she would have been like. Rebecca was only three when she died and had no recollection of her at all. She watched the other mums in the street taking their kids to school and wondered what it would have been like to mix with the other children in class. She had a succession of private tutors in a succession of different RAF bases and her standard of education was high but she had been deprived of her childhood. Now she was deprived of her father, her brother and her lover too. A grandfather, an uncle and a new dad. She was planning to tell Danny this weekend. She had toyed with different ways of breaking the news to him. Over breakfast, after making love, casually whilst out shopping or at the rugby club during a match. She amused herself with Dan's imagined responses. She knew that he would probably cry and try to hide the fact with one of his stupid, funny remarks like "are you sure its yours?" She wanted so much to give Dan something special in return for everything he had given her. He had always been so selfless, so thoughtful and tireless in supporting her. Rebecca also wanted to be the mother that she herself had never had. She wanted a little girl. She would call her Emily. An old fashioned traditional, feminine name and she would be beautiful. She would at last have a normal family.

Rebecca's heart leapt as the phone went.

" Becky, it's Roger. Have you heard anything yet?"

" No nothing at all. It's driving me crazy." She lied.

" You must call the police, I've told you. The longer you leave it the worse it may get."

Roger had spent the previous day with Rebecca and insisted that she report Dan missing to the police. She had argued against it, making various excuses. In keeping with Ruth's demands, she had not given Roger the full truth about the phone call two nights previously. She could not afford to lose Danny. Not now.

Rebecca placated Roger and promised to keep him informed as and when she heard anything . She hadn't been out of the house for days and needed some groceries from the shop. Her bearded collie 'Biggles' hadn't had a walk for two days. She figured that life had to go on and decided to take him over the park first. He was such a comfort and joy to her. She had questioned the wisdom of having a dog originally, being away from home so much, but Biggles had lots of friends who were willing to look after him down at the depot. The night watchman, old Ted, had become quite fond of him and Rebecca was always made to feel quite guilty each time she repossessed him, taking him back to the flat. Old Ted, whose hearing was not so good despite the device in his right ear, thought he was called 'big holes' due to the ones he was forever digging in the yard.

Rebecca was still looking out of the window as the grey BMW pulled up outside, but she paid no heed to it.

" Hello fella." The postman bent down and gave Biggles a good old rub. "Morning Becky. Haven't seen Danny for ages. Hope he's OK." Rebecca answered with a simple

" Yes he's fine thank you." She made her way along the small footpath that led through the children's play ground and on into the open fields near the downs. She and Biggles quite often made it to the top of the hill and the view was exceptional. There was a little bench at the top and Danny had delicately carved both their initials into it in those early romantic stages. It was in fact quite a local tradition and soon, there would be very little actual bench left to sit on.

They made it to the top field and Becky let Biggles off his lead. He could get up to no real trouble here and could run around all day while she admired the view and gathered her thoughts. She was never out of touch though. Her airline bosses in Europe had provided her with a global service mobile and quite often called her from far off places.

Becky went over the moss-encrusted outline of Danny's carved heart as her mobile rang and shattered the peace of the surrounding countryside.

" Put the dog on the lead."

" I beg your pardon?"

" Put the dog on the lead and tie him to the fence post. We must talk." Rebecca swung her head around and saw a blond woman leaning against the stile in the next field down, talking into her mobile.

" Biggles! Biggles! Come here boy, don't play me up, not now." As soon as the dog was secure, the woman crossed the stile and made her way up the field and sat down next to Rebecca.

" Where's Danny, is he safe?"

" He is for now, and he'll stay that way, but only if you co-operate with us."

" Look, what's this all about? What do you want of us and why have you framed my brother?"

" We need you to do a job for us. Shall we say that your family are insurance policies and we are keeping them safe until you redeem them."

" And just how do I do that?" Asked Rebecca. Ruth handed her an envelope.

" We need some information. Its all in there." Rebecca opened the envelope and took out a list of demands. There were several requirements, the first being details of 'RADNET' and it's effective coverage within specific areas of Europe. The list went on requesting details of customs procedures for flight crew, technical information on various airports throughout Europe and names of key personal associated with them.

" Why do you want to know all this?"

" The 'why' does not concern you. You may not know all of this information first hand but you are well connected in the industry. You will have to find out from the people who do know."

" And just how am I supposed to do that?"

" That's your problem. But you will do it, if you want your family returned safely."

There was no doubt that Rebecca Washington was virtually aviation's first lady in Europe and she was indeed well connected. Who ever this woman was, she thought, she had certainly done her homework.

Ruth punched another number into her mobile. She spoke in German when it answered. Shortly after she held the phone to Rebecca's ear.

" Hello, Danny, is that you? Are you OK? Where...." Ruth pulled the phone away and began to speak in German once again. She eventually hung up.

" Where is he, you haven't hurt him have you?!"

"Calm down Rebecca. He's OK. However you must understand the power and resolve of the people that I work for. They won't hesitate to hurt him if you don't comply with our requests.

Back in Bradwell, Franco was having a similar conversation with Danny. He was so relieved to hear Rebecca's voice but distressed at the thought of any harm that may come to her. Johan was at hand to restrain Dan if he over reacted.

Ruth was playing an elaborate game of 'second guess'. She had both Rebecca and Danny believing that the other was hostage and that their fate was dependent on the others co-operation.

" I suggest that you provide me with the radar information first. We shall be watching you Rebecca. Any unusual contacts that you make will result in harm to your loved ones. You love your dog too don't you?" She said threateningly. Poor Biggles had been jumping and straining at the leash and had now resorted to whimpering.

77

" You are only to contact legitimate sources for this information and I stress that any strange behaviour will be punished." Ruth walked over to Biggles and stroked him with implied menace.

" Stay away from my dog. I'll do as you say."

" I'll be in touch within a few days. You should use your time wisely."

Ruth made off down the hill and Rebecca wrapped her arms around her dog and began to cry.

Once back indoors, she made a cup of tea and composed herself, allowing some time to think. She picked up the phone.

" I want to speak to Lawrence Carlton please. It's extremely urgent. My name is Rebecca Washington." After a pause she said " Please get him to call me as soon as possible. I stress, it's very urgent."

CHAPTER 23

The Bulldog looked magnificent, resplendently regal with its proud, sculptured lines highlighted against a backdrop of larger tube-like airliners, which were altogether mundane by comparison. She certainly attracted more than her fair share of attention as she followed taxiway Delta to the arrivals building at Venice's Marco Polo Airport, which traditionally was more accustomed to dealing with the bulkier, commercial traffic. To the onlookers, it appeared that the little craft was being given the red carpet treatment and that there must be someone famous on board. In the event, the single occupant was not so much famous, but very important. Just how important he would prove to be, Lawrence Carlton was unaware of at this time.

Whereas there would normally be three or four Boeings, mingled amongst the odd Airbus A330 with a sprinkling of Bizjets thrown in for good measure, all taxiing and lining up for a swift succession of departures and arrival at this busy Airport, all had held back on account of this majestic little Bulldog. The viewing gallery was crammed with sightseers jockeying for position as they were convinced that *'Golf Lima Charlie's'* occupant must be someone worth catching a glimpse of for all these other aircraft to be holding their position. In truth, the reason that Lawrence and his aircraft were afforded a clear field was quite simple, 'Wake Turbulence.' (*) Arriving and departing passenger aircraft would create a massive 'wash' that would certainly be disastrous for an airborne light aircraft such as the Bulldog. Even taxiing would be quite hazardous and this was the real reason why the commercial traffic was held back. There were specific, published tables of 'Wake Turbulence' clearance distances between this blend of traffic for the controllers to refer to and the 747s could only sit and watch and enjoy the spectacle also.

Lawrence was quite used to this kind of reception and thoroughly enjoyed the attention that he and his Bulldog were rightly awarded.

Lawrence held a diplomatic passport and passed through customs unhindered.

There was no need to book in at an hotel, as he would not be staying overnight. Instead he paid the cab driver and walked across the Piazza St Marco and into the cathedral of the same name.

At thirteen hundred hours exactly, in a synchronised manoeuvre, the congregation rose to its feet, the choir began to sing and the refectory door opened allowing the procession of priests, altar boys and nuns to make their way up the central aisle towards the altar to celebrate mass. The afternoon ceremony was an elaborate affair conducted in full gowns and with the complete choir in attendance.

The cathedral was adorned with religious icons, paintings, statues etc. and there were several small crypts where worshippers would light candles and make offerings towards their chosen patron saint. The air was filled with a blend of candle smoke, frankincense and a damp, musky aroma, which captured the essence of the hundreds of years of worship that had taken place there.

Lawrence rose from his pew as the procession reached the altar and entered one of the confessionals at the back of the cathedral. These large, ornately carved mahogany structures were almost like enclosed sentry boxes designed to accommodate a priest and a penitent Christian only. On confessing their sins, the priest would offer absolution and the sinner would be duly forgiven of them on payment of several Hail Mary's and usually, at least one Lord's Prayer.

Lawrence knelt and said:

" Forgive me father for I have sinned. It has been 2 years since my last confession. The sky is blue over Lake Geneva on a summer's day."

The reply was just as strange.

" Have you got my money?"

" Have you got my information?" said Lawrence

" All that you need is in this envelope." A leather-gloved hand pushed the A4 manila envelope under the small dividing curtain designed to afford some small level of dignity and privacy between the confessional's occupants. Lawrence opened the envelope and studied its contents.

" This is good" he said and passed a smaller package through the hatch.

" How quickly can you be operational?"

" Two full days from your 'go ahead' and on receipt of the balance."

" I'll pay fifty percent now and the rest on completion. If that is not acceptable to you then the project is off. Do you understand?" There was a slight pause before the stranger, who was obviously no priest, answered.

" If the balance is paid in American dollars."

" Not a problem. In that case, get your colleagues in position. I will be in touch in the usual fashion shortly to tell you when to 'go'."

Lawrence rose and left the confessional backwards uttering a very audible

" Peace be with you Father" as he left.

CHAPTER 24

Senor Alberto Mendez had been relieved of his immediate duties in Palma in light of recent events, and was seconded to Brussels to concentrate solely on the *'Destiny'* issue. Little more was known about the recipe of the drug but its lethal nature was re-affirmed daily with the autopsy reports arriving on a regular basis. Byotek HQ was the obvious place for a strategic headquarters and the shrewd, elderly Spanish gentleman was best placed to make full use of its resources and lead the team. That team had already made significant enquiries by the time that he arrived and placed his weathered, leather attaché case on his already busy desk.

"Gentlemen, to work!" he announced, with no formal introductions to delay him further.

The report that immediately caught his attention was one concerning a list of pharmaceutical companies that legitimately manufactured the drug Phlolariscene, a powerful growth stimulant that had shown up as a trace element in *'Destiny'*

One particular fertiliser company based in France had recently increased its production of 'Agriterre 250,' an unusually potent phosphorous organic fertiliser that required special handling and administration and was consequently rarely used on the general market. Byotek listed this company in connection with 'Phlolariscene,' which was also an integral element of the fertiliser. On investigation, most of the other companies listed had reported that, due to the unstable nature and handling difficulties of Phlolariscene, they had ceased production of the substance. This particular firm however, had not, they had increased their output yet there appeared to be an imbalance between the amount of Phlolariscene being produced and the amount actually used in 'Agriterre 250.' It could be argued, Alberto thought, that their increase in productivity was due to the cessation of output from the other firms. However, he decided to pay a personnel visit to 'Mediculture 3000' in Grenoble to investigate.

Alberto Mendez had arrived unannounced at 'Mediculture 3000,' purporting to be a sales representative from a packaging firm. His reception was less than friendly and he was told that he would have to make an appointment for another day as no one could see him at such short notice. Explaining to the young female receptionist that he had come a long way and that he was in need of refreshment, she had directed him to a cafe some five minutes drive away. Alberto nodded but asked if he could use the toilet before he left. He was an old, overweight gentleman, he explained, and was having trouble with his prostate. The young girl dutifully escorted him to a set of swing doors at the start of a long corridor and was about to accompany him to the rest rooms when the switchboard began to ring. Alberto indicated that he could manage to find his own way and promptly disappeared into the corridor as she returned to the reception. A full ten minutes passed before she decided to track him down. Alberto had made full use of his excursion and had plundered a filing cabinet or two. Up to now, Byotek had very little to offer the investigating team other than a fragmented chemical analysis and a couple of oblique riddles that were received on the 'Net.' The despatch notes that Alberto now held were the first positive lead.

The young, French receptionist had a penchant for stilettos and the unmistakable click of her heels along the corridor warned Alberto that she had come looking for him. He quickly folded the despatch notes and placed his hand on the door handle as it was twisted from outside. The door swung open and the girl began to complain loudly asking him what was doing in there. Alberto apologised, quoting his advancing years and frailties, saying that he was lost. The girl had noticed that the filing cabinets had been interfered with and whilst trying to block his exit, she had called out loudly for assistance. Alberto continued to apologise saying that he was just a stupid old man and pushed by her, making his way along the corridor back to reception. He had broken into a half jog and had noticed at that point that his bladder was indeed that of an old man. As he reached the main door out into reception he heard voices behind him and there were obviously several bodies now in pursuit. He fumbled for the keys of his rented Peugeot and unlocked the door with some speed, closing and locking it after him. The ignition had barely engaged when a hand tugged at the driver's door and another on the passenger side but he had already hit the central locking button preventing the doors from opening. As he drove off, he saw three men in his rear view mirror, standing in the car park as the young receptionist wrote down his registration. One man began to dial a number on his mobile phone.

Alberto had seen a lot of life, and death of course, during his years as chief medical examiner in Palma. Nothing could shock him anymore and he had learnt the skills of detachment necessary for him to function properly within the ghoulish parameters of his job. He had always managed to keep the horrors of his career within the domain of the workplace, leaving them at the door when he left. This time, however, he couldn't help but feel a deep involvement, which drove him to become involved beyond his normal remit.

Two days prior to his visit to Grenoble, he had been called back to Palma to direct the autopsy of another drug related death. The indications were apparently such that 'Destiny' was the probable killer. Alberto enquired as to why his colleague, Juan Enriquez, could not carry out the autopsy in his absence. Juan was more than capable of performing the surgery. The administrator calmly explained that the corpse was that of Juan's daughter, Juanita.

Alberto performed the autopsy with the grace and precision of a ballerina. He had always maintained a deep respect for the bodies he encountered and duly dissected on his slab, ever mindful that he was in charge of someone's beloved. He had dealt with deaths by natural causes, 'RTAs,' suicides of various natures, cot deaths, shootings, drowning and many drug overdoses. The cot deaths were the ones he had found most distressing, until now.

Juanita s beautiful young body lay lifeless before him and he began his autopsy by wiping a virgin tear from an eye that had seen so much death and tragedy yet had remained dry until this point in his career. Juanita had always called Alberto 'Uncle' and he thought of her as the closest thing that he would ever have to a daughter. Alberto's hitherto emotional detachment had extended to his personal life, and he had never formed any bonds, nor had he married.

When the review board played back the cassette tape of the autopsy as they always did, Alberto Mendez was heard to be crying throughout his commentary.

The Peugeot was a comfortable car but not that fast to carry Alberto far enough away from the offices of Mediculture 3000 as quickly as he desired. The excitement was far too much for a man of his advanced years. He had checked his rear view mirror consistently for the last fifty minutes and was reasonably confident that he had not been followed but he couldn't be sure. His swollen bladder was now beyond uncomfortable and was in fact quite painful. Established well en route to Paris, Alberto decided to pull into the services at Dijon for relief.

On exiting the gents, feeling considerably lighter, he sat at the table in the crowded restaurant and ordered coffee. He unfolded the papers that he had taken from Mediculture and began to read. Suddenly, he leapt to his feet and began to run to the door as the waitress returned with his coffee.

" Cafe monsieur!" She shouted.

" Non, non. Ou est la telephon ?" he replied with some urgency. The waitress pointed to several kiosks in the crowded reception area and left his coffee on the table. Each booth had at least two people queuing outside and Alberto was extremely agitated. Eventually after a little shoving and declaration of position in the queue, he entered the booth and closed the door behind him. Alberto dialled the international operator and requested a number in Brussels. He had just been connected to the Byotek office when he heard the sound of the kiosk door being opened behind him. Without looking round he shouted "Non. Ferme, ferme." The next sound he heard was a rather peculiar hissing noise. In the second before his death, he realised that it was the sound of the air rushing out of a large cut in his windpipe.

Mario Marcantonio slipped away quietly wiping the blade of his knife on the papers that he had just taken out of Alberto's hand. He stopped by his car, clicked his lighter and cremated the blood stained documents.

CHAPTER 25

" Sardinia!" Danny was reasonably surprised by the destination given to him by Ruth. He had suspected that their pickup point would be somewhere on the Italian mainland. Ruth had presented him with all the charts and information necessary for him to plan the journey and he pondered the complexity of the trip. He had read many accounts in the aviation monthlies of intrepid 'PPLs' who had crossed continents in their light aircraft and he had marvelled at their achievements, yet, here he was faced with the daunting, yet curiously exciting prospect of just such a trip. Whereas these others had made regular scheduled stops on their journeys, this trip was to be flown without any at all. He studied the charts and nervously pushed his hair back several times.

" I want you to work out a plan to get us there as quickly and as discretely as possible." said Ruth." We will need to fly as low as we can to avoid radar and obviously, we must route over rural areas in case we are spotted from the ground." Ruth was a capable pilot but her skills where simple compared to those of Danny's. Mario had done his homework and thoroughly researched Danny's background for her. She was fully briefed on his capabilities and she was confident that he could come up with the best course available. He was undoubtedly the best man for the job.

"This is going to take a while" he said." We'll need GPS too. You'd better get a couple of compatible units with moving map displays. There are a lot of mountains in the way in the south of France! We need to install a good 'SAT NAV' system." (Satellite navigation, or 'Global Positioning System' GPS for short, was introduced by the Americans just prior to the Gulf War. They sent aloft a constellation of twenty-four strategically placed satellites to circumnavigate the globe. Ground, or aircraft based receiver units, some actually displaying a moving map of the current location, given line of sight to at least three, but preferably four of these satellites, would reference their position to within an accuracy of two metres. GPS was just one of the recent technological advances that helped the allied forces 'see off' the Iraqi dictator and provide him, in fact, with the 'Mother of all defeats.')

Ruth nodded her approval and made a note in her filofax that she always carried with her.

"I'll need an 'up to the minute' Metfax to complete this" said Dan." When do we go?" (Not only is it a legal requirement but a sensible one too, for any pilot to get a weather briefing before any intended flight.)

" I'll give you the notice that you need when you need it. Do what you can for now." said Ruth.

Wind data was vital to any calculations concerning such a trip. Winds that could vary in direction and strength aloft could seriously affect the progress of the journey and the amount of fuel required. Light aircraft were particularly vulnerable to being blown off course and basically acted as a weathercock in windy conditions. They seldom flew in a straight-ahead approach, crabbing into the wind instead, to offset any drift. If the True Airspeed (TAS) of an aircraft was, for instance, 100 miles per hour and it was flying into a direct headwind of 10 miles per hour, then its progress over the ground would in fact be only at 90 miles per hour and the converse would apply too. Over a long journey, these winds could have a considerable effect.

Danny had never flown to the south of France before but a quick glance at the chart suggested that he would have to route south through the Rhone valley. He had remembered reading about the 'Mistral', a powerful wind that belted southwards down this gully between the Massif Central to the west and the Alps to the east. It would be fine on the southerly outbound leg. The wind would actually carry them with it, increasing their speed dramatically. The trip homeward however, could be difficult, particularly if they were carrying a heavy cargo.

Dan laid out the charts and set about the task. He opened a new file in his 'Pocketflite' programme of his 'palmtop' and entered the aircraft's call-signs at the top left hand corner followed by their cruise speed and fuel consumption figures on the right. These were the starting points for any plan. Next, he began to draw a line on the chart in red chinagraph pencil that represented his planned track. Chinagraph was easily removed with a cloth and Dan had to make many alterations as he encountered obstructions en route, having to draw a course around them instead. Low flying was dangerous, doubly so in unfamiliar terrain. Normally, he would work out the figures for the 'MSA' column next. 'MSA' stood for 'minimum safe altitude' and it was a priority detail to note any obstructions en route and allow a safety margin of at least five hundred feet above them as a lowest height to observe and fly. In this case, as Ruth had instructed him to work out a low level passage to enable them to fly under the radar, MSA's were pointless so Dan had to be careful to avoid any such masts or towers that lay in the way of his route. He meticulously identified each one on the charts with a circle.

Along with the growth in the usage of mobile phones, came an accompanying proliferation of ungainly transmitter pylons dotted across the countryside where one would least expect them. They popped up so quickly that many did not appear on the latest edition aviation charts. Danny made a mental note to be vigilant and wary of these. If the visibility were at all doubtful then low flying would be particularly hazardous. The most commonplace fatal accident statistic was usually associated with flight in undulating terrain under restricted visibility. Known as 'CFITs' (Controlled Flight Into Terrain,) the pilots were simply unaware of their position and haplessly flew into the ground or the side of a mountain. Danny was only too aware of the statistics due to his association with 'GASIL.'

Danny considered that they would have to navigate along horizontal corridors above the MSA's but below the radar coverage. These lower and upper heights appeared to overlap in places and Dan was kept quite busy rubbing out and re routing his track lines. He would have to guesstimate the line of site of the radar by studying the hills and mountains in the vicinity of the major airfields and attempt to build a picture of these three dimensional corridors. Not every airfield was equipped with radar but the major ones certainly were. Danny also considered that they would have to fly to the right of any line features that they may be following (roads, railways, rivers etc.) as it was a standard procedure to do so and he was mindful of the fact that any other traffic that they may encounter, would be doing just that but coming the other way.

It would take Dan a full five hours before his plan was ready.

Ruth appeared several times at his shoulder but said nothing, not wishing to break his concentration.

The duly completed flightplan, now resident only in Danny's organiser, was the most comprehensive he had ever done. He had actually benefited from the experience, as the exercise could only raise his level of awareness and general airmanship. Had he chosen to do the calculations in the traditional fashion, by using the plastic, circular slide rule that was the mainstay of a pilot's kit, it would have taken him considerably longer. In this case, he had simply entered track, true airspeed, fuel consumption, and waypoint data into the programme and, at the single touch of the 'calculate' button; he was presented with the required flight information. It would take only moments to add the wind data at the required moment for the final headings. It would prove to be a simple matter to download the plan into his GPS system when it arrived. Using this software was simple and expeditious and Dan had another reason for using it which he wasn't about to divulge.

Ruth had asked him to print out three copies of the plan. One for himself and one for her. The third copy was a mystery. No doubt, it would be for whoever would greet them at their final destination in Sardinia.

Danny connected the organiser to the Macintosh and highlighted the 'Print' option. The printer noisily announced itself active and the first of the three copies began to appear. Danny made a point of leaving the office and generally inspecting the work he'd done on the Pups. He was actually quite concerned about the fuel lines running from the cruise tanks and hoped that he wouldn't have any 'vapour lock' or similar problems with the supply. He then went back into the office and reappeared with the first hard copy of the flight plan, which he duly presented to Ruth. Franco and Johan, curiosity getting the better of them, peered over her shoulder for a first look.

" This won't be an easy flight" he informed Ruth." It would be quite demanding under normal circumstances, but to fly low and avoid surveillance is going to be practically impossible. I've had to guess about the radar coverage."

" I'm waiting some further information concerning the radar," said Ruth." I hope to have it any day now" believing that Rebecca would oblige under the circumstances.

Danny returned to the office to collect the next issue.

The organiser was in fact a mini, multi tasking computer that basically meant that it could perform several functions at the same time. As the printing continued,

Danny returned to the main system screen and selected 'E-Mail.' On pressing 'enter' a prompt appeared asking for the 'E mail' address.

A few days previously, whilst Danny had been sitting in the office with Franco, considering his choices for the aircraft's new call signs, he had managed to make a note of the address at the top of the programme that Franco had been viewing. Danny quickly inserted

'Bio.Ecom@/brus*gov' and hit the 'POST IT' icon. An error page appeared stating 'ADDRESS FAILURE – PLEASE CHECK AND TRY AGAIN' This was followed by 'RETRY OR ABORT?' Dan hit 'POST IT' again and the error message reappeared. At this point, he could hear movement in the hangar and he strained his neck so that he could use his peripheral vision to look at the keyboard and the door of the office at the same time. He scrolled back a page and checked the address just as Ruth called to him. He noticed an erroneous '6' in his address and realised that he had missed the shift button when hitting '@'. The upper case of '6' was '@' on his organisers non-standard keyboard.

" Danny!" Ruth was feet from the office door. He hurriedly hit 'POST IT' once again and as Ruth and the others came into the office, 'SENDING MAIL' flashed up on the screen of his organiser .To his horror, the Macintosh began to display the transmitting pages of the plan. Not appreciating what was in fact taking place, Ruth looked at the Mac just as the last page flicked out of sight. A 'bleep' from the organiser was accompanied by a 'MESSAGE SENT' display, which Danny quickly cleared. At this stage, he was a little flushed and there were obvious signs of sweating that Ruth had noticed.

" Are you OK Daniel?' she inquired sarcastically.

" I guess I've been working hard and late these last few days and it's beginning to catch up on me," he replied. He was unsure whether her concerns where due to her suspicions concerning what had just taken place, or if they were in fact genuine. She could not afford her flight leader to go sick at this stage.

" Rest for the remainder of today" she said as she looked again at the screen of the Mac. Fortunately, at that point, the printing had just finished and the sudden lack of the printers chatter diverted her attention to it.

" I'm fine" Dan said to aid the distraction" but I will rest tonight. We will need life- jackets too incidentally. There's a lot of water to cross between France and the island."

Danny figured that it would be at least a day or two before they set off. Ruth had to supply the Sat Nav units and he would need at least an afternoon to fit them properly. The Pups were now as ready as they would ever be for the journey. He had thoroughly serviced them too and the cruise tanks were duly charged with 100LL Avgas. Avgas differed from mogas (motor gas) as it had a lower lead content and different burn characteristics. Mogas was produced under less stringent quality controls and had the potential to contain more water, which could freeze in the carburettor causing serious problems. The high lead content of mogas could also foul the plugs and vaporisation could occur causing vapour locks in the system. This could lead to fuel starvation and engine stoppage. Ruth had provided two large drums of Avgas and the Pups were fuelled and ready.

Danny decided that rest was indeed a priority. He had all but finished the immediate jobs at hand and recognised the importance of being alert for whatever awaited him over the next few days. His newly acquired camp bed was reasonably comfortable and he chose to retire early.

Franco had been busy assembling his makeshift laboratory and there was much activity in that corner of the hangar. Suddenly, Danny was aware of a putrid smell filling the room and he rushed to the door as Ruth and Johan held handkerchiefs to their mouths and rushed to open windows.

" We'll need masks" exclaimed Franco as he wiped the tears from his eyes that were continuously running. Ruth had supplied him with a small sample of *'Destiny'* resin to test the manufacturing procedures.

" Go back to bed Danny" said Ruth." This doesn't concern you."

CHAPTER 26

When Lawrence Carlton eventually returned to Brussels, he was met personally by his 'Girl Friday,' his long-term personal secretary Margaret. She had always been loyal to Lawrence and had been at his 'beck and call' for many years. In fact, she had become a rock for him, particularly after the death of his Beloved Barbara. It was quite obvious to most but, sadly, not to Lawrence, that her attentions for him went beyond those of a personal assistant. Margaret had tried to detach herself recently from the unrequited feelings that she had for Lawrence but the underlying sense of attachment was too strong. She concentrated instead, on managing those emotions beyond sight, if not of those around her, but beyond he that she loved, for fear of rejection.

Once clear of the terminal building, Lawrence directed the chauffeur to take them both straight back to the office despite Margaret's protestations that he should take some rest. She had soon realised that it was futile to argue with him when he was in one of his stubborn moods, so she decided to work late with him and give him as much assistance as possible. There was always more than enough to do but Margaret was skilled in prioritising his duties and she began to prepare a schedule for him.

" Oh, and a Miss Rebecca Washington called. She said it was urgent."

"Rebecca called! Why didn't you tell me earlier?" He admonished.

Margaret was aware that Lawrence's attentions seemed to be a little more than those of a business nature where miss Washington was concerned. She had met her on one occasion in Whitehall and noted Lawrence's reaction the first time he had seen her. She was undoubtedly a very attractive woman and Margaret had felt a particular jealousy stir within her. The very mention of her name still filled her with envy. If only Lawrence would react to her in the same way she mused.

Lawrence shot Margaret a glance as if to reprimand her for demoting the importance of this message to halfway down the agenda when it should rightly have been a priority. He stalled her briefing session and dialled the number.

" Rebecca, it's me Lawrence. I'm sorry for the delay but I've only just got your message."

Margaret busied herself with her notes appearing to be uninterested but was in fact hanging on to every word that he said. Lawrence was absorbed with the phone call and Margaret noticed the overly concerned look on his face.

"Rebecca. Calm down and listen very carefully to what I say." Lawrence looked up at Margaret and she now gave him her full attention realising that there was a problem. When the job had to be done, Lawrence could always count on her for her support.

" You must do as they say for now. If they call again, tell them that you are working on their demands and stall them as long as you can. I will return to London

89

tonight and I'll come to you first thing in the morning. I want you to arrange a meeting with all the drivers at the depot for eleven A.M. Now, is your fax switched on?" he inquired." Good. I'm going to fax you a copy of the 'Radnet' chart for Western Europe. That should keep them busy. I'll see you tomorrow morning. I'll come straight to the flat." As he hung up, Margaret expected him to fully brief her, as he normally would on any important matter. Instead, he offered her a dismissing glance and asked what was the next item on the agenda. Not wishing to appear as inconvenienced as she was, Margaret continued with the briefing.

" Oh yes, and Gabriel Dupont from the Byotek office dropped this in. He said that it had been received in their office by mistake and that it was obviously meant for 'Radnet.'" Lawrence looked over the flight plan and dismissed it.

" It means nothing to me. Probably another Internet stray." He filed it in the bin. Lawrence had learnt to make rapid judgements concerning the mountain of paperwork that he had to deal with. It could soon mount up and clutter the office so he was adept at dealing with it as quickly as it arrived instead of laying it aside for further deliberation. Margaret continued with the business at hand and a further two hours passed before Lawrence declared that enough was enough for one day and that he would treat her to dinner before he set off for London. Margaret declined, attempting to punish him for his associations with Miss Washington but she soon realised that it was she herself who would suffer. Why couldn't she just be thankful for what she had of him, she chastised herself? Why must it be all or nothing?

As an educated, otherwise sensible and intelligent woman, these irrational notions and her strange behaviour immensely bothered Margaret where Lawrence was concerned. There was no doubt, that despite her attempts at denial, she was still very much in love with him. Lawrence, sensing that she was upset by something, offered to walk her to her car instead. This time she gratefully accepted the offer and placed her arm in his as they walked along the endless corridors towards the car park. She normally cursed the miles of plain carpeting between her parking space and the office but she now cherished every step as she clung to her love. She kept the conversation polite and asked Lawrence if his head felt any better having declared a headache earlier. Before he could reply, she changed the subject dramatically. Lawrence was a little startled that she hadn't waited for his response about his head.

" Oh, I nearly forgot to tell you! Have you heard the terrible news about Senor Mendez?" Lawrence had attended several seminars in the great hall and had become acquainted with this particular gentleman. " He's been murdered!" Margaret went on to explain exactly what had happened and wished that she hadn't mentioned it at all because Lawrence was so shocked at the news that he stopped dead in his tracks and let go of her arm.

" My God, I can hardly believe it. What a terrible thing. I had coffee with him only last week" he declared. They continued to walk and resumed their arm in arm embrace and Margaret explained what she knew.

90

" Apparently, he was working on this *'Destiny'* thing, strayed beyond his duties of analyst and tried to play amateur detective. He ended up getting killed for his efforts. He was obviously getting close to something or someone, but he didn't let anyone know what he was doing until it was too late. It's so sad."

Suddenly Lawrence stopped dead in his tracks once again. Margaret asked him what was wrong but he replied with a 'shoosh,' followed by a

" What did you say?" This was somewhat of a rhetorical question and after a moment's reflection; he suddenly turned around and began to walk back the way that they had come.

" What is it? What's the matter?" said Margaret.

" I need to go back to the office. Something you said." Lawrence was deep in thought and Margaret could hardly keep up as he was practically running now. Lawrence got to the office door first and tapped it with his fist.

" Damn!" he said as he realised that Margaret had the keys. She arrived shortly afterwards, slightly out of breath and curious as to what on earth had gotten into him. Margaret shut the door behind them as Lawrence fumbled in the bin.

" What did you say that drug was called, the one Senor Mendez was investigating?"

" Err, *'Destiny'* I believe." she said. Lawrence pulled the crumpled flight plan from the bin and smoothed it out on the table.

" If I'm not mistaken" he said as he paused and tapped his right index finger loudly on the table… "Margaret. Look at the call signs at the top of this flight plan. You say that this was received at Byotek and they presumed that it was for us here at Radnet."

" Yes, that's right."

" I could be imagining this, but what does that say?" Lawrence pointed to the first call sign on the top of the flight plan form. Any ICAO (International Civil Aviation Organisation) flight plan would be headed by the respective aircraft's call sign.

" Uhm, Kilo Alpha Romeo Mike Alpha and Kilo Zulu Mike Echo Tango" she replied.

" Yes but what do they say?"

Margaret was confused but Lawrence persisted. As a pilot, he was used to spotting and using acronyms and mnemonics.

" Unless I'm mistaken, doesn't the first one abbreviate to 'karma' and the second to 'kzmet'?" he asked.

" Well yes, but what's so important about that." Margaret inquired.

" Karma my dear, is Hindu for '*Destiny*' and kzmet is an abbreviation for 'Kismet which is the Muslim word for virtually the same thing. I think you better get me Gabriel Dupont on the phone. This was meant for Byotek after all!"

Gabriel Dupont arranged to come straight over to the office. Lawrence told Margaret to go home but she insisted that she stayed. She was rewarded instantly with an unusually personal gesture from Lawrence by way of a thank you. He reached out and touched her right cheek softly, saying:

" Thank you Maggie, I really don't know what I would do without you sometimes." He suddenly snapped back to his detached, formal self but Margaret noticed him blushing slightly. This was the first time that Margaret had received any form of intimate gesture from Lawrence and here she was on the receiving end of two. Not only did he touch her so gently but also he had never called her Maggie before. She was flushed with excitement, and the awkwardness that they both felt was only broken by the arrival of Gabriel Dupont.

Gabriel Dupont was ex Belgian military and now a key figure in the narcotics bureau of INTERPOL. He was tasked with not only the day-to-day running of Byotek, but also the investigation into '*Destiny*', which had now turned into a specific murder inquiry with the demise of Senor Mendez. He was very excited about the news that Lawrence had told him as it was the first real lead he had. Gabriel appeared to be a little out of breath as he knocked and entered Lawrence's office in one swift movement. He had obviously broken into a trot along the corridors in his anxiety to get there.

Lawrence offered and poured three scotches and was a little surprised that Margaret had accepted. He was beginning to see a new side to her, which he found quite interesting. She, in turn, was feeling very privileged, being allowed to stay whilst Lawrence told his incredible story to Mr Dupont. He left nothing out and told him of his initial meetings with Miss Washington in connection with her missing father Douglas. He explained how her brother Peter was apparently set up and was now in a prison in Madrid and, finally, how her boyfriend Danny had now been abducted. Mr Dupont studied the flight plan.

" This is excellent!" he declared" we now have somewhere to begin. I should have noticed this before when it arrived but I just naturally presumed it was meant for Radnett. Have you any idea who sent it?"

" Well, my guess would be Danny Michaelson." said Lawrence." Given the demands made of Miss Washington by this blond woman, I'd say that the whole thing has been a set up from the start. You've been looking for the supply route to northern Europe and I believe you've just found it."

" No, I believe that you just found it!" Replied Gabriel. I am very grateful monsieur. Sardinia would not have been my guess though. Sicily maybe or even the Camorra in Naples, but Sardinia is a surprise. When will this flight take place do you think?"

" Within the week I would imagine. They are waiting for some specific details concerning radar coverage. I was going to fax some over to England but maybe I should stall for a day or two until we decide what to do. What do you think Gabriel?"

" I think that we must think very carefully my friend, before we bait our hook. This is one very big fish and we don't want to lose him. Oh, before I forget, there is another matter with which you may be able to help." Gabriel took some notes out of his brief case and laid them on the table for the others to see. "Until now, this has been the only thing that we have had to go on. Senor Mendez was working on the chemical analysis of *'Destiny'* before he was killed and he had sent out global requests for help identifying the ingredients in this drug. The mortality rate is increasing every day and we must develop an antidote or some form of treatment as soon as possible. At this time, we simply do not know what we are dealing with. We have identified several ingredients but the formula is still unknown to us. However, we have received this cryptic message, twice now in fact, on our main Byotek terminal but it means nothing to us. Maybe you can make something of it as you did with the plan. "He pointed to the message that he had received a week previously.

' LOOK TO THE FUTURE, THE FUTURE IS AT HAND. LETTERS ONE TO SEVEN WILL HELP YOU UNDERSTAND.'

"'I'm sorry" said Lawrence." I was never very good at crosswords or conundrums"

" Not to worry my friend, you have been more than helpful." Gabriel began to pack away the papers strewn over the desk when Margaret stopped him.

" Well, I am good at crosswords. Let me have another look at that please, and your other notes too." Margaret studied the notes before her as Lawrence admired her new found, uncharacteristic boldness." This is strange. Its as if some one is trying to help but they won't go the whole way and tell you exactly what you need to know. Why don't they just come straight out with it?"

" We're dealing with the Mafia don't forget," said Gabriel." We believe that this message is from some one on the inside who is taking serious risks as it is."

After a few moments Margaret continued.

" Oh yes, I see. Look. I think I know what this means 'LOOK TO THE FUTURE, THE FUTURE IS AT HAND' - the 'FUTURE,' gentleman as this refers to, equates to your *'Destiny'* does it not? And the answer to the problem that you seek, is 'AT HAND.' Lawrence, you surprise me, you're good at mnemonics. You should have spotted this one ages ago. *'Destiny,'* gentlemen, is a mnemonic for it's own makeup. Look, let me see if I can explain 'LETTERS ONE TO SEVEN WILL HELP YOU UNDERSTAND'. Don't you see? From your chemist reports you have already identified several compounds, now, if I write them down... 'LETTERS ONE TO SEVEN' should help us understand. There are seven letters in *'Destiny'* if I'm not mistaken.

D... For doll. You have already identified the presence of the narcotic pep pill 'Doll.'

E....Nothing as yet, OK lets see how we get on with...

S....STP. There you are, 'STP' a known hallucinogen. Lets see how we get on with

T....Sadly, no 'T'. Oh yes, here you are. There's a report from Glasgow about a drug which heroin addicts inject but which causes arterial blockage by clotting. Trimazopin.

I... I for insulin. The report states that 'insulin controls the amount of sugar in the blood. Too much will induce hyperglycaemia resulting in a further hallucinogenic state and probable kidney and liver damage.' Ooh, nasty. Lets see what Mr 'N' has in store for us

N... Nor adrenaline.' To expedite the migration of the drug through the system through increased metabolic rate.' Well that fits too. So far so good! OK then, lastly we have

Y....There it is. At the bottom of the lab reports. 'Yhoba'. What on earth is 'Yhoba?' exclaimed Margaret. She continued to read aloud. Powerful sexual stimulant derived from the root of the Yhoba bush. Used extensively by the Uharu bush tribe of northern Africa during mating season!" Margaret allowed herself a somewhat irresponsible but none the less entertaining thought, that she could do with a supply of the latter to lace Lawrence's morning coffee with.

" Well gentleman, there you have it, well almost. We don't have an 'E' as yet."

Gabriel Dupont was dumbfounded. His jaw dropped to the floor in disbelief. The secretary from the office along the corridor had pieced together in moments, a riddle that his own technicians and detectives hadn't even touched upon.

" Margaret, you're a genius!" exclaimed Lawrence. He leant over and gave her a no holds barred kiss directly on the lips. Margaret almost dissolved with embarrassment. Gabriel leapt to his feet and seconded the gesture.

" Gentlemen, please!" she said attempting to regain her composure. She buried her head in the reports to hide her blushes. After a moment she said:

" There's still something that bothers me about this. I'm not quite sure what it is.' LOOK TO THE FUTURE, THE FUTURE IS AT HAND. LETTERS ONE TO SEVEN WILL...... That's it! Why *letters* one to seven? Why not letters D to Y. Letters, after all, are letters, not numbers."

" I'll tell you why!" said Lawrence who had been studying the report also," because it's a formula too. Margaret, you're wonderful! You've done it again. It's simple. Look, doesn't this Byotek circular urgently request not only the nature of the compounds but their quantities too? That's why they're numbers and not letters. Its simple look. " As a pilot, Lawrence was comfortable kicking figures around at a moments notice and the significance became clear. " One part doll. Two parts 'E' whatever 'E' is. Three parts STP. Four parts Trimazopin. Five parts Insulin. Six parts Nor Adrenaline and seven parts Yhoba. Wow. Seven parts Yhoba. No wonder these autopsy reports talk of massive prolonged erections! Well Gabriel, I trust you consider your visit worthwhile? It's a shame that we couldn't identify the missing 'E' for you. Suddenly, Gabriel grabbed the lab reports from the desk.

" My God! Maybe I'm not so redundant after all," he said in his unusual Anglo/Flemish accent that was somewhat comical. "I think that I've just had a flash of inspiration too!" He declared as he grabbed a telephone and ordered one of his lab technicians to report in immediately.

" Just a hunch,' he said. " Now, Lawrence, we must work on our other problem, our 'big fish'. Let us see if we can catch him in your 'Radnett.' Please excuse my pun."

The three were now in very high spirits and awarded themselves further double scotches. The phone rang shortly afterwards. The technician was now in the lab and Gabriel told him that he would be there in ten minutes.

" Margaret, it is time for you to go to your home. You are a very pretty lady and a very clever one too. We must not overwork you. Please allow me to offer you the services of my chauffeur. He will take you home and collect you in the morning." Gabriel had obviously been very taken with Margaret and was acting in a particularly chivalrous manner. Margaret began to politely decline but stopped herself, quickly realising that there may well be gains to be had from the 'old jealousy angle' as her Mom would have put it. She reminded herself that she had been drinking also, so she accepted his offer graciously and left the office on Gabriel's arm noting Lawrence's reaction as she left.

Lawrence picked up Danny's plan and began to make some notes of his own. After a while, he went over to the main chart table and unfolded edition twenty-one of the half million series, *Italy and the Adriatic.* He paused a while and then unlocked the safe, taking out the manila envelope given him by the mercenary whom he knew only as 'Broussard,' in Venice. He laid its contents, and Danny's flightplan on the table and continued making notes. Forty-five minutes later, Gabriel Dupont made one of his grand entrances and startled Lawrence in the process. It was not lost on Lawrence that he had now entered the realm of the underworld and that he was embroiled in a massive Mafia plot to undermine the economy and the structure of the European Economic Community. People not unlike himself, were being murdered. As the door swung open, he was delighted to see that it was Dupont who was bursting in and not some Mafioso hit man. Gabriel was wearing a larger grin than the one he had left with. Lawrence felt a strange sense of jealousy stir within him, the like of which he hadn't felt since those early days in Cambridge with Barbara. He assumed that Gabriel's grin was on behalf of his new association with Margaret. He was wrong.

" Lawrence my friend, we have it!"

" Have what?" inquired Lawrence.

" We have found our missing 'E'. "

" What is it?" he asked anxiously.

"'E." came the reply.

" Yes. 'E' I know. But what is 'E'?" he asked again.

"'E' my friend is 'E'." Gabriel was playing games with him now." Lawrence, you surprise me. You pilots are supposed to be experts at mnemonics and abbreviations."

" OK Gabriel. You've made your point so what is 'E' an abbreviation short for?"

" Well my friend, the answer came to me as you and the beautiful Margaret were astounding me with your aptitude. There was a programming fault in Byotek you see. We had instructed it to analyse individual compounds that collectively made up *'Destiny'*. It was looking at the wrong level. All your pilot-talk set me thinking. 'E' as we see it in *'Destiny'*, is already an abbreviation for a drug which has commonly become known simply as 'E'. *'Ecstasy'* my friend, *'Ecstasy'!* We had the answer at our fingertips all the time. Byotek was looking for single elements and it didn't recognise *'Ecstasy'* in its complex form. It appears that *'Destiny'* is a new potent version of that old designer drug which we do in fact, know a lot about.

All of my chemists are now back in the lab, as we speak, working on an antidote. This is a good day my friend, a good day!

As Gabrielle sat next to Lawrence at the map table, they both raised a glass in honour of Senor Alberto Mendez

CHAPTER 27

RAF Bradwell Bay was opened on November the 28th 1941 and became operational in April 1942, playing an active role throughout the war as an independent fighter station until its closure in June 1946. It was built on an area of marshland formerly known as Dengie flats, where an air firing range previously existed. A small landing area was originally provided for refuelling purposes only but with the increase in hostilities in Eastern Europe, the strategic, east coast position of the field was soon to be realised and thus, RAF Bradwell Bay was formed.

The station played host to a variety of air craft throughout its operational life but the Boston 111 bombers of the Canadian 418 squadron operated from the field throughout the major part of the war, playing various important roles as short range, light bombers. The 'Bostons' were often accompanied by Spitfires 'riding shotgun', protecting them from attack by Mescherschimdt fighters. Douglas Bader often flew from the base with the Bradwell wing spitfire squadron.

RAF Bradwell Bay was equally renowned for its squadrons of De Havilland Mosquitoes that were based there. These incredibly fast, deadly accurate bombers were paramount in the war effort. Mosquitoes were 'sortied' for many specialised important tasks but one unfortunate role that they often played was that of mercy killer. When allied pilots, troops or French resistance fighters had suffered relentless torture at the hands of the Gestapo and were destined a slow, agonising death, the mosquito would fly right up the high street and knock on the door of the particular Nazi HQ, delivering its angel of death with pinpoint accuracy, by way of a 1000lb payload. These 'wooden wonders' as they were often called, as they were made almost entirely out of plywood, would make low level pathfinder runs, offering the beginnings of what we now know as 'smart bombing'. During the gulf war, smart bombs would track the beam from a high-powered laser and would devastate the illuminated target. Mosquitoes would actually mark their targets in a similar fashion by flying low over the intended site, in advance of the bombers, marking the target area with red flares. Outriding mosquitoes would drop yellow and green markers to the left and right to identify the perimeters of the destruction zone in order to minimise civilian casualties.

In the early hours of a May morning in 1943, one particular Mosquito was returning from such a mission and flew over Bradwell requesting permission to land. As the clearance was given, the aircraft collided with a mine- laying German Heinkel HE 111.

Many allied aircraft, having completed their runs, were followed back to base by the Luftwaffe, only to be picked off when they were at their most vulnerable, on final approach to the field. Many of our bombers were lost to these 'goal hanging' marauders (*). However, in this particular incident, the unfortunate Mosquito crashed into the underside of the Heinkel, which displayed no lighting for obvious reasons, and duly lost its tail fin in the process. Without any control surface in the lateral axis, the crippled aircraft duly crashed. The two man crew of this stricken Mosquito landed in the mud flats in the sea off Pewit Island in the bay itself. Many other airmen were returning to the base at that time on foot and from their position on the sea wall they could hear the cries of the two crashed pilots who were stuck in the mud. It was still dark and, as the station neither possessed nor could find a boat, these spectators could only stand and listen to the cries of their colleagues as the muddy waters rose and eventually engulfed them.

From a similar position on the path, now overgrown and neglected, inhabited only by mosquitoes of Mother Nature's kind, Danny surveyed what was left of runway 03.

" You've gotta be joking! There are more holes in that runway than in a pincushion. Its totally overgrown and I'm not at all happy about these pylons all over the place."

" Well it's all we've got" said Ruth; " We're just going to have to make do."

Ruth and Johan followed Danny down the embankment and on to the apron of 03.

" Bloody rocks all over the place too! These will all have to go." Dan kicked a reasonably sized flint into touch.

" Depending on wind and air temperature, we're gonna need six to seven hundred metres uninterrupted take-off roll. We've only got a fraction of that. It's just impossible! If we've got a southwesterly tail wind, which is normal here at this time of year, forget it! Its suicide!"

Ruth, although disturbed by the news, respected Danny's opinion. He was in too deep at this point to be unnecessarily obstructive.

" How much run do we need if we had a strong head wind, say twenty knots?" she inquired. Dan tapped the buttons for his 'pocket flight' programme to make the necessary calculations.

" Four hundred metres maybe. Anyway, it's not gonna be a headwind, it's gonna be a tailwind which means that, if it's twenty knots, we'll need at least a thousand metres. No chance!" Ruth repeated 'four hundred metres with a head wind.' she turned and looked over Dan's shoulder. He turned to face the way she was looking and it suddenly dawned on him what she had in mind.

" Now you have gone crazy! Did you happen to notice, lady, that there's a big line of pylons coming out of the power station, crossing right over the runway. Hey. Ruth!" he shouted." You must be joking!" Ruth had already begun to pace the reciprocal length of 03 in the opposite direction, towards the power lines. Danny caught up and joined in the count alongside her.

" Four hundred and seventy two paces. That's enough."

" And what about the pylons!" Danny argued.

" Well you said it Danny boy, they're big ones. We'll go under them."

Danny realised that Ruth was serious and he had no option but to consider this alternative. He let out a submissive sigh and strained his neck back to survey the height of the cables.

" Maybe" he said." But there's no margin for error at all. Well have to stay low to get under them but then look, there's that grain silo at the end of the runway. What do you suggest we do about that?"

" Well just have to go around it." Said Ruth matter- of- factly."

" Oh right, its aerobatics now is it?" Dan retorted sarcastically.

Ruth ignored this last remark and spoke to Johan in German. He looked around and nodded in approval and Ruth suggested that they walk back to the hangar.

" Johan and Franco will see to the undergrowth and the rubble on this stretch tonight. I suggest that you install the Sat Nav units this afternoon and we'll do the pre - flight brief this evening." Danny looked surprised." We go tomorrow." Said Ruth.

" Tomorrow?" Repeated Dan.

" If all goes to plan, yes. We'll leave as soon as there's enough light to see us under the cables."

Dan spent the afternoon installing the GPS units into the Pups, fitting their permanent antennas and making final checks to his electrical and mechanical modifications. He would have no time to flight test the 'mods,' and the extended flaps bothered him. They had proved effective on the radio controlled models but the real size versions had caused him some problems. He was afraid of the very real possibility of 'tearing them off' if they were deployed at too fast an air speed although he was sure that they would be very effective for the STOL requirements. As the afternoon wore on, Danny felt that he had done all he could do, physically, to the Pups. He decided that he should spend the rest of the time considering how and where to fly them.

Under the watchful eye of Franco, Danny retired to the office and considered the route. The next thing that he needed to do was to get an accurate weather forecast. From the Apple Mac, he could poll the met office fax machine and receive a printout of various types of weather report formats. He punched in the codes, which instructed the met office fax to send him the satellite picture covering the region, followed by the forecast for the next twenty-four hours. More or less as predicted, the winds forecast were 265 degrees at 25 knots, very slightly off Westerly. If Ruth went ahead with her crazy 'underneath the arches' take off plan then they would be rolling on a heading of 210 degrees for take-off, with a serious starboard cross –wind component. Danny pondered the wisdom of this scenario. The take off would still be into a head wind of sorts, which would provide enough lift for the short distance available but too much lift to get under the cables. The right hand crosswind component meant that the right wing needed to be dropped and held into wind on take off. He summarised the situation on the desk note pad as if to legitimise the problems:

1) Short runway.

2) Uneven surface - possibility of fouling.

3) Strong crosswind.

4)Cables to go under.

5) Grain silo to go over/around.

6) Compromised take off/starboard wing drop.

This was not adding up well for Dan. His skills would be challenged to the full and, as yet, he was unaware of Ruth's capabilities. He felt a certain sense of responsibility towards her. Without her, he had no way of knowing how or where Rebecca was.

Dan entered the new wind data into his pocket fliteplan and re calculated. Although the figures were not radically different to his original ones, they warranted reprinting. Dan hooked up his organiser to the Mac in usual fashion, still under the watchful eye of Franco, and hit 'PRINT'. The organiser responded with the customary bleep and the printer went about its business. Suddenly, another series of bleeps sounded that Danny was unfamiliar with. A 'MAIL RECEIVED' page flashed onto the screen and set Danny's pulse racing. Dan's blood raced through his veins and he felt that Franco could surely read his mind. The fresh copies of the flight plan were resting in the print tray and, once again, Danny actively distributed them to the others, shutting off his organiser and placing it in its usual top pocket of his denim shirt. He had asked Ruth to provide him with a change of clothes on her last expedition. She'd actually done a good job and had chosen what Danny probably would have done himself. He was never far away from a denim shirt and the new one was fine. Two rugby shirts, a pair of Levi's and white trainers were also well chosen. She had also thrown in two pairs of white boxers and brown socks for good measure. Danny was quite impressed and very thankful for the change of underwear although, without a hot bath or shower, which he hadn't had for days, there seemed little point in changing.

Whilst Johan and Franco worked on the runway, removing weeds, collecting rocks and filling some of the larger holes with them as evenly as possible, Danny and Ruth went over the proposed plan and tactics. Danny, with his instrument rating and experience, was to act as flight leader in the superior equipped *'Mike Alpha.'* Ruth had no problems with this, as she had never undertaken a flight of this magnitude before. The Sat Nav units were programmed with the relevant waypoints and grid references. If they were to fly under the radar, the chances were, that they would also be too low to track the VOR beacons. 'VOR' (Very High Frequency Omni-directional Radio Wave) navigation beacons were used for most cross -country flights of any substantial distance. An instrument called the OBI (or Omni Bearing Indicator) mounted in the aircraft would locate and track one of 360 'radial' signals, representing degrees of the compass from a specific beacon and the flight would progress onto subsequent ones for the entirety of the journey. The 'VOR' line of sight was similar to that of the radar and Danny figured that he could kiss the beacons goodbye as well. He prayed to himself that the GPS units wouldn't go 'off the air' in the vicinity of any mountains.

Although Danny would make the command decisions, Ruth was at pains to remind him of the consequences of any failure to co-operate.

" The sooner we get the job done, the sooner you can be reunited with your precious Rebecca," she said.

The next two hours were spent familiarising themselves with the route. Finally, Ruth suggested that they rest, as the next few days would be very demanding, mentally and physically. She took her copies of the plan and left.

Danny had wondered what became of her of a night-time. She just seemed to come and go without warning. There were many other buildings remaining on site but, from what Danny could see from his little fresh air sessions, they looked virtually uninhabitable. As well as the silver BMW, which had brought him here, Ruth had been driving a large transit type van for the equipment deliveries. He wondered if she had been sleeping in that.

As the light failed, he descended into his camp bed. He had been waiting for an appropriately private moment to investigate the surprise E-mail that he had received earlier. He switched on his organiser and entered the 'E -Mail' directory. It took a few seconds to load onto the screen and he anxiously began to read the message. Suddenly, he was disturbed by the sound of the door opening. He had no time to exit the message quickly enough, so decided to bluff his way forward by pretending to be studying the plan. Ruth had returned to the office and slowly shut the door behind her, dropping to her knees beside Danny's bed.

" Still working Daniel?" This was more of a statement than a question. This bought him some time to switch off his unit. Before he had a chance to reply, Ruth said

" We're going to get to know each other very well this next week Daniel." She paused for a reaction and got none." I imagine that you miss Rebecca a lot don't you Dan? I don't know why." Danny presumed that Ruth was using Rebecca's name by way of a threat once again. It soon occurred to him that, in actual fact, Ruth was coming on to him.

" There's no need for us to be enemies Dan. Especially tonight." she declared." Everyone needs a little bit of love now and then. That bitch doesn't deserve you Danny." Danny was totally taken back by the remark." Anyway she's not here Dan but I am. I always get what I want and I want you!" Danny felt the bile rise in his throat as Ruth said

" Make love to me Danny".

Danny lashed back.

" I could never make love to someone like you. You repulse me. Rebecca is more woman than you'll ever be!" he replied. " Shut the door on the way out." Ruth stood up and spat on the floor at the end of the bed. She slammed the door as she left. Dan felt sick at the very thought of what she had suggested. It was as if she wanted to take him away from Rebecca in every possible way. After the insult that he had hurled at her, he presumed that she wouldn't be back any further tonight to bother him. So once again, he flicked open his organiser. This time, uninterrupted, he read the contents of the E-mail twice. He couldn't believe it the first time.

CHAPTER 28

" What is it then?"

" You don't get paid to be nosy, just get ya' boys together and make sure you finish the job on time, OK!"

" Not being nosy Guvna'. Just wanna' do a good job that's all. It would help to know what it is we're makin' so that we can make a good 'un, that's all."

" Well you don't need to know. Just get on with it."

" Must be important, to drag us outta' bed in the middle of the night, like. It's for the government you say?"

" That's right. What's it to you who it's for?"

" Well the boys are a bit worried see, what with all that Matrix Churchill arms to Iraq affair. We don't wanna' get caught up in any bother ya' see Guvna'."

" OK, out with it. What do ya' want?"

" Well, its gotta' be worth more than the usual Guv', being as it's for the government as like, and a rush job 'n all."

" OK Jarvis, you've made ya' point. Double pay."

" Well Guvna, me and the boys see, we don't want no trouble. We'll do a good job and we'll be totally discreet, but it'll take five of us, I'd say..... Ten hours flat out."

" How much man, how much?"

" One weeks wages each Guvna."

" Forget it!"

" OK Guv'. We'll just come back for normal shift tomorrow."

The night foreman turned to walk towards the door and knew that he wouldn't get halfway.

" Damn you Jarvis. OK. But you do it on time and do it right or you don't get a penny. You understand? Go to it man."

The Sheffield foundry always had a night shift in the old days. In fact, there were many similar steel works in that part of town back then, and they were all open and running both day and night. At night, the kilns and castings would light the sky with their sparks and fill the air with their sulphurous discharges. Nowadays, all that had gone. Most of the works had closed and those that were still open struggled for a four-day week. Old Jarvis was left over from those industrious times and his father before him. They both knew steel. It was in the family blood. Sadly, it was in the family lungs too. The old man had died of emphysema and Jarvis never went far without his inhaler. Even though the foundry fumes had destroyed most of his lungs, Jarvis took a deep breath and revelled in the smell of employment.

As the shift worked through the night, drinking tea and water and taking salt tablets to replenish the body's losses due to severe sweating in the extreme conditions of the foundry, the twenty four by nine by thirty foot structure began to take its form and shape. Working from hastily drawn up plans and to scant briefings, ropes were attached to pulleys, which, in turn, were attached to the harness, which was duly fitted to the finished structure. Jarvis and his team completed the job in eight hours twenty minutes, collected their week's wages each and went home to shower and sleep.

Lawrence had not slept for over twenty-four hours. He had felt the worst at 6 am that morning as Gabriel and he worked on their own plan, however, Margaret had returned with a change of shirt and casual clothes for him at 7am. A hot shower, followed by a pot of equally hot coffee, revived him enough to make the trip back to England.

The engineer had fuelled the and pre-flighted the Bulldog with a flight plan already filed and accepted for Lawrence's immediate departure to Rochester England.

Lawrence was duly met at the small British field by Rebecca and an official of Marconis, the company who owned and operated the small grass airfield. Rebecca dispensed with the formalities and kissed him on the cheek. She was very pleased indeed to see him. The company technician settled for a handshake and a 'I'm very pleased to meet you sir'. The company limousine chauffeured them to the depot and Lawrence brought a very distraught Rebecca up to date, confirming that his meeting at the depot was scheduled for 11am.

As they pulled into the yard overshadowed by the cathedral, Biggles ran out to greet them, closely followed by old Ted who had no control over the dog at all. The yard was particularly busy this morning with shipments arriving for ongoing dispatch from all over the UK. Plant machinery, mountain bikes, Danish furniture and a wide variety of commodities were being transferred from their smaller factory vans to the monster trailers and removal lorries of the firm, ready for international dispatch. As Rebecca and Lawrence emerged from the limousine, the frantic activity in the yard ceased and the drivers left their duties, following on into the warehouse. There were already many people seated inside and Lawrence surveyed those that had gathered and acknowledged certain persons with raised eyebrows and a nod. The remaining eleven company drivers, from a team of twenty, the others being abroad on deliveries, were all present, and surprised to be in the company of two police officers; one high ranking Customs official, a Ministry of Defence spokesman, the Marconis technician and seven rough and ready military types. Old Ted invited himself in, and Biggles was eventually allowed in also, to stop him barking at the door.

" Good morning gentlemen and Miss Washington of course. Thank you all very much for coming," said Lawrence." As you all know by now, we are involved in somewhat of an international incident. I can tell you that every effort is being made to get Peter released from Prison. In the interim, I have arranged for him to be moved to a more suitable environment than that of Madrid Central Prison. Now, before I go any further with this briefing, I must ask those of you that haven't already done so, to sign a copy of the official secrets act. What you are about to hear is an issue of national security, and you are to be bound to silence on threat of imprisonment.

Later that day, two megaliths from the 'Forward Fast' Freight company fleet left the yard and the remaining drivers went about their duties as normal.

CHAPTER 29

Danny was awoken, not by the customary black boot, but by the sound of the hanger door being noisily pulled back. He felt the in rush of the crisp morning air as it surged under the ill fitting door of the office and he sought refuge under his blankets until his senses sharpened. Once dressed, he went out of the office to see the others busy pre-flighting the Pups, which had both been hand towed out onto the apron. He grabbed a cup of strong black coffee from the bench and joined them to oversee their inspections. Danny usually did his own pre flight inspections, trusting no one else with this important task.

In his early days as an instructor, Danny had learnt a very potent lesson with regard to the unforgiving nature of aviation. Having instructed a pupil to 'pre flight' the aircraft whilst he himself finished his coffee in the comfort of the clubhouse, Danny installed himself in the right hand seat, believing that the walk round inspection that precedes any such flight was complete and thorough. The airfield was particularly busy that day with aircraft arriving and departing on a regular basis due to the pageant scheduled for that weekend. Several flights were lined up before and after him at the hold, awaiting departure clearances from a clearly over stressed air traffic control officer. The taxiway joined the active runway mid point and Danny asked for 'Backtrack' (*) from the controller. This amounted to a request to join the runway mid way along its length and taxi the craft back to the very beginning, making use of the full length of tarmac available. Due to the proliferation of aircraft in the circuit, the controller denied the request and told Dan 999to go from midpoint or not at all. He duly accepted and was half way along his take off roll when he realised that something was wrong.

" Take her off at sixty knots" he told the student who appeared to be having some difficulty. It was at ninety-five knots (110 miles an hour) that Danny intervened and attempted to get the Pup off the ground before it careered into the rapidly approaching hedge that was looming at the end of the runway. The control column appeared to be jammed (*) but Danny managed to pull it back enough to give the aircraft sufficient lift to clear the hedge. The elevator was stuck in an ascending configuration that sent the Pup into a vertical climb attitude so severe that the craft almost flipped over onto it's back. It soon became apparent that the student had missed the control lock on the elevator during his walk-round inspection. A simple bolt that acted as a locking mechanism for the control surfaces of the aircraft whilst it was parked, that should have been removed before take off, almost led to their early demise. A cool head and Danny's thorough understanding of aerodynamics saved the day, the aircraft and their collective bacon. The elevator was stuck and was of no use whatsoever. Danny simply rolled the Pup through ninety degrees, effectively flying it sideways with its port wing pointing at the ground. In this attitude, the rudder that would usually provide control in the normal horizontal axis, now became a surrogate elevator. It was not the best circuit or arrival that Danny had ever flown, with the pup side slipping and landing heavily half onto the runway and half onto the grass. It was one, however, that both men walked away from and one that taught Danny to always do his own pre flight checks. Today would be no different.

Without saying a word, he watched Ruth sitting at the control seat in '*Mike Alpha*' as she scanned the cabin for anything untoward. Danny hadn't given her any particular reason to be suspicious but she was naturally cautious and searched the cockpit thoroughly. She looked up to see Danny watching her, paused to stare at him and continued with her task. Eventually, she spoke.

" Of course, you will be searched thoroughly before take off as well. You'd better forget all about that bitch Rebecca if anything goes wrong." Once again, Dan failed to rise to the remark and said nothing but he did note the sentiment behind her comments. Ruth had mentioned Rebecca many times before but never with such a personal attack on her. Danny put it down to his rejection of Ruth the night before. She was obviously not used to being turned down. Danny acknowledged the remark with a shrug only and returned to the coffee pot to replenish his cup as Ruth tested the flaps. The noisy motors engaged and the flap actuators laboured under the stress of the larger than normal load. As Dan poured out his coffee, he noticed Ruth's filofax open on the desk beside the pot. With his back to her, he was only assured of her whereabouts by the sound of the flaps being tested. He wasted no time and flicked to the front of the book. Where the normal owner's details would usually be found, there was nothing but blank spaces. Turning to the back however, he found just what he was looking for, an international driving licence. 'Ruth Piva -Vasquez'. He repeated the name to himself several times to commit it to memory and turned the file back to the page where he had found it open. Danny then actively joined in the pre flight and checked the petrol tanks for any sign of contamination. Water easily condensed in the tanks overnight and collected at the lowest points in the fuel system. These points were usually fitted with drain plugs and Dan drew off samples in a test tube and held them up to the hangar light as it was still dark outside. Oil checks were next followed by brake cylinders, tyre pressures, (especially high today for the short take -off), pitot tube, and general walk-round. Everything seemed to be in order.

Both craft were now ready, and Ruth and Danny loaded their flight bags and positioned their charts on the empty right hand seats. Headsets were plugged in and kneeboards were duly loaded with their own copies of the flight plan. Flasks of strong sweet coffee, along with bread rolls and biscuits were also carried to provide energy and caffeine for the expected eight to nine hour journey. There would be no refreshment stops on this route and plastic urinal bottles were carefully stowed within hands reach. Danny flicked on the master switches of both aircraft in turn and assigned a common frequency to both radio sets to enable in flight communication between Ruth and himself.

Still under cover of darkness, the four bodies towed the Pups out onto the threshold of runway 'TWO ONE,' using the hand towbars, and aligned them with '*Mike*

Alpha' in front and *'Echo Tango'* behind. Acting on Danny's instructions, Johan marched up to the sea wall embankment and drove a makeshift flagpole into the ground. The white sheet flag would hopefully act as some wind direction indicator in lieu of a proper sock.

When he returned, and acting on Ruth's instructions, he thoroughly frisked Danny from head to foot. As Danny then climbed into his lightweight, unobtrusive life jacket, Ruth took Johan aside and spoke to him in German. Danny looked up as the pair seemed to be engrossed in an in depth discussion. Eventually, Johan threw his hands in the air and gave in, agreeing to whatever it was Ruth wanted. She turned and walked back toward Danny.

" OK Danny, this is it. As soon as dawn breaks, we begin to roll." Ruth was now obviously nervous about the departure. Danny was to go first and circle the bay whilst Ruth caught up.

" OK Ruth, listen to me. This is what I want you to do." Suddenly, Danny found himself once again, unexpectedly in the role of instructor. There was no point leaving Ruth to her own devices at this stage. If the nightmare scenario occurred and anything went wrong with Ruth's take off, then Danny feared that he would never see Rebecca alive again." After start -up, do your power checks at the same time as me. Leave your carb-heat control out while I take off, in case of any ice build up if I'm delayed. Don't forget to push it in before you roll as you'll lose power with it still out. You're positioned ten feet or so behind me and the extra distance will be useful. It's a short field takeoff. Remember your training. I'm sure you did it. Both feet full down on the brakes. Ten degrees of flap, no more or there'll be too much drag. Apply full power and hold on the brakes until it's straining at the leash OK? Brakes off, and lots of right rudder 'cos it's gonna yaw left with a vengeance. Get it off the ground at 55 knots if you can. It'll be heavy with all the gas but I want you to get rid of the ground friction as soon as possible. Just ease the stick back as soon as you're rolling and get her airborne quickly. When she's unstuck, fly her in ground effect, five feet above the floor, that's all. Let the speed build to eighty knots before you pull her up into the climb. You've got a narrow corridor between the cable end of the runway and that bloody silo. You need to get in it at speed to be able to pull up in time and miss the thing. You should be at no more than twenty feet under the cables and you need 80 knots. Do you understand?"

Ruth nodded. She was obviously uncomfortable with her own departure arrangements.

" Your break point is the flag, if your not off the ground by then just throw it away. Power off and brake, then give it another go. Speaking of the flag, look where the wind's coming from. (*)"

It wasn't quite dawn yet, but the silhouette of the flag was clearly visible against the blue grey backdrop of the sky." You've gotta' crosswind too. Right wing down and into wind OK? Not too much in your take off roll or you'll scrape it along the floor. Just watch out for any gusts." For once, Danny had delivered a serious briefing. No jokes or anecdotes of any kind, just pure, common sense airmanship. Ruth was comforted by

this thorough advice and she didn't feel as alone as she did five minutes previously."
Get strapped in and wait for my signal for start up. We'll radio check then power check,
and then roll. Good luck."

This was a strange moment for Dan. He had to remind himself that this woman
had abducted both him and Rebecca, and had threatened them both with their lives, yet
he felt a very peculiar sense of comradeship with her at this point. Like it or not, they
were indeed a team and would have to act as one if they were going to pull this off.
Adding further to his surprise, Ruth responded with a' Good luck' as well,
complimented with a small peck on his right cheek. This was a small sign of gratitude
for the concern that Dan was showing her.

They climbed on board their respective Beagle Pups, locked the hatches,
checked the harnesses, strapped their kneeboards to their respective knees and sat in
silence. There was a steady hum from the great nuclear power station that seemed
totally incongruous with the bleat of the early rising coot that busied itself on the
marshland. As dawn broke, the full splendour of Bradwell Bay became apparent and it
was hard to imagine the bombers that rolled off the very runway where the two Pups
now lay waiting. A thin mist came in off the sea and carried with it a scent of salt
mixed with various agricultural smells that didn't quite fall into either pleasant or
unpleasant categories. They were just pure Mother Nature, and Danny prayed that she
would be on their side today.

Minutes rolled by, and with the gradual increase in light, it was difficult to
judge just exactly when the right moment would arrive to start up. They were
eventually prompted by Franco who jolted them back to alertness by suddenly
appearing in front of them and pointing his thumbs up.

' This is it !' Dan said to himself. He looked back over his left shoulder and
received the necessary acknowledgement from Ruth.

" OK. All switches up, mixture rich. Six primes of the throttle, select left mag,
clear prop, hit the button." The Rolls Royce Continental engine turned slowly at first
but after three more primes with the throttle, it duly caught and roared into life. Danny
looked round again to check Ruth's engine was also running and he switched on the
radio.

" Kilo Zulu Mike Echo Tango. Radio check. Over." Seconds later Ruth replied

" Kilo Alpha Romeo Mike Alpha. Your radio's a five. Loud and clear" Danny
paused and chose his words with caution.

" So Ruth Piva-Vasquez this is it. We're off to Sardinia to collect your
'Destiny.' Before I go a step further I want some assurances." Ruth was stunned by his
opening address

." How did you know my name?" she replied.

" I saw it in your filofax this morning on your international driver's licence.
Ruth Piva Vasquez." he taunted. "Careless of you to leave it lying around."

" So you know my name. What of it? And if you want assurances, I can assure you of the consequences if you don't co-operate."

" I want to know that after our trip across France, down through the Rhone valley and onto Sardinia and back again with this nasty drug of yours, that both I and Rebecca Washington will be released." Danny let go of his transmit button and waited for the reply.

" Don't waste my time Danny. Start your roll."

" I'm going nowhere until, I get your assurances. Its 5.25 am on Thurs. the 6th of July and I'll stay here until next week unless I get my assurances." Both Danny and Ruth were aware that their engines were running and that the longer they stayed there arguing, the more likely they were to arouse suspicion.

" You crazy bastard !" replied Ruth" Yes, yes. You and the bitch go free."

" And what about Peter Washington. You stitched him up good 'n' proper didn't you?"

" Ha! He was like a lamb to the slaughter. Poor bastard was a pushover," she replied. "We watched him for weeks. It was so easy. He stays in a Spanish prison unless we get this done."

" OK then. After our flight plan is complete you'll arrange to have the charges dropped. I want you to arrange a leak in your cartel confessing to the frame up, totally exonerating Peter OK?"

" OK Danny whatever you say- just get on with the flight."

" No. I just wanna' hear it from your own lips first." He badgered. " I just can't believe the lengths you went to to set him up and use him. What type of person are you Ruth Piva Vasquez?" Danny was deliberately baiting her.

" I'm Mafia. That's what I am and you'd best remember that. Peter was week and he paid the price. I played him from start to finish. The poor bastard was still in bed dreaming of me while I was outside planting the heroin in his truck. Still, at least he was more of a man than you. Four times he did it! In just one night!" Danny was getting just the answers he wanted." Yeah, I'll get him off the hook if the job's done." said Ruth.

" There's also a small matter of my licence and reputation too. So Baker was one of your boys was he?"

" That was a classic," Ruth laughed" He just walked right in and closed you down in hours. There isn't anything we can't do. Do you understand that Danny ? I've had enough of the third degree now. Start your roll before Franco suspects any trouble. He wont be as tolerant as me. Remember, he's in charge of Rebecca now."

" OK. It's not necessary to threaten me any more. I just wanted you to spell it out that you'll put things right. I'll do as you say. OK then, back to business. Remember everything that I've told you. Here goes."

Danny covered the toe brakes, selected both Mags' and gently pushed the throttle forward for his power checks. 1800 rpm on the gauge, final Carb' heat check and select both magnetos individually to check the drop differential. Finally, throttle fully forward for full power check then backward to check for slow idle in the same way that a car must tick over at stand still. Lastly, the all-important 'full and free' check of the control column. Danny checked that Ruth had completed her vital checks also and hit ''transmit.

" *Kilo Mike Alpha* rolling." The thrust built to a peak and he removed his feet from the brakes. 'Kilo Alpha Romeo Mike Alpha' began to roll.

CHAPTER 30

At 5.25 on Thursday the 6th of July, Rebecca Washington draped herself over the bathroom basin and vomited. The accompanying nausea, coupled with the shock of the previous week's events made her unusually, violently ill. She had anticipated that pregnancy would be difficult but she was totally unprepared for the scale of the morning sickness. Rebecca cried between wretches. Not only did she feel ill, but also she felt terribly alone. Never before had she felt such a sense of helplessness and isolation. She wanted Dan. She wanted him there to help her through her sickness and pain. She had nobody at all to turn to, now that both her brother and her dad were missing also. The stomach cramps intensified and she feared for the child that was growing inside her.

" This can't be natural," she said to herself, questioning this 'morning sickness' process and the purpose it served." It can't be doing either one of us any good" she thought. Eventually, the spasms ceased and she washed her face with cold water. She reminded herself that she would have to be strong now, for everyone's sake, but especially for that of her unborn baby.

Rebecca made her way back to her bed only to find that Biggles had beaten her to it. She reclaimed enough of the mattress to lay out fully and went back to sleep. She awoke naturally, some three hours later. No alarm clock, phone or tail wagging dog. She simply awoke. Rebecca picked up the phone to check for a dial tone in order to see if it was working properly. She repeated this exercise several times over the next hour as if to prompt a call. Lawrence had promised that he would call her as often as possible from his mobile, but she was not allowed to have his number. Her orders were to stay at home and rest. There was nothing that she could do now. Rebecca had taken some leave that was owing to her but her airline bosses had said 'OK. But please switch your mobile on from time to time. You know that the whole place falls apart when you're not about.' She felt a little guilty that she hadn't told them of her pregnancy at that time, and that it was unlikely that she would be returning at all. She wanted a normal family life now. 'Any way' she thought 'Danny should be the first to know'. She had told her bosses nothing of what had happened but Peter's arrest was mentioned on a national news report and they had got wind of it. One had called, offering his support and extended her leave on compassionate grounds.

Rebecca showered, dressed and breakfasted on grapefruit, toast and black coffee. Even the milkman had deserted her this morning and the doorstep had nothing to yield. The newspaper, however, had arrived and she settled onto the couch to read it. She felt sure that something may have broken by now and she scoured the pages of the tabloid for any sign but found none. She placed her coffee cup back on the occasional table and picked up her mobile phone. She was now 'up and about' and ready to face the day. She switched the phone on, placing it back on the table and was startled as it rang immediately. A pre recorded voice said

" You have a new message waiting............. You have a new message waiting."

Becky was confused. She could hear Danny's voice. She ran over to the window to ensure a stronger reception. "Kilo Zulu Mike Echo Tango. Radio check. Over"

"Kilo Alpha Romeo Mike Alpha. Your radio's a five. Loud and clear."

" So Ruth Piva Vasquez, this is it. We're off to Sardinia to collect your *'Destiny.'* Before I go any further, I want some assurances..."

Rebecca listened intently as the message continued and finally stopped. Another digital voice came on the line and said

" Press one to delete, two to save, three to review or simply hang up.''

Rebecca pressed 'three' and listened to the entirety of the message once again. She eventually did hang up and, with her pulse and thoughts racing, she sat back on the couch to figure out what to do next. Rebecca had been listening to a recording of Danny's 'RT.' transmissions of earlier that morning. When Ruth had originally instructed him to re-tune the radio frequencies away from the usual aviation 'VHF' band to avoid detection, he chose 'UHF' instead. His background as a Telecom engineer proved extremely useful and he was fully aware that mobile phones also operated in the Ultra High Frequency range. In the brief moments when Franco and Johan had left him unattended, Danny managed to retrieve the remnants of his smashed mobile phone that had been dumped in the bin in the corner of the hangar. It had been a simple matter to locate and remove the modulator and connect it 'in circuit' inside the back panel of *'Mike Alpha's'* radio unit. Every time that Danny pressed the' transmit' button on the joystick, the modulator would send a pulse to a radio transmitter mast and ultimately, Rebecca's phone would ring. He was confident that, at 5.25am that morning, Rebecca would be asleep and her phone would be switched off. This would divert the messages into her call-back voice bank automatically and they would be digitally recorded for eventual playback. Danny had chosen his words very carefully that morning and effectively let Ruth hang herself by getting her to admit openly, on the air, her involvement in Peters arrest and incriminate herself in the process. She had responded beautifully, just as he had planned and he was sure that this dialogue would be sufficient to obtain Peters release, if it had indeed been captured by the voice bank. Danny had also clearly marked the telecommunication masts on the charts that both he and Ruth carried. He had told Ruth to be wary of them during the low flying phases of the trip and that he had highlighted them on the maps where possible. In fact Danny had marked them so that he could arrange always to be in the vicinity of one en route to ensure safe transmission of his messages. He could now stay in touch throughout most of the flight, broadcasting his position, although unable to confirm whether or not his transmissions were in fact being received. Pilots often transmitted their position reports' blind' in the hope that someone would hear them and a possible dangerous situation would be avoided.

Rebecca dialled the international number once again and Margaret answered.

"Lawrence Carlton's office, can I help you?" Rebecca explained to Margaret exactly what she had heard.

"My God! That's incredible" said Margaret." don't worry Rebecca, I will pass this on to the relevant people immediately. You will probably receive a call from Mr Dupont from Interpol shortly. His office is only along the corridor and he has been working closely with Lawrence on this matter. Tell me the name and number of your telephone company." Rebecca gave Margaret all the relevant details and Margaret in turn, told her to also inform the local police inspector who was in charge of her security arrangements. Lawrence had arranged for representatives of the local constabulary to be present at the briefing previously held at the depot. They, in turn, had organised discreet surveillance for Rebecca. A plain clothed, armed WPC had been placed with the family next door and two officers were working undercover as builders on the new housing estate over the road. Rebecca was carrying a small device with her at all times which acted as a panic button. A single press would send a radio signal to the pager units carried by the police officers who could respond within moments.

Lawrence and Gabriel, who were heading the operation, were unsure at this point, exactly what Ruth's role in the operation was. They presumed that she was acting purely as a link woman for the cartel and had no idea that she would actually be piloting one of the aircraft.

Using a secure, coded satellite link, Lawrence responded to the page signal that Gabriel had sent him. Lawrence carried a pager that worked on a vibrating principle owing to the sensitive nature of the operation. An unwelcome series of audible bleeps at the wrong time could seriously compromise his situation, so Lawrence was alerted by a tingling sensation to his left waistline, where the unit was strapped.

"Ruth Piva Vasquez." Began Gabriel." I have a full dossier on her. Born in Buenos Aries 1961. Italian mother and Argentinean father. He was killed in the Falklands conflict in' 82. Mother and daughter moved back to Italy in '85 and spent five years in Rome and eventually settled in Napoli where her mother apparently still lives. She has a previous record of petty drug dealing and served four years of a seven-year sentence for extortion. Sent down April 27th '90, released Feb. 16th '94. Has held a private pilot's licence, issued in South America, since '84, although it was revoked in '90 on her committal. Well my friend, if nothing else, we can arrest her for being illegally in charge of an aircraft without a current licence!" Gabriel joked." She is actually quite a clever woman by the look of this too. She is fluent in Italian, French, German and English and studied law in Argentina, obtaining her degree in early '84 before they left the country for Italy. She has never actually practised it but has definitely broken it a few times my friend! What on earth makes a women like this go off the straight and narrow, huh?" Lawrence was as bemused as Gabriel. This was not the CV of the usual criminal type that they had encountered.

"I imagine that she was recruited by the mob during her years in prison. She would undoubtedly be an asset," he suggested.

" This is possible, yes, but there is more, Lawrence. Whilst she was incarcerated, she was not idle my friend, oh no, not at all. Listen to this. During her four years in prison she studied pharmacy and obtained honours in her degree. This contributed to the parole board's decision to release her three years early. If I were a Mafia Don, I would waste no time recruiting this particular lady. Her picture shows her to be very attractive as well. I will radio fax it to you shortly along with the other information that you require. Now, how goes it with you my friend?" Gabriel inquired.

" Everything is running to schedule so far. We hope to be in place by tomorrow afternoon. I will keep you informed of our movements."

"I am worried about Danny's transmissions, Gabriel. We don't want anything to go wrong and jeopardise our original plans."

" Don't worry, our experts are at the phone company now and have set up monitoring equipment. Nothing can go wrong. They have assured me that these transmissions are simply 'one way' telephone calls and Rebecca has been told to keep her phone switched off so that the divert to the voice bank is automatic. Incidentally, we have made her land line a secure line and it has been checked for a tap, its clean. She is a lot happier now that she knows that Ruth is not about but she is very distraught about Danny. I have assured her that the police officers are close by if there's any trouble. She is safe my friend."

" I just hope we can keep our heads down until they've actually got the stuff on board, there's no point blowing our cover until we're sure about where it's coming from and exactly whose behind it. Are your people in place in Sardinia?" asked Lawrence.

" I have five teams on the island but it is a big place my friend. It is nine thousand, two hundred and ninety nine square miles, Lawrence. They could come in and out without our getting a glimpse. My guess is that they will come in along the western seaboard of Corsica. Incidentally, the French are keeping a good look out for them, and head for the south west of the island. It is generally very mountainous but there is a lowland plateau, the Campidano, which runs North West to South East heading into the province of Cagliari. Cagliari is also the nearest port to Sicily and we think that *'Destiny'* arrives in Sardinia by sea. Remember that the families are known to run several ferry companies in and out of the islands, and the Campidano is an ideal passage for an aeroplane. There is little place else for a small craft to go to on the island."

" Gabriel, you must realise that you're going to lose Danny's transmissions the moment he leaves mainland France. He'll be low over the water to avoid the radar, and the telecommunications network certainly won't be within reach. We may just have to rely on our original plan. What other messages have you received since the first one?"

" Well, nothing of too much importance, nothing for us to act upon as yet. They had some trouble with the take off this morning and some further problems at le-Touquet, but they are in the air now and on their way. You must remember that they are not going to be making the normal amount of calls. They will only effectively be talking to each other en route when they have to. I doubt if there'll be much by way of friendly chatter. We estimate the journey will take eight, maybe nine hours. That is a long time, my friend. There will be periods of long silence I'm sure. They will be tired and hungry and I hope that they didn't drink too much before they left!"

" What of Peter Washington, he's off the hook now isn't he?" Enquired Lawrence.

" He is indeed, but we are not arranging for his release as yet. We don't want to alert the wrong people. The Spanish ambassador has been summoned to the Foreign Office in London and I believe, even as we speak, he is being briefed on the situation. Peter will be informed of events but kept isolated and afforded every comfort. We need not worry about him anymore."

" What about Roger at the flying school. He's at a standstill isn't he?"

" As yet we have told him nothing. We think it's best that he goes on believing that he has problems for a while. It'll just arouse suspicion if he opens the club again. All in good time my friend."

" Gabriel, I must go. Keep me informed of any developments and keep your fingers crossed for me!"

" I shall my friend. Take care and God be with you."

CHAPTER 31

Danny's departure was anything but discreet. As his momentum built and his air speed indicator began to rise, a flock of lapwings that had settled at the end of runway 'two one' scattered and took to the air with scant regard for power cables, noise abatement procedures or anything else. In a flurry of madness, Mother Nature was rudely woken from her slumbers.

Keeping a wary eye on the overhead power cables and the grain silo, Danny waited for his speed to build to the anticipated 55 knots in order for him to gently rotate *'Mike Alpha'* off the ground. He eased the stick back slightly to reduce the friction and protect the nose wheel from the lumps, bumps and holes in the officially disused, brow beaten runway. Suddenly, the Pup simply leapt off the concrete and launched itself into a high elevation attitude that put it on a direct collision course with the impending power lines.

" Christ!" shouted Danny as he struggled to point the nose down in the little available distance left before impact. The new, larger flaps had proved to be extremely efficient, and the cruise tanks fitted behind the seats had obviously altered the centre of balance, dragging the rear of the aircraft downwards and increasing the angle of attack of the wings. These two factors conspired to catapult The Pup uncharacteristically into the air only moments after it had begun to roll. Danny had to act quickly. Not only was he in danger of hitting the cables but, due to the severe angle of attack, he could easily 'stall' the aircraft at any moment with catastrophic results.

Watched anxiously from the ground by his three abductors, Danny punched the stick forward, pointing the nose acutely towards the ground, which seemed to be close enough to touch anyway. The Lapwings scurried 'to and fro' immediately ahead in the line of Danny's flight path, in the same fashion that a dazed rabbit would dance in a crazed frenzy, bathed in the glare of the oncoming car headlights. 'The last thing I need now is a bird strike!' he thought. Danny had no time for considered reactions. Acting on impulse alone, instinct told him it would be better to 'go agricultural,' a term he often used when instructing. Better, he felt, to deal with a collision on the ground, in a controlled fashion, rather than hit the cables in mid air and drop like a stone.

The ASI read 80 knots as the Pup went into a steep dive, under, but barely avoiding the power lines. There was no time for a flare, just a violent, stick back manoeuvre to try and limit the force of impact with the runway. *'Mike Alpha'* announced itself back on the ground with a single 'yelp' from its tyres and promptly bounced back into the air, re-launching itself in the style of a Harrier jump jet. Fortunately, Danny had not had any time to cancel the flaps and their ten-degree 'take off' setting, which had proved far too severe in the initial takeoff, added to the effect. The flaps, combined with the 'slingshot' launch, sent the Pup high into the air, comfortably clearing the grain silo.

"Shit! That was interesting " He said with his finger on the transmit button. "I suggest you try that a slightly different way." Dan assured Ruth. "You wont need any flaps at all to start" he declared. "Just trim the nose forward and watch for those bloody cables." He had at least proved the performance value of his modifications.

Now safely at 2000 feet, Danny put himself into an orbit, directly over the mud flats where the stricken Mosquito lay un-recovered, affording himself a good view of the field as he reconsidered the take-off technique. "OK Ruth. Listen carefully. The numbers have changed now. Leave the flaps alone until you're directly under the cables. At that point whack 'em down ten degrees. I want you to start your roll and keep the nose wheel down on the ground as long as you can. Just hold her down and wait for seventy knots on the ASI and then gently take her off and take aim. Get those flaps down quickly under the power lines or you wont clear the silo. You'll need the extra lift at exactly that point. You wont have to worry about the birds, I think I've frightened them off for good!" Ruth declared herself ready and pushed the throttle forward taking an instinctive deep breath. She pressed the transmit button and said

" Rolling." Danny watched from above and saw 'Echo Tango' racing along the runway.

"Wait, wait" he urged. "Wait ... Now! Pull her off now!" However 'Echo Tango' appeared to be stuck to the ground like a Grand Prix contender. He hit 'transmit' again. "Now Ruth, take her off now!" Still Ruth held the runway and she was way past the flag marker point. "Abort!" Cried Dan. "Throw it away!" he yelled. There was no reply. Ruth was still on the ground with no sign of slowing down. 'Echo Tango' literally drove under the cables at 95 knots. Ruth then dramatically yanked the stick back and took off like a rocket, virtually vertical. She had chosen to ignore Danny's advice on all counts. She figured that speed was her only option to enable her to pass under the cables and perform the manoeuvre she needed to clear to the left of the Silo. The induced drag of the flaps would simply have slowed her down and she needed every drop of motion. With initial momentum on her side, she threw in a ninety degree left bank pulling back on the elevator at the same time to pull her into the turn. The steely 'clunk' made by the protective skid at the back of the aircraft, (which was used to receiving the odd 'bloody nose' from less than perfect landings,) as it glanced of the silo wall, once again scattered the bird life, which had only just resettled after Danny's failed attempt at a discreet departure. The minor collision and resulting vibration however, dislodged the residual grain from the rim of the structure, which sprinkled downwards, calling its feathered guests back to an early breakfast.

"Jesus!" Danny blasphemed as Ruth regained her composure and enough height to join him in his orbit.

With Danny established as point, they duly descended to six hundred feet above sea level with Danny to the right and Ruth slightly to the rear and left, anxious to stay below radar but above the visual range of any boats in the bay that may want to note their call-signs and duly report them if they suspected them of breaking the 500 foot low flying rule. (An aircraft should never pass within 500 feet of any person, vehicle, building or structure in any direction.)

The two Beagle Pups headed east, out into the channel, passing Clacton on the portside and leaving Bradwell bay behind for the birds.

Several hundred miles away, Emil Broussard, the mercenary that Lawrence Carlton had spoken to in the confessional in Venice, discretely positioned himself on a ridge and assembled his portable satellite antenna dish. The digital camera connected to it was trained on what he considered to be a suitable landing site for the Bulldog in accordance with Lawrence's wishes. With a single press of the 'send' button, Broussard sent him several appropriate, celestial photographs.

Elsewhere, as the two giant 'Forward Fast' trucks pulled up at the customs post, their drivers were expecting the usual 'UCD' and were both well armed with import / export licences, carnets, dispatch and order notes. All of the necessary paperwork in fact, and some that wasn't really, (thrown in to confuse any irksome official,) was readily available for scrutiny. The border post official singled out the leading vehicle and requested a visual inspection of the documented cargo. Electrical goods, mountain bikes and select wooden furniture. The crew had been expecting this and the cargo had been loaded in a fashion whereby examples of the merchandise were readily visible from the back door. Stacked high to the ceiling were ornate chests, bureau's etc., delicately packed and positioned and held in place by rows of cardboard cartons containing televisions, hi-fi's and desktop PCs. Separated by a row of wooden pallets was a rack containing four rows of mountain bikes. As the back door of the massive removal van was eventually unlocked and swung open, the intimidating array of goods stacked to the ceiling, prompted no more than a second glance from the customs officer who obviously did not want to be involved in any laborious search that would result in him breaking into a sweat. After all, with the new EEC directives on freedom of movement, his checks were usually less stringent than before and this cursory inspection would surely satisfy his superiors that he was pursuing his duties as expected.

The two trucks were swiftly cleared through customs with their documentation approved, having been given the same level of attention as the cargo search. The schedule was strict and could not be interrupted. Thankfully, their journey was resumed without any serious delay.

Precisely one hour and ten minutes after leaving the border, the two vehicles, which, until that time, had travelled across Europe in convoy, parted company and went their separate ways. The lead vehicle continued south whereas the second transporter headed west and up into the mountains. Arriving at its destination just after dark, the driver parked in the trees adjacent to the clearing that had been chosen primarily for its seclusion and elevation but also for its sympathetic nationality in the event of anything going wrong. The four-man crew left the cab to survey the area whilst Lawrence Carlton assembled his own satellite dish, connected his own laptop checked his watch and waited.

CHAPTER 32

The plan was to fly directly out into the middle of the channel and turn south, following the clearly defined dividing line between the London and Brussels FIRs (flight information regions) initially, then follow in turn, the London / Paris boundary for as long as possible. This would not only keep them the furthest distance from the respective national radar services, but also pose an interesting question of jurisdiction should they be detected in these initial stages.

Passing Cap Gris-Nez to the portside, the most northwesterly point on the French coast and the aiming point for most GA aircraft coasting out from Folkestone wishing to make the shortest channel crossing, the Pups would follow a well-trodden route, blending, if necessary, with the proliferation of 'G' registered aircraft heading for Le Touquet. (GA = General Aviation – the term most commonly used to refer to privately owned, light aircraft)

Despite the early hour, Danny expected a fair volume of other aircraft to be in the area already. Le Touquet was virtually an aviators Blackpool. The moment the sun came out, so too did virtually every UK PPL, heading for this popular resort, known also as 'Paris Plage.' Mile upon miles of desolate, sandy beaches trimmed this beautiful coastline and the town itself offered the finest restaurants, pretty gardens and girls too making 'Le-Touq' as it was colloquially known, a prime destination. Danny calculated that a course flown via Le Touquet would most probably go unchallenged if noticed at all, and the area just south of the town would prove an excellent entry point into France for the start of their long journey.

The one, unfortunate, possible disadvantage to anyone travelling by air in this particular region was the French coasts propensity for sudden, dense sea fogs which had stranded many a day tripper, much to their inconvenience but as much a delight to the local hoteliers and bar keepers. This particular morning was to be no exception and as the brace of Beagles flew west abeam Boulogne, the visibility became anything but.

Ruth followed Dan into the opaque mass of a classic, early morning, Le Touquet fog. Even though Dan had his IMC rating a (instrument meteorological conditions- an initial instrument rating) he still found it quite disconcerting and very disorientating to be suddenly plunged into the thick white stuff. His imagination, although he reasoned it to be caution, presented him with various nightmare scenarios of mid-air collisions and spatial disorientations that would turn his world literally upside down without him realising it. His IMC rating was useful but without the help of an air traffic controller watching and directing him from his radar screen, he felt a little anxious. His instrument training had taught him to focus on the primary instrument, the AH (Artificial Horizon) at all costs and trust the information it was giving him even if he believed his arse to be where his head used to. The AH was hardly rocket science. It was primarily gyroscopically driven but contained a weighted pendulum which, all things being equal, religiously and stubbornly pointed the way Danny didn't want to inadvertently go; down! He watched it like a hawk.

"I don't like this at all. It's getting thicker by the second and we're only at 500 feet." declared Dan. " It's far too risky to fly blind at these low levels and we can hardly ask for radar assistance." A radar service would usually be sought under such conditions from the nearest ATSU (Air Traffic Service Unit) but the Pups were doing their best to avoid the very thing that they actually needed the services of at this point. They would also have had a hard time explaining their presence in the area without having filed an international ICAO flightplan.

"We're gonna have to go over the top" said Dan, postulating that safety was paramount and it would be better to climb through and out of the fog rather than risk low level passage through it.

" How high is over the top?" Asked Ruth.

" Dunno,' a thousand, fifteen hundred feet at a guess. I don't see that we've got any other option."

" But the radar? "

" Sod the radar! Even if we do show up, they're not gonna know who the hell we are. They'll just think we're day trippers. "

" OK. What do we do?" enquired Ruth, taking him at his word.

" Just keep your head for now. If it gets too 'claggy,' concentrate mainly on the artificial horizon but maintain your height and heading at all costs. Watch your DI (direction indicator) and your Altimeter. In fact," he added " as we're so low, concentrate on your VSI (Vertical Speed Indicator) 'cos that tends to react quicker than the altimeter. Remember; 'Height and heading,' Height and heading." His instructor had drummed this into him when he was a student. " Standby 'one' while I figure out the next move."

Ruth soon realised the just how difficult it was to fly solely on instruments. She had limited experience in these conditions and never felt comfortable in the situation. She felt as though all of her instinctive senses and reactions had failed in an instant so she intently scanned the instruments then scanned them again and again. Each sweep gave her a different reading and it was obvious that she wasn't holding the sky at all. As her tension built and muscles constricted, every tendon seemed to add its own opinion of which way up she was and added further unwanted control inputs into the column.

"Danny, I've completely lost visual with you now. I'm not very comfortable with this! You were above me to the portside when I saw you last but I can't be sure where you are now in relation to me" she said. "I seem to be flying lots of different heights and headings right now." She said with an honest and pragmatic candour.

"Just do as I tell you and stay calm," replied Dan recognising that she was about to get into trouble. "Things only go wrong when you panic. I'm currently at five hundred feet about to start climbing to one thousand. Follow me."

Danny and Ruth were about to receive their first lesson in loose formation flying – don't do it in fog.

Danny trimmed *'Mike Alpha'* until the ASI read 75 knots. This gave him a comfortable six hundred feet a minute climb rate. Ruth, being unfamiliar with the performance of a Pup, instinctively chose to climb at 60 knots, achieving a 900 hundred feet a minute climb rate, at a steeper and faster angle of ascent, which put her on an imminent collision course with the undersides of Danny's aircraft.

"Ruth, It's just occurred to me. What speed are you climbing at?" Before she could answer, Danny heard the 'rasp' of metal on metal as his 'AH' went crazy in an instant. "Christ, I've been hit!" He shouted as if to verbally confirm the gravity of his situation. In an instant, his aircraft plunged back into the milky depths and disappeared from Ruth's sight just as quickly as it had appeared. The initial impact pushed him into a spiral dive to the right but as he battled to regain control and his orientation, *'Mike Alpha'* suddenly, and just as violently, then rolled to the left.

The first 'crack' of impact flushed an overload of adrenaline into Ruth's system and stung her into action. It had been too late for her to take any avoiding action but, in an attempt to limit the impact, as *'Mike Alpha'* suddenly appeared from nowhere directly above her, she instinctively rolled sharp left. The initial 'crunch' preceded split seconds of anxiety, which seemed frozen in time as 'thud' followed 'scrape' and 'grind' then suddenly 'silence' as *'Mike Alpha'* ricocheted off into the fog.

Snowy white flecks peppered Ruth's windscreen, gouged from the paintwork covering the paper thin aluminium roof that was all which stood between her head and Danny's Pup at the moment of collision. As she threw the control column to the left, both hands yanking her aircraft away from Danny's, her starboard (right) wing flipped *'Mike Alpha'* over to the right and into a spiral dive. One thousand feet above sea level offers very little by way of room or time to recover from a steep dive and Dan was acutely aware of this. The 'AH' was of no use to him as the violent manoeuvres had caused it to 'topple' and it too was in a state of complete confusion. With no visual references to relate to, Danny had no option but to 'ride it out' until he could establish exactly which way he was heading and recover accordingly. His first instinct was to let go of the stick and simply let the aerodynamic forces push the control surfaces of his craft back into their rightful positions and 'let the thing sort itself out' as he would have put it.

"Danny! Danny!" Ruth yelled anxiously over the 'RT' but there was no response. Dan had other things on his mind.

Danny caught a second breath as *'Mike Alpha'* did indeed seem to be 'sorting itself out' as the violent roll to the right slowed and stopped, however, he dropped it again when the aircraft proceeded to roll just as violently to the left.

" Dan, are you OK?" Ruth continued without any response.

'*Mike Alpha*' continued to plummet earthward at a speed far in excess of its VNE. In a matter of seconds, the fog thinned and the visibility began to increase as Danny wrestled with what appeared to be a jammed control column. He quickly shot a glance to his left and an upwardly stuck aileron proudly presented itself and offered its person as being the cause to his out-of-control-roll-to-the-left problem. The severity of the impact had induced his initial roll-right, then, as his speed had increased, the offending control surface became effective and swung him the other way. Almost deafened by a beating heart that threatened to rip itself out of his chest at any second, Dan's attention was first drawn to the VSI which was unwinding itself furiously, almost shouting at him to 'Straighten up and fly right.' Secondly, a picture appeared in his windscreen that reminded him of a Salvador Dali painting. All the right bits were there but they just didn't seem to be in the right places. Sea where the sky should be, Fog where sand could usually be found, no sky at all, ever shifting, rearranging, nauseating. A collidescope of shifting images, all giving him different advice. Suddenly something new, a sign to point the way, as if a disembodied arm had reached into the surreal painting to lend a hand and tell him where he was.

Just north of le Touquet, the mouth of the river Canche joined the sea and its sudden inclusion in the picture sparked the cognitive beginnings of Danny's salvation. Danny had indeed been a Le Touq'day-tripper in his time and the beaches and the river were more than familiar to him. As recognition dawned and familiarity became a comfort, instincts reappeared and Danny's sense of 'which way is up' returned along with his premise of keeping a cool head. Despite Ruth's constant bleating in his headset, he prioritised his actions and ignored the impulse to tell her to shut up. 'Aviate, Navigate, Communicate,' he remembered. She was last on the list. His mental process sharpened, quickened no doubt by the rapidly approaching 'Dali' that confronted him. He had to concentrate on the jammed control column that wouldn't let him 'aviate.' Why wouldn't it? It's Jammed! Why is it jammed? The thoughts marched through his mind like an invading army. What is it jammed on? The Flaps? Something is jamming the aileron against the flaps! Instinctively, as the beach-like scenario in his dead-ahead turned into an actual beach, he grabbed the flap switch and engaged the motors. Slowly, grinding, whirring, resisting, then suddenly yielding with a 'snap,' the flaps lowered and the aileron stubbornly reacted to his inputs. Both hands now on stick and pulling, pulling, backwards. Resistance but reaction. Stability but tremendous speed. Now Constable not Dali, the image was perfect and he was part of it. No longer an observer, Dan was thrust into the picture as he raced along the surface of the beach in cushioning ground effect and he found himself on finals for 'Paris Plage.'

The immediate coastline in the vicinity of the Canche offered a vast expanse of level beach that was half sand, half mud. Although not the best surface to land on, it was the only one available and Danny had no choice but to affect a touchdown. He figured that the soft texture would offer some braking effect. He cut his engine to idle to make his arrival as discreet as possible and to add the breaking effect of a slow turning propeller also. For once, the weather Gods had smiled on him and his approach was directly into a head wind, which in itself would have induced a slower touchdown. *'Mike Alpha'* began to regain her composure and started to fly again like a Beagle Pup, albeit a little concussed. The flare was normal with a touch down on the main gear that produced little of a rollout as the wheels dug in to the soft mud and consequently brought the nose wheel slamming down shortly afterwards.

Meanwhile Ruth was in the incipient stages of panic. Not only was she terribly shaken by the collision but she had also lost her Sat. Nav. unit .The comforting three inch square, rudimentary 'Lowry like' picture that had told her precisely where she was and gave her a simple outline of the coastal features, had vanished along with Danny. The screen flashed up a 'WARNING / NO COVERAGE' and she soon became disorientated and isolated. Common sense told her to climb, to clear the fog first then reappraise. As milky white gave way to translucent blue, she established an orbit then hit the RT button once again fearing the worst. To her surprise, the response was rapid.

"It's ok. I'm down in one piece, just!" Replied Dan. " I guess you've got no GPS?" He said dryly.

"I haven't, how did you know?" said Ruth.

"I've just taken what's left of your antenna out of my aileron linkage, that's how." He retorted. "It got jammed in the slot between the flaps and the aileron when it ripped itself off your roof. It gave me some anxious moments " he declared.

" Are you Ok?" enquired Ruth with a perverse sense of concern, worrying primarily about the success of the mission but with an underlying anxiety for Dan to whom she was becoming ironically fond of. For some time now, Ruth Piva-Vasquez had an alternate agenda of her own, to deliver retribution to the Washington family. She wanted revenge. She would take from them as they had taken from her. She wanted Dan. Originally she had just wanted to take him from Rebecca to deny her her loved one, but now she wanted Dan for herself.

"Yeah, I'm alright, but I'm stuck on the beach. Things seem to be OK with the aircraft and I've got 'Full-and-Free' back again. I might have a problem getting airborne as I'm a little dug in right now" he continued.

"What do I do now?" enquired Ruth. " I'm 'on top,' at fifteen hundred feet in the clear blue."

"OK." Responded Dan. I want you to go to two thousand five hundred feet and orbit right. That'll keep you over the sea in this general area and give you a good clearance from the top of the fog so that you can see me coming if I can manage to get back in the air. Just keep a rate one-turn going until I get back to you. Ruth climbed as instructed and went into a fifteen-degree angle of right bank, which would turn her full circle in sixty seconds equalling a rate one-turn.

Danny scoured the immediate area of the beach and eventually came back with three appropriately shaped large rocks. He positioned the largest under the nose wheel and built the sand up behind it to form a prominent wedge. The other two had a flatter surface to them and Danny dug the sand away from in front of the main gear and placed them in front of the wheels. He hoped that, once full power was applied, the nose wheel would ride up the wedge, lifting the main gear onto the flat rocks and he would gain enough momentum to commence his take off roll. Recounting his experience at Bradwell earlier, he was hopeful that the over zealous flaps, combined with the headwind, would be enough to get him aloft.

Danny climbed into the cabin and checked his 'Harnesses and Hatches,' which were all duly secure. He started the engine and checked the gauges for any abnormal readouts. He prudently went over the departure routine in his head by way of simulator practice, as it would be his second unconventional take-off that day. It would amount to the 'short field take-off' technique that he had readily taught his students over the years but with a few extras thrown in. Dan would keep the flaps up initially to reduce drag whilst rolling off the rocks but would have to slam them down immediately afterwards to produce the lift. This lift would effectively reduce the aircraft's weight and friction as it rolled over the sand. He covered the brakes with his toes, pushed the throttle gently forward to the 'stops' and held his breath as the Rolls Royce continental engine wound up to twenty two hundred rpm. As the thrust built along with his tension, and at the moment when he felt that he could elicit no more from his craft, which was again straining at the leash, he jerked both his ankles backwards as if in some weird aerobic workout manoeuvre, and let go the brakes. The Pup bumped its way over the rocks and viciously slued off to the left. Danny had no directional control of the craft whatsoever, with the steering nose wheel being totally ineffective over the uncompromising sandy surface. Within moments, the speed built and sent the Pup hurtling along the beach towards the mouth of the river. Danny held the flap switch backwards, almost breaking it off with his urgent heavy handedness. As the flaps began to deploy, the aircraft began to slow down considerably under the effects of the induced drag. Danny had no performance figures or precedents to go by other than the Bradwell incident. He simply had to run with the take off and react to the aircraft's movements as and how they occurred.

As the flaps came down and as misfortune and the River Canche loomed ominously, lady luck intervened by providing the fourth rock of the day along with a strong gust of headwind at precisely the same time. The resulting bounce, as 'Mike Alpha' hit the rock at 65 kts, coupled with a strong cushion of air beneath the flaps, launched her unceremoniously into the air as if she were plucked from the surface by the hand of God.

Momentum carried her swiftly to 100 feet but then her nose suddenly dropped as if she were a balsa wood model that had just been hand launched, soaring, diving, swooping then properly airborne and climbing.

" OK Ruth, I'm in the air, but only just!" Ruth's sigh of relief was a complex one. Not only was she pleased to hear that Danny was OK but she was ever mindful of the consequences had 'Mike Alpha' been discovered on the beach. Answering to the authorities would be easy in comparison to the consequences of failing the 'Family.'

" Good, we're behind schedule and need to get on with this" she said with as much detachment as she could muster. Ruth had always kept her feelings behind a brick wall, choosing it's tough hard exterior as her chosen façade, leaving a barren courtyard within that denied her fulfilment and enrichment. When she was a child, Daddy was always too busy to be there when she needed him and it hurt so badly. Now he was gone forever and she kept the pain caged within, alongside all the other emotions that she feared to feel except Revenge. Sweet revenge. She knew that the best form of protection was attack and attack she did when anyone tried to get close. She was terrified that anything she might say to Danny would reveal a crack in that wall, not only to Danny but to herself also.

"What's the next move?" She asked curtly.

" Away from each other I'd say" said Dan with his singular wit. " I suggest we try and keep clear of each other until we're properly visual. This is what I want you to do now. Roll out of your turn at 270 degrees - Westerly. I'm tracking the coastline heading 180 degrees - Southerly. That should give us some separation while I climb through this crap.

" I've got you!" Ruth suddenly declared. " I'm rolling out now." She was anxious to get out of the turn as quickly as possible as the constant turning had left her feeling nauseous.

" You can't possibly be visual with me" replied Dan. "I'm not out of the clouds yet. You must be tracking someone else. Confirm your heading?"

" 270 degrees." Ruth replied.

" OK. Just hold it this time." Reaffirmed Dan. " 270 degrees and 2,500 feet. Remember, height and heading!"

" Copy 270 degrees at two thousand five" she read back.

Moments later, 'Mike Alpha' punched a hole in the cloud layer and leapt into the clear blue skies like a dolphin bursting out of the ocean.

"I'm out" said Dan. Moments later "I think I have you to my starboard. Turn a right orbit for identification. Ok. That's you. Roll out 230."

"230 copy"

As 'Echo Tango' duly rolled onto 230 degrees 'Mike Alpha' levelled out at two thousand five and pulled alongside, announcing his arrival and complimenting it with a thumbs-up. For a moment, he thought that he saw Ruth smiling as if she were genuinely pleased to see him.

" As you said, let's get on with this" he retorted.

Danny fixed their position on his GPS as being south of Le Touquet and calculated a new heading to get them back on track. In a graceful, synchronised manoeuvre, The two Pups peeled left, diving back into the white expanse of cloud and headed off onto the next leg of their journey.

CHAPTER 33

Once again, the lights were on in the laboratory long after every one else had gone home. Vittorio Bartelli worked late into the night. Originally, it had taken him six whole weeks to invent '*Destiny.*' This time, the Mafia Don had given him just one, but this time it would be easier. The lessons learnt in the creation of '*Destiny*' would not be wasted and the Byotek programme was proving to be invaluable. On this occasion though, its services were being put to a more sinister use. Its vast database of substances and compounds were readily available to Vittorio and he could assess combinations of them and their effects, digitally on the screen instead of spending tedious, hazardous hours in the laboratory with the real thing. It had only taken a day to combine the first three elements.

RANITADINE...A generic name for stomach acid inhibitors used in the treatment of ulcers. It would be included in this instance, to prevent the acid mixing with, and attacking, the other compounds.

ETHER...To induce drowsiness.

VALLIUM...To retard the system, contrary to the adrenaline compound present in '*Destiny.*' This would render the body vulnerable and consequently, the other substances would stay in the nervous system longer.

Vittorio worked through the night, sleeping for an hour or two on the couch in his office. He had not visited his wife for days. She would understand if she was able. He had a job to do.

That morning, Vittorio, a deeply religious person, had gone to mass at St. Peters Basilica in the Vatican. He watched his two daughters kneel at the alter rail and receive Holy Communion. Vittorio decided to abstain from receiving the sacrament on this occasion. He was not in a state of grace. He would have to confess his sins and receive absolution before he could accept the body of Christ. The conflict of emotions overwhelmed him and he was quick to wipe the tear that sprang from the corner of his left eye before his daughters noticed. As the choir began to sing 'Ave Maria,' accompanied by the two, physically dominating pipe organs that stood like sentinels on either side of the alter, Vittorio held his hands together in prayer and said ' forgive me lord. What I do, I do in the name of my wife, my sweet Sofia.'

Having crossed the Austrian border, now separated from its sister truck, the lead vehicle continued south, onward through Slovenia and headed for the border with Croatia. It had no intention of trying to cross over. It would have not been allowed through anyway in the absence of a Red Cross or the prescribed 'UN' markings designating it as part of an aid mission. The bulk of its load would be delivered later that day to a warehouse in Ljubljana in the centre of the country but it had a particular duty to perform first.

The southern foothills of the Alps extended deep into Croatia where they became known as the 'Dinartic' Alps. The dividing line between the two countries was often to be found lying along miles of this mountainous, impassable terrain.

The 'Forward Fast' freighter rolled on towards the border town of Delnice and drove high into these mountains above the village. The driver chose his spot carefully and pulled off the road. From his vantage point he could see the customs post clearly with his field glasses and he noticed the blue berets of several 'UN' peacekeepers mingling with the troops and officials from both sides of the border. They were clearly engaged in a dispute, shouting, pointing and barracking each other with the 'UN' commander trying to do his level, diplomatic best to intervene but failing miserably.

This was as good a time as any. Binoculars now trapezeing from side to side, dangling by the cord around his neck, the driver ran the full length of his vehicle banging the sides as he went, prompting those within into action. Once again he swung open the slab-sided back doors, this time without the prying eyes of any customs official. He removed a large retaining pin from the bottom of the rack, which held the mountain bikes, and slid the assembly backwards, aided by the four soldiers who had been secreted behind it since they had left Rochester. The four mercenaries immediately began a routine of stretching, filling their lungs with an abundance of clean, fresh mountain air. Rucksacks were passed down from inside the truck and equipment was given a final check. Maps were referred to and watches synchronised in a briefing that lasted no more than ten minutes. The four soldiers each took a mountain bike, checked the tyre pressures and swung them aloft, to rest across the backs of their respective shoulders until such a time as they would be needed. The commanding officer reminded them that they had a schedule and a rendezvous to keep and that they had to cross fifty miles of mountainous country by twenty hundred hours. He barked 'Let's do it' and the 'pay as you go' militiamen ran off down the forest-covered valley towards the Croatian border.

The area of war torn middle Europe, formerly known as Yugoslavia, was no stranger to conflict and aggression. Its history of oppression and tyranny began several hundred years ago when the Turks invaded and claimed the land as part of their vast Ottoman empire. The root causes of the current hostilities dated back to that period offering differences of religion as the main protagonist in the conflict. In truth, the religious excuse was simply a facade. The Turks, in an effort to further the causes of Islam and convert as many of the indigenous population as possible to the faith, offered incredible tax incentives to any person becoming a Muslim. Deep social rifts began to appear. Those who worked in the affluent cities and towns were undeniably better off having converted to the faith, whereas farmers, or those who simply lived off the land, had nothing to gain by the transition as they were tacitly poor and remained as they were.

As the Turkish invaders were eventually suppressed and ejected from the lands, the newly formed confederate states of Yugoslavia began a new period of existence that was inherently flawed from the beginning. Interwoven throughout the lands were communities of 'have and have nots' based on the so-called nature of their creed and not on their skills or merits. The obvious resentments ran deep and festered until the domino effect of rebellious breakaway states in other former communist countries reached out and lit the fuse in Croatia and Bosnia Herzegovina. The scale of bloodshed was astonishing. How could anybody begin to unravel the mess and find a solution to a problem so complex? Many tried and failed. Many ambassadors from many countries, under the auspices of the United Nations, tried and failed. Meanwhile, the killing went on. Whole villages were rounded up and driven away, never to be seen, or heard of again.

Orbiting American spy satellites eventually detected the sites of mass graves and broadcast the pictures to the civilised world which looked on in horror, aghast at the spectre and depth of evil and appalled at the lack of intervention by the super powers. 'Guilty by complicity' was a charge often levelled at the 'UN.' No one-member state had the courage to take the necessary, even if drastic measures required to stop the killings and put an end to the abhorrent 'ethnic cleansing.' Almost to late, and after much prevarication that equated to thousands of innocent lives being lost, did the UN forces intervene, exceeding their usual role of ineffective 'token policing presence only' to one of aggressive military authority.

After several, hollow threats by the United Nations peacekeepers, Wing Commander Douglas Washington became one of the first pilots to actually lead the threatened air strikes and, sadly he was the first to be shot down. He and his co-pilot safely ejected but were soon captured by the Bosnian Serbs. Milosivic denied all knowledge of his captives, keeping them hidden until such a time that he may need them and subsequently use them as political pawns.

Not wishing to be drawn into the conflict, neither Britain nor France, who also had a couple of airmen shot down, dared to be seen to officially engage the Serbs in open warfare to recover their servicemen.

Emil Broussard was a mercenary. He had not renewed his contract with the French foreign legion when his eleven-year term of duty finished. He loved the job, but as a player on the open market, he could do things his way and offer his services to the highest bidder. He was a professional and expert in the skills of subterfuge amongst other things.

Emil supported himself on both elbows, as he lay secreted on the verge of a hilltop on the outskirts of the Bosnian town of Bihac. Pinned beneath his elbows, spread on the ground in front of him, was a spy satellite photograph. As a chill, mischievous wind, that carried with it the bitter- sweet scent of the local lavender laced with the despair of the region, tousled his hair and whistled through the trees, inviting tumbling leaves to constantly invaded his photograph as the Turks had invaded before, Emil ran his tongue around his cracked top lip to offer it the moisture that it so eagerly desired.

He raised his binoculars and checked the face of the man seven hundred yards away with the face in the photograph and confirmed that it was indeed that of Douglas Washington.

The missing, British pilot was shackled by the ankles to a post in the centre of the wire fence enclosed compound and was appeared to be having some breathing difficulties. His co-pilot, Gil Pertwee, was restrained by the wrists, as his leg appeared to be broken. Both men showed signs of facial bruising sustained either in the crash or possibly at the hands of an interrogator. Both would need urgent medical attention.

Emil checked his watch and buried his rucksack in the hollow in the ground that he had prepared earlier. His small, hand held, satellite-driven tracker unit, pointed him in the direction of his rendezvous and he ran off to keep his meeting.

At 19.40 hours, exactly on schedule, at the prearranged spot, four heavily panting military personnel riding mountain bikes, leapt ballet like from the brow of the muddied track, entered the clearing and formated on each other in a precision, Busby Berkley style manoeuvre. Emil acknowledged their arrival and indicated his presence by a careful set of bird like whistles before he emerged from the undergrowth to greet them personally. It had been over a year since Emil had last seen Jacques, Oliver, Chuck and Andre and the reunion was sweet but minimal as indeed the fond farewells had been fourteen-months prior. With only a knowing glance and shake of the head, camaraderie such as this needed no more, no less.

The group of five mercenaries then made their way back to the hilltop overlooking the compound and took up their observation position as Emil began his briefing.

" Three guards round the clock, patrol changes every six hours. I've spotted three different shifts, so there are nine Serbs in total. All carrying automatic weapons."

" Great! All we've got is Ether and air guns! Replied Jacques.

" I've told you. No killing unless survival is dependent on it. Absolutely no shooters. Knives only if absolutely necessary. Any unjustifiable homicides and you answer to me. Is that clear?" Enforced Emil. "Need I remind you that one careless blunder could plunge the whole of Europe into another world war. That means no more private jobs for a while!"

Emil briefed his squad and instructed them to sleep in a two-hour rotation. The whole operation, if properly executed, should take no more than eight minutes and they would go at dusk.

Twenty minutes before dawn broke, Emil woke the others and recovered his equipment from the hollow. Still under the cover of both wind and of darkness, the four mercenaries slid snake-like down the hill and eventually took up their designated positions at the compound leaving Emil to observe and direct from the ridge. Through his night scope attached to the rifle, Emil could see every movement made by the squad in a greenly surreal panorama that almost detached him from the harsh reality that was about to unfold, as if it were some poor quality news broadcast that he was watching on

TV. His neck swung back and forth as if he were watching a game of tennis, alternating between the night scope and normal vision to consolidate his sense of perspective and coordination, assessing range and trajectory.

Still resting on his elbows on the verge of the hill, once again licking his lip, though this time through force of habit, he saw the four men below him each signal 'ready' in the pre arranged fashion. He moved his sights to inside the compound and confirmed that there was nothing there that he wasn't expecting to see - three guards in the usual places. Emil emitted a single owl like hoot and watched as the first Serb guard was brought to his knees with an arm clenched tightly around his throat whilst an Ether covered cloth was held tightly over his nose and mouth.

Emil was probably the highest paid mercenary in the business and rightly so. He was also probably the best connected and well respected amongst his colleagues. He could arrange and command a specialist team to deploy at short notice any where in the world but his fees were immense. Lawrence Carlton was specific about his requirements. Money was no object and each of these men had been carefully chosen for their particular talent and they were the 'best of the best.'

Emil's own particular skill was that of a marksman and it was time to prove himself once again. This time, he licked his finger, denying his upper lip its quotient of saliva, and thrust it towards the Gods. The resultant chill over his knuckle told him what he wanted to know about the wind speed and direction and he calibrated. The same finger then wormed its way into the trigger well of his rifle and patiently awaited its next instruction. Emil moved his sight to the Serb sitting at the bench only a few yards from where the captive pilots remained shackled. He framed him carefully in the night scope, as if he were about to ask him to say 'cheese.'

The high velocity tranquilliser dart arrived with a thud, puncturing a capillary in his neck, spilling a teaspoonful of blood onto the lapel of his olive green military fatigues. Paralysis was instant but unconsciousness would take a few seconds longer. Unable to assist or react at all, in the moments before he passed out, the Serbian abductor could only sit motionless and observe as his colleague leapt to his feet under the inspiration of fear and confusion then stark realisation of what was happening. He ran towards his captives fumbling for his pistol, stopping only to kick Douglas Washington broadsides across the jaw. That split second of gratuitous violence would cost him his life.

As Emil unleashed his dart, Andre, squatting on the roof of the barracks, in a well-rehearsed spontaneous manoeuvre, dropped a gas canister into the air vent then leapt to the ground to cover the door and anyone who came through it. Emil quickly dropped the first rifle and picked up the second that lay cocked and ready beneath him. Chuck had begun to scale the perimeter fence as soon as the attack had began and was busy cutting the barbed wire crown that encircled it. His job was to then take his long handled cutters to the chains restraining both pilots and concentrate on cutting them free while all hell broke loose around him and the others covered his back.

It was now a race to see who could get to the pilots first. As Doug Washington's top lip burst and splattered a cocktail of spit and blood onto Chuck's boots, his Serbian attacker raised his pistol to fire point blank into his forehead. A momentary glance to his left dutifully presented his profile into the arc of the cutters, which swung up through his chin, removing his nose and his right eye with the first blow. Despite Emil's warning, the second blow was effectively a mercy killing, which the Serb was grateful for, stemming his pitiful cries but not the flow of his life-blood.

The barracks door swung open and two Serb guards stumbled out coughing and rubbing their eyes from the effects of the gas. Andre dragged the first one out of the line of fire and administered his Ether as the second tranquilliser dart ruptured the skin of the next. From the other side of the arena, the latrine door suddenly burst open and a pistol shot cracked the fragility of the covert operation as it reverberated through the valley and announced the whereabouts of Serb number six. Oliver had remained hidden as ordered and would only intervene in the event of things going wrong. His chosen skill would only be required in that event. The sight of Andre clutching his shoulder in a Napoleonic gesture, as the bullet passed through it, was justification enough and he sent his bowie knife cart wheeling through the air and into the Serbian skull that fired it.

Then silence, except for a barking dog in the distance and the laboured, blood-spraying wheezes made By Commander Washington as he fought for every breath.

" Douglas Washington?" Chuck enquired by way of an introduction. The Pilot, in a state of shock, could only nod a 'yes.' " Its OK sir, we're hear to take you home!"

As Chuck attended the shackles of both pilots, a clean up operation began in the yard. Oliver took the morphine from his first aid kit and injected Jacques, and then dressed his wound to stop the immediate bleeding.

Four unconscious bodies were dragged into the barracks, further sedated, gagged, loosely bound then placed into the recovery position. Two lifeless ones were seated and secured at the open-air bench with ropes holding them in position. Two mannequins of death, pretending not to be when viewed from a distance. Emil maintained his position but broadened his watch to sweep the valley and surrounding area for signs of the third guard shift that had remained unaccounted for.

Jacques helped Gil Pertwee unceremoniously to his feet only for him to scream in agony as the left one failed to support him and he dived back onto the ground as a consequence. Doug Washington took two steps and, fighting for his breath, sank to his knees also.

"What do we do now Chuck?" enquired Jacques.

Chuck paused momentarily for thought and focused on the Can of Ether that hung from Jacque's belt.

"Forgive me sir," said Chuck. "You'll be safer this way." He said as he held the cloth over Douglas Washington's airways. Gil Pertwee nodded his head in approval and offered no resistance as the vapour toured his sinuses and awarded him pain-killing sleep.

The four mercenaries arrived back at the verge of the hill carrying the two unconscious pilots over their shoulders, inert, as were the mountain bikes before them.

" I said no bloodshed!"

" Emil, we had no choice. The situation went up in our face. We had to react immediately." Said Chuck.

Emil had seen exactly what had happened and knew that they had no other option, yet he still voiced his concerns despite his acknowledgement.

"We will have the British government to answer to!" He declared.

"How so?" Replied Oliver who was usually the quiet, well tempered and best educated of the group. When he spoke, the others readily listened. "We left no clues and the Serbs have denied any knowledge of these Airmen. They can't suddenly change their minds and confess to a breach of the Geneva Convention. Catch 22!" He laughed.

"Catch 22 indeed." Emil reiterated, realising the irony that would also drive the Serbian search parties to track them down and revenge the death of their two colleagues. " We must move quickly. Dawn is breaking and we have casualties that will slow us down. Chuck, Oliver, Andre. You three make your own way back to Croatia. He needs proper care for that wound. You'll have to deal with it yourselves. Remember, we're not supposed to be here. Don't get caught." He ordered. "Jacques and I will take the pilots to the pickup point. Your money will be in your Swiss bank accounts in one week as per usual. Thank you again my friends."

The usual exchanged glances, and handshakes gripped like the beginning of an arm wrestling bout, saw the group split into two and go their separate ways.

Emil sedated his charges once again. It would be a long cold night with no assurances of rescue tomorrow. They would camp at the pickup point, set up the satellite dish and wait. He was seriously concerned about the health of the two pilots. Pertwee had developed gangrene and would no doubt lose his leg. Douglas Washington's breathing was shallow and erratic. He wondered if they would last the night.

CHAPTER 34

The mist began to thin, burning off as the sun came up and rubbed the sleep from Mother Nature's eyes. The Pups had a reassuringly good 'visual' with each other as they flew over head Compiegne, north of Paris.

With Ruth's GPS non serviceable, Danny had elected to make some changes to the planned route. If the weather deteriorated and the aircraft were separated once again, particularly in the mountainous region of southern France, then Ruth would need a helping hand to navigate through the basins and passes of the Rhone valley. The answer was quite straightforward. The great infrastructure of the N17 motorway dissected the entire length of the country as if it were the largest snake on the 'snakes and ladders' board, changing it's designation as it went but still linking Calais on the north coast with Marseilles on the south. Its passage took it directly through the low ground of the Rhone valley and on towards the coast. It would be a simple exercise in VFR navigation to follow it. Ruth was naturally suspicious of this intended course change but Danny's suggestions were practical and made sense.

"Trust me, it's a positive move. I don't know why I didn't think of it before?" Danny argued. "The motorway is the most direct, and lowest for that matter, route through the mountains. It's a slightly shorter course too, so we can make up the time that we lost at Le Touquet."

Originally, they were due to fly to the west of Paris, routing Chartres, Orleans, Bourges then entering the valley between the Massif Central in the west and the Swiss Alps in the east, north of Lyon.

"But were now going to route north of Paris and directly through the radar systems at Lille and Beauvais to say nothing of 'Charles de Gaulle.' They will spot us miles away!" Ruth challenged as she checked her chart.

" But that's the whole point, don't you see?" countered Dan. "We're never gonna be sure that we're not being picked up anyway. It must look double suspicious if we keep popping up and then disappearing from the controllers screen like an errant space invader. I think its better that we switch the transponders back on and squawk 7000. Let them see us." (7000 is the general 'conspicuity' code that would appear on a controllers screen to let him know that an aircraft was there without specifically identifying it.) "That way, we'll just blend with everybody else and not draw attention to ourselves".

Danny had made his point and Ruth saw the common sense behind it. They couldn't guarantee that the whole journey would be flown underneath the entire 'Radnet' and it would indeed be suspicious if they kept flashing on and off the controller's screen. Better that he saw just another set of 7000 figures, alerting him that there was traffic in the area and he could at least direct his commercial traffic away from them in the usual fashion and maintain a degree of safety.

Ruth had no logical grounds to disbelieve Danny so she cautiously agreed to the course change under the circumstances, recognising also, that she had no other choice if the mission was to succeed on schedule. However, what she wasn't immediately aware of, was the gift that she had earlier handed Danny on a plate, scoring an own goal in the process, by ripping off her GPS antenna. This was the most credible excuse that Danny had for changing course and she had readily accepted it. What he wasn't so quick to point out however, was, that by following the proposed route along the motorway, they would also constantly be within the range of a proliferation of radio masts that adorned the route in support of the mobile phone networks. By following the motorway through France, Dan could be assured that his transmissions were undoubtedly being picked up elsewhere.

Dan had never made such an extensive journey in his life and he would need all of his skills, along with his wits, not only about him, but sharpened and polished. He had followed 'line features' as they were known (roads, rivers, railways,) before, but never for such a distance. He remembered the rule for such a piece of navigation; 'When following a line feature, keep it on your left.' This, of course, would maintain separation from another aircraft following the same feature but in the opposite direction, also keeping it on his left. If they were to follow this motorway all the of the way through France, they would surely encounter such a situation.

The Pups climbed to a respectable three thousand five hundred feet, duly squawked 7000 and announced themselves to a host of Radar controllers across the country in the process. It had occurred to Danny to squawk 7500, which was the universal emergency code that indicated a hi-jack. This would have inevitably resulted in French Mirage Fighters being scrambled to intercept, but the consequences of that were unimaginable. The mission would fail and he may never see Rebecca again. Better, he reasoned, to run with it for the present and just hope and pray that all of his transmissions were being intercepted, but, by the right people.

Danny had decided that they should cruise at Three thousand Five hundred feet as this altitude would keep them within comfortable visual range of the motorway and within the line of sight of the radio masts. It would also be in compliance with the 'Quadrantal' (*) rules, fitting in with any other GA traffic in the area. Now that they had made themselves known, Danny thought it would be prudent to stick to the rules and 'blend.'

The 'Quadrantal' rule system was a simple tactic employed by pilots to ensure a basic level of separation between themselves, without the assistance of an Air traffic controller, whilst cruising low level. The circle representing the face of a compass would be divided into natural, ninety-degree quadrants. Flights in the o to 89-degree quadrant would fly at odd thousands of feet; 90 to 179-degrees would fly at odd thousands of feet Plus five hundred. Quadrant three would be flown at even thousands of feet and the last sector at even thousands plus five hundred. This would ensure a minimum separation at all times between aircraft on converging courses. The Pups

160-degree course took them into the second quadrant and consequent odd thousands plus five hundred. 160 degrees also routed them directly over the French town of Reims, famous for producing many Cessna aircraft in addition to those made in the states. In fact, production had recently re started at Reims and it was commonplace for light aircraft to be seen in the vicinity.

The journey progressed without incident, saving a slight easterly detour to avoid the Paris TMA (*T*erminal *M*anoeuvring *A*rea) (*), which also began at three thousand five hundred feet. Being based in Essex, Dan was very aware of the constant infringements of the Stansted Zone and how seriously the authorities took it. He wasn't about to 'bust' the Paris one so they went around it.

As the journey progressed, Dan stressed to Ruth the importance of a strict fuel management regime en route. Both the Pups were fitted as standard with long-range tanks in the wings and the barrel-like cruise tank that Dan had retrofitted to each in the rear of the cabin. Three percent of the fuel on board would be required just to actually carry its own weight and as the flight progressed, constant re-trimming and careful selection of the various tanks was required to maintain the necessary balance as the fuel burnt off.

In accordance with normal good practice, regular 'FREDA' checks were also carried out to make sure that all was well in every department. (FREDA was the acronym for *F*uel- check contents- pressure- tank selection and pump, *R*adio- check correct frequency engaged, *E*ngine-check instruments for temperatures and pressures- *D*irection indicator – aligned with compass as its gyroscope could wander, *A*ltimeter- check height and regional pressure setting in the subscale - this could be easily obtained by tuning into the frequency of a local major airport where the information would be regularly given to the other traffic.)

Danny had no appetite at all but realised the importance of keeping his blood sugar levels high, aware of the energy that he was expending due to the stress alone. He had requested several bars of chocolate for the journey and, now that they were established comfortably in the cruise, he unwrapped one, began to eat and relax a little.

Suddenly, Dan's GPS bleeped alerting him that he was approaching an 'SUA' (*S*pecial *U*se *A*irspace.) They were now in the approach to Lyon, which sat squarely in the gorge between the two mountain ranges. The airspace at Lyon airport was class 'D' and would require a clearance to pass through it. This would mean passing pertinent details to the controller and was obviously out of the question and, again, he couldn't risk a zone infringement. A similar situation presented itself to the east with the Geneva control area. Danny grabbed his chart, comparing it with the moving map display on his Sat Nav. The GPS only displayed the aircraft's proximity to airspace and showed no topographical features at all. Careful comparison with the charts showed that there was only a narrow corridor between the Geneva zone to the east and the Lyon TMA to the west. This corridor would take them, in part, away from the safety of the valley that they had been following and over the higher extremities of the Alps. It soon became apparent to Dan that he would have to do something and do it quickly as the high ground was in sight and approaching fast.

"Ruth, we've gotta climb, now! Make it sixty knots OK, do it now!" Danny was engrossed with his charts, cross-referencing and double-checking, and not keeping as good a lookout as he normally would. One of his favourite sayings to a student was 'measure twice and cut once' so he checked the charts once again to make sure that he hadn't missed anything.

"Danny, have you seen what's in front of us?" said Ruth

Directly in front of them was a layer Cumulonimbus. Thunder clouds. These were to be avoided at all costs. The up-drafts within these heavily bruised storm clouds were so violent that they could rip the wings off an aircraft and they would undoubtedly make matchwood of the Pups, to say nothing of the risk of lightning strikes.

"Christ, that's all we need." Dan exclaimed. "We're gonna have to avoid those somehow. Standby." Dan had some quick thinking to do. Another glance at the chart confirmed his suspicions that there was no room to manoeuvre around the storm front, with control zones every which way and an Alpine mountain range thrown in for good measure. His thoughts returned to the countless accident reports and statistics that he had help compile for 'Gasil.' He had no wish to add himself to the 'CFIT' column.

They would have to go 'over the top' and there was little distance left to affect a normal ascent. Two thousand feet above them was a dense formation of ordinary white cumulous clouds that sat like a floret of cauliflower on a dish of sky blue. "OK, here's what we do. On my mark, apply full power and initiate a tight climbing spiral to Port. You will go first and I'll orbit at three thousand five to give us some separation. We'll have to go through the white stuff above us first then we can go over the storm. Just keep the climb going, and keep it tight, like a 'rate one' OK? Remember, when we lose visual, the mountain range is to the East and the control zone to the West. If you're unsure and disorientated, err to the west not the east. Control zones are softer than mountains as a rule."

Ruth began to climb in small circles as directed, like a reverse helter-skelter that took her vertically upwards in the planned corridor. "We can go to ten thousand feet in these Pups if need be. Lets hope we come out on top before then." Danny spoke to her as she climbed to reassure her with his presence. "Don't panic Ruth, just keep the circles tight OK. I'm two minutes behind you climbing at sixty KTs with no fear of a repeat performance of Le Touq'."

Just as quickly as Ruth had disappeared into the Cauliflower, she seemingly re-emerged 'on top' with a sigh of relief mixed with gasp of wonder as the Alps suddenly presented themselves to her in their full panoramic splendour. Lake Geneva jostled with Mont Blanc for her attention whilst the Matter horn to the west simply demanded it.

"Danny, I'm through and clear at eight thousand. This is just awesome " she informed him. " The storm front peaks at six thousand I'd say, so we're well clear."

"Go to Nine thousand to give me some clearance. I'll be through in two and we'll head south over the first range." Replied Dan.

Ruth rolled out of her spiral climb and headed directly for the range, her confidence growing by the minute and her senses suspended in the majesty of the mountains.

"Not a good idea!" Dan said stirring Ruth back to reality as he caught up and saw her attempting to cross the mountains in her dead-ahead.

"Why not? "

"You never, but never cross a mountain range at right angles." He replied. "Don't just fly straight at it. Always cross at forty-five degrees, sideways. That way, if you get into any trouble, you can turn away quicker." Sound advice from Dan the instructor.

Danny's GPS fixed them ten miles west of Le Bourget. *'Mike Alpha'* and *'Echo Tango'* established themselves on a heading of 180 degrees, due south towards Grenoble. A carefully, although rather hastily, re-calculated course that took them over mountains, over storms, between control zones and through the most demanding flying of Danny's career. His learning curve was steep and as determined as his resolve to see Rebecca again. The notion was as clear to him as was the image of her face that had been etched in his mind and carried in his heart from the day that he had first seen her.

Without any further problems, Grenoble, then Marseille, then a roll left in formation out across the ocean towards Sardinia.

CHAPTER 35

"That's it, I'm afraid we've lost them!" Exclaimed Gabriel Dupont.

The offices of 'Talk Mail International' in Reading, England, had been virtually taken over. As well as Gabriel Dupont, there were several Scotland yard officers, a criminal psychologist, two SAS team commanders, several of the companies own technicians along with various engineers from BT. Most of the general secretarial and white collar staff, with a few exceptions, had been told to stay home as a matter of security.

As the reel-to-reel tape recorders spun alongside their digital counterparts, laser printers busied themselves producing hard copy transcripts of Danny's 'RT' transmissions.

"Damn!" Gabriel rapped his knuckles on the desk as if it had somehow offended him. "They're out of range. I guess they're out over the ocean now." Raised eyebrows around the table seconded his suspicions. "Have you had any luck with 'Italcom'?" Enquired the Belgian sleuth. His colleague explained that he wasn't sure if the Italian phone company were just being obtrusive or simply didn't know what they where doing. He suspected the latter. The Italian Government, in their long running but freshly invigorated battle against the Mafia, were offering every assistance to the campaign realising that their domestic problem was beginning to overflow into the rest of Europe. However, their working practices, where there were any, weren't quite in line with Brussels where it counted.

"They keep going on about the mountains. It's very difficult for them to maintain a proper coverage, so they say, because of the bloody mountains. I guess they've got a point but it sounds like a case of 'lack of investment' to me, they should wack up a few more masts!" The engineer said letting his frustration get the better of him. "They have assured us that they will pick them up again in the Campidano plateau though. Apparently, they have several transmitters there, that's if they've got any bloody electricity;" he said, his cynicism providing an encore. Gabriel bent over the chart table, holding his tie back with his left hand as it swung over the map and putting the index finger of his right over the relevant part of the island of Sardinia in an attempt to physically connect with it.

"So now we must be patient my friend huh?" Replied Gabriel. He turned again to the reams of printed dialogue before him. Talk Mail Int' were equipped with the latest IBM voice recognition software and it was a simple matter, once educated to the phonetic inflections in Danny's voice, to convert the digital recordings into files and subsequently print them out.

Alongside Gabriel at the table, also engrossed in the transcripts, were Susan Meadows, a criminal psychologist and Ian Royal, an MI5 officer who was effectively Gabriel's English counterpart. Both Gabriel and Ian had worked together on numerous occasions and it was Ian who had co-ordinated the English side of this operation. Susan Meadows was a brilliant crime analyst. She had graduated from York with a degree in psychology and had written a 'milestone' paper entitled *'The Criminal mind, it's motivation and management.'*

Susan possessed an apparent sixth sense, often providing the Police, through analyses and insight, with the vital missing link in their investigations and she was highly respected. Clairvoyant she was not, and although several such 'mediums' had indeed effectively contributed to criminal investigations, particularly those where a great trauma had occurred, and especially in the United States, the UK authorities found themselves open to ridicule and to accusations that they were 'clutching at straws' when they used the services of such a person. Scotland Yard preferred a more scientific, respectable approach to 'clutching at straws' and employed Susan to provide a psychological personality profile of the given offender and she had proven her worth many times.

Gabriel was sceptical this new method of Police work. He reasoned that you cannot rationalise the criminal mind, which by its very nature was irrational, but he tolerated Susan's presence as it was specifically requested by Lawrence Carlton for whom he had much respect.

Whilst Susan and Ian buried their heads in the printouts, Gabriel picked up the phone and dialled an international number. When he was connected with the Interpol switch board he gave his name and code number and quoted a divert reference. He was eventually patched through to the officer in charge of the SWAT teams that were on the ground in Sardinia.

"Sebastian? Gabriel Dupont. They are on their way. We lost them twenty minutes ago when they went over the ocean. Are the French set up in Corsica?"

"Oui. The coast guard has been informed but, again, it is a big place and we cannot be sure where they intend to land. Everybody here seems to be making excuses of one sort or another but I am confident that we will catch them." Sebastian replied.

Dupont explained that it was imperative that everybody kept out of sight until after the pick up. No over zealous detectives were to jeopardise the operation until the drop had been made and the main suppliers were present. Gabriel wished Sebastian luck and stressed that he wanted to be informed of any developments, no matter how small or seemingly insignificant.

Gabriel drank another black coffee and pulled the customary grimace as he sipped. His reputation as being somewhat 'wiry' and difficult had preceded him

"In Belgium we drink real coffee" he ungraciously announced to the embarrassed secretary who had provided it. He re-read the transcripts and pondered over every paragraph looking for double entendres or any specific information that he may have over looked. " What is this all about?" He said to Ian. Gabriel was referring to the remarks made by Danny about 'why me?' "Am I missing something here?" Said Gabriel.

"I know what you mean" responded Royal. "I sensed something unusual too. She does seem to be harbouring some kind of grudge doesn't she? Danny was right. The whole set-up seems a bit elaborate for what they're trying to achieve."

Royal looked back over the pages of transmissions. "Look! Here, and here!" Ian counted four separate incidences of Ruth referring to Rebecca Washington as a 'bitch.' Gabriel stood up to look and pushed his hair back, deep in thought, arrogantly snapping the fingers of his other hand as if the secretary should know that he wanted more coffee despite his earlier rudeness. Susan said nothing and carried on reading. Gabriel then referred back to his own copy, reviewing the appropriate passages.

"Ah yes, look!" said Gabriel. "Twice she has called Peter Washington a bastard as well. What is happening here my friend huh? Vasquez seems to be, how shall I say, holding a grudge towards the Washington's but not actually towards Danny himself, in fact she appears to be quite complimentary of him at times." Once again, Gabriel scrolled through the pages of the print out. When he found the relevant paragraphs that were bothering him, he read them out aloud. 'Why me? What have I done to deserve this?' he continued... 'You! Your a bonus Danny.'

"Ian, you see this section here. The woman appears to be somewhat in admiration of him. Let me see, ah yes, then there is this ominous passage.... 'There are some scores to be settled.' There is something very strange going on here. Something that we are all missing. What do you make of this Miss Meadows?" he obligingly asked her, as she had been silent until now, and, convinced that her presence was indeed a waste of time, he offered her some rope with which to hang herself by inviting her to contribute something that he was sure she didn't have. Susan Meadows was aware of Gabriel's scepticism of her science and she felt that he was also naturally sexist, having been anything but polite to her until now. She considered her answer carefully before she spoke. Instead of entering into a debate on the matter, Susan confidently and eloquently offered an explanation instead.

"Vasquez wants Danny for three reasons. One, because of his skills as a pilot. Two, because she's attracted to him and three, and most importantly, because she wants to take him, 'that which is dear,' away from Rebecca." Gabriel was, again, less than gracious with his reply.

"This you can tell because of your degree?" Gabriel said sarcastically.

"This I can tell because I'm a woman!" She retorted successfully and instantly won the admiration of everyone within earshot as she scored a direct hit in the centre of Gabriel's pomposity.

"Touché!" Said Royal, delighting in the spectacle of his Colleague from across the channel being put in his place. Gabriel recognised that Susan had won the round and offered her 'the floor' with a wry smile, acknowledging her bull's-eye.

"Go on Miss Meadows please."

"She wants to take him away from Rebecca to 'settle a few scores' quote, and, having got to know him, she realises that Danny is indeed a real bonus, far more so than she had expected. She has a growing affection for him, which is very apparent from these transcripts. He is obviously a very skilled pilot too and the right man in the right aircraft for the job."

"I agree. He seems to be a brilliant, intuitive young man. I hope to be able to meet him someday" interrupted Gabriel in an attempt to disrupt the flow of her synopsis. Susan continued regardless.

"... And he is obviously a very attractive man with personality, integrity, he's devoted and sincere. His loss to Rebecca would be extreme. I believe that Rebecca Washington may have caused Vasquez some injustice in the past, taken something dear from her and Vasquez is killing two birds with one stone, getting the job done and getting even with Rebecca at the same time." Royal stood with his mouth open, impressed to the hilt by the young graduates delivery. Gabriel was surprised also, by the concise, positive manner of her address and awarded it with an acknowledging smile.

Gabriel put the printout down and opened his briefcase. Royal gave him a questioning look. "Just a hunch my friend, a little hunch!" Said Gabriel as he opened the folder and re read his file on Ruth Piva-Vasquez. His look turned to one of deep consternation and he grabbed the phone.

"What? " Said Royal, surprised by the urgency.

"More than a hunch now my friend, an educated guess." Said Gabriel as he dialled the number.

"What? What? " Persisted Royal.

"Danny hasn't done any thing to deserve this at all my friend, of that you can be assured and he is indeed a bonus, a brilliant young man and an absolute bonus. You are a very clever young lady too Miss Meadows but you're assumptions are only half correct." He broke off and spoke into the telephone. " Ministry of Defence, records please."

Gabriel spoke at length to many officials at the MOD. Much rank pulling was done; military verses civilian and lots of 'you have no authority' type conversations took place. Ian Royal listened intently, somewhat perplexed, whilst Susan continued to make notes of her own. Eventually, Gabriel's authority was established as absolute. "Just get them on the phone!" He demanded. " It was along time ago and international relations are re-established I can assure you. Call me back." Gabriel gave the operator the number and hung up. Royal was at bursting point and getting a little angry at the lack of an explanation.

"OK! OK! Calm down my friend. Danny doesn't deserve any of this, oh no. His only crime is to be engaged to Rebecca Washington. On that point you are correct Miss Meadows." Much to Royals' frustration, the phone rang and cut short Gabriel's explanation.

"Thank you, thank you. And the precise date? Date?" Gabriel repeated. The Argentinean military clerk was a little put out by the brusque nature of his inquiry. She had been told to co operate fully by her superiors but her loose English, coupled with the annoying echo that accompanied such international calls, made the conversation very difficult. " Eduardo Piva-Vasquez, yes that's right. Thank you, you have been most helpful." Gabriel terminated the call then re-dialled the MOD at Whitehall as his Belgian bulldog features took on an even more serious demeanour. He barked his requests down the phone at the records clerk.

"That's right, June the 8th 1982, Bluff Cove. The day the Sir Galahad sunk. Two Argentinean planes shot down...My God!...Yes, yes thank you. That's all I need to know." Gabriel slammed the phone down and shouted across the room for everyone to hear. Royal stood in stunned silence and Susan looked up from her notes as Gabriel leapt to his feet.

"Ruth Piva's father was an Argentinean pilot in the Falklands war. He was shot down and killed over Bluff Cove whilst attacking the sir Galahad on the 8th June 1982 by a British Sea Harrier piloted by one 'Douglas Washington!' Exactly thirteen years ago today. Unlucky, not 'for some,' but for Rebecca and Peter Washington I suspect. I believe that they are in great danger. You must alert your officers in Rochester at once and get me the Spanish ambassador!"

CHAPTER 36

Leaving the French mainland, heading out over the sea towards Sardinia, the Pups settled into straight and level flight at one thousand feet above sea level. The journey so far had been anything but straightforward but as they headed due south across the Ligurian sea with no mountains or similar obstacles to worry about, Danny tried to unwind a little and consider what may lay ahead in Sardinia. He had his new instructions to follow and there was a strict schedule to adhere to. His decision to follow the autoroute through France had been a good one and they had made up the time lost at Le Touquet. Ruth had initially been sceptical about the detour but eventually agreed that it was a good move. She did, however, question the wisdom of returning by the same route. She felt uncomfortable at the thought of flying full in the face of every one and anything with a full payload of *'Destiny.'* She asked Danny several times about the return journey but he wouldn't be drawn on it saying only that they would talk about it later, on the ground, where he could study the charts more easily. She had no reason to doubt his response.

With an estimated one hour left to run before arrival in Sardinia, the French island of Corsica appeared in silhouette off their port wing. Danny had been reviewing his instructions on his pocket organiser and switched it off to save the batteries for when they would be needed most. He could not afford for it to crash, not now that his life depended on it.

Danny had not been told exactly where on the island of Sardinia that they were supposed to put down. Ruth had withheld their ultimate destination from him for obvious security reasons. She had told him that she would take over as lead flight when the time came and Danny's job was to simply get them to the island. He had studied the charts however, back at Bradwell and he had a fair idea where they would eventually land. He too, like Gabriel and Lawrence, reasoned that the Campidano plateau was the obvious choice with its lowland passages and the port of Cagliari at its apex, providing an ideal drug supply route via the ferry lanes that linked the islands. Their current heading of 160 degrees would take them in a straight line from their point of departure in France right on through to the Campidano. This track would also keep them out of visible range from anyone on the island of Corsica.

Suddenly, and somewhat prematurely, Ruth declared that she would take over as lead flight.

"Ruth, that's Corsica not Sardinia!" declared Danny.

"I'm aware of that." She replied. "Just do as you're told and follow me." Danny was suddenly thrown into a panic. Any unscheduled changes to the flight could prove hazardous to his own contingency plans. It was obvious that Ruth also had a little trick up her sleeve but Danny had no choice but to comply with her instructions for the time being.

Danny rolled the Pup right and allowed 'Echo Tango' to advance to lead position. Shortly afterwards, Ruth instructed him to turn left twenty degrees and follow her lead. Danny's GPS was fully operational and the moving map display indicated that their new heading appeared to be taking them away from the Campidano. Ruth made several more course changes until they were heading due east. Danny checked his chart against his GPS and it appeared that they were in fact heading for the north of the island and not the south as he had originally expected. It was only a short time later that the northern coast of Sardinia did indeed begin to appear. All but the southern plateau of this Italian island was rugged and mountainous. Danny checked his charts for a suitable landing zone but found none, other than the plateau in the south. As they continued east, he figured that they would probably turn south at some point, flying along the eastern shores of the island instead and enter the plateau from the opposite direction. Still they flew east.

"You realise that we're in fact leaving Sardinia behind now don't you?" Said Dan, still playing the role of chief navigator.

"As I said, just do as you're told and follow me. We're just about to find out if your fuel calculations are correct or not. There's been another slight change of plan I'm afraid." Ruth offered no more by way of an explanation and simply steered the two aircraft onward east and away from the island of Sardinia.

CHAPTER 37

"What! You mean to say that you have lost them?" Gabriel was furious. It was not the call he had been expecting. Sebastian was quick to respond in his own defence.

"We could not lose them Monsieur, as we never had them in the first place!" Gabriel, who was well known as somewhat of a hot head, although his frustration in this instance was understandable, duly registered Sebastian's annoyance. Gabriel eventually conceded that it was nobodies fault and pacified Sebastian by addressing him as 'my friend' several times in his usual fashion. Sebastian went on to explain exactly what had happened.

"The Corsicans received a few short transmissions an hour ago. Not much was said but it would appear that Vasquez has taken control of the flight and is leading them away from Sardinia. My guess is that they are heading for the Italian mainland. They were not on the air long enough for us to auto-triangulate a fix of their position but she indicated that they were heading east."

"Do you think that she suspects anything?" Gabriel had an awkward habit of thinking out aloud. His colleagues always found it difficult to know if he was actually posing a question that they had to provide an answer to or whether or not he was just 'airing' his thoughts. Before Sebastian could reply anyway, the Belgian detective continued. "I think that this is a shrewd woman my friend. She too is full of surprises huh!" Sebastian was unsure as to how or whether to respond at all. His Belgian superior was just using him as a sounding board. Eventually he decided to come back with a polite 'yes, she's...' but, once again, Gabriel cut him short with his vocal deliberations. "Vasquez never intended to land at Sardinia. No she's too clever for that my friend. It's a simple matter of security. She wouldn't tell Danny exactly where the pickup would be would she? She has caught us all wrong footed my friend!"

" I guess so." Said Sebastian who had just decided to go along with anything his superior said.

"So it's plan 'B' after all Sebastian!"

Danny checked the fuel gauges and his figures once again.

"We've enough for ... I'd say one hour thirty minutes tops. I can't be sure of the wind though. Where ever we're going, it better be within spittin' distance!" Danny said voicing his concern. The Italian coastline was clearly insight now and Danny presumed that their point of arrival would be somewhere on the mainland. Once again he had miscalculated. Ruth instructed him to turn right ninety degrees, which now pointed them, due south. 'What is she playing at?' Danny said to himself. He had laid out his chart on the passenger seat beside him and once again orientated it to position it in the direction in which they were travelling, in keeping with good navigation practice. It was immediately apparent that they were on a direct heading for Sicily. Danny hit the transmit button "God woman, well never make it to Sicily! We'll go to dry tanks half way there and ditch in the sea!" Danny felt a sense of panic for the first time and was minded to leave this crazy woman to her own devices and make for dry land on his own.

"Relax Danny. I'm not stupid. I've done the figures too. Were not going anywhere near Sicily, in fact, were almost home now. Follow my lead." A well executed steep turn left sent the aircraft eastwards once again, towards the Italian coastline. Ten minutes later, Ruth revealed all.

"OK Danny, this is it." Danny had his thumb on the chart, plotting their position to second-guess his GPS. As Ruth turned left towards their new island destination, the 'Satnav' fixed itself squarely on approach to the small Italian island of Capri.

"Capri, we're actually landing in Capri?" Danny managed to mention the destination twice in the one sentence for 'God speed' over the airwaves.

"Affirm." Came the standard 'RT' response.

The two Pups flew low across the bay passing several fishing boats lazily at sail. Guiseppe Marcantonio looked up from his newly refitted vessel, picked up his radio transmitter handset and excitedly made his call, remembering to push all the correct buttons as Mario had shown him. As the two aircraft passed over the quayside and up over the village of Niapello, Danny scanned the terrain for any sign of a suitable landing site but saw none. Ruth lead them north of the town, passing over the spire of 'Our Lady of Suffering' and onwards east into the dense tree lined valley. They passed over the orange grove at eight hundred feet above sea level and, as the mountain range loomed ahead, Ruth suddenly rolled the aircraft left, pulling back on the stick to pull her tightly into a 180-degree reciprocal turn to point her due west. She then declared that it was time for their 'Downwind' landing checks.

"But where? I can't even see the field!" Cried Danny perplexed.

"You will Danny, trust me. Do your checks! It was mnemonic time in earnest. 'BUMFHH.' Again, Danny said it out aloud. Somehow it took on more importance when stressed vocally instead of remaining just a notion on the tongue. The downwind landing checks were usually completed whilst flying the reciprocal length of the runway on the 'Downwind' leg, in order to ensure that the craft was fit and configured, in plenty of time, for landing. In this instance, the checks would have to be done instinctively as Danny re-scanned the panorama for sign of a landing strip but saw only an ocean of green treetops before him.

" Brakes – pressure, check. Undercarriage – down and fixed, check. Mixture – rich, check. Fuel - cock on both; pump on; sufficient for landing, check. Heat - Carb' heat control; - pull, no icing detected, check. Harnesses and hatches - secure, check."

148

With Ruth now positioned 'number one' on finals, both Pups, duly configured for landing, flew along the deep, sheer sided valley with nothing but the green baize covering of the orange groves beneath them. The new saplings provided by Mario and planted by the villagers earlier in the season, had flourished and were rich in stature, leaf and yield.

" We can't put down in that," cried Dan, nervously.

"Just shut up, listen and watch!" Came the curt reply. "It's a very short field Danny. I'm going in first to use all the available length. You're the expert so you'll come in as number two. You'll have to touch down exactly on the threshold or you'll run into me on the ground." The only reply that Danny could muster was

"What threshold, I cant even see the field?"

"You will, any second now" replied Ruth.

Danny blinked in disbelief. The trees of the orange grove directly in front them suddenly began to part as if some biblical event was taking place. Thirty or so of the village people, arranged into two teams, tugged hard on the ropes just as Mario had taught them. The network of pulleys and cantilevers began to tighten and the supple branches of the Moroccan orange trees began to bend and moan as the leather harnesses came to bear once again, this time imposing their full authority. The system had been used primarily to shake the fruit from the trees into the nets below during harvest. This time there would be no shaking or relaxing. No resistance just submission as the ropes demanded that the trees 'stand aside' to reveal a neat little landing strip beneath that had been totally obscured until then.

Ruth had landed the Cessna at the grove many times and was familiar and reasonably comfortable with the approach although remaining vigilant and focused for the skilful manoeuvre. She was, of course, unfamiliar with the Beagle Pup and it's new larger flaps so she made sure that her approach speed was a perfect sixty knots. She applied a cautious three quarter flap setting to slow the aircraft down and gather pools of air beneath them to cushion her landing. The nose of the aircraft pitched down in consequence and gave her a better view of the field for her arrival. Although her approach speed was good, her actual touchdown was misjudged and late, arriving halfway along the strip. The upward gradient of the field however, combined with her slow speed, produced the required braking effect in the time and distance available and 'Echo Tango' drew to a timely halt. Danny, however, was feeling less than comfortable about the landing. Obviously shaken by the sudden appearance of the strip and still worrying about the consequences of the changes to the flightplan, he was not particularly composed or 'set up' in the approach, as he normally would be. Danny selected full flaps and as the motors engaged and dutifully lowered them he noticed that his airspeed was high at over seventy knots. Suddenly the nose of the aircraft ducked forward and 'Mike Alpha' dived toward the ground.

"Christ!" He shouted as his undercarriage ripped through the upper branches of the perimeter trees sending oranges bouncing in all directions. He thrust the throttle fully forward with his right hand whilst yanking the control column fully back with his left, in a sharp movement reminiscent of punch from a Thai boxer, and headed back into the sky.

"Going round!" He shouted more as a force of habit than a procedural courtesy.

The valley was too narrow at the western end for Danny to execute a '180' so he continued west until clear and out over the bay. Guiseppe saw the silhouette of *Mike Alpha* in the clear waters appearing as if she were a great foraging manta ray, moments before her engine announced her presence above him.

"OK Ruth, I'll try that again and a little differently this time." Said Dan over his radio, contemplating exactly what difference to make.

On many occasions, Danny had seen the Hercules pilots perform the *Khe Sanh* manoeuvre at the summer air shows in Britain and it was his favourite routine next to the 'showstopper' from the Harrier jump jet. *Khe San* was a USAF airfield in Vietnam that was surrounded on all sides by Vietcong guerrillas. Arriving aircraft on a normal approach were effectively sitting ducks, being particularly vulnerable to small arms fire. A new landing technique was needed and rapidly developed to solve the problem. The arriving Hercules would remain at a safe altitude, out of fire range, until almost over the threshold of the runway at which point the pilots would literally dive the machine towards the ground pulling the nose up only moments before impact, executing a perfect touchdown and roll out. It was a stunning spectacle and always a highlight of the show to see the display pilots throwing the mighty Hercules aircraft about performing the legendary *Khe Sanh* manoeuvre.

In the absence of a Harrier, The *Khe Sanh* manoeuvre was Danny's next best choice. He'd never actually tried it before but this trip had been unconventional throughout so he decided to try this radical approach.

Guiseppe pushed the button on his handset one more time and reported to his son that *Mike Alpha* had indeed returned to the valley and that he should hear its engine any moment now.

Danny set up a long and low approach with three quarters flap and a more than usual throttle setting. With this configuration, he literally dragged the aircraft along the tops of the trees at a perfect sixty knots. His *Mike Alpha finals Khe Sanh* call left Ruth and the others a little perplexed as they watched anxiously from the ground for him to appear.

Whilst hardly on the scale of 'Khe Sanh' but a similar manoeuvre none the less, Danny consoled himself with the thought that at least nobody was firing at him on this occasion. He locked his vision onto the rectangular hole one mile in front of him that he must pour through like floodwaters down a drain, clinging to the very contours of the opening. With his hand firmly on the flap selector switch, he began the mental countdown that had one attempt only to provide him with the exact moment to deploy the flaps.

150

As the edge of the green carpet rapidly approached, Danny anticipated a two second delay for the motors to engage and lower the flaps to their full extent. He counted out aloud so there could be no miss-order of his thought process. 'Five, four, three go!' The motors whirred and the flaps deployed suddenly thrusting the nose of the aircraft down in a violent tilting action that painted his windscreen green once again, filling it with the bloom of treetops punctuated by the dash of orange fruits. The knee jerk reaction to pull hard-back on the column limited the penetration of his nose wheel into the Fauna and saved his life. A second later, an inch deeper would have resulted in the nose leg snagging in the branches and cart wheeling the Pup onto it's back, fracturing its spine and rupturing the cruise tanks. Danny's biggest fear was to be trapped in the wreckage of an aircraft, doused in Avgas with prayer alone to stifle the flames and his screams.

'Mike Alpha' tore through the remaining fifty yards of Moroccan sapling, scattering fruit, leaves and the local bird life. Its undercarriage slapped and snapped an arrival announcement to Ruth and her colleagues who were anxiously awaiting it's appearance on the ground which, in the event, suddenly appeared in the forward view as the aircraft broke through the final barrage of twig and leaf that battered it's airframe. Leaf gave way to grass and speed gave way to sloth as 'Mike Alpha' abruptly came to a standstill halfway up the slope as if it were a fast jet landing on an aircraft carrier, having been gently placed there by the velocity arresting courtesy of the supple perimeter saplings. 'Not exactly stylish or what I had in mind' thought Dan, but an absolute 'greaser' of a landing if not in the conventional sense.

Ruth had watched Danny anxiously from the safety of the surrounding shrubbery. She had exited from her aircraft immediately after landing in case Danny had run into her from behind. Mario stood beside her in the grove and noted with surprise, the look of concern on her face as Danny aborted his first landing run and her subsequent look of relief as he eventually stepped down from the Pup unscathed. Mario broke off his stare and snapped his fingers to the others who then let go the stays to the pulley system. The orange trees gently flexed back into position and formed a fauna covering that made the Pups invisible from the air and also from space. The spy satellites would provide a picture that would be of agricultural interest only.

"It's been a long few days Ruth," said Mario as he kissed her on each cheek. "How was the flight?" He enquired.

"We had some minor technical problems but it went mostly to plan" She replied with a flush that did not go unnoticed by the Mafia hit man.

"And Michaelson. Did you have any trouble with him?"

"No, but he's no fool. He has done what we have asked of him so far. He believes that we are holding his girlfriend so he does what he's told. He's a first-rate pilot and mechanic. We couldn't have made the run without him." She said, inadvertently declaring an interest in Danny that went beyond her remit. Mario menacingly looked Ruth directly in the eyes as he reminded her of her duty of debt to the family.

"He will obviously be a great loss to you I'm sure, but you must carry out your orders to the full. Your mother wouldn't like it if you failed us. Do you understand?" Ruth looked over at Danny who was being escorted into the villa and slowly but reluctantly replied

"Yes, I understand. He'll die when the times is right."

CHAPTER 38

Rebecca couldn't concentrate on the book so she put it down once again. This particular novel was in French. She often read books in foreign languages. Not only could she enjoy the story but she could also polish her linguistic skills at the same time. On this occasion though she just couldn't keep her mind on the plot so she eventually gave up on it, choosing to work in the kitchen for some active distraction instead. She punched the 'on' button of the TV set as she got up, hoping to catch the regional news for any bulletins concerning Peter. She then turned her attentions to her curry club recipe book. Danny's favourite food was curry and Rebecca was well practiced in the art of blending exactly the right amount of spices to keep her man's taste buds in love with her along with the rest of him. She took comfort from the familiarity of preparing the Massala, which offered a tenuous link to her missing love whom she imagined to be sitting at the breakfast bar dipping his finger in the sauces and earning a loving slapped wrist for his interference.

Rebecca suddenly dropped the bowl, her involuntary action spilling chopped onions and garlic over the work surface as the shrill, piercing ring of the telephone cut through her late afternoon melancholy and sent the adrenaline coursing through her body. She had been waiting for the phone to ring all day and now that it was begging for her to answer it she became unable to move, momentarily gripped with terror as she imagined the worse kind of news that the caller may deliver. Her pulse became almost visible and her heart thumped like the kick of a bass drum at a rock concert. Her stomach played host to a thousand butterflies as the blood flow deserted it, rushing instead to her arms and legs in a primeval 'fight or flight' physiological response. All systems 'stood down' however as she grabbed the receiver and bathed her ear with the balm of a familiar friendly voice;

"Hi Becky, its Roger. Have you heard any news?" The sense of relief was overwhelming but countered by the frustration of still not knowing if Danny was safe or not. Rebecca didn't like lying to Roger but it was justifiably necessary. She kept her replies as near to the truth as possible and explained to him that she had reported Danny missing to the police and that she was expecting a call anytime now.

"What's happening at the club?" She enquired politely. The news had just come on the TV and she was absorbed with the headlines, not really paying much attention to Rogers' reply.

"Absolutely nothing!" Said a frustrated and confused Roger. "I've got members complaining all over the place and to make things worse, the CAA are giving me the run around saying that they don't know of a 'Mr Baker.' I'm on my way now to see my solicitor to get him to sort it out."

Biggles ran to the door and started barking, making it very difficult for Rebecca to continue her conversation.

"Biggsy!' Stop that! Sorry Rog,' I'm going to have to go. The dog can hear someone on the landing. The milkman always comes late on a Thursday to get his money, so I'd better go" she said, anxious to disengage from Rogers's problems as she had enough of her own and, besides, she didn't like having to lie to him. "I'll call you as soon as I have any news." Rebecca hung up on Roger whilst he was still in mid sentence,

"But Becky, it's only Weds..." Becky grabbed her purse as the doorbell rang. With one hand on Biggles' collar she half opened the door and extended the other with the correct change in it for the milk bill. She suddenly remembered that it was in fact Wednesday not Thursday and she looked up to see Johan bursting through the door. The first shot sent Biggles to the floor with a loud yelp. He lay there bleeding and panting heavily.

"I've got a message for you bitch," said Johan pointing a small handgun squarely in her face. "This is for Ruth's father, Eduardo Vasquez. Your father murdered him in the Falklands and now it's his turn to grieve!"

The second shot was louder than the first. Rebecca's fight or flight response could never be powerful enough or quick enough to save her. It could never have out-run a bullet under any circumstances and Johan was at point blank range. Stunned by the noise of the blast but feeling no pain, Rebecca opened her eyes, which stung along with her nasal passages as she coughed misty cordite from her lungs. She was momentarily detached from the events within the room, but as her senses gathered and her eyesight refocused, she saw Johan lying in a pool of blood next to her dog.

The MI5 officer stood over the body pointing his gun at it with both hands whilst the WPC ran over to Rebecca shouting

"Police! It's OK! Police! Just stay still Ma'am." The detective who had fired the shot kicked Johan several times, checking for a response, then rolled him over with his boot. The bullet had hit him in the back of the head and as Johan was turned around, it was obvious that the front right half of his face was missing along with any sign of life.

" It's OK, he's dead."

CHAPTER 39

It was a matter of survival. With the dwindling fish stocks and less and less demand for the ever-decreasing yield from the grove, the citizens of Niapello soon became practised in the art of 'asking no questions.' They cared not where the money came from, as long as it continued to do so, to repair the church, to replant the grove and to re-equip the village's small, archaic fleet of fishing vessels. Tradition in the islands was such that, in the event of a crisis, the villagers would close ranks and support each other in any way possible. This ultimate community spirit was a logical extension of their daily way of autonomous life. They had long operated an alternate economy based on reciprocal favours rather than a purely monetary regime that would be subject to the usual taxation. The village elders reasoned that 'x' amount of lire within the community, changing hands several times, subjected to the usual heavy taxes on each transaction, would soon turn into 'no' lire. Far better, they thought, for the mechanic to fix a car for someone who could repair his roof in return and keep the money on the island where it belonged. The system worked well and the villagers worked hard. When the opportunity arose for the town's problems to be virtually eradicated overnight, no questions were asked. It was simply a matter of survival and survive they must.

The villa had not been used for some time, as it was virtually derelict and in need of serious attention before it could become habitable again. The building materials had arrived effectively at the same time as the saplings from Morocco. All that the villagers had to do was make the necessary repairs themselves. No money changed hands. There was none to try to hide, none to make excuses for and none to pay tax on. Instead, the men folk worked diligently and collectively until the once ramshackle building in an advanced state of decay, was fully functional again.

The expected yield from the new trees would produce a legitimate source of income for the town and most of the villagers would be involved in one capacity or another in the growth, harvesting, packaging, transportation and eventual retail of the fruit. They had already begun to assemble and prepare the wooden cases for package and export of the oranges at the end of the harvest. The grove had once been a vineyard and the vaults contained extensive wine cellars. Instead of barrels though, this time, the basement was filled with large wooden crates although the musty smell of ancient grape still remained.

Mario pointed to the two wooden chests that he wanted and the men from the village eagerly removed them from the stack and began to unpack them. As the lid came off the first container, one of the elder workers began to cough uncontrollably and his eyes began to stream as the fumes from the resign rose into his face. Mario shouted at the men calling them 'imbeciles' and accused them of rough handling the goods, damaging the packaging. He then instructed them to carefully load the contents

155

of each carton into the back of the aircraft and respectively refuel them. The men eagerly busied themselves in compliance.

Danny sat on the edge of his bunk and ate the bread and salami he had been given. The others drank wine but Dan would never drink before a flight even if it had been offered. 'At least eight hours between bottle and throttle' he would tell his students. More if they had consumed a lot of alcohol in the last twenty-four hours. He was quite happy just to eat and drink the water, of which there was plenty. Besides, he needed his wits about him and his senses sharp for what lay before him. His simple bed was in the corner of the room occupied also by a dozen or so men folk from the village who had been charged with keeping an eye on him. He felt slightly intimidated by them but reminded himself that, if all went to plan, the nightmare would soon be over. Once again, he discretely reviewed his instructions on his organiser. They were far too complex to commit to memory but he tried. His disciplines learnt whilst instructing had taught him to avoid short cuts. Although mnemonics were fine, 'always refer to the checklists and flight plans where possible' he would teach them. 'It just might save your life' he would stress.

Danny quickly changed file on the unit as Ruth appeared in the room. In a strange way, he was pleased to see her. Through the course of the flight and the problems that they had endured and overcome, Ruth and Danny had developed a perverse sense of camaraderie. He was unaware at this stage of her hatred and sinister intentions for Rebecca though. The E-mail that he had received from Gabriel on the last night back at Bradwell had given him hope of a way through this nightmare although he wasn't sure if he could be courageous enough to adhere to the complex and bizarre instructions. He couldn't be certain that his transmissions were being intercepted but he had placed most of his faith in 'Plan B.'

"Danny, we must go over the details for the return trip. We leave again at first light." Ruth had acquired a detailed 'Met' report covering the region for the next twenty-four hours. Noting the wind details, Danny discussed the various options and considerations and the return route was soon established. Danny had suggested that they fly north west, passing between the Italian mainland to the east and Corsica to the west, entering France at Nice and weaving their way through the valleys and passages of the Alps to Geneva and then onwards north to Lille, eventually   returning to Bradwell. He suggested that they confirm specifics en route in case of any diversions or further problems that they may encounter. Ruth felt that he was being a little evasive but he reminded her that the outward-bound trip went 'hardly to plan.'

Both Danny and Ruth were exhausted. The mental exertion alone of ten hours flying was intense. Danny was anxious to complete the briefing and retire as soon as possible. It was imperative that he was refreshed and his senses sharp for tomorrow. As Ruth rose to leave, she turned back towards Danny pausing for a moment before she spoke. She seemed to stumble over the words and Dan waited expectantly. He was a little surprised by her parting remark.

" I wish it could have been different Danny."

Ruth was fully aware of the consequences of failure. The family had helped her when she was in trouble and now it was time to repay the debt. That was the system and the family did not tolerate failure. She had become quite fond of Danny and really did wish that things could have been different.

As dawn broke over the field, the pups were already fuelled, loaded and lined-up ready for take of. As the engines were started, the trees were pulled back in readiness for departure.

"OK Ruth, no power cables this time. We both know how efficient these flaps are so lets use them. Full flap, OK? No need to watch the air speed indicator, she'll just fly herself off when she's ready. Just help her over those trees with a little bit of 'backwards' on the stick."

The early morning tranquillity of the grove was fully compromised by the roar of two Rolls Royce Continental engines turning at two thousand seven hundred and fifty revs per minute. Danny and Ruth gracefully launched themselves into the mini mist that always hung close to the trees at that early hour and swiftly semi circled the Pups back over the grove towards the coast. Mario stood on the veranda of the villa as the sweet scented fog swirled over the field and settled on the strip where moments earlier the pups had proudly stood in readiness. As the saplings dovetailed back together, life became normal once again in Niapello. Heads were raised as the craft flew over the town and blind eyes were duly turned as the town's folk went about their business.

"OK Danny. Level at five hundred and take up a heading of 310 degrees" said Ruth, assuming the role of flight leader.

The imposing spectacle of Mount Vesuvius loomed out of the half-light; the ever present sentinel guarding the bay. Ten minutes later, as the aircraft established themselves straight, level and comfortable at five hundred feet, the sun leapt into the sky as if it too had suddenly been launched aloft from a place of rest. Various little islands were dotted in the sea beneath them, each with its own communities, traditions, orange groves and secrets.

Danny and Ruth had said very little to each other for the initial part of the journey and Ruth was flying point. As Danny trailed behind, he carefully trimmed 'Mike Alpha' for straight and level, hands free flight and switched on his organiser. He had password-protected the file and his anxiety coupled with the small buttons on the unit and the thump of a spiralling thermal, led to his mis-entering of the code. 'Access denied' flashed across the screen. The sudden adrenaline rush sent his metabolism into full alert and he tried again. He carefully entered *'PLAN B'* for a second time and the file dutifully presented itself before him. Danny entered the four-digit code '3333' into his transponder as directed and switched the unit from 'standby' to 'on.' He entered the new radio frequency into the standby bank in readiness for the appropriate moment and he checked his position on his GPS. Danny punched the new co-ordinates into the machine and held his breath as he hit the *'Go To'* button. The GPS took several seconds to make the necessary calculations then presented Danny with a new set of figures and an arrow pointing in the relevant direction. A final check of the chart to confirm his position then Danny gently steered *'Mike Alpha'* five degrees to starboard. Ten minutes further on, he instigated another five-degree right turn, which had shortly put a considerable distance between Ruth and himself. When radio silence was finally broken, he didn't want to risk being in visual range of Ruth in case she attempted any drastic retribution. Danny composed himself and announced 'this is it!' out aloud to himself as he took the first steps towards starting *'PLAN B.'*

CHAPTER 40

The previous evening, whilst Danny had been discussing the return route with Ruth, Don Prizzi was entertaining a guest at his villa on the island of Sicily. He often entertained in grand style and his wine cellar was the envy of the island, boasting a vast collection of rare and vintage bottles from all over the globe. He had been saving one select bottle for this particular guest and was looking forward to opening it.

'Godfather' Don Marineo had long been an irritation to the Prizzi household and many of the other families had also begun to regard him with caution. His arrogance and self elevated position of superiority had gotten out of hand in the last two years and he acted as more of a dictator rather than playing the traditional role of figurehead for the brotherhood. Many had begun to question their collective choice of 'Godfather' and with the renewed onslaught against them by the Italian authorities Don Marineos' arrogance was singled out for blame. The various factions and fraternities of the Mafia had put their' 'wagons in a circle' and within this new atmosphere of co-operation and communication within the brotherhood, Don Prizzi felt that this meeting was long overdue.   .

The Godfather was initially suspicious of the invitation but his ego eventually overrode his cautions and he accepted, believing rather, that his rival was jealous of his success with '*Destiny*' and that he wanted to play more of an active role in its production.

The black Lincoln Continental settled in front of the steps of the Prizzi villa and a servant approached the car to greet and assist the visitor from the vehicle. Two of the Godfathers own over-zealous bodyguards leapt from the car and prevented the servant from getting any closer. Don Marineo exited from the back of the Lincoln and dismissed his men when he saw his host appear on the steps. The two men kissed each other on alternate cheeks.

"It is a great source of pleasure to me to have you in my humble house on this occasion."

"I am honoured to be here Don Prizzi" replied the godfather, surprised at the depth of hospitality.

The two men were led away by servants, through the reception area where a string quartet played Mozart, Don Marineos' favourite composer, and on into the beautiful oak panelled dining room where a veritable feast awaited them. Don Prizzi employed a full time French master chef who was attended by two sous-chefs of Italian origin who could turn even the most humble pasta dish into a culinary masterpiece. Three servants attended the tables busily, proffering course after course on silver platters. There were many different types of wine especially selected from the cellars and displayed in a large rack at the side of the room. The two Dons sampled many and as a further gesture of friendship and hospitality, several bottles were sent down to Don Marineo's bodyguards who were leaning against the Lincoln, smoking and laughing.

The evening progressed smoothly and much alcohol and food were consumed. As the two Dons conferred and discussed family business, the servants took the opportunity of a quick cigarette break before they cleared the desert course. Laughing and joking, they joined the Godfathers staff leaning against the Continental and offered them more Frascati. Ten minutes passed before the headwaiter announced that their break was over and that it was time for them to go back to work. He took the last puff of his cigarette and dropped it to the floor, grinding out the last embers with his foot. The others acknowledged the cue and followed his lead as he leapt into action.

The Garrotte had long been the traditional method of execution used by the Mafia. A thin but strong cheese wire, ended with wooden handles and wrapped tightly around the neck ensured a swift death. Suffocation, usually followed by the severing of the jugular vein, delivered a prompt, determined demise. The three body guards slumped to the floor within seconds of being throttled, their death-rattles accompanied by the sickly sweet smell of blood mixed with the outpourings from their bowels, their anal sphincters losing control and opening within moments of the blood supply being cut to their brains.

The headwaiter swore profusely as he attempted to wipe his shoes clean before he served the next course.

Inside the villa Don Marineo complimented his host on the variety and quality of his wine cellar.

"You have a fine liking for wines Don Prizzi, as you have for women too, as I recall" the Godfather offered.

"I always have a well stocked cellar; it is one of life's more favourable pursuits, along with the fairer sex of course." Don Prizzi was aware of the Godfathers fondness of the grape and knew which buttons to press to engage his guest in a round of 'one-up-man-ship' concerning the riches of his cellar.

"I too have a comprehensive selection in my cellar" replied the Godfather. "I pride myself on knowing my wines and I can name the origin of most with a simple taste. You must come visit me my friend and we will test your own palette on my collection."

Don Prizzi had done his homework. He had taught his children the wisdom of the saying 'know thy enemy' and was about to confirm the theory. He knew of the Godfathers fondness of Mozart and had flown in a string quartet from Vienna especially for the evening. He was also aware of, not only Don Marineos passion for wine, but also of the depth of his egotism. Recognising that the Godfather had taken the bait, he pressed his guest further

"Well now, for you my friend, I have something most special. Let us test your palette here and now with something that I have saved especially for this occasion. I am sure that you will agree that it is a very rare blend. Enjoy!" He raised the bottle and filled the Godfather's glass to the brim and encouraged him to drink. Don Marineo drank and offered no immediate comments. He regarded the wine curiously instead. As he helped himself to a second and third glass, his host began to talk of more serious matters.

"So, you are very proud of your recent achievements no doubt?" Don Prizzi asked rhetorically. The Godfather acknowledged the remark with aloud guffaw filling and raising his glass once again.

"Destiny, prepare for your destiny" he laughed. The Don was in the advanced stages of being drunk and made little sense.

"It was a wonderful twist don't you think, to call my creation, my....., I beg your pardon, *our* salvation, *'Destiny.'* "Another glass and the bottle was almost finished.

"You have gone to a lot of trouble for me tonight Don Prizzi. The Mozart did not go unnoticed and the food and wine has been splendid although I must admit that I have not come across this particular grape before. It is most unusual. Yes, a lot of trouble indeed my friend and I am asking myself why, after all this time, you should go to such lengths to please me. There is obviously something that you want from me. Confess to me Don Prizzi. The real reason that you brought me here and provided this wonderful meal was to relax me and take advantage of my over drinking. I know you of old my friend and you want something. Feel free to approach me but be warned, I have had a long association with 'the grape' and although I may appear a little relaxed, I am still in command of my senses. You want to share in my Good fortune don't you? My 'Destiny!" The Godfather roared with laughter and began to choke himself. Moments later he regained his composure and washed away his cough with the last few drops from the bottle, excusing himself as he poured. Don Prizzi waited a moment before responding.

"On the contrary Godfather, I want nothing to do with your drug but it is ironic that I am in charge of your own destiny at this precise moment." The Godfather looked very puzzled. Don Prizzi continued. "I too have not been idle. I have invited you here tonight to introduce you to my new product. The Prizzi household have developed a new drug too." The Godfather stopped in his tracks, coughing once again as his happy facade turned to a look of concerned curiosity.

"I'm sure that your family are very proud of your achievements Godfather and I can honestly say that my own family will be proud of mine too after this evening." The Don pushed a piece of paper in front of his Godfather and stood over his shoulder as he read out aloud

" 'R' for Ranitidine. A stomach acid inhibitor.

'E' for Ether. To induce drowsiness." The godfather looked confused. The Don continued

"Yes, your family must be very proud of you.

" 'V' for Vallium. To relax the system. How many children have you now Don Marineo? Five? Six?" Before the Godfather could answer, Don Prizzi continued.

" 'E' for Elderberry wine. A potent inclusion to disguise the taste of the other ingredients. I knew that you couldn't resist the challenge of a new bottle Marineo." This time, he had dropped the customary, respectful 'Don' from his address.

" 'N' nitric acid. A Particularly nasty substance I'm sure that you would agree. Did you ever meet my family Godfather?" he enquired. He already knew the answer. The godfather was very confused and his head was spinning. He began to reply

" I don't believe so ...." Don Prizzi interrupted him and continued reading from the paper.

" 'G' - Gelatine for arterial blockage. Yes you have. You have met three of my sons tonight. They have been serving us all evening and shortly they will be serving your three sons.

'E' for Ecstasy, the drug that started it all. "

The Godfather was having trouble breathing and was very puzzled by the line taken by his host. He managed a polite but futile comment

"You have three fine sons Don Prizzi. I did not know that it was they who were serving us. You should have told me."

"That is right, you 'did not know.' There has been much that you 'did not know' and as Godfather, you should have known. Now it is too late. "

The Godfather began to feel threatened and tried to call out to his bodyguards managing only a few shallow breaths instead. He suddenly felt very ill and was unable to move.

"Yes, three fine sons. I did have four but, of course, 'you did not know.' Are you feeling all right Don? You are looking a little ill." The Godfather had began to have serious breathing difficulties.

"It must be the wine, this last bottle was one too many for me. I confess that I know not what it is. Tell me where it comes ...." The godfather was interrupted before he could finish his sentence.

"Yes four sons. Four fine sons. My youngest Antonio was a fine boy. Handsome like his father. Loved to drink and party like his father. And finally

'D' for 'Destiny.' Most appropriate don't you think? My chemist was anxious to include it. By now I imagine that you must be feeling quite ill. Antonio loved girls and they adored him too. Just like his father." Don Prizzi talked slowly and deliberately making sure that the Godfather understood every word. He kept checking his watch.

"I imagine that your lungs are probably filling with blood as we speak and breathing will become most difficult shortly. Yes my Antonio was the apple of my eye. He wanted to start work for the family this summer but I told him to go off and enjoy himself, drink a little, make love a lot. Oh, I don't think that you recognised our wine waiter tonight either." Don Prizzi rang the bell to summon him into the room.

"Antonio went to Malta two months ago. He asked me for more money so that he and his friends could go over to Ibiza." The godfather coughed and wiped a streak of blood from his nose as Don Prizzi looked at his watch once again before he continued.

"Nose bleed, exactly on time! A marvellous piece of chemical engineering I'm sure you'll agree. Ah, Vittorio come in. You do recognise Vittorio Bartelli don't you? Our illustrious wine waiter. You may recall that you ordered your henchman Mario Marcantonio to cut off his wife's fingers." The godfather was manifestly terrified and the look of horror was transfixed on his face.

"Yes, Antonio was my pride and joy. I only wish that I could have been there at the end, as they pulled him from the foam. The pathologist, Senior Mendez, wrote that his death was due primarily to suffocation but, if he had lived, the lack of blood supply to the brain would have left him as a cabbage. He actually drowned in his own blood. He commented that he would have suffered excruciating pain as his arteries blocked and ruptured.   I didn't even get a chance to say good-bye. That is what I find most distressing"

The blood had begun to haemorrhage from the Godfathers mouth and nose as the nitric acid attacked his lungs. At that moment, Don Prizzis' remaining three sons, masquerading as waiters returned to the room.

"Ah, the last course. You are very lucky Marineo, you will get the chance to say goodbye to your sons." The waiters laid the three silver Platters on the table and removed the lids. The heads of the three Marineo boys were virtually the last things the godfather saw before his lungs filled with blood and choked him.

"Oh, and one last thing. You wanted to know the name of the wine, the sweetest bottle on earth." With his dying breath, Don Marineo watched as Vittorio Bartelli turned around the bottle that he had been drinking from. The label said simply

'REVENGED'

CHAPTER 41

The 'hard' and software systems that comprised the mechanisms of 'Radnet' were not subject to any 'UCD,' cross border hold ups, or regional scrutiny at all. The 'Net' covered the whole of Europe comprehensively and was the only true example of a workable, federalist enterprise that was beyond denunciation. It worked and it worked well and nobody had anything but praise for it.

Air Traffic Control at Rome's Fiumicino Airport picked up the first signal. It was then relayed simultaneously to centres at Ajaccio on the island of Corsica and Porto Torres on the island of Sardinia. They in turn relayed it to Genova, then Milan and finally onto Venice. Air traffic controllers at Venice, acting under instructions from Interpol at the behest of Gabriel Dupont, altered the frequency of the transmission, boosted the signal and relayed it once again.

Securely hidden high in the mountains to the west of Lublianja in the country of Slovenia, Lawrence Carlton and his team, in their remote moments of isolation, were startled by the audible alert heralding the arrival of a coded message via the satellite link. They had waited patiently and eagerly for the signal, which, until that point, they could never have been certain of arriving at all. Lawrence lifted the lid of the laptop and was prompted to enter the appropriate code to gain access to his programme. 'PLAN 'B'' was duly typed and accepted and the screen changed to one resembling a cross between a traditional radar controller's display and that of the new generation of 'moving map' Sat. Nav. screen. This new 'Desktrak' programme was the first of its kind enabling integration between the land based 'Radnet' system and the 'Global positioning' network of satellites. A traditional use for the GPS system would be to fix and plot the position of the airborne receiver unit itself in relation to the satellites, for its own navigation purposes only. Under this new procedure however, the ground based radar network would initially establish the whereabouts of the subject instead; the frequency of that signal would then be changed and re-transmitted celestially. The GPS satellites would then blend the data with their own, overlaying the subjects position on a moving map and finally sending the information earthwards to a designated remote tracking station.

Laurence Carlton was the designated station in this instance and the numbers '3333' were clearly displayed on his laptop, overlaid on a map, which detailed the western coastline of Italy. The 'Desktrak' programme indicated that Danny was about to cross the coast at Anzio, approximately ten miles South of Rome, heading North East. This was the moment that Lawrence and his team had been so eagerly awaiting and proof at last that Danny had in fact received the E-mail hastily sent by Gabriel and himself from Brussels.

Lawrence shouted 'Go' to his team and the men went into carefully rehearsed assiduous operation. The back doors of the freighter were again swung open and the three-deep wall of cardboard boxes that had greeted the customs officer at the Austrian border were removed by the team who had formed a human chain for the task. As the last carton was removed, a false bulkhead became visible which divided the vehicle across its width fully from top to bottom. The fixing bolts were quickly and easily removed, followed swiftly by the bulkhead itself, to further reveal a structure that had been hastily created in a Sheffield steel foundry several nights before. The whole, intricate assembly was mounted on greased runners, which slid the whole framework forward in a similar fashion to the operation of an automated car wash. Now poised at the back of the vehicle, the team took careful hold of the ropes and braced themselves to take the tension when the last of the retaining pins were released. Lawrence supervised the operation but added his weight to the ropes as the cradle holding his treasured Bulldog was swung from its forty-five degree angle to a horizontal position allowing the craft to be gently lowered to the ground.

Even if the great mountain range had not been there to obstruct the flight path, permission for flight in this part of the world would never have been granted so it was decided therefore, to freight the Bulldog over the Alps to its current vantage position instead. The thirty-three foot wingspan of the Bulldog precluded it from being loaded in a horizontal aspect into the freighter, which was the largest of its type available, so the cradle was designed to hold the aircraft diagonally sideways from bottom left to top right in a fashion that would not stress the airframe at all. It was a marvellous piece of practical, precision engineering that slid readily back into place once the Bulldog had been despatched. Its services would not be required for any such homeward journey.

After a quick but thorough 'walk round' check, Lawrence installed both himself and his laptop into the Bulldog and went through his start up checks. As he did so, the rest of the team carefully refitted the bulkhead and reloaded the boxes containing Hi-Fi's, TV's, computer games etc. in readiness for delivery to a warehouse in Lublianja later that day. A legitimate order for the goods had been placed with all the necessary paperwork in order and at hand, which qualified the vehicle's presence in the country, providing an adequate alibi if they were suddenly challenged. Gabriel was renowned for being thorough and, indeed, he had been once again.

The normal take-off roll for the Bulldog was 450-500 hundred metres depending on load and wind strength. The plateau offered less than one hundred. Lawrence had once had a holiday in Jordan, which had unexpectedly coincided with the annual world hang-gliding championships. He and Barbara had spent a whole afternoon watching these intrepid 'Indiana Jones' types throwing themselves off mountains in gravity and death defying manoeuvres, strapped to their kites, which plummeted initially before recovering to 'commit aviation' as he put it. The principle would be the same on this occasion. A Bulldog, however, weighed considerably more than a hang-glider 'but,' as Lawrence continuously reminded himself out aloud for reassurance, 'the principle was exactly the same!'

The engine proved to be a little harder to start than usual. Normally, only a handful of primes would be necessary to rouse the 'Dog' but on this occasion, the beast wouldn't budge from its slumbers, rousing anxiety only, amongst the crew.

Because the aircraft had been transported several hundred miles in an adversely inclined position, whatever fuel had originally been left somewhere in the system of pipes and pumps, normally aiding a rapid ignition, had either drained away or vaporised. There were some very anxious looks on the faces of the crew who were packed and sitting ready in the cabin of the truck; ready for an immediate departure of their own once the Bulldog was airborne.

Lawrence primed the system with ten strokes of the lever once again and hit the start-up button. He was very conscious of over-priming the system, as the manual warned of a propensity for engine fires when flooded. Between each attempt, he pulled the mixture lever back to 'IDLE-CUT-OFF' and hit the start button again. Turning the engine over with the mixture control set in 'ICO' would purge any excess vapour from the system, reducing the risk of fire before starting afresh. Of course, every subsequent attempt drained not only excess fuel but precious life from the battery also. Lawrence had no contingency plan in the event that it should go flat. Some older aircraft were fitted with special ports, well away from the propeller, to enable safe connection of jump leads for just such an occasion. It was nowadays an altogether sad and senseless omission that these ports were missing from the newer aircraft, an absence that was as unforgivable as that of a missing starting handle on latter-day cars. Nobody in their right mind would want to go near a spinning propeller to retrieve their jump leads from inside the engine compartment.

Every futile attempt to start the engine drained the resource a little more until finally, it had no more to give. The battery was flat. The propeller settled in 'the vertical,' like a watch that had stopped at six o'clock. Lawrence slapped his thighs accompanied by a particularly out-of-character cuss as two of the crew climbed down from the truck to assist.

CHAPTER 42

Danny felt his muscles tighten as the call he had been expecting came through.

" Danny, where are you? I've lost visual."

This was the confirmation that Dan had been waiting for, verifying that he was now at a safe enough distance from Ruth to begin his next manoeuvre.

In the panel in front of him were three switches that he had fitted to both aircraft back at Bradwell. One of the duplicate trio in the panel in front of Ruth was a dummy. Danny had told her that the new switches were to operate the new fuel pumps that he had installed along with the cruise tanks. He explained to her that the fuel system had had to be totally redesigned and that the pumps were necessary to ensure correct flow and pressure in the system during certain phases of flight. She knew nothing of these matters and readily accepted his explanation. In fact, only two of the switches were necessary to operate the pumps. Danny had carefully avoided his own third switch up to this point but it was now time to see if it would work as planned .

" Come in Danny, I can't see you "

Ruth had already completed a full rate one orbit to the left and could see no trace of *'Mike Alpha.'* In the absence of any 'RT.' response she could only presume that Danny had met with some sudden mishap and she began to retrace her route calling him again over the radio. Her own adrenaline rush stimulated her imagination and she distressed herself with dark imaginings of the retribution that her own family would suffer at the hands of Mario should the mission fail.

As rational thought began to replace her panic, she began to reason that if Danny had experienced any engine problems, then he would have undoubtedly informed her over the 'RT.' Conversely, if he had been having problems with the radio itself, then she would have easily been able to see him during her manoeuvres.

The obvious explanation soon presented itself to her and she pressed her transmit button once again. "OK Danny, I know you can hear me. What's going on?" Still there was no reply. She waited a few moments for a response, still hoping that there was an innocent explanation for Danny's absence. Danny had no reason to respond at all and simply listened to Ruth beginning to panic. "You know what the consequences will be for failure to cooperate. C'mon Danny, speak to me."

Danny remained calm and quiet. It was only when Rebecca's name was mentioned that he became agitated. " Have it your way Danny, but just remember that you'll have very little to return home too if you do in fact make it. There certainly won't be any Rebecca waiting for you!" This time, Danny just couldn't sit there without making some attempt at an appropriate response.

" I've had enough of your shallow threats." he said " I'm not dancing to your tune any longer. I know that Becky's OK and you've got no hold over me at all now."

"What do you mean? How could you know anything? Becky's far from OK Danny. Look, it's not to late Dan. Just come back with me as planned and it'll all soon be over."

"No chance, you're on your own now. Get lost, literally!" With that, Danny leant forward to change radio frequency to the new one that he had waiting on standby, as per his instructions. Before he changed channel he heard Ruth's final remarks.

"So be it. The bitch is probably already dead. "

Despite having already been assured of her safety, Danny felt a wave of panic wash over him coupled with a desire to be sick. The little nagging doubts made him stop and momentarily reconsider his course of actions but he was in far too deep to change anything now. He pressed his transmit button one last time

" Go to hell you evil bitch! "

Danny hit the button and changed radio frequency. He couldn't bear the sound of her threatening voice any longer and in a split second, her sickening tones were replaced with complete, pacifying silence. He grabbed hold of the third switch and said 'Fuck you' as he slammed it down positively.

CHAPTER 43

"I just can't believe it. She's never played up before!" Lawrence had one hand aloft, holding the engine cowling open whilst checking the fuel line with the other. "There's plenty of gas in here. There's absolutely no apparent reason that I can see, except for Sod and his law, why this engine won't start. The Batteries totally shot now so the only way we're going to get this aircraft started is to hand swing it. Any volunteers?" he asked.

Hand swinging a propeller was not one of life's safer pursuits, particularly for the unpractised and especially when it was attached to a mighty Bulldog. The team members looked at each other to see who was willing to draw the short straw. There was no time for deliberation or hesitation so the team leader swiftly offered his services. It was actually a straightforward procedure but obviously extremely hazardous to the 'swinger' whose successful attempt would leave him staring at a pair of whirling meat cleavers. Normally, a pair of chocks would be inserted under the main wheels to prevent the craft surging forward once started. The problem would then be that someone would have to remove them whilst negotiating the 'food blenders.' There were no chocks readily available anyway on this occasion so they would simply have to proceed as best they could.

Lawrence briefed his team leader on the appropriate action and settled back into the cockpit in readiness.

"Remember, once she's spinning clear to the left OK!" he stressed.

The crewman took up his position. He looked rather awkward, with his feet already pointing in the direction that he was intending to leap, giving him the appearance of a child's twisted doll. He grabbed the top blade with both hands and waited for a 'thumbs up' from Lawrence who had switched on the ignition and primed the fuel system. The first swing took an almighty effort to turn the Avco /Lycoming IO-360 engine that had been dormant for some while. As the top blade began to move and lurch downward, the crewman dived to his left in anticipation and made an ungraceful, grass arrival on all fours. What he hoped would be the roar of a propeller was in fact a roar of laughter from the rest of the team who had witnessed his unnecessary nose-dive whilst the propeller remained idle. He felt like a goalkeeper experiencing the embarrassment of diving prematurely to the left as the ball passed him to the right during a penalty shoot. Dusting himself down and acknowledging the spectacle with a half smile, he grabbed the top blade, now in a better ten o'clock position and tried again. His practise leap had not been wasted as he discovered when, on the second attempt, the propeller tore into the fresh mountain air immediately in front of him and begged the aircraft to advance towards his flesh. Lawrence arrested the initial forward motion with his toe brakes and pulled the throttle fully backwards having left it cracked open initially to help the start-up. He looked up just in time to see the soles of the crewman's boots as they flew to his right in a leap of Olympic proportions. This time nobody laughed, as the 'swinger' seemed to land quite heavily. The truck driver ran over to help haul his colleague out of the way and lost his baseball cap in the process as the powerful prop-wash rushed backwards with a vengeance bathing, not only the airframe, but anything in it's path with it's maelstrom. Another 'thumbs up' from Lawrence and a final 'Good luck' response mouthed by the team, saw the Bulldog tear off the edge of the mountain in simply a moment. The whole crew ran over to the edge to watch what followed.

The Bulldog needed fresh air to rush over its wings at sixty knots at least to encourage take off and flight under normal conditions. At the moment that it dived over the edge of the plateau it was only travelling at only thirty-five. The aircraft was in fact 'stalled' at that point, Bernoulli's principal (*) having yet to take effect. The Bulldog simply nose-dived into the ravine like a roller coaster having reached the pinnacle of its travel with nowhere else but 'down' to go. The ferocity of the dive shook Lawrence and he grabbed the stick with both hands leaving none to catch his stomach if it did indeed exit from his mouth as he felt it would at any moment.

It took only seconds, but ones that seemed like hours, for the air speed indicator to confirm the required sixty knots. Laurence pulled the craft out of the dive with only three hundred feet between himself and the tops of the fir trees in the valley below. Normal flight characteristics were soon in place and Laurence took up his new heading as the team he had left behind boarded the truck to begin the next phase of 'Plan B.'

CHAPTER 44

Danny's training as an electrical engineer had been fun. He was so interested in the subject that studying the volumes of manuals required to pass his exams had been anything but a chore. Being able to combine both of his hobbies by building remote control kit planes was purely paradise. He had learnt to construct them long before he had learnt to actually fly himself. Fitting the remote circuit board in the panel behind the third switch had been easy. The relay unit inside Ruth's transponder had been a little harder, not from the design point of view, but physically trying to accommodate the hardware inside the casing proved difficult. When Danny hit the third switch, a signal was transmitted to a relay unit fitted inside of Ruth's transponder which switched it from 'Standby to 'On' and re-configured its code internally to squawk ident '7700' despite the reading on the front panel. Danny had no way of gauging if it had worked but if it had, every radar controllers screen within a hundred mile radius would be glowing with the international distress squawk '7700.' An airliner that had been hijacked or was in some similar level of distress usually squawked this code and a normal reaction would be for an intercept jet to be launched from the nearest military facility to investigate.

Ruth had no idea that she was now fully visible to the whole 'Net' and she had no inkling of what was about to follow. She had suddenly begun to feel nauseous and was finding it difficult to think straight. She was terrified at the consequences that may befall her for failing in her mission so she decided that damage limitation was the best strategy. 'Maybe Danny won't make it back, at least not before me' she thought. 'If I can just make it back with at least one cargo of resign then all is not lost' she reasoned.

Ruth decided that her own 'Plan B' would be to continue with 'Plan A' but without Danny. Danny had repaired her GPS aerial at the grove before departure that morning and the unit was fully functional again, so she at least had her guiding 'Satnav.'

As Ruth took up a new heading and mentally prepared herself to cross the Alps, she had no idea that two intercept F16 fighters had just been scrambled from USAF Sigonella air force base, ironically, on the island of Sicily.

CHAPTER 45

Back at Bradwell, Franco had set the laboratory up as charged and had little else to do until the resin was delivered. He had argued with Johan the day before when the German had told him that he was going off to 'do a little job,' as he had put it. Franco reminded him that his 'job' was to maintain security at Bradwell and not to go off doing other 'little Jobs' the moment Ruth went away. Franco eventually conceded, actually feeling glad to see the back of the German oaf for a while but he was now getting a little edgy, as the idiot hadn't returned as promised.

Franco had not been privy to Ruth's instructions for Johan to assassinate Rebecca. He would not have approved of Ruth's personal agenda in this regard, which would only serve to jeopardise the mission. He imagined that Franco had probably found himself a 'bit of skirt' and stayed the night, accounting for his delayed absence. Franco smiled to himself as he imagined the fury that Johan would face if he wasn't there when Ruth returned later that day. He stood on the breakwater and took long drags on his mini cigar as he looked out over the bay. He knew nothing of the dramatic history of the area but couldn't help but feel touched by the tranquillity offered by the landscape. He felt a sense of sadness that the beauty spot was spoilt by the presence of the power station, which seemed somewhat incongruous with its surroundings. Still, he was a scientist and he knew of the sacrifices that had to be made in the name of science. For countless years he had studied for his masters degree in physics. He followed it with a similar qualification in chemistry and a degree in maths was not far behind. He had made sacrifices in the name of science. Personal ones. He had given up all hopes of having a normal family life. He couldn't even hold down a relationship for any length of time, as there was always too much work to do. He was only human after all. The court had branded him some kind of monster but it was only one 'little' rape, yet all his qualifications were taken away from him. He had served only seven months of his ten-year sentence when his Godfather had intervened and secured his release. Franco had a good position now, working for the family and felt honoured that he was to be put in charge of the UK operation.

If all went to plan, he was expecting the Pups to return later that afternoon. There was little for him to do in the laboratory until then so he had taken the opportunity to stretch his legs along the embankment. He decided to walk back along the runway kicking away the odd stones that Johan had overlooked when clearing it. He was far too far away to have disturbed them yet the flock of Lapwings that had been settled all afternoon at the hangar end of the runway had just taken to the air. Franco checked his watch and prepared an appropriate 'what time do you call this' type speech for Johan as he walked back to meet him at the hangar. Johan's silhouette was clearly visible against the stark contrast of the ocean as it shrouded his appearance through the workshop window.

"So, you have at last decided..." Franco rounded the corner of the workshop door, his reprimand in full swing when he realised that the body in front of him was not that of Johan's. He had obviously caught the intruder by surprise also. Franco found it difficult to focus on the figure that was standing in front of the window. His back was to the door and, as Franco entered, the intruder turned around and shouted 'SAS officer, freeze!'

Franco was better positioned to let off the first shot. His Luger was bulky but effective and he quickly fired through the pocket of his Barbour raincoat without raising the gun fully to horizontal. The Bullet entered the thigh of the SAS officer and incapacitated him immediately. The thought process was almost instantaneous. Franco had always had a responsive mind and it took only seconds for him to evaluate the situation and determine that he was a sitting duck whilst he remained in the hanger. The open ground was not a particularly desirable alternative but that was effectively all that was left by way of an escape route. Again, his mathematician's brain told him that he stood a better chance if he could get to the power station. SAS officers never worked alone, he knew that. They would no doubt be hidden in the line of trees to the south of the field. He would have to act fast if he was to have any chance at all of reaching the station.

Franco leapt over the injured officer who was holding his leg in agony on the workshop floor, and climbed through the window at the back of the building. As he was halfway to the breakwater, he heard the first warning.

"SAS, stop or we'll shoot." His response was to turn around and send two further bullets stinging into the corrugated iron walls of the hanger. He had barely made it over the ridge of the sea wall as a volley of automatic rifle fire dug into the embankment below him. The only possible refuge that he could find would be within the power station and he ran along the overgrown path towards it, stooping as he went.

Bradwell power station was one of Nuclear-electric's seven Magnox variety nuclear reactor plants. It was connected to the national grid on the first of July 1962. Bradwell Bay was chosen for the site as it offered many significant benefits. Firstly, there was an unlimited supply of cooling water from the bay. The station would use up to 227 million litres an hour! Secondly, the area, which was of nominal agricultural value, offered good access for sea transportation of spent nuclear fuel to Sellafield in Cumbria and lastly, there was a very stable, geological substrata which was capable of supporting heavy plant. It had been an obvious choice for RAF Bradwell Bay as well as the power station. It was no surprise that the Mafia too had recognised its strategic positioning.

"You cannot allow any situation of that nature to develop Captain. Do you understand? This is a nuclear reactor site. The consequences would be incalculable if there was to be an accident of some kind. This man must not be allowed any where near it. Do you understand?" The power station manager had made his position very clear. The SAS Commander hung up his cell phone and made a call on his short-wave radio instead.

"Under no circumstances is he to reach the station. Take whatever action necessary."

"Sarge' says 'take him out' if necessary. You'll probably get just one shot. You'd better make it count!"

Corporal Lance Billings Smith had been part of the Squadron of Special Air Services who had helped recapture Goose Green in the Falklands conflict. The engagement had been bloody and the casualties heavy. Nothing could compete with the horror of that battle except the possibility of a nuclear incident at Bradwell bay. He was comfortably positioned lying between the trees at the south side of the field. The leather strap of his automatic rifle was carefully entwined between his left wrist and right elbow generating a steadying tension between them. He was focused on the five-yard break in the embankment just before it joined the immediate grounds of the station. Franco was last spotted four hundred yards to the right as he leapt over the ridge. He could have actually gone the other way and made for the mud flats. They had no way of telling.

'Five yards.' The Corporal was responsible for just 'five yards' of overgrown footpath. He had had his own mountain to sentry at Goose Green, now they had given him just 'five yards.' The eyepiece of his rifle had been pressed hard into his right eye for ten minutes or so and the eye had begun to water and haze over. Suddenly, there was an ear-shattering burst of gunfire that lasted no more than one second. The lapwings had suddenly taken to the air and several of them had been cut down in a frenzy of feathers.

"It's only the birds! Christ, you shot the birds!" Shouted the orderly. Corporal Lance Billings Smith rubbed his right eye, stood up and emerged from the conifer trees.

"Christ Corporal, keep ya' head down!" Shouted his colleague. The Corporal kept walking, crossing the runway and ploughing through the remains of several slaughtered Lapwings. The others caught up with him, turning as they went with there rifles primed in an effort to cover him. Lance said nothing until he got to the footpath.

"Five little yards!"

Franco lay dead on the bay side of the path, peppered with bullet holes.

CHAPTER 46

The city of Rome was clearly visible from Danny's port window as he passed to the southeast. The many splendid, spectacular, historical buildings were laid out on a platter before him, like decorations on a wedding cake. The vast Vittorio Emmanuele 11 monument dominated the skyline, its white walled splendour a stark contrast to the crestfallen neighbouring Coliseum. Away in the distance, past the Pantheon, he could clearly see the dome of St Peters Basilica and the other statue crested buildings of the Vatican.

Danny had been to Rome once before. He was totally captivated by the city, it's ancestry and it's spirituality. The Trevi fountain was the most beautiful thing he had ever seen apart from Rebecca, whom he had only just recently met at the time. Danny had thrown three coins in the fountain, having seen the film of the same name, and made his wishes, which subsequently came true when Becky declared her undying love for him. Danny told himself that when all of this was over, he would return to the city and propose to Becky in front of the fountain.

He pressed his transmit button once again.

"Carrier pigeon on frequency. Come in Bird dog." There was no reply.

Danny was flying off into the unknown. Based on the strength of the Bradwell E-mail that he had received and put his faith in, he continued northeast, transmitting his message every few minutes. If no contact were made by the time he left the Italian coastline then his GPS and his initiative would be his only companions. His 'Plan 'B' instructions had run out at this point and, so to, had the coverage of his charts. Ruth had provided them for the southwest coastline of Italy only.

"Carrier pigeon on frequency. Come in Bird dog." Again there was no response.

Danny knew that a level head would be his salvation. He recalled his basic geography and remembered that once he crossed the eastern shores of Italy he would be flying over the Adriatic sea, at which point, he should be very careful not to go to far east as he would stray into Balkan airspace. That would be very unwise at this time he figured, so his contingency plan would be to follow the Italian coastline northwards then eastwards where he hoped to find and arrive at Venice. In the event that he did land there, he hadn't quite figured out what he would say to the Italian customs authorities who would find him with a full cargo of *'Destiny'* resin. He would have to cross that one when he came to it.

"Carrier pigeon on frequency. Come in Bird dog." This time, Danny received an ear full of static by way of a response. He had been expecting some interference from the mobile phone network now that he was over the mainland.

Suddenly

"Carrier Pigeon, this is Bird dog! Danny, are you OK?" The response sent Danny's heart leaping from his chest.

"Yes! Yes! Lawrence is that you?"

"Lawrence Carlton at your service Dan."

"Thank God. Christ, this has been a nightmare! Please tell me that Becky's OK, she is isn't she?" Danny asked anxiously.

"She's fine Dan, just fine. She's a little shook up and misses you like crazy but she's fine. I'll fill in all the details later, right now we've got a job to do."

"I just can't believe all this is happening. God, its great to hear your voice Lawrence. Where are you, what am I supposed to do now?" Danny enquired, overwhelmed with nervous relief.

"Just keep your head Danny and keep your heading too. You won't be able to see me just yet but I'm tracking you quite clearly. I fix you about three miles south of Ancona. Just keep up your current track and we should be visual in ten minutes or so. We've been monitoring your transmissions and we know the whole story but we're not quite 'home n dry' yet. The British Government has further need of your skills."

Over the next ten minutes. Danny told Lawrence everything that he could remember starting with the problems with Baker at the flying club in North Weald, through his abduction and onto his landing at Capri.

"Dan, according to this, we should be visual any time now. We're actually on collision course so I'd like you to turn right ten degrees but keep a look out for me over your left shoulder. Is that clear?"

Danny's windscreen was again covered in dead flies. There were thousands of them in this part of the world and most of them appeared to be mashed onto his windscreen. He had already cleaned it at the grove that morning yet it was practically opaque again with a layer of squashed, juicy bugs. A single dead insect stuck to the windshield could easily obscure an approaching aircraft until it was perilously close. With closing speeds of approx. two hundred and fifty miles an hour it was imperative that he established visual contact as soon as possible.

"Ah, I've got you Dan. I think it's you. Rock your wings for me. Yeah, got you. We're about two miles adrift. Keep your heading and I'll come around behind you."

The Bulldog was a full thirty knots or so faster than the Pup 100 and would have no problems catching up.

"Well I'll be damned if I can see you." Replied Danny. "My windshield's a mess. I've never seen so many bugs before."

The Bulldog duly passed to Danny's left, turned one hundred and eighty degrees and eventually pulled alongside. Lawrence held his right hand up in a half wave/ half 'I'm pleased to see you too' gesture.

"A friendly face at last" replied Dan as he waved back.

As the two aircraft fell in to tandem formation, Lawrence Scrolled through the menu options on his *'Desktrak'* programme which was flashing madly indicating arrival and contact with '3333.' He entered '9999' and the unit took up the task of tracking its new target. Seconds later it displayed a new set of bearings and 'ETA's.'

"Thirty seven minutes to destination Dan. I'll brief you as we go."

CHAPTER 47

Ruth felt sick. She had always been terrified of Mario. He had beaten her up badly once before when she had failed to entertain an important client of his to the man's complete satisfaction. She had accompanied him all day to the race meeting and laughed at his dreadful jokes, which he cracked relentlessly. She dined with him at Sabatinis in Rome that evening and hid her disgust and embarrassment as the fat pig belched his way through four courses. His breath stank and his manners were like that of a Viking. She later refused to sleep with the man so he raped her. The scratches that she left in his cheek took two weeks to heal properly. The bruises that Mario left on hers took six.

Ruth also felt very confused. She found herself experiencing an emotional rush that made the tears well in her eyes and a lump develop in her throat. Rational thought had abandoned her. A conflict of emotion raged within her and she leapt from one train of thought to another and back again. She began to talk out aloud to herself as if she were her own mother lecturing her about what she should do. She loved him but she hated him. Because of him, she would now have to face up to Mario once again and she couldn't take another beating. Why then, if she hated Danny so much was she crying? She loved him because he was the first good man that she had known. She hated him because he gave Rebecca everything that she needed and that she herself had never had. She hated him because he was un-hateable and she felt more comfortable hating men.

"I do hate you, I do. If you were here now I would kiss you. Just who do you think you are, going off and leaving me here? I love you Danny. Mum, is that you Mum? What are you doing here? Have you seen Danny?" Ruth wept. In between the phases of crying she began to laugh. She would then suddenly return to whimpering as her delusions increased.

The package containing the *'Destiny'* resin had been loaded carelessly into the luggage space behind her seat. Mario had chastised the worker in the cellar for not taking enough care when removing the package from its wooden crate. The man had not taken kindly to being embarrassed in front of the others. He didn't care much for Mario anyway. He had always been wary of the boy who stole oranges from the grove when he was the manager there and responsible for the losses. He knew that the towns-folk made excuses for the cheeky little boy Mario, with his impish looks and golden tongue, but he knew that behind the angelic face and loveable, roguish personality that seemed to captivate everyone else, was an evil, cold-hearted villain.

It was he who had taken the girl back to her parents in the village after Mario had abandoned her in the grove. Francesca adored Mario. He was her first love and whilst her heart was filled with love and romance, Mario had just one thing on his mind. The other boys had bet him that the virgin Francesca would still be so at the end of the summer. He had sweet talked her for weeks and believed that she was ready to succumb. She wasn't but that didn't stop Mario. Enzo had found her lying under a tree crying, her dress stained with blood from the savage intrusion and her underwear missing, which Mario had taken as proof of his wager. Enzo helped the girl to clean up and took her home. He knew that she wouldn't say anything. Nobody would have believed this of the 'wonderful' Mario Marcantonio. She would have been ridiculed and outcast.

In his anger, Enzo had carelessly thrown the resin package into the back of the aircraft in defiance of this fraudster. He knew in his heart that no good would come of this madness and that ill fortune would befall the village in divine retribution. As Ruth had circled, frantically searching the skies for a sign of Danny, several tears in the wrapping had developed. Although the apertures were only small, the fumes had been gathering for some time in the cabin and Ruth was overcome by them. She suddenly threw up. Mother nature and fate had both conspired against her this time, blending unrequited love with noxious substance. In her compromised state of mind, instead of finding a place somewhere between love and hate, she spent moments experiencing extremes of each instead.

"Danny, is that you my love? Where have you been you bastard?"

Something suddenly caught her attention and she looked out to see an aircraft taking up formation off her port side. Danny had come back for her after all. He was signalling to her, rocking his wings. He obviously had radio problems. Yes, that was it! She was so very pleased to see him although she was still feeling very confused. She thought that she could suddenly see two of him framed against the vivid blue sky.

"I'm so tired Danny. Hold me Dan, Love me Danny, I hate you!"

Ruth was unconscious as her aircraft plunged into the ocean. The intercepting American pilots from USAF Sigonella had no idea who Ruth was or what she was carrying, or indeed the nature of her distress squawk. They watched helplessly as the Pup ditched in the ocean.

"Eagle one, did you see anyone evacuate the aircraft before it sank?"

"Negative."

CHAPTER 48

It was a matter of honour. Yan Slavic had become a soldier immediately after leaving college and long before the current civil war had started. He quickly rose through the ranks to reach officer status. His family and village were proud of him and those who served under him admired his leadership skills and his strength in combat. This particular situation, however, was a disgrace. He would rather have been killed in battle than suffer the shame of failure in such a fashion. It was a simple enough task, to guard two captured airmen, yet, to have his whole squad overcome in a matter of moments, was an absolute humiliation. Pride was a powerful motivator and, in this instance, it would come after the fall and not before.

Yan was also very shrewd. From humiliation, he hoped would come commendation and recognition. That they had been attacked was undeniable. The circumstances and outcome of that aggression however, were, as yet, unpublicised and known only to Yan and his platoon. It was his intention to recapture the two prisoners along with their liberators and profess to his superiors to have survived the onslaught, capturing the unknown aggressors and finding favour and accolade instead. The alternative was disgrace.

Although they had at least half a day's head start, Yan was confident that he would catch up. He knew that the failing health of both the airmen would slow them down and they would not be as familiar with the territory as he was. Yan and his colleagues studied the maps laid on the table.

"There will be only two possible ways out of the country for them" said Yan. "They will not go south nor east, that would only take them further into our heartland. No, They will go west to the sea or north by foot over the mountains. This terrain offers no way out by air for a suitable aircraft other than a helicopter, but these people are obviously no fools. A helicopter would be a sitting duck for our forces."

Yan studied the map further before he made his decision. "We will split into two groups of three. I will go west towards the coast with Stefan and Milan, as I am sure that they will head for the coast. The other three will go north. Ivan, you must stay here and tend the injured." He traced a line from the compound towards the Adriatic and the path lay directly along the valley floor. The others looked at each other seeking reassurance but it was obvious that they were having serious doubts about the proposals.

"Captain, this is a vast area and we are only in groups of three. Even if we are lucky enough to find them, we don't know how many of them there are. We could be heavily out numbered." Yan explained that *they* would have the advantage of stealth and surprise this time. The enemy would be travelling as light as possible with limited arms. *They* however, would be fully equipped. He reminded them that it was a 'matter of honour' and they must not, and would not fail. No one questioned him again.

Yan and his men had no trackers or hi tech equipment to assist them at all. What they did have, however, were dogs. One of the assailants had obviously been injured in the attack and his blood stained jacket was left behind along with the bowie knife that they had retrieved from Lanic's shoulder. The wooden handle of the knife was worn and a cloth had been tightly wrapped around it to assist the grip. These would be sufficient for the dogs to recognise the scent. The hounds were given a last sniff and they tore off into the forest with the men close behind.

The morphine had run out. It was of no matter to Gil Pertwee. The fever was raging and he had hardly survived the night. Every once in a while, without rousing from his unconsciousness, he would scream and protest at the pain then fall silent for a while until another wave of subliminal suffering manifested itself with a further tortured yell. The lack of sedation was of more concern to Emil. He felt sure that the crippled airman's cries of anguish would surely deliver them back to the Serbs who were no doubt in pursuit and not far behind. His depleted first aid supplies now offered only a solitary rolled crepe bandage, which he thrust into Pertwee's mouth to stifle every scream as it occurred, removing it only when he fell silent to assist his breathing.

Douglas Washington was lucid but unable to move. General exhaustion, malnutrition and pneumonia had rendered him immobile. Doug's biggest problem was the onset of hypothermia, which would kill him if he spent a further night on the mountain. The last few days had also taken their toll on Broussard. His training and years in the 'legion' had taught him to survive by eating berries and insects. A stranger to this part of the world, unfamiliar with its indigenous plant life, he had obviously eaten something offensive causing him bouts of diarrhoea during the night and he had begun to recognise the initial stages of dehydration. Emil conserved his energy, moving only when necessary. He licked the morning dew from the leaves, offering a few of the precious, captured raindrops to his sick companions also.

'Today,' Emil concluded, they would face their own 'destiny.' It would offer them death or liberation.

The three fugitives were sufficiently hidden in the under growth at the perimeter of the clearing. A small handgun with eight rounds of ammunition, a Swiss army knife and Emil's' failing strength were their only defences if needed.

Emil raised his field glasses once again scanning the surrounding area. It was moments later that he first heard it. He swept the area with his glasses but could see nothing. He heard the bell once again and seconds later, the first goat came over the hill followed by several others and two herders. They were heading straight for the clearing in a direction that would lead them towards his sick companions. Emil had come to far, only to be discovered by two shepherds. He would have to do something and quickly. Emil knew that the sight of two NATO Air Force uniforms would send the goat herders running off for help. He, however, was dressed in non-specific military fatigues and could readily pass as an errant soldier in need of help.

Emil summoned his remaining strength and rose to a squatting position. Douglas Washington had seen the shepherds and managed to nod an approval to

Broussard, as he seemed to know what he was thinking. At that moment, Pertwee let out an agonising cry that tore through the fresh mountain air like the squawk of a crow. The two Serb goat herders stopped dead in their tracks and looked over towards the undergrowth where they were hiding. Pertwee had unwittingly made the decision for Emil who promptly leapt to his feet and limped out into the open ground where the shepherds could readily see him. The limp was designed to show them that he was injured and in pain and that it was he who had yelled out. It would also hopefully throw them off their guard, believing that he was in need of assistance and incapable of attacking them.

Emil had hastily inserted the bandage roll into Pertwee's mouth to prevent any more untimely screams but he decided to shout out himself just in case. "Hoi, hoi!" he yelled, waving his arms at the two men to attract their attention. He mustered the biggest smile that he could manage in an attempt to show them how pleased he was to see them. The two goat herders just stood completely still where they were, curiously transfixed as Emil lumbered towards them. As he was just yards away, once again Gil Pertwees' agony rose to a scream that the gag could not prevent, alerting the shepherds to his presence in the undergrowth. One of them immediately pulled a knife in readiness for the approaching mercenary. At that point, Emil abandoned the limp and simply pulled out his handgun from inside his jacket. There was no resistance at all, just an astonished submission from the two goat farmers who readily laid face down on the ground with their arms and legs spread-eagled. Emil tethered their hands and reassured their safety with several 'Oks' and led them back to the woods where he tied them securely to a tree. He turned to Doug and received another nodding approval.

"Goats!"

Emil was totally surprised by Doug's announcement. "Goats milk" he wheezed again. Recognising how rich, nutritious and needed it was, Doug had found the breath to alert Broussard to the opportunity of some much needed sustenance. Most of the herd had stayed together in the middle of the clearing but one or two stragglers had begun to stray and a couple had wandered over to the hedge. It was a simple matter for Emil to grab one by its rope collar. He rummaged through his rucksack and found a suitable receptacle for the milk and chuckled as he said to Doug

"Billy-can, what else!"

He'd never actually milked a goat or anything such before and he crouched beside the animal, looking towards the shepherds for advice and a certain amount of approval. The herders nodded and smiled nervously as the juice began to flow. Emil offered the first drops to them in acknowledgement of their assistance and as an indication that he wished them no harm.

Pertwee was next. Emil gently raised his head and poured some of the sweet, sticky liquid into his throat. Even though he coughed most of it back up again, he ingested a small, beneficial amount. Douglas drank slowly, catching his breath between sips and nodded when he had drank sufficient. Emil returned to the animal, which gave a further small amount of milk. He readily accepted it and drank before releasing the creature to wander off to find the rest of the herd, which had now begun to disperse.

Emil checked the battery life of the transmitter once again then he settled back against the oak tree. He checked his watch and closed his eyes for a moments rest.

"Air rifles? I don't understand Captain, why air rifles? Why not high velocity firearms with silencers?" The question bothered Yan as much as his subordinates. Something was nagging in the back of his mind and he stood a while to consider exactly why.

"Why indeed air rifles?" he repeated and pondered. The dogs had found the discarded tranquilliser rifles quite quickly. The hollow that Emil had dug was next, containing empty ration containers and surveillance photographs but nothing to help the Serbs establish the identity of their attackers.

"They did not use traditional firearms presumably because they didn't want to kill anybody initially," reasoned Yan to his men as he was beginning to formulate an impression of what had actually happened. "I believe that Lanic fired first and they responded swiftly as only they could under the circumstances. No… they did not want to kill us but things went wrong." After a few more moments' deliberation, Yan concluded, "These are people who do not want or cannot afford to be drawn into this war…" It began to get clearer to Yan as he spoke out aloud. "Because… they are part of the UN and because if the United Nations declare war on Serbia, then the rest of Europe will join in and our Russian friends will not stand by without helping us. Because gentlemen…of World War Three! That is exactly what they don't want and exactly what we do! Our lands will fall without help from the other communist countries. Gentlemen, listen very carefully to me. We will all receive great honour and do our country a great service. We can draw the west into this war quite simply by capturing and executing these men who are undoubtedly British along with their Air force colleagues. The British will not stand by and see their soldiers killed without a fitting response. Their government will have to retaliate but we will argue that these deaths were quite legitimate as we were attacked first. Gentlemen, we will be heroes!" Yan picked up his field radio and called his team that had headed north. He instructed them to 'kill on site' and return only with dead bodies.

Yan was no stranger to the hills. He had often hunted there, as a boy and he knew exactly the right paths to take.

They had been searching for hours along the stream in the gully between the hills when suddenly; one of the tracker dogs began to bark ferociously, way ahead of them in the forest. Yan and his companions immediately dropped to a stooping position and listened. The dogs were going crazy. They were trained to respond in this fashion only when they had come into contact with the scent that they had been tracing.

The Serbian soldiers leapt to their feet and ran through the forest with their rifles cocked in readiness to finish the job that the dogs had started. They were obviously tearing their prey apart.

Yan was the first to arrive at the scene and signalled his men to circle left and right. The five dogs had their victim pinned to the ground and were tearing at the flesh. Yan raised his rifle to shoulder level and signalled the others to join him. With the dogs firmly in his sights he ran into the middle of the affray shouting at them to 'leave.'

All was not as it seemed. As Stefan and Milan pulled the dogs away, the torn, bleeding, crippled body of a goat tried desperately to get to its feet and escape to safety. It finally fell down, terminally wounded, bleating in terror as the bloodhounds were held at bay. Yan kicked one of the dogs shouting 'stupid creatures.' He didn't realise that, far from being stupid, the hounds had actually attacked the goat that Emil had milked earlier as his scent was still on the animal.

Yan took a small handgun from its holder and improvised a silencer by holding his jacket over the barrel as he sent a small bullet into the animal's brain killing it instantly. The sound of a muffled gunshot was a familiar one in the hills in recent times; the sound of an agonised dying goat was not and would only arouse suspicion.

As the dogs calmed down and the soldiers prepared to continue their search, Yan's field radio crackled into life. The team that had gone north reported that they had found the dead body of a soldier that had apparently only just recently bleed to death. They believed that it was probably the one that Lanic had shot. His Uniform was unusual, being neither Serb nor Croat. They reported that the dogs had a strong scent and were tracking well.

Yan kicked the goat to make sure that it was actually dead and out of frustration that he had made a wrong decision. "Well, it would appear that I was wrong" he explained to his colleagues. "I felt sure that they would head west, towards the sea but it appears that they went north after all. The others have found a dead soldier; the one that Lanic shot. He will be very pleased when I tell him. We will go back around the hills to the north to join them."

The three Serbs went back down the hill and Yan stopped to wash the goat's brains off his hands and face in the stream.

There were many sounds that the hills had to offer. Other than those proffered by nature herself, the sounds of war were familiar to Yan and his men. It was quite commonplace for a fighter to roar overhead and the dull thud of the far off guns, relentlessly pounding Bihac and Banja luka, seldom stopped. This particular sound was different though. It was unfamiliar and Yan stopped washing to listen to it. The others stopped to listen too. Faint at first, it appeared to grow louder and come closer. It was similar to a band saw that relentlessly went about its business without stopping for breath. Yan stood Upright and identified the direction from which it came. He recognised the sound only seconds before the two light aircraft came into sight. They came from the west, over the top of the trees and began to descend onto the very mountaintop from which Yan and his men had just left.

"I knew they were here, I knew it!" he shouted as they released the dogs once again and ran after them with their rifles cocked and ready once again.

CHAPTER 49

The Morgana berthed in her usual fashion at Palermo, Sicily and Mario skipped through customs to make a familiar rendezvous with his suppliers. His Godfather would be very pleased with him and he was anxious to report his progress to the Don. Everything was going to plan and on schedule.

The underground laboratory on the Marineo estate, high in the mountains, would soon have to increase its production of the resin. Once *'Destiny'* was established in the UK; mainland Europe, France Germany and Holland would follow. Mario was going to suggest to the Don that the vaults of the villa in Niapello's orange grove would make an excellent production site also. His village would, at last, be financially secure and the people would bestow great honour on both him and his father.

Mario walked out of the terminal and on towards the black limo parked in its usual place. Instead of being shown into the back seat as normal, the driver, whom he did not recognise as one of the regulars, gave him the customary shipment case and told him that the Godfather was unable to see him today and that he was to make his delivery as normal. The chauffeur watched Mario return to the ship and waited until it sailed before he made his phone call.

" He is definitely on board, yes, and he has the case. The rest is up to you."

Mario was a creature of habit and routine. Once again he made his way straight below decks and into his cabin. He stored the aluminium case under the bed and poured himself a whiskey. Since his recent notable successes and consequent newly found favour with Don Marineo, Mario had begun to take liberties with his position as chief engineer. The title was effectively a 'front' now and he played less and less of an active role. His knowledge of the fleets engines and workings however, was still superior and, although he spent most of his time in his cabin, he was still at hand in case of any serious problems. Leaving orders not to be disturbed unless really necessary, Mario closed his eyes for his usual short sleep.

The Morgana sailed south towards Malta and, once again, Mario woke automatically at the correct time and swung himself upright on the edge of the bunk. He checked his watch and reached down for the case, duly removing the model aircraft components ready for assembly in the usual fashion. Mario had assembled many of these little craft within the last couple of months and the process was now quite familiar, the delicate touch required being in total contrast to the brutal skills required of him as a Mafia hit man. Mafia executions were usually savage and demonstrative and there was no doubting Mario's prowess in this department yet he was gentle and methodical with the craft, which he fully assembled within ten minutes.

Another check of his watch revealed that it was almost time for the delivery. He took the remote unit from the case in readiness and then loaded the bag containing the *'Destiny'* tablets into the fuselage.

Still perched on the edge of the bed, Mario pressed the red 'master' button on the remote to activate the system. As he did so, he felt a sharp pain in his right thumb as if a needle had pricked it. He looked at the rubber button and noticed that there appeared to be a tiny hole in the centre of the cap. He then noticed that his thumb had formed a tiny bubble of blood at its tip. He curiously broke open the two halves of the simple aluminium case to reveal a small vial of liquid attached to a hypodermic needle. By pressing the button, the glass vile had initially been broken, releasing its contents into the needle, which had then duly pierced his thumb at the zenith of its travel. The nerve gas took only seconds to take effect. Instead of inducing unconsciousness, the special preparation rendered him immobile and speechless although still in contact with his reasoning and tactile senses. It was as if he had been chemically chained and gagged.

Moments later, his cabin door opened and a large man entered carrying a small black brief case. The visitor closed and locked the door behind him and laid his case on the table. Mario could only look on helplessly as the man opened the case and took out a framed photograph, standing it in an appropriate position on the table. He then placed a candle beside the picture, which he lit. Mario felt the words of panic and confusion form in his back throat yet they did not arrive at his mouth. The stranger then took a holy bible from his case, knelt and spent the next few minutes reciting chapters from it, interspersed with prayer and a final act of contrition. Eventually he turned and spoke to Mario.

"Do you recognise the lady in the photograph?" Even though he did not, he had no way of indicating a negative reply. The controlling muscles of his face had frozen, fixing him with a steadfast, sardonic grin. "Let me help jog your memory" said the stranger.

Vittorio Bartelli took a pair of gardener's secateurs from his case and snipped off the little finger from Mario's left hand, which he placed on the table next to the photograph. The pain seared through Mario's body, which was unable to provide the scream that he required to dissipate the agony. "I want you to say her name." Vittorio placed the next finger along into the jaws of the cutters. "Come now. Do you mean to tell me that you cut off the lady's finger without even knowing her name?" Vittorio knew full well that Mario was incapable of speech. A loud snap heralded the removal of another finger, which was subsequently placed alongside the other one on the table. "OK, so it was only one little finger" another dropped to the floor "but you took so much away from her with it, and you didn't even know her name." The fourth finger was a little more difficult to remove taking several attempts and ultimately requiring a two handed grip on the cutters. Mario now had only six fingers left.

Vittorio's skill as a chemist had been challenged in producing this particular nerve agent. The Biotech programme had been invaluable in suggesting an African tribal poison, Curare, as a prominent ingredient in his potion to achieve the required effect. He had designed the drug to not only immobilise Mario but to deny him unconsciousness when his system craved it.

187

"Let me give you a clue. 'S'... 'O'... With each letter, Vittorio removed another finger. " 'P' 'H' 'I' 'A' - SOPHIA!"

All of Mario's fingers were now lined up on the table next to the picture of Sophia Bartelli. "You didn't even know her name. Such a beautiful name but more so than just a name. The word Sophia means Beauty. It means passion. It means love and devotion and all that is good. Such a beautiful word. Were I to allow you to live, it is a word that you should learn, for, to me, it means life itself. For you, it will mean the opposite. I will watch you die with it on your lips but you will never have the privilege of saying it."

Vittorio did not speak again. He took the *'Destiny'* pills from the model aircraft and thrust several into Mario Marcantonio's throat and he sat back to watch him die.

CHAPTER 50

"It's a very short field Danny. Full flap and wheels down on the threshold OK?"

"Believe me, I've had some practice!" replied Dan.

Even though Danny was the only instructor of the two, Lawrence had spent hours studying the field from the spy satellite photographs and took the initiative as flight leader.

"We wont have time for backtrack either," Lawrence continued. "We go in one way, turn straight around and go out the other, despite the wind."

Emil Broussard was the first one to hear the aircraft as they approached and he let out a 'Thank God' as he leapt to his feet. He immediately helped Douglas Washington to his and, despite his protestations, pulled Gil Pertwee to a sitting position. Emil had discussed the operation over and over with Lawrence and knew that the aircraft would arrive from the south if indeed they arrived at all. He had settled the pilots in the undergrowth at the north end of the field to minimise the distance and time spent on the ground.

The Bulldog came in first, a little too high, touching down rather later than expected a fair way along the field. Lawrence Had to 'swan neck' the aircraft in the same fashion that a slalom skier does towards the end of his run, to avoid running out of space. Moments later, Danny's Pup slipped over the edge of the trees, touching down exactly on the threshold, rolling and braking in time for a well placed arrival alongside the Bulldog.

Emil grabbed a fistful of Pertwee's jump suit and, with a mighty tug, swung him up and over his shoulder. He stumbled slightly whilst getting to his feet but made a recovery and set off towards the Bulldog. Emil had previously agreed with Lawrence that both He and Danny were to remain at the controls, no matter what, ready for immediate take-off if there were any problems. Lawrence had managed to pull back the Bulldog's canopy in readiness and Emil lumbered up onto the wing, slipping Pertwee, who was screaming incessantly, over the edge and into the spare seat.

"Go! Go!" he yelled as he jumped clear. Lawrence slammed the canopy shut and applied full throttle. The Bulldog skewered unevenly over the grass until Lawrence corrected and straightened the nose wheel at which point, it quickly gained speed and launched itself off the field with only a minimal clearance between it and the treetops at the southerly end.

Yan and his two military associates were half way up the hill when they heard the Bulldog overhead in a steep climb. They fired several shots at it, hitting fresh air mostly, with only a couple of bullets actually piercing the airframe.

Douglas Washington had been reserving what little energy he had left for exactly this moment and had taken several laboured steps out into the clearing. He quickly turned around as he heard the gunfire. Emil dropped to the floor instinctively but leapt to his feet again when he saw Douglas standing, vulnerably, in the open ground. He ran into Doug as if he were about to rugby tackle him to the floor but swept him up and over his shoulder instead without stopping, and continued to run towards the Pup.

Danny had already released the door catch in readiness but the Pup was actually facing the wrong way for departure. If he turned the aircraft around, ready for its takeoff run, the open, passenger door would be on the wrong side. Emil would have to carry Doug further, needing to go around the aircraft to gain access. Danny chose to stay positioned as he was and pick up his passenger first before manoeuvring. He had unbuckled his own harness but had strict instructions not to leave the controls. As Emil, whose strength and energy reserves were now faltering, staggered towards the Pup, Danny lent sideways towards the open door ready to assist. Emil's 'fireman's' lift eventually deposited the stricken airman, who was desperately fighting for breath, onto the starboard wing. As Danny leant further across to help him into the cockpit, he saw three soldiers run into the clearing at the southern end of the field.

Emil unceremoniously pushed Douglas into the cockpit, leaving him in a half standing position as he slammed the door shut. "Go. Now!" He ordered.

Emil jumped to the ground and took up a position between the aircraft and the approaching Serbs, effectively shielding the Pup from attack. He raised his arms in acknowledgement of the fact that he had nowhere to go and would submit readily to capture. The first bullet hit him in his left thigh. The second bullet arrived moments later and lodged itself in his stomach. He fell to the ground bleeding profusely and writhing in agony.

Danny had started his takeoff run and was actually heading directly towards the Serbian soldiers. A normal take off roll would place him more or less parallel with them at the point of rotation. He had cast aside his headset on arrival and the engine noise in the cockpit was severe. He was desperately trying to fly the aircraft with his left hand, pull Doug into the passenger seat with his right and scan the instruments at the same time when a side cockpit window suddenly shattered as a bullet passed through it. Danny looked up and out to see the Serbian sniper kneeling in front of him in the distance, with his rifle poised at shoulder level.

Although a fast moving target, the Pup was now only one hundred yards away from the Serbs and closing. Yan steadied himself and tracked the aircraft in his rifle sights. With his simple, bolt action rifle, he would have time for one, maybe two more shots before the aircraft became airborne. He would have to make them count.

Danny was engrossed by the spectre of the soldier pointing a rifle at him. The harsh reality that someone was trying to kill him welded his concentration to the job at hand. Remembering how the new flaps had propelled him into the air at Bradwell, his first instinct was to slam them down and get airborne as soon as possible. A nagging doubt froze his hand to the flap actuator switch before he could actually lower them. Instinct told him that he would be better off keeping a lower profile for as long as possible so he chose to hold the Pup on the ground as the speed rapidly increased, aiming the aircraft directly at the sniper instead. It would be a Mexican standoff.

Danny yanked Doug's collar and pulled his head forward to remove him from the line of fire. The instrument panel was hardly bullet proof but it was the best protection that the aircraft had to offer him so Danny made sure his passenger was hidden behind it. Danny chose to sit erect and stare his attacker in the eye. He also figured that the only weapons he had were the whirling metal blades of his propeller. Spinning at 2,700 RPM, they would also offer him some nominal protection against any shots fired, deflecting them at least he hoped.

As Yan inched to the right and repositioned for a broadside shot, Danny gently pushed his left rudder pedal to maintain his head-on collision course with the Serb whose finger had began to tighten around his trigger. It was now a matter of whose nerve would hold longest in an adult version of the game of 'Chicken.'

The yards between them slipped away and eventually the first shot rang out. Emil always carried a small handgun and, with a single shot that was borne of the skills of a lifetime and an absolute desire for accuracy focused by his intense pain, from his supine position in the mud, he sent the solitary round stinging into the chest of the Serb commander who fell directly into the path of Danny's propeller, decapitating him instantly.

One of the two remaining Serbian soldiers reacted by sending a volley of bullets in Emil's' direction, running towards him as he did so. Emil lived long enough to see 'Mike Alpha' eventually get airborne with its freshly acquired red livery.

The last Serb who was some twenty yards away from his commander when he died, instinctively raised his own small firearm and began to empty his magazine into the now airborne Pup, which presented more of itself as a target as it flew directly overhead.

Most of the rounds passed harmlessly through the skin of the fuselage. One, however, chose the skin of the Pilot, entering his upper back from the left side, shattering his shoulder blade before passing out the front of his chest and lodging in the instrument panel.

The pain was intense. Danny had never known such a level of physical trauma and he instinctively grabbed hold of the wound with his right hand, desperately trying to stem the blood flow, letting go of the control column in the process. A momentary pitch downwards was rectified by Douglas Washington who found the strength and courage to resume the flight. He initiated a steep turn right and immediately took the Pup out of gunfire range.

Inspired by his sense of freedom, Douglas Washington once again took on the mantle of hero for which he had been decorated on many occasions. This was Doug's environment. It was simply a natural motor function for Doug to fly an aeroplane and he could do it in his sleep. It was as natural to him as breathing, although he was currently having severe difficulty in that department.

Doug took the Pup to a safe height before he considered what to do next. Danny was conscious but so consumed with pain that he was of no use at all. Doug had no visual with the Bulldog but noticed a pair of headphones that had hastily been discarded in the well between the seats. As he held them closer to his ears, he could hear someone transmitting. Doug pulled the set properly into place over his own head.

"*Mike Alpha*' come in. Danny, are you OK? Over."

"Station calling this...is Douglas Washington. Danny's hit, I'm ...in control."

"My God! Douglas, this is Lawrence Carlton in the Bulldog. What's your exact situation sir?"

"My companion...has gunshot wound...shoulder...losing a lot of blood." Douglas fought for the breath to finance every word. "He's on the edge of consciousness. 'I'm...in control, severe...breathing difficulties. Re...request instructions. Over."

Lawrence had not considered the eventuality that Danny would be injured. Douglas Washington was obviously very ill himself and his breathing difficulties would only worsen in the thinner air offered at the altitude that they needed to fly at to avoid small arms fire. Lawrence's own passenger was also in severe distress and could offer no assistance. Weeks of planning had gotten him this far and Lawrence wasn't going to lose anyone at this stage. He was just about to find out if he had the 'right stuff' that pilots were rumoured to be made of, namely, a cool head and a steady hand.

"Douglas, is your GPS on the air?" he enquired.

"...N ...egative." came the laboured reply.

"OK. I want you to put your transponder on and squawk **9999**."

Both Lawrence and Danny had switched off their transponder units when they had first made contact with each other, to cut down the amount of spurious signals that they were sending in the war zone. Lawrence set his '*Desktrak*' to receive and track '9999.'

"OK Doug. I'm tracking you quite clearly. Turn left ninety degrees onto a heading of due west. Head straight for the sea. Do you copy?" There was no reply for several agonising moments as Douglas searched for the breath to answer.

"Affirm...Two seven zero...degrees."

The Bulldog was still over Croatia, at least ten minutes from the coast and Lawrence was certainly not going to initiate an orbit over a war zone in an attempt to let the Pup catch up.

"Once we're out over the ocean we'll attempt to establish visual. Just hang on Douglas. We're nearly home and dry. Medical help is waiting. Lawrence could barely comprehend the reply as Doug's breathing was deteriorating rapidly.

'*Desktrak*' showed both aircraft to be at three thousand feet and climbing, approx. five miles apart. Suddenly, Lawrence noticed that '*Mike Alpha*' was rapidly losing height. The programme indicated a descent rate of twelve hundred feet a minute. The Pup was obviously in a nosedive.

" *'Mike Alpha'*- Doug! What's going on? Declare your status!" Lawrence tried many times to raise Doug but there was no reply. The Pup was going down.

"Mike Alpha, Douglas, for Gods sake! Pull up! Pull up...Christ! I've lost them!"

Lawrence watched helplessly as the screen showed *'Mike Alpha'* to be in a two thousand foot a minute nose dive, far exceeding its VNE speed. The small crafts airframe would not stand up to the ferocity of the plummet and the wings would surely be torn off.

Lawrence accepted what appeared to be the inevitable and he was overwhelmed by a sudden guilt. His thoughts curiously turned to Rebecca. It was as if he had encouraged her to gamble a husband to gain a father but now she had actually lost them both. What would he say to her? How could she ever forgive him? Another thought then entered his head. One, which had been trying to surface for some time now but needed prompting by a disaster such as this. Margaret. Sweet, supportive, devoted Margaret. Lawrence had known for some time of her feelings towards him and he had been strangely jealous of her liaison with Gabriel. He had suppressed his reciprocal emotions for two reasons. Firstly, as a sign of respect for Barbara, and secondly, because he could not endure such a level of loss again in the event that anything should ever happen to a new love. Detachment had been his companion for many years now and he felt safe within its walls. It had brought much loneliness at times but it had also offered him a certain security within his new strength of character while he grieved for his dead wife. The realisation now however, was dramatic. In the face of death, Lawrence knew that it was time to let go of the past and seize the fragile future with two firm but gentle hands. If he managed to return safely, he would ask Margaret to marry him. Barbara would understand.

CHAPTER 51

USAF Sigonella was situated in Sicily on its eastern borders, just inland from Catania. Until now, its main claim to fame was to launch two intercept fighters that forced a fleeing aircraft containing Abul Abbas and three of his 'Palestine Liberation Front' terrorist colleagues, to land there after they had hijacked the ferryboat 'Achille Lauro' and murdered the passenger Leon Klinghoffer. The wheelchair bound elderly Jewish gentleman had been shot in cold blood and his body thrown overboard somewhere in the Syrian sea. The Hijackers subsequently sought refuge in Cairo after sailing the ship through the Suez Canal and the Egyptians obligingly provided them with an aircraft for their escape.

Ronald Reagan and Colonel Oliver North had decided to force the plane down at Sigonella but found themselves facing the wrath of the Italian army when they tried to arrest the terrorists at the Sicilian base. A stand off ensued with both sides holding the other to arms. The Americans eventually capitulated and Abul Abbas was freed to resume his journey and eventually enjoy his liberty in Yugoslavia.

It was now time to even the score.

The base played host most weekends to the various marines, seamen and officers who would normally occupy the great carriers and battle ships such as the 'Ma Baker' and the 'Missouri,' that routinely patrolled the surrounding seas.

The revellers were flown in by helicopter in shifts that would provide them with a weekend of complete abandon with all of the base's facilities at their disposal.

The Crater club hosted a band and a DJ every night and there was no shortage of American girls who worked as civilian operatives on the base, who were eager to party with the guys.

Naval commander Chuck D. Vine was in the club when the call came through. The club steward 'Ski' had just taken down the sign on the wall, which informed the patrons of the style of music being played there that night. He replaced the 'VARIETY' sign with the one that said 'ROCK' just as the guitarist tore into the solo in 'Freebird.'

"Say again, the damn band just got started."

The caller repeated his message as the commander stood holding the phone tightly to his ear whilst the first finger of his free hand was pressed firmly into his other one to dampen the noise. "Goddamn!" was his initial, incredulous reaction. "And on whose authority?" he enquired

"The President of the United States sir" came the unmistakeable reply.

"This better be for real son!"

"The necessary codes are with your ship already Commander. You are to return immediately."

Chuck D. Vine hung up and rubbed the back of his neck.

"Goddamn!" He repeated to the amazement of his onlookers. The wizened-faced naval commander chewed on his cigar as he walked back over to his colleagues who were still sitting at the bar consuming large doses of Michelob beer and larger amounts of 'Lynyrd Skynyrd' provided by the band. "Sorry boys; all leave's cancelled. Believe it or not, we've gotta job to do! We're goin' straight back to the 'Bute.' "

The 'Bute' was the crews' nickname for the formidable aircraft carrier from whence they had come, which some also called the 'Brute' due to her massive firepower.

The announcement that 'leave' was cancelled was greeted with a mixed bag of reactions ranging from slight curiosity as to 'why,' through deep consternation, to 'too drunk to care.'

Chuck was momentarily distracted from his thoughts by a commotion that had broken out over by the DJ booth. A particular marine was hassling the DJ to play his favourite record 'right now' despite the fact that the band was in the middle of it's set. His persistence eventually led to the arrival of a Military Police officer who cautioned him and delivered him back to his friends on the dance floor by way of a slightly painful arm lock. This was a standard incident for officer Lopez on a Friday night in the club. He tried to be particularly tolerant with these boys though. He knew what it was like to graft for six weeks on a ship without setting foot on dry land. The boys worked hard and played hard and they were 'just lettin' go some gas,' he would argue.

Suddenly, Officer Lopez felt a sharp burning sensation in his right shoulder. It took a few moments for him to realise that he'd been stabbed.

"Will Ya' look at that crazy son of a bitch" said Chuck who had seen the troublesome sailor pull the knife and attack the MP. As a crowd gathered around the affray, Lopez turned, grabbed his assailant by the throat and pinned him against the wall.

"You crazy mother! I warned you once. You're gonna pay now boy!"

Showing great restraint and nursing a flesh wound only, Lopez cuffed the marine's hands and read him his rights. The sailor spat in his face and Lopez ducked away wiping the curiously claret stained spit from his cheek with his sleeve.

"Hey Lopez" an onlooker shouted. "Ya' hit him too hard. Ya' gone broke his nose!"

"I never touched the mother and he's lucky I 'aint" he replied. The marine's nose had suddenly begun to bleed profusely and Lopez wondered if he had inadvertently head butted him in all the commotion. The marine began to cough and splutter then his mouth suddenly opened and erupted all over the MP, covering his jacket in blood.

"Holy shit! This boy's sick. Get a medic in here!" cried Lopez.

By the time the paramedic had arrived, the marine had already bled to death on the floor of the club.

"Drug overdose I'd say sir."

Chuck Stood over the body appalled at what he saw, as the medical officer explained further. "Looks like another '*Destiny*' related death Sir. We've had three in the last month." The medic told the commander that there had been several reported incidences at other US air bases throughout the Med' over the last couple of weeks. It was a virtually unknown substance and they had no effective remedy as yet. The commander listened intently to what he had to say. When he had finished, Chuck replied

"Don't you worry about it son, I've just been given a cure."

The commander snapped his fingers and left the club with his officers, leaving the medic wondering just what he had meant.

The special 'Ops' room on the 'Bute' went to green 'level one,' alert readiness. The commander went over the charts once again and confirmed the co-ordinates with his officers.

"OK, go to Def' Con' two."

"Def' Con' two sir, affirm" was the read-back confirmation. Level two secured the doors of the control room preventing any entry or exit. It also reduced the lighting level to a red hue, which left the radar screens prominently visible. Armed guards were placed at every ten yards around the room and the US Battle Cruiser 'RETRIBUTION' became fully at Battle stations.

"Well boys, one way or another, I imagine we're gonna make the papers tomorrow. Keys Captain?" The first officer unbuttoned his regulation khaki shirt and removed the chain that had hung around his neck since he had first accepted his commission. "Insert on my mark. Three two one, Mark!" Both the commander and the first officer inserted their keys instantaneously. "Turn on my mark. Three two one, Mark!" Both men stood down from the console. Chuck spoke to the weapons room on the intercom and confirmed their readiness.

"OK Boys, I thought we'd had enough of this sort of thing in the Gulf." As he pressed the red launch button he declared

"It's time for some more D. Vine Retribution!"

The phone on the great oak table rang twice only before Darius Marineo answered it. His father and brothers were away on business and he stayed behind to manage the estate in their absence. He did not have the stomach for violence that the rest of his family seemed to posses but his business acumen secured him an important administrative role in the family. He had spent six months establishing the laboratory and it was now fully productive.

196

"Father?" His Father and brothers had not returned home when expected and Darius presumed that it was he who was calling. The voice at the other end took a moment to answer.

"Listen very carefully to what I have to say." The American accent secured his attention immediately. "You people have crossed the line this time. You have killed Americans and we will not tolerate that. Peddle your filth amongst yourselves. You have fifteen minutes to evacuate your women and children. God Bless America."

High above the island of Sicily, an American Stealth bomber monitored the launch of the two Tomahawk guided missiles from the US Battle Cruiser 'RETRIBUTION.' The 'Bute' was situated in the Ionian sea between Greece and Italy, its presence in the area being at the behest of the UN security council to add weight to its operations in Bosnia if required. The missiles' progress was beamed back to the 'Bute' by the Stealth and Chuck and his officers watched their flight path on a large, upright, see-through, glass display.

"Their home and dry Gentlemen." Said Chuck. "Nothing can stop them now. I doubt if these guys will have any 'chaff' at hand' he laughed. "I only hope the damn things get round that mother of a mountain!" he laughed.

"That mountain's actually a volcano sir. Mount Etna I believe, sir." Replied the first officer.

"Volcano did you say?" The Commander looked suddenly pensive. "Is it active? "

"I believe so sir." As he replied, the first officer realised just why Chuck D. Vine had enquired.

"Abort!" Ordered Chuck suddenly.

"Sir?"

"Abort Goddamn it! The sulphur and phosphorous fumes from that thing is gonna blitz the guidance system. We're gonna have a disaster here! Abort!"

"Sir, with respect we just can't self destruct now. 'Toms' are over Catania at this moment and there's gonna be some 'fall out' debris with possible civilian consequences."

" Then go to manual for Christ's sake, just get 'em away from there!"

The first officer entered the relevant codes and the system eventually surrendered control to him via the joysticks on the panel.

"Got one, got … two sir. We have manual on both sir. Instructions please."

"Christ man, just fly 'em outta there!"

"Where… exactly sir?"

The Commander hastily dismissed his first officer from the console by pulling him out of his seat by his collar and took charge of the control columns himself. Chuck had helped extinguish the oil fires that the retreating republican guard had left burning all over Kuwait a few years before hand. He was familiar with the missile systems and had flown several manually into the heart of the infernos, duly 'snuffing' out the flames.

"With respect sir, that's a densely populated area. Destruct is not an option." Chuck didn't answer. He fixed his gaze on the screen and suddenly threw both columns to the right.

"Now back, that's it. C'mon beauties. We're gonna stick 'em in the hole boys" he declared to the bewilderment of his subordinates.

The brace of Tomahawks climbed up the southern edge of the volcano and as they rounded the apex of the vast crater, Chuck thrust the columns forward, sending them both plummeting down into the molten lava that filled its belly. The 'Ops' room officers looked stunned and waited for the mountain to erupt at any second. Chuck let go the sticks and stood up smiling. He noticed the look of horror on his crews face.

"It's OK boys, I'm not stupid. I disarmed them first! Now, get me the 'Stealth' on frequency."

The federal drug administration had waged a year long, ruthless campaign against the drug cartels. The Cosa Nostre were pursued at every turn and FBI officers had infiltrated the organisation and others, in an attempt to stem the relentless flow of narcotics to its shores. They had extended the operation to Columbia and challenged the drug Barons on their home ground taking, not only their liberty, but their homes and possessions and those of their families and friends too. The message was loud and clear.

War raged about the city of Medellin and gun battles were commonplace between FBI agents and dealers trying to protect their growing fields and production facilities from attack. 'Biotech's' 'soft' option approach to the drug problem was supported by a very 'hard' military one.

The brief from on high was to stamp out the trade, 'whatever it takes.' The Sicilian problem was a logical extension of their general offensive and the committee of Senators, Military advisors and Federal officers that had gathered in an office deep in the Pentagon, unanimously sanctioned the attack.

Chuck D. Vine looked at the telex containing his orders once again.

" 'Whatever it takes' now I take that to mean 'whatever it takes' don't you son?" The first officer of the 'Bute' was twenty-five years the junior of his commanding officer and this was his first posting since graduating from naval college. His Degree in no way qualified him to give the supportive 'yes' that Chuck required of him. Only thirty years experience in the job, reading between the lines of the many orders received, and knowing just exactly how far to go in their application before the Pentagon denied responsibility, would justify his answer. He only had six months and the best reply he could muster was a delayed 'Er...'

198

"Don't worry son" continued Chuck. "It's my arse in the sling!"

The Stealth crew had watched in amazement as the two Tomahawks disappeared into the molten magma of Mount Etna. The 'HSD' (heat sensing display) was sensitive enough to detect any small amount of body heat radiating from an individual or creature from a distance of over three miles. The screen was a kaleidoscope of colours, the shades of red usually being the most intense areas of heat that were portrayed. The crew had never seen a 'white' register on the display before, but then they had never flown an operation over an active volcano before either. In fact, the heat radiating from the mountain was too much for the sensors to decipher so they defaulted a 'white' on the display.

"I have the authority Captain; Order number Charlie one Alpha Zulu three six two. 'Whatever it takes.' Now are you gonna make an issue of this son?" The menace in Chucks voice was enough to persuade the stealth Captain to comply.

"I guess not Commander but my own orders were to act as reconnaissance only."

"That's yesterdays news son. Today, I call the tune, is that clear?"

"I suppose so sir. Can I have that security clearance once again sir? Thank you sir." Chuck repeated his authorisation code and reaffirmed his seniority.

" Just what do you want us to do sir?"

"I believe you boys have got one or two 'GBU 15s' up there. Is that right?"

"Affirm" came the reply.

"OK. I want you to spend one of them for me. I'm sending you the data now, standby to receive."

'GBU 15s' were laser guided bombs. The crews that carried them nicknamed them 'Good-Bye Units' as nothing would survive their arrival. They were the epitome of 'smart' weaponry and had a devastating effect. Until now, they had only been used in a war zone. One, however, was about to go 'civilian.'

The Stealth flew at a height that made it invisible to the human eye as well as being 'cloaked' to radar screens. Its presence was undeniably felt though, should it decide to attack.

The 'HSD' was trained on the particular estate high in the westerly, mountainous, Mazara region of the island of Sicily. The zoom function rapidly brought the villa into close-up and myriad colours portrayed intense activity in and around the grounds. Several vehicles were seen to be leaving the area in a hurry. The pilot in the command left-hand seat had strict instructions to launch exactly on the hour. A ground based back up squad would move in after the attack to clean up. Two buttons were all that were necessary to wipe out the Marineo estate. The first would pinpoint the laser beam onto the target and the second would send the 'GBUs' straight down the line.

"Here's one for the record books," commented the Stealth Captain to his co-pilot as he locked the laser on target with button one. Button number two sent a very potent message to the laboratory and survivors of the Late Don Marineo. The bomb arrived swiftly and efficiently. It pierced the concrete casing of the underground factory like a hypodermic piercing flesh. The chemical stocks ignited instantly and sent a fireball bursting out of the air vents, which scorched the estate, reducing the villa to ash in moments. The heat was so intense that the concrete laboratory melted, entombing Darius and his chemists who had thought that they would be safe within.

At two minutes past the hour, Commander Chuck D. Vine spoke to the stealth captain on the radio requesting a damage report.

"We have a 'White' sir; our second today!"

CHAPTER 52

Hypoxia is a condition where the available oxygen in the blood is insufficient to meet the tissues requirements. The sufferer will normally display a blue tinge to his lips and fingertips as the haemoglobin in the blood remains in a deoxygenated state. The onset of the condition can be rapid and unless the correct action is taken promptly, the outcome will always prove to be fatal. The early signs will include a euphoric sensation similar to that of being drunk, followed by muscular and further serious, mental impairment.

There have been many Hypoxia related aviation tragedies. In 1979 a King Air 200 aircraft decided to carry out a decompression exercise at 30,000 feet over Exeter Airport. The onset of Hypoxia was so rapid that the crew lost consciousness without even recognising the symptoms. The aircraft continued the flight under its own volition and crashed after running out of fuel, several hundred miles away in France. All on board were lost.

Many things can increase susceptibility to Hypoxia, namely; altitude and its associated decrease in oxygen and pressure, illness, the cold, fatigue and drugs.

Douglas Washington scored highly in all departments. The nature of his illness added a few more bonus points too; Pneumonia. Doug had no first hand experience of Hypoxia but was ever mindful of its existence. A young recruit under his charge eventually left the RAF for a job with a civilian airline. What was left of his body was flown back from France and buried in his hometown of Exeter.

Doug had decided to put more of a 'vertical' and less of a 'horizontal' distance between the Pup and Croatia. He had to take *'Mike Alpha'* out of small arms fire range as soon as possible and he considered that the best option was 'up.' This would mean staying over the country slightly longer but he would hopefully be at a safe enough height until out over the ocean where he could level the aircraft, open the throttles and 'get the hell out of there.' Ground to air missile attacks were unlikely as heat seeking devices failed to recognise the nominal heat given by the exhausts of small, propeller driven aircraft.

Danny was barely conscious as the craft climbed through five thousand feet and he was still losing a lot of blood. Douglas Washington was Hypoxic. He had expected it.

During the climb, Doug had opened the direct air vent in the panel in front of him to assimilate every ounce of oxygen that he could. However, he battled to remain conscious at the controls until they were at a safe height above the war zone.

Lawrence Carlton was frantically trying to raise him on the 'RT' but Doug had neither the breath nor the opportunity to return the call. His fingers had turned blue with the illness and the cold and his diminished powers of reckoning made the workload in the cockpit overwhelming. Even the simplest of tasks seemed beyond him. His last rational thought was to dive the aircraft rapidly to a lower altitude. Recognising the signs of the advanced stages of the condition, Doug knew that his requirement for oxygen was immediate. Diving 'Mike Alpha' rapidly from five thousand feet would ram the airflow into his system through the small, open window port, at face level directly in front of him.

Lawrence was about to change radio frequency and continue the journey homeward on his own. His responsibility now lay towards Pertwee and his worsening condition, which was the only priority. Suddenly, the radio crackled and he heard the familiar wheeze that preceded Douglas Washington. A glance at *'Desktrak'* showed that the Pup had pulled out of the dive and had levelled out at five hundred feet above the Adriatic. The rumours about Douglas Washington's legendary handling were obviously true. Moments later, Douglas made a slow but definitive statement as to his condition

"Lawrence... reports of my ... death have been.... Somewhat exaggerated!" Lawrence felt the laughter begin in the very pit of his stomach and rise to erupt from his mouth. The release and sense of wonderment shook his entire body as the stress manifested itself in uncontrollable rounds of guffaw. Fighting for his own breath, between the spasms of giggling, nervous relief, his eventual response was an equally appropriate classic quote

"Washington I presume!"

The two craft quickly established visual with each other, taking up a frail formation as they headed for safety. Douglas followed Lawrence's instructions and changed to the new radio frequency.

Douglas turned to Danny, who was virtually unconscious, and with his last reserve of breath, said

"Hang on son.... We're going home."

CHAPTER 53

"Mayday, Mayday, Mayday! Venice. Bird-dog and Carrier Pigeon. Inbound to you. Urgent medical attention required. Gunshot wounds. Oxygen, morphine and blood transfusion required. Currently over Adriatic, abeam Porec heading three one zero degrees at six hundred feet with estimated twenty-five minutes to run. Inbound to you. Need full emergency services in readiness. Over."

"Bird -dog, Venice. Lawrence, it's Gabriel speaking. It is good to hear your voice my friend! We have been holding our breaths and praying for you." Lawrence resisted the temptation to make comment about the 'holding of breaths' and was sure that the remark was not lost on Doug. "You are cleared 'straight in' Lawrence and full emergency services are on standby. There are many people waiting here for you. Come on home my friend."

Rebecca had been sitting anxiously with Gabriel and the others for what seemed an eternity, waiting for some news. She panicked when she heard the incoming transmission requesting 'urgent medical attention.' The tower was a hive of activity and no one responded when she said

"Shot! Whose been shot?"

She sat on the sofa giving and taking comfort from 'Biggles' who was nursing a broken leg from Johan's gunshot. The dog had not left her side since the incident. Her brother Peter held her hand, attempting to ease her distress. He had been unceremoniously dragged from his Spanish cell in the middle of the night a couple of days previously and put on board an aeroplane to Geneva where he was met by a British government official. He was duly debriefed and re briefed on the current situation and shuttled to Venice for an emotional reunion with his sister.

Marco Polo airport at Venice had blocked the arrival of all incoming flights until the Mayday was cleared and the situation concluded. The authorities could not afford civilian losses under any circumstances so the commercial traffic was put in a holding pattern over Austria, well away from their control zone.

The holding Airline pilots listened intently to the radio as the drama unfurled before them. The very mention of the word 'Mayday' (from the French 'm'aidez' or 'help') was enough to strike terror into the hearts of any pilot. Coupled with the words 'gunshot wounds,' everybody on frequency dared not make a sound.

"Doug, can you manage this?" Asked Lawrence.

"...Affirm...try and...bloody stop me!" was the asthmatic but authoritative response.

The two aircraft had eight miles to run and Lawrence 'called in' their position as 'long finals,' in keeping with standard procedure. He kept his finger on the transmit button as he went through his landing checks, prompting Doug, who was unfamiliar with the general operations of a Pup, to follow his lead. Just then, Danny spoke, managing to bypass his pain momentarily

"Flaps. Watch out for the flaps. They're not normal. No more than ten degrees." Doug looked out of his right window and watched the trailing, inner wing segments duly lower as he pulled the lever. The nose of the aircraft dramatically pitched down and Doug re trimmed as a matter of some urgency. He nodded his acknowledgement and thanks to Danny for the advice. Without it, there could well have been a further calamity, with full flap possibly resulting in a pitching-over or cartwheel.

At four miles out, Lawrence upgraded his call to 'Finals,' adding

"We're home 'n' dry!"

He spoke too soon.

With *'Mike Alpha'* three minutes behind, the Bulldog flew its final approach perfectly and uneventfully, landing safely then executing an immediate left turn off the runway and onto the adjoining apron. Once stationary, Lawrence released his harness, pulled back the canopy and jumped onto his port wing to anxiously observe the Pup's arrival, as the Paramedics took charge of Pertwee.

There was a strong, twenty-five knot cross wind component that had provided some significant buffet on arrival for the beefier, more powerful Bulldog. This would undoubtedly make things difficult for the Pup.

Unbeknown to Lawrence, the Bulldog had sprung an oil leak. One of the bullets that had entered the engine canopy on departing Bosnia had made a lucky strike. Now in its standing position on the apron, the oil leaked onto the red-hot exhaust manifold of the aircraft and was instantly repelled in a cloud of thick white smoke, giving the appearance that the Bulldog was on fire.

As Douglas Washington spent the last of his energy and resolve keeping the Pup perfectly lined up with the runway, despite the crosswind, an over zealous fire tender driver, seeing the smoke billowing from the Bulldog, pulled across the runway in front of the arriving Beagle Pup, to attend to the apparent fire.

"Bloody idiot, get out of the way!"

Lawrence waved his arms and shouted at the assiduous driver who was oblivious to the impending collision.

On the other side of the field, at a safe distance, were other fire, ambulance and police crews, primed and ready for any eventuality. Rebecca, Peter, Margaret and Gabriel waited anxiously inside a Range Rover that sat on the apron with its engine running, in readiness to provide a swift reunion for the riven family and friends.

Rebecca watched with terror from inside the vehicle as the arriving Pup tried desperately to veer right to avoid the fire truck. Douglas had actually cut back the power in readiness for touchdown, just as the fire truck pulled out in front of him. He slammed the throttle forward to increase the power but it was already too late. Before he could pick up enough speed to be effective against the crosswind, a gust blew him broadside into the tender. Rebecca screamed, turned and buried her head into Margaret's shoulder to avoid the spectacle of the disaster, which sent the other crews rushing to the scene.

The Pup had smashed into the top of the truck, tearing off its port undercarriage and sending the aircraft over the top and into a vicious, flat spin. Danny was thrown against the wall of the cabin and let out an agonising scream as the craft spun on its axis, scrapping along the runway for two hundred yards before coming to a standstill.

Another fire truck was quickly on the scene, swiftly followed by a Policia vehicle containing two 'Carabinari' officers, (Italy's quasi-militia police force,) several other ambulances and ancillary vehicles, all with flashing lights and beacons of varying colours and intensity.

A fuel line had ruptured during *'Mike Alpha's'* skating session and the sparks had readily ignited the Avgas. This time, the flames were clearly visible as the airframe quickly became engulfed.

"Get them out! Please somebody, get them out of there!"

Rebecca had jumped out of the Range Rover and ran screaming towards the crippled Pup. Gabriel gave chase, caught up and restrained from her getting any closer to the blazing aircraft.

Douglas Washington was the first to emerge. As the fire crews sprayed the aircraft, covering it with white foam, he managed to unlatch the door and collapse onto the wing. One of the Carabinari was there to catch him and assist him to the nearby ambulance. Doug protested as he was dragged away, indicating that Danny was still in the burning aircraft.

Danny's port door had buckled in the crash and would not open. The second Carabinari grabbed an axe from one of the fire crews and hacked away at the hinges as the cockpit began to fill with black, acrid smoke. Danny's lungs were stinging with every breath. The door was eventually ripped off and the overly heroic Italian dragged him out by the jacket and lifted him onto the awaiting stretcher before returning to the blazing aircraft once again, despite the shouts from the fire crews that she would 'blow at any moment.'

The paramedics hastily attended Danny and Doug in the back of the ambulance. Doug was given the oxygen that he craved and morphine for his pain. Danny's condition was serious. As one medic hastily cut away his clothing to gain access to his wound, another thrust a hypodermic containing adrenaline into his chest to arrest his failing vital signs. Rebecca, who had broken free from Gabriel, jumped into the back of the vehicle and grabbed Danny's hand.

"Oh Danny, I love you so much. Don't give up on me now!" She pleaded.

In the moments before he lost consciousness, Rebecca placed his hand on her stomach so that he could feel the two bumps that were growing inside her. "You're going to be a father; twice!" Danny battled the onslaught of unconsciousness, managing to open his eyes and give her a long, wide, joyous smile. Before he passed out, he managed one of his familiar, audacious replies,

"I heard you the first time!" Rebecca cried tears of joy as he fell silent.

"He's going to be ok. Let him rest," said the doctor who recognised her need for reassurance.

Rebecca turned to her father whose face was mostly hidden behind the mantle of an oversize oxygen mask

"Welcome home Granddad. No more flying for a while OK! We're going to be a normal family now. Please!" She laid her head against his chest and tears of joy peppered his light grey jump suit.

Lawrence stood beside the smouldering remains of *'Mike Alpha,'* trying to catch his breath after running a laboured two hundred yards from the Bulldog. There was still a lot of commotion and activity going on, with the rescue services anxious to clear the field as soon as possible to enable the civilian flights that were clogging the skies over Austria, to land and despatch their passengers.

As the ambulances sped off to hospital with their respective patients, Lawrence was suddenly left feeling somewhat neglected. He looked round to see Gabriel and Margaret standing together talking by the Range Rover. His heart sank realising that he was too late. Years of prevarication would now reward him several more of heartbreak.

Margaret suddenly disengaged from Gabriel, as his conversation was still in full swing, leaving him a little surprised and indignant. She stood transfixed, simply staring at Lawrence, who searched her gaze for forgiveness and confirmation. The connection was unbroken as they both began to walk slowly towards each other. Margaret spoke first with an uncharacteristic boldness an unreserved honesty

"Lawrence Carlton. I love you and always have. Now what are you going to do about it?" Lawrence couldn't believe his ears nor his eyes as his usually docile, shy, personal assistant boldly put him on the spot

"Marry you I guess!" He replied.

"Well that's that sorted!" She said as she threw her arms around his shoulders and kissed him in a fashion that she had only ever read about in books.

"Ha...herm!" Gabriel coughed an interruption. "May I be the first to kiss the bride and congratulate the groom?" After kissing Margaret, Gabriel threw an arm around Lawrence and kissed him on both cheeks. "It is good to see you my friend, very good indeed" he reaffirmed. Lawrence gave his good friend an earnest smile and a look that conveyed, not just an honest 'pleased to see you too' but also a heartfelt condolence for his coming second in the race for Margaret's heart. Gabriel was as sincere and genuine with his response. "Do not apologise to me my friend. I am extremely happy for you both. You are indeed very lucky though Lawrence. Margaret is quite a lady, but you will be pleased to know that I too have got my girl Lawrence." Both Margaret and Lawrence raised their eyebrows in surprise and anticipation. "The

Coast guard picked up Ruth Piva-Vasquez this morning and she has been singing like a bird ever since. We have both her and her mother in protective custody. Come my friends, we have much to celebrate."

EPILOGUE

The Camorra were a society of criminals similar to the Mafia but based in and around Naples. The insular organisation was not as extensive as that of its Sicilian counterpart but it was just as ruthless and violent. There was certainly no love lost between the two and no sign of anything approaching honour between the two societies of thieves. The Camorra had followed with interest the many clandestine operations of the various families within the Mafioso brotherhood, eager to capitalise on any situation that they could for themselves.

After leaving Marco Polo Airport, the Policia Vehicle left Venice and sped along the E70 motorway, which would eventually take them to Naples. The two Carabinari were equipped with UZI sub machine guns and they would not think twice to use them if any body tried to stop them. There was too much money involved. The Camorra had promised them a lot more work if they completed the job properly this time. The Camorra could easily pick up where the Mafia left off. They had the necessary personnel and expertise. It was their destiny. All that they needed was this one last package of resin that the Carabinari had pulled from the burning wreck of Beagle Pup

'G-KARMA.'

REFERENCE SECTION

This section will provide further, detailed information on the aviation topic mentioned within the story, where such an explanation is required to embellish the coverage within the text, which is kept to a minimum to avoid distraction from the flow of the plot. Further reference should also, and always, be made to UK AIP or the ANO for full and legal definition.

Where appropriate, explanation of complex and unusual concepts is given in layman's terms with simple analogies included to dispel any inherent mystique.

The relevant topic is indexed by the page number whereby it initially appears in the story suffixed by (*), for quick and ready reference should you so desire.

PAGE 1
MAYDAY PROCEDURES.

There are two levels of emergency call, the highest priority being the 'Mayday' 'distress' call and the lesser priority being the 'Pan/Pan,' 'urgency' call.

A 'Mayday' call, which specifically should be repeated three times in succession, 'Mayday, Mayday, Mayday,' is used when the level of 'distress' threatens imminent, serious danger, requiring immediate assistance. Once a 'Mayday' (from the French word m'aidez meaning 'help') or a 'Pan Pan' call is made, no other stations are to transmit on that frequency until the 'Mayday' or 'Pan/Pan' is cancelled, or a particular station is asked to assist in some manner or another.

A 'Pan Pan/Pan Pan/Pan Pan' (also repeated three times in succession,) call is used in the event of a condition or situation being determined to be 'urgent' but not requiring immediate assistance. This can, of course, be upgraded to a 'Mayday' should the situation worsen, requiring immediate assistance.

The 'Mayday' call should be made in accordance with convention, stating the following information in the order shown. This, of course, can only be done if the brevity of the situation allows, remembering that the priority at all times is to safely fly the aircraft.

Remember 'Aviate, Navigate, Communicate.'

A) 'MAYDAY,MAYDAY, MAYDAY.' (Or 'PAN PAN /PAN PAN / PAN PAN.'

B) State the name of the station that you are calling I.E. A local airfield or the emergency service frequency on 121.5 MHz.

C) State your aircraft's callsign and type.

D) State the nature of the emergency I.E. 'engine failure' or medical incapacitation of whatever nature.

E) State intention I.E. 'Attempting forced landing in farmer's field.'

F) State current or last known position. Current height and heading if appropriate.

G) State pilot qualifications I.E. if instrument rated or not, student pilot etc.

H) Any other useful information to assist the emergency services. I.E. 'Two passengers on board, one is suffering a heart attack.'

A cool head will undoubtedly assist the delivery of a 'Mayday' call, which, in this conventional format is somewhat protracted.

If the seriousness of the situation precludes the pilot from delivering this message in full, prudence would suggest that 'Callsign' and location of intended forced landing site would be the desirable items to transmit in the first instance. This will help the emergency services in their efforts to locate you and offer any medical or practical assistance that you require.

Further reference should be made to CAP (Civil Aviation Publication) 413.

PAGE 2.
RADIO TRANSMISSIONS

Only one station can transmit on any one frequency at any one point in time. Any transmissions requiring a response therefore, should be suffixed by the term 'OVER' which determines that you have finished your own transmission and that the frequency is now clear for your incoming response. Should you determine that your transmission is finished and that no response is required, then you should suffix your call with 'OUT.'

It is prudent to point out that the archetypal phrase 'Over and out' which prevails in films and fiction is a misnomer and a contradiction in terms, 'Over' declaring that you want a response and 'Out' declaring that you don't.

'Yes' and 'No' have no validity over the airwaves, the correct terminology being 'Affirm' and 'Negative.' It is also noteworthy that 'Affirmative' was used until recently, however, a common, unintentional malpractice amongst pilots is to get slightly out of sync between the spoken word and the operation (depression) of the transmit button. This will manifest itself by chopping off the beginnings and endings of words. It was therefore determined that due to this phenomena, the perception of '...ative' could have been either 'negative' or 'affirmative,' leading to a dangerous ambiguity. This is now resolved by the clearly defined terminology 'Affirm' and 'Negative.'

It is not uncommon for a stuck transmit button to jam a frequency with its carrier wave and it is good practice to check the free travel of this item periodically.

Should a normally busy frequency suddenly be deafeningly quiet, it would be prudent to check once again in case your last transmission left the button depressed consequently jamming the frequency.

Note that English is the international language of the air.

CALL SIGNS

Aircraft call signs are their unique, identifying registration numbers that are the equivalent of a car's number plate.

The prefix identifies the country of origin I.E. G-BTDR whereby the 'G' denotes Great Britain.

The full call sign should be used when initial contact is made with a radio station. The receiving station will then usually abbreviate it in his/her response for expedience, referring to the prefix and the last two letters only. A typical example of this would be as follows:

The transmitting aircraft would make the initial contact

"North Weald Radio, Golf Bravo Tango Delta Romeo"

In response, North Weald would usually reply

"Golf Delta Romeo, North Weald Radio. Pass your message."

The abbreviation is at the prerogative of the controller and unless he initiates the abbreviation, then the full call sign must be used. This is in the event that two aircraft of the same *abbreviated* call sign are under his control whereby, to maintain identity, the full call sign remains in use. This, in fact, is not uncommon.

Technically, the abbreviation must contain the prefix; it is not uncommon however, to hear only the last two components being used

"Delta Romeo – out."

PAGE 3
TROUBLE CHECKS.

In the event of any airborne engine failure, a cool-headed application of these typical problem checks can hopefully identify the problem.

It is good practice to carry a list of these checks, pertinent to the particular aircraft, readily accessible, attached to your kneeboard for instance, in the unlikely yet possible incidence of such an emergency.

Another good practice is to learn the drills as a 'touch item' routine, verbally declaring the item and touching it at the same time to promote a familiarity and awareness of the location of each item on the list.

The first thing to do at the onset of any rough running would be to check for the presence of carburettor Ice. This is undoubtedly the most common offender in the engine trouble department. Ice can build up in the carburettor even in the most unexpected of conditions. This will eventually choke the fuel supply and result in engine stoppage. Regular application of the Carb' Heat Control is a vital action in flight and should be performed every ten minutes or so during flight and also at low power settings (i.e. on final approach) where the heat from a slower running engine is nominal.

Care must be taken to return the control to 'OFF' when full power is required as hot air reduces the engine power at a given throttle setting. Always check that the Carb' Heat control is 'OFF' for takeoff and 'OFF' for the very last segment of the approach to the runway when coming in to land as you may need full power to 'Go Around' in the event of a missed approach or similar event that will preclude you from landing.

Usually a 'plunger' style knob, the Carb' heat control, once pulled, directs hot air into the carburettor to melt any ice build up. This should be applied for al least a full minute at a time or in accordance with any particular instructions for the relevant aircraft.

If this fails to rectify the problem, the next best thing to do would be to trim the aircraft for the best glide speed and then pursue the trouble checks, which, typically, should consist of the following:

One of the fuel tanks could have run dry so turn the selector cock to 'both' and switch on the fuel pump. Check the gauge. Have you run out of fuel? Note that reference solely to a fuel gauge is negligent in the extreme as they have a propensity to fail. A thorough pre flight check should always include a visual inspection of the fuel tanks to determine that enough fuel is present.

Records should also be kept of any fuel uplift and fuel burn rate. This can be a comforting reassurance should your gauge suddenly fail in flight giving you the impression that you are empty when you can calculate otherwise if this information is at hand.

Catastrophic fuel leaks are rare and would be visually evident or 'strong on the nose' in some incidences but not always. A good visual check is therefore recommended as such a leak would present a serious fire risk. A distress call would be prudent in such circumstances followed by an immediate forced landing.

It is unforgivable for a pilot to allow his aircraft to run dry unless a leak can be blamed. The gentlemen from the CAA will no doubt wish to talk to you if you are negligent in this department.

Vital action checks, immediately prior to flight, require that you isolate the magnetos individually and check that the differential in the readings falls within the published parameters. It is not, however, a recommended procedure to individually check the 'mags' in flight because, if indeed, one has failed then, by selecting it individually, you will invite an engine stoppage that otherwise would have been avoided by leaving the selector on 'Both.'

PAGE 7
·
'V' SPEEDS.

For safe operation, each particular design of aircraft will have speed considerations and impositions placed upon it for its various stages of flight. These are usually prefixed with a 'V' and some typical examples follow.

VSO – This is the all important 'stall' speed of the aircraft with the flaps lowered. This is denoted by the lowest (speed) end of the white band, which appears on the 'ASI' or Air Speed Indicator. In simple terms, flight below this speed is impossible and great care should be taken to maintain an airspeed in excess of this figure.

A simple analogy could be drawn with that of a bicycle, which must be pedalled at a certain rate for it to achieve motion.

VS1 – This is the stall speed with a cleanly configured airframe, I.E. no flap lowered. This is indicated by the lowest (speed) end of the green arc and it should be noted that this speed is higher than VSO, illustrating that slower flight is possible with lowered flap.

VFE – This is the maximum speed allowed with a full deflection of flap and it is denoted by the highest (speed) end of the white arc.

In brutal terms, if full flaps are lowered at a speed in excess of this amount, the normal flight characteristics of the aircraft would be compromised and in a worst-case scenario, the actual flaps could be physically torn from their mountings.

The white arc then, denotes the flap operating range and care should be taken to observe their operation within its limits.

VNO – This speed denotes the maximum speed in the normal operating range and is represented by the (highest speed) end of the green arc. The green arc then, denotes the normal speed range of the aircraft with a clean airframe, I.E. no flaps.

VNE – After VNO, flight speeds enter the range of the yellow, cautionary arc and at its highest (speed) end lies VNE – the never exceed speed. Flight beyond this could have catastrophic consequences on the airframe.

VNE can all-to-easily be achieved by pointing (diving) the aircraft under full power. Any such manoeuvre should always be accompanied by a reduced throttle setting.

OTHER V SPEEDS NOT NORMALLY FOUND ON INDICATED ON THE ASI.

VA – Maximum manoeuvring limit, I.E. during aerobatics or similar.

VR – This relates to the Rotation speed during the take-off roll whereby airflow is sufficient for the nose of the airplane to be raised for the initial phase of flight to begin.

These speeds should be contained within the aircraft operations manual, which should always be consulted before any intended flight.

It should also be noted that these indicated *'stalling'* speeds are not absolute as the stall is always achieved at the same angle of attack of the wing and not always at the same indicated airspeed.

Various considerations should be taken into account in this regard such as steep turns, which are analogous with a line of ice skaters whereby the inner skater can remain virtually stationary whilst the outside participant spins with a considerable velocity.

The inner wing in a steep turn can similarly stall whilst its outboard counterpart is in full flight.

Weight, power settings and airframe contamination, be it frost, snow, mud or bugs can all have a detrimental and punishing effect on these figures and the consequent flight characteristics.

PAGE 8
'Q' CODES

QNH – this code refers to a setting in the altimeter subscale, which will configure the unit to register 'Altitude,' that is, height above 'mean' sea level, 'mean' being the average taken between low and high tide. This setting should be used when cruising across country whereby the important consideration is separation and collision avoidance from other cruising traffic that will be using the same pressure setting.

Using mean sea level as a datum, air traffic controllers can duly segregate traffic in their care, passing this QNH setting to their respective charges and advising them duly of any avoiding, controlling action, knowing that their vertical measurement reference is synchronised.

It should be noted that the altimeter is essentially a barometer in principle and works on a pressure principle. Air pressure can readily change and vary from local region to region and a 'regional' pressure setting should be obtained from the controlling service from time to time.

QFE – This is an airfield pressure setting passed to the pilot by the controlling service at the airport/field where the intention is to land.

This will configure the instrument to indicate 'height' above the ground.

For example; if an aircraft was intending to land at an airfield which itself had an elevation of 'three hundred feet' above sea level, and that aircraft had cruised 'cross-country' on a 'QNH' setting to get there, it's altimeter would indicate 'three hundred feet' once the aircraft has actually landed and is on the ground.

Of course, the prime consideration for an 'inbound' landing aircraft is the actual vertical distance between itself and the runway, not the sea. A greater sense of perspective is achieved by reconfiguring the altimeter for 'QFE.'

QDM - Not to be confused in any sense with an altimeter setting, QDM is a 'magnetic' heading to steer by the aircraft, in zero wind conditions, to reach the DF station. 'DF' stands for the 'Direction finding Station.'

Some airfields posses equipment, which enables them to auto-triangulate or ascertain by various means an aircraft's position from the source of it radio transmissions. Once this position is ascertained, it is a simple matter to pass the QDM to the disorientated pilot who will be home in time for tea.

Realistically, QDM is the most often requested bearing from pilots who are lost or 'temporarily unaware of their position' as the more politically correct would put it.

QDR – Is the 'reciprocal' magnetic bearing of the aircraft in relation to the DF station.

QTE - Is a 'true' (I.E. no magnetic variation) bearing of the aircraft in relation to the DF station.

QSY – Without literal translation, 'QSY' usually prefixes an intention to change frequency from one station to another i.e. 'Golf Delta Romeo QSY to North Weald on 123 decimal 52.' This will usually prompt an acknowledging response from your current station such as ' to North Weald on 123 decimal 52. Goodbye' releasing you from their attentions/ control. It should be noted that, once established with a radio station, an aircraft should request an ongoing frequency change before actually doing so. This frequency change can either be acknowledged and sanctioned as per the above example or it may in fact be denied, the controller requiring you to stay with him/her for a while longer.

'QFO!' For definition please consult the text on page 8. This code has no legal definition although many have been known to utter it!   ·

PAGE 8
SEA HARRIERS

A Royal Navy Sea Harrier is essentially the same aircraft as an RAF Harrier, the main difference being the tactical use of the aircraft. Sea Harriers are used for air-to-air combat whereas the RAF harrier was mainly used in a ground attack role.

PAGE 9
COLLISION AVOIDANCE.

Converging Aircraft should each turn *right* to avoid each other. Committing this simple fact to memory is a lifesaver.

Consider the logic of turning right (starboard;) the pilot in command sits on the left (port) and by turning right, each pilot then passes on the visual side of his counterpart.   ·

Analogous with the logic of driving in a foreign country; a left-hand traffic pattern is complimented by right-hand drive cars whereas a right-hand traffic pattern utilises left hand drive cars. One convention is the same however, that is, in either case, the driver sits centrally on the 'off-side' of the road in question, providing a better perspective of any oncoming traffic.

Starboard / right is denoted by the international convention of the colour green.

Left/ portside is denoted similarly by red. This is best remembered by the prompt 'have you any red port left?'

A last due point of note to consider in the realm of collision avoidance and general conspicuity is 'relative motion.' If two aircraft are on similar converging courses and a constant relative bearing exists between them, then 'relative motion' masks the threat of collision. Contrary motion will provide the visual stimulus to detect another aircraft, however the converse applies making the 'relative motion' traffic difficult to detect in the early stages. In this situation, nothing in your immediate visual panorama seems to be moving in relationship to anything else, in essence, providing nothing to 'catch the eye.' This phenomenon increases the risk of collision by delaying your reaction to it.

Typically, in a situation such as this, the other traffic will appear to remain in the same segment of your windscreen although its size will eventually rapidly increase in perspective, as it gets closer to you. Do not underestimate closing speeds of aircraft and do not overestimate your reaction time to this potential hazard. I have my own acronym emblazoned across my kneeboard to remind me of this threat; CVVV 'Constant Visual Vigilance Vital.'

PAGE 16
COLLAGE AIR SQUADRON

The 'Collage Air Squadron' actually exists in its proper title of 'University Air Squadron' for the same reasons given in the text. It also has employed and enjoyed the services of many 'Bulldogs' and 'Chipmunks' for many years and long may they do so.

PAGE 23
'TOUCH AND GOES'

The practice of 'touch and goes' is paramount to, not only the student pilots regime, but to that also of any pilot who wishes to stay proficient in his skills and maintain his currency. Essentially, a take-off followed by a landing accompanied by a radio call such as ' Golf Alpha Mike, touch 'n' go.'

Many hours will be spent pounding the circuit in this fashion during the initial stages of training. This will compound the basic necessary and essential skills required for the most demanding phases of flight.

A golden piece of advice would be to maintain a strict balance between the number of take-offs and landings!

PAGE 28
GAS DETECTING TECHNOLOGY

This technology actually exists and was commonly used during the Gulf War in hand-held, ground-based operations.

PAGE 35
CIVIL AVIATION AUTHORITY AND GOVERNING BODIES

A governing body called ICAO, which stands for 'International Civil Aviation Organisations', regulates global flight.

The CAA is the UK government-sponsored Department charged with overseeing all Aviation matters within UK airspace and for 'championing our cause' abroad.

The American equivalent is the FAA – the Federal Aviation Administration.

Each country across the world has an equivalent organisation, some of which operate their own set of rules and procedures that are slightly different in some respects to the ICAO standards.

This, of course is illogical and potentially hazardous. Recently, European state members have instigated a body called the JAA, which stands for 'Joint Aviation Authorities,' in an attempt to harmonize policy and procedure.

In the UK, the CAA oversee other bodies who are answerable to them, namely the PFA (Popular Flying Association) and the BMAA (British Microlight Aircraft Association.)

The PFA are responsible for issuing the permits and engineering advice to homebuilt aircraft or some factory built types that no longer have factory backup or spares. They also actively promote the essence of private flying, maintaining the interests of the private pilot at all levels.

The PFA rally, held annually in July, is the largest aviation event held globally outside of the United States.

PAGE 42
CIRCUITS and 'PPR'

In Accordance with Rules 17 and 35 of the air, essentially, all aircraft shall conform to a pattern or 'circuit' formed by others intending to land at that aerodrome unless the Air Traffic Controller advises otherwise.

These circuits are conventionally oblong shaped, like the rim of a shoebox, with each leg having it's own name. This will assist the controller and all traffic in the vicinity by pinpointing the exact location of an aircraft within the circuit pattern, which is usually flown at 1000 feet on the 'QFE,' i.e. above ground level.

Although oblong in shape, it is quite common for pilots to be advised to fly a 'wanky' version of this pattern, usually for noise abatement reasons and in an effort to avoid a particularly sensitive neighbour or farmer etc.

On departure, the circuit legs, which should be flown at right angles to each other where possible, are called; Upwind, Crosswind, Downwind, Base and Finals. It is a legal obligation to declare your position at the 'Downwind' Leg, and on turning 'Finals.' You may well be asked to declare your position at any point in the circuit.

Circuits are conventionally flown left hand, in keeping with the logical visual positioning of the pilot in the left hand seat. However, circuits can and are, flown either left or right-hand and the circuit direction for each available runway is predetermined. The pilot is well advised to establish this by either contacting the aerodrome before departing for it, or to consult any of the readily available flight guides, which list this information.

Each Airfield will publish and operate it's own preferred circuit joining procedures also which should also be established before setting off.

Some airfields are 'PPR' which means that prior permission must be sought (by telephone) for any inbound flight where all pertinent information in regard to circuits, noise abatement and preferred circuit joining procedures will be passed.

This also a useful exercise to determine the opening hours of the café as well.

PAGE 45
RULE 5 THE 'LOW FLYING' RULE.

Rule no 5 lays down the law with regard to 'low' and 'close' flying and it is to be heeded.

An aircraft must never fly within 500 feet of any person, vessel or structure with some notable exceptions, essentially when taking off or landing in accordance with normal aviation practice. This rule applies in **all** directions! For example, this does not just apply to height or altitude but horizontal separation also. Should you so desire to fly up the English channel at such a nominal altitude (height above sea level remember) that your wheels are getting wet, this is acceptable practice as long as you maintain a minimum 500 feet horizontal separation from any oil rigs, tankers, ferries, buoys (and girls), piers, wind surfers, swimmers etc.

There is an incumbent responsibility upon the pilot to fly at all times at a height over any settlement that will enable him/her to glide clear in the event of an engine failure.

Single engine VFR (Visual Flight Rules) flights over London, for example, are banned because, owing to the controlled airspace above, which precludes flights at such a height, gliding clear is impossible.

This 500-foot in any direction rule effectively creates a 'dome' of protection around any such person, vehicle or structure.

For more detailed information on rule 5, please consult the UK AIP and the ANO (Air Navigation Order.)

PAGE 58
FLIGHT PLANS

Contrary to popular belief, it is not necessary to compile and lodge a flightplan every time you take to the air however, it remains discretionary and you may do so if you desire..

Aircraft should, however, 'book-out' before every flight, noting simple pertinent details such as Callsign, aircraft type, Pilots name, destination, time of departure and number of persons on board. Similarly, they should 'book-in' at their arrival point. This basic information will facilitate any level of search and rescue that may be necessary as well as maintaining an accurate record of movements for the particular airport/field concerned.

Any international flights, that is, flights that cross an International boundary or UK FIR (flight information boundary) must file an ICAO (International Civil Aviation Organisation) flightplan.

To reiterate that, although under no obligation, private pilots can choose to file a plan for any flight.

Again, not a legal requirement, but it is strongly recommended that a plan is filed for flights that intend to progress 10 nautical miles or more from the coast and over sparsely populated or mountainous regions.

The ICAO flight plan is a thoroughly detailed account of your intended flight, listing all the essential information. Broadly speaking, this covers not only specific details of persons aboard, aircraft specifications, route, timings and fuel endurance etc. but also safety items such as life rafts, locator beacons and the like.

This flightplan must be opened and closed in the appropriate manner to avoid an automatic scrambling of the search and rescue teams should your aircraft and journey not comply with your scheduled arrival.

For precise information consult the ANO / UK AIP.

There is always someone available at a licensed airfield that can help you with the correct compilation of the ICAO flightplan, which comes in the standardised form of a pre-printed lose leaf page with check boxes and simple to follow 'fields.'

PAGE 70
SHORT FIELD TAKE-OFF

A short field take-off essentially requires the best of a normal take off technique with a few extra parameters.

Attention should be paid to wind direction especially, keeping as much into wind as possible for extra lift.

A prime flap setting, usually ten degrees is required, remembering that more flap generates more lift but as a secondary, undesirable component, they also generate drag, which will slow down a take-off roll.

A higher than normal nose attitude is preferable and a sooner, rather than later, lift-off is recommended as soon as minimum flying speed is reached.

The main feature that differentiates a short field take-off from a normal one, is the practice of applying full throttle whilst holding the aircraft at a standstill with the toe brakes until it is 'straining at the leash.' This is reminiscent of Fred Flintstone who would frantically pedal his 'rockmobile' from stationary until 'warp-drive' kicked in and launched him on his way.

At the appropriate moment, release the brakes and maintain full throttle whilst correcting any immediate yaw to keep the aircraft rolling straight in its mission to get airborne ASAP.

'STOL'

'Short Take-Off / Landing' is a desirable characteristic for any aircraft, enabling it to simply take-off or land at the smallest of strips.

The important ingredient here is the 'power to weight ratio.'

The new breed of composite aircraft score highly in this department and coupled to a variable pitch propeller, this becomes a winning combination.

Analogous to the gearing of a car, a variable pitch prop' with a 'fine' setting will allow the engine to produce more power and RPM at a given throttle setting that a coarsely set one. Fine pitch is desirable for take-off when maximum RPM is needed. Rather like trying to drive in the fast lane of a motorway in first gear, this 'fine' setting is absolutely useless in the cruise but is good to 'get you going' initially from standstill.

A coarser setting will literally 'grab' more air for less RPM and thrust it backwards over the airframe resulting in a faster speed. This will also produce a better fuel consumption.

223

PAGE 70
FLAPS and AILERONS.

Flaps are inboard segments of the trailing wing edge which deflect to various settings symmetrically, simultaneously and sympathetically unlike their outboard counterparts also on the trailing wing edge, called ailerons. These work in contrary motion to each other I.E. if the left hand aileron is deflected upwards then its right hand counterpart will be deflected downwards. It is the ailerons working in this fashion that bank or roll the aircraft.

Flaps have a dual function; they can induce more lift at a lower airspeed and can also increase the drag component, acting as a virtual 'airbrake' to slow the aircraft down. They should be operated strictly within the limits denoted by the white arc on the air speed indicator.

Flaps can be lowered by either a mechanical motor coupled to a switch in the cockpit, which can lower them (simultaneously) to any degree from 'off' (clean) to 'full' with the actual degree of deployment usually displayed on a gauge, or by a simple lever, similar to a car's handbrake lever, which has pre-determined stages or notches to access.

PAGE 71
DANGER / PROHIBITED / RESTRICTED AREAS.

Various levels of restricted airspace are to be observed and are clearly marked on aviation charts which are to be carried on every flight as a legal obligation. These areas are three-dimensional with their boundaries and heights annotated on the charts.

Practically, a danger area (marked 'D') would be something like a military firing range, or a captive balloon flying area etc. whereas prohibited areas (marked 'P') would usually be over a prison or Buckingham Palace or sim.

A restricted area (marked 'R') is one wherein flight must be in accordance with various conditions promulgated in AIP RAC 5-2 notices or 'NOTAMS.' 'NOTAMS' are 'Notices to airmen' which are published when specific information becomes available of an important nature. These will be posted on the notice board at the airport/field and should always be referred to before flight along with any weather forecasts for the appropriate region.

An example of a 'NOTAM' would be to advise of 'Purple Airspace,' temporarily restricted due to a Royal flight. Further examples may be notification of a 'Red Arrows' display in a particular area or even notification that a particular radar service has been withdrawn or even a particular runway at an airport being closed for repairs.

Bird sanctuaries, gas venting stations, areas of intense aerial activity (AIAA,) gliding sites and military training areas are further examples of restricted airspace which are clearly given dimensional limits and boundaries and duly marked on the charts.

It is sometimes possible to cross a danger area using 'DACS,' a 'Danger Area Crossing Service.' A radar based service that is sometimes, but not always available for a given area. Care should be taken to make contact with 'DACS' before entering the area or simply 'go around' as a safer option.

It is worth noting also that danger areas etc. are not always active and passage 'through' as opposed to 'around' or 'over' may be permitted by the controlling DACS station but, conversely, it may not.

PAGE 79
WAKE TURBULENCE

Small aircraft, or more pertinently 'light' aircraft, are very susceptible to 'Wake turbulence.' This type of disturbed air takes the form of vortices that are generated by larger aircraft that take off at a steep angle of attack.

The frenzied pool of air that falls as residue from these aircraft can take several minutes to settle and small aircraft are best advised to wait until the air settles once again before attempting a departure as 'Wake turbulence' is not a desirable medium to support flight.

PAGE 97
'RUN AND BREAK'

Following on from the topic raised in the last paragraph of page 88 concerning the 'picking off' of allied aircraft on finals at their home base, the term 'Run and break' requires description and definition.

To reiterate that allied aircraft were at their most vulnerable when coming in to land, configured for slow flight on finals for touchdown. They were easily and readily picked off by the Luftwaffe and many of our aircraft were indeed lost in this fashion.

The 'run and break' was devised as a counter measure and essentially comprised a manoeuvre whereby the landing aircraft would start a full throttle 'run' along the runway from a predetermined point called the 'initial.' This 'initial' point was usually a mile out from the extended runway centreline. The aircraft would fly a line parallel to the runway, 50 yards or so to the 'dead side' (i.e. not the 'live' circuit side) at a low level.

At a certain point along the runway's length, the aircraft would pull sharply upwards in a spiralling turn towards the live side and fly an elliptical circuit that would bleed the speed off and make the aircraft vary hard to target as it spiralled in for landing.

It should be noted that the RAF dropped this practice in 1945 although a similar manoeuvre, performed at a much higher altitude, remains.

PAGE 106
BACKTRACK.

Quite simply, this term relates to the practice of taxiing the wrong way along a runway, usually done for one of two reasons:

1 - Taxiways from the apron to the active runway seldom deposit an aircraft exactly at the threshold, some even giving access to the 'active' halfway along its length only. Some aircraft elect to start their take-off roll from this midway point whereas others prefer to 'backtrack' to the absolute beginning to make prudent use of the full length available.

2 - Conversely, some aircraft require a longer roll-out on arrival and miss the taxiway requiring a subsequent 'backtrack' to enable them to depart the active and onto the taxiway.

'Backtrack' permission should always be sought from the controller who may indeed refuse if the circuit is busy.

'FULL AND FREE'

A vital action before take-off is to always check for 'full and free' movement of the control column.

When checking for 'full and free,' especially in an unfamiliar aircraft, the perceived movement of the column should be cross referenced with a visual external check of the actual degree of movement of the relevant control services to make sure that they do indeed correspond in the correct sense.

This item is omitted from the story on page 95 for dramatic licence but is emphasised within the same chapter on page 99. It must always be performed before taking an aircraft into the air.

PAGE 108
WINDSOCK.

Windsocks are simple but invaluable, low science devices used to gauge wind speed and direction. They are, of course, common sights at airfields but what is not commonly known is that they are calibrated to be fully inflated at a wind speed of twenty-five knots. This would be indicated by a 90-degree deflection from the pole, placing the sock parallel with the ground. In broad terms, half of this deflection would indicate a wind speed of 12.5 knots.

An ideal interpretation of the information given by the sock would be for the pilot to fly his aircraft literally straight up the narrow end. This would give him maximum airflow over his airframe and preclude any element of crosswind, which is undesirable.

In reality, runways seldom line up with the sock so a prudent choice of runway, where a choice is available, to maximise an 'into wind' take-off and minimise any crosswind component, is advisable. It is also advisable to avoid colliding with the sock on take-off.

PAGE 136
QUADRANTAL RULES.

It should be noted that the description of the Quadrantal rules appearing within the text on this page, pertains to flight in UK airspace only. Whereas flight over most European Countries employs a slightly different, more elaborate 'semicircular' version of these rules, it was felt prudent to use the Quadrantal rules throughout flightplan as the book is aimed at potential UK pilots who would be better served by an understanding of them in the first instance.

It is emphasized however, that any flights outside of UK airspace should be flown in accordance with the rules of that particular Country and these should be determined before departure.

PAGE 137
AIRSPACE

To the lay observer, the eternal expanse of clear blue sky offers unlimited freedom and inhibition, punctuated only by the odd fluffy white cloud.

In reality, such observation will liberate the eyeball only, as many complex restrictions apply to those who wish travel 'by sky.'

The airspace above the UK is divided into two primary regions: the London and Scottish FIRs (Flight Information Regions,), which extend from the surface up to 24,500 feet. Above this lies the UIR (Upper Information Region), which extends to 66,000 feet.

Within the confines of these defined regions, further subdivisions exist. The next division would be to classify airspace as either 'Controlled' or 'Uncontrolled,' the latter being termed the 'Open FIR.'

Controlled airspace is further divided into levels or classes, reflecting the nature and level of activity. For instance, Heathrow operates some of the busiest airspace in the world and as such is determined class 'A.'

Controlled airspace operates the following classes, each with it's own set of rules, regulations and restrictions, far too protracted to evaluate here:

Class 'A' / 'B' / 'C' / 'D' / 'E.'

Uncontrolled airspace operates classes 'F' and 'G.'

In addition to these divisions exist Control Zones, TMAs (Terminal Manoeuvring Areas) ATZs (Aerodrome Traffic Zones,) MATZs (Military Aerodrome Traffic Zones which include a stub,) Airways, prohibited, restricted and danger areas.

The skies above us still represent the last 'great freedom' but each year this liberty is further eroded as more and more of the World's Airspace is grabbed by the controlling authorities to keep pace with the ever growing proliferation of commercial traffic.

PAGE 170
BERNOULLI'S PRINCIPLE

Although A little complex in it's entirety, Bernoulli was a venerable gent whose theory remains at the very heart of the principle of flight.

A common misnomer is the belief that air pressure under a wing is the determining force in flight, literally pushing an aircraft skyward as indeed your hand would be pushed should you care to dangle it at the correct angle from a car window whilst in motion. Although a 'pushing' component exists beneath the wing, Bernoulli discovered a 'sucking' one above it.

Essentially, a wing with a high camber on its upper surface will encourage the air to flow over it at a higher velocity than that of the air passing below it. A higher velocity results in a lower static pressure and the wing is virtually sucked from an area of high pressure below to an area of low pressure above.

The all-important angle of attack determines this velocity and the subsequent 'lift' or 'suck' along with the design of the particular aerofoil (wing) in use. This can be experienced by varying the 'dangle angle' of the hand from the aforementioned car, practised only with great caution and at the hand owners own risk however.

The information contained within this book is designed for enlightenment and entertainment and is not intended to replace any formal training, which is required for the safe and legal issue of a pilots licence. It will, however compliment such formal training offering a simpler, practical level of understanding. Reference should always be made to the UK AIP, copies of which can be found at any licensed airfield along with details of the ANO or where it can be found.

Any amendments or additions to this section will be posted on the website at:

www.imaji-nationpublications.co.uk

ABOUT THE AUTHOR

'**Flightplan**' is the first title from Mike Jordan with others pending, including the follow-up thriller '**Deadline.**'

Mike has worked within the entertainment industry as a pop musician and promoter since 1976. During this period, he has toured extensively for, amongst others, the US Air force, appearing at their various facilities throughout the Mediterranean, which have provided him with the inspiration for the backdrop and settings for this novel.

He is based in Essex where he achieved his coveted PPL in 1995 in a Beagle Pup.

His chosen charity is the Essex Air Ambulance Appeal and he campaigns on their behalf.

He spends his time between the stage, the studio, the office and the sky, where he can often be found aboard his treasured Pulsar.

The Author with Sky Sports Beagle Pup G-AXPM

ACKNOWLEDGEMENTS

My sincere thanks and gratitude to all those who have assisted or contributed in anyway towards the publication of this book, especially,

Robin Hodson for his grammatical guidance, Robin Hughes and Dennis Goss for their technical expertise, Alan Crouchman for his historical and knowledgeable observations, Chas Stirling for his invaluable input and assistance, my friend Alan Gill, a true gentleman who was always on the end of the phone or the drive when I needed him, Jane Pengelly for the encouragement, Kevin Regan for the brutal observations in the initial stages, Roger Hayes for teaching me to fly a Beagle Pup, British Royal Naval Captain Richard Sharpe for the poignant interview with regard to the Sir Galahad, Jane's fighting publications and information group, especially Duncan Lennox for his Missile expertise, Dave Wylie for the detailed information on RAF Bradwell Bay, Sue Carter information officer at Bradwell Power Station, British Telecom for their 'UHF' technical guidance , Royal Air Force Hercules Pilot Brian Skillicorn for the detailed explanation and terrifying demonstration of the 'Khe San' manoeuvre, the US Air Force, The US Military Police, especially officer Lopez, British Airways Rome flight crew, Nortel for providing the essential trips to Rome, the various chemists who assisted in the creation of *'Destiny'* who wish to remain anonymous!

Thanks to 'Biggles' for playing himself, aided and abetted by his brother 'Groucho.'

Heartfelt thanks to Pete Kenneby for the refuge, solitude and friendship, also to my wife, parents and family for their patience, support, love and dedication and to all those who have provided the inspiration and motivation for me to pursue north of my original target, the project, and bring it to a conclusion through many frustrating years of research, re-evaluation and re-write!

Special thanks to the management and crews of the Essex Air Ambulance for their skill, dedication and humanity and to all those who have contributed to the appeal.

THE ESSEX AIR AMBULANCE APPEAL

The Essex Air Ambulance comes in the shape of a Bolkow 105 stretch helicopter bearing the callsign G–ESAM and is typical of many such units that operate across the UK. It is surprising to note however, that these intrinsically vital, life saving machines and their crews are funded solely by charity, receiving not a single penny from Government or NHS trust coffers.

The Aircraft is based at Boreham Airfield near Chelmsford and can reach the farthest point of Essex within 15 minutes of becoming airborne.

The Essex Air Ambulance generally services 5 hospitals within the County, namely Broomfield (Chelmsford,) Harlow, Basildon, Colchester and Southend. The average flight time from the scene of an accident to the nearest of these facilities is only 6.5 minutes, the top speed of the aircraft being approx. 150 miles per hour, approx 2.5 miles per minute. The helicopter can, of course, opt to deliver its patient in cases of extreme emergency, to the nearest hospital, be it within the boundaries of Essex or not, Addenbrookes in Cambridge being a regular example.

The crew of 1 pilot and 2 paramedics attend an average 3 to 5 missions a day, flying an average 10 hours a day, 7 days a week in Summer and 8 hours a day, seven days a week in winter. 14 paramedics work a rota of 5 days per month average with 2 pilots working 4 days on, 4 days off supported by one full time engineer.

The aircraft is designed to carry 2 patients at any one time. It is interesting to note that Road Traffic Accidents (RTAs) account for 45% of all 999 calls, 22% of which involve children. Horse riding accidents account for 20% of 999 calls whereas heart / stroke problems at work account for 30%. Others account for the remaining 5 percent including spurious, non-vital 999 calls such as nosebleeds!

The Essex Air Ambulance costs a staggering £65,000 a month to keep it in the air, that is approx £2,137 a day / £365 an hour and a phenomenal £780,000 per annum. The Aircraft receives 8 days a month flying sponsorship from the AA and the remaining £574,848 has to be found purely through donation. Various fund raising events and road shows take place throughout the year, details of which can be obtained from the Essex Air Ambulance HQ on 01245 444460 where direct donations can also be made.

The man responsible for raising these funds, co-ordinating and galvanising the general public of the County into contributing to their most vital asset, is a certain Mr Lee Gillam who can also be contacted on the above number. Organising the Appeal is, in itself, a full time job. It should be noted, however, that Lee is also one of the aforementioned 14 paramedics who contribute their skills, courage and kindness with a vocational, relentless dedication that often accompanies the saintly.

On behalf of the people of Essex, for the many lives saved, to Lee and his colleagues we say 'Thank you.'

As well as raising the profile of the Appeal, five percent of the net profits of all book sales of 'Flightplan' will also be donated annually to the charity.

Please give generously.

Thank you,

Mike Jordan

The story continues

Coming soon, from the same author

'DEADLINE'

For more information:

www.imaji-nationpublications.co.uk